W9-AQA-562

WHIRLWIND

Further Titles by Hilary Norman from Severn House

The Sam Becket Mysteries

LAST RUN
SHIMMER
CAGED
HELL
ECLIPSE
FEAR AND LOATHING

Standalone Titles

RALPH'S CHILDREN
WHIRLWIND

WHIRLWIND
Hilary Norman

Severn House Large Print
London & New York

This first large print edition published 2017
in Great Britain and the USA by
SEVERN HOUSE PUBLISHERS LTD of
Eardley House, 4 Uxbridge Street, London W8 7SY.
First world regular print edition published 2016 by
Severn House Publishers Ltd.

British Library Cataloguing in Publication Data
A CIP catalogue record for this title is available from the British Library.

ISBN-13: 9780727893130

Severn House Publishers support the Forest Stewardship Council™
[FSC™], the leading international forest certification organisation. All
our titles that are printed on FSC certified paper carry the FSC logo.

Typeset by Palimpsest Book Production Ltd.,
Falkirk, Stirlingshire, Scotland.
Printed and bound in Great Britain by
T J International, Padstow, Cornwall.

For Helen.
With so much love, always

Acknowledgements

My special gratitude to the following (in alphabetical order):

David Balfour, for sharing his knowledge; Howard Barmad; Jennifer Custer; Daniela Jarzynka; Pippa McCarthy; Special Agent Paul Marcus; Nick Pin, for his kind and expert help; Sebastian Ritscher; Helen Rose; Dr Jonathan Tarlow; Euan Thorneycroft; Jan Wielpuetz. And Jonathan. For everything, and much more.

Author's Note

Shiloh, Rhode Island, is a fictitious place, as are all characters.

As for the weather, my 'Blizzard-to-End-All-Blizzards' was created before any mentions of the very real 'SantaBomb' or 'Snowmaggedon: Parts I or II'.

He craves the dark, needs it, loves the way it wraps itself around him like the death-sweetest, foulest, most perfect swaddling blanket.

In darkness, he is most fully himself.

Not a good person. Not a *normal* person, but an intelligent one, fully cognizant of what he is.

A psychopath.

A monster, at times. Both in the light, and in the dark.

He does his best work though, his *killing*, in the dark, where he's most wholly alive. And if, by chance, they die before they reach his Erebus, then sometimes he kills them a second time. Because he needs to do it. Wants to do it. To do that to *them*.

In the light, even among people, he always feels alone, but darkness brings comfort. There's no fear in it for him, it is simply home and infinity, its possibilities endless, its sounds fantastical, the scurrying and squeaking within and the soft, distant sounds from without, in the other world.

He might have liked to have been a mole.

Except that moles are gentle creatures, and he is not.

Though it isn't just the darkness that brings him to life.

It's the killing.

Which brings the only light worth seeing:

1

star-bursts of ecstasy bright enough to burn his corneas.

He is an insane person, he knows that.

Sometimes, that knowledge brings with it a measure of pain.

Not for much longer.

One

1965

The mother was never quite certain if her son's voice truly soared above the others in the choir of St Matthew's, and it was not, of course, right or proper to let her pride show, or even to feel it. Her husband had once said that a choir dragged from a congregation as limited as Shiloh's could have little to commend it.

'All the boy needs to do is hold a note in all that caterwauling and he's going to sound like Johnny-fucking-Mathis,' he said.

She seldom dared to argue or to admonish him; she knew her place.

But he was wrong about their son's voice. And on this Good Friday, right or not, she felt pride to the very depths of her soul, listening to him singing 'We glory in your cross, O Lord' with the other choristers.

Pride not the only sin she was guilty of.

'*Wives, submit yourselves unto your own husbands, as unto the Lord.*' Ephesians, chapter five, verse twenty-two.

She tried not to complain, but sometimes it was hard.

'*Let your ways be known upon earth,*' her son and the choir and congregation sang.

The mother sang too, returning her thoughts to

3

the service and their lovely church, gazing around at its peaceful walls and up at its vaulted ceiling – before allowing herself another snatched glance at her boy, for whom she thanked God every single day.

And did so again now.

The boy felt the glow.

Of singing for the Lord. And for his mom, too, because all this was thanks to her. For reading to him from her Bible when he was a little kid, explaining it to him, making it easy, telling him the stories in her own words too, which was why, later on, while other boys at school were swapping Spider-Man or Hulk comics, he'd be daydreaming about Joseph and his coat or Daniel in the lions' den.

Or about how best he could serve Him.

His dad hated it, got mad if he caught him reading the Bible, then took it out on his mom. Which was why he'd started taking it to his secret place to read.

No one – not even his mom – knew about that place.

Safer that way, because soon as anyone knew, they'd stop him going there, for sure.

He'd been there when the Angel had come.

He thought, later, that it might have happened so he could help his mother, because of how mean his father was to her sometimes, and because she deserved better than him.

Not his place to think that, but honoring his father wasn't always easy, and it hurt to see how

4

sad his mom looked sometimes. Except when she was here, in church.

That had to be why the Angel had come to him.

He'd known right away that it was the Angel of the Lord.

That voice, so loud in his head. Louder even than the banging of his headaches, left over, his mom had once explained, from the sickness that had nearly killed him as a baby. So loud, filling his whole *skull*, that it was impossible to tell if the voice was male or female, but the boy figured it had to be male, because the angels in the Bible always were . . .

Not that it was important.

It was what had been *said* to him that was important.

What the Angel had told him to do.

The boy had no words to describe how important that was.

And how terrible.

His very own covenant.

Which *maybe* made some kind of sense because he lived in a village called Shiloh, which was the name of the place in the Bible where the Ark of the Covenant had first been kept. And he wondered for a while – trying to keep from thinking about what he had been told to do – if anyone living in any other US towns named Shiloh might have gotten messages from the Angel too, had maybe been given the same command.

To give up what they loved most.

He wondered if they felt the way he did about it.

5

Part resentful, part afraid, part awestruck.

Mostly awestruck. At having been *chosen*.

Which meant he had no choice. None at all.

And now he was almost out of time.

Because tomorrow was Holy Saturday.

Two

Reverend Thomas Pike's soft rubber-soled foot-steps were almost inaudible as he entered St Matthew's at six p.m. on Saturday evening.

The church – his church as he privately thought of it, his appointment as vicar having been approved by the diocesan bishop himself – was empty, awaiting the start of the Easter Vigil, just two hours away.

It would be dark then, as they began, but for now the vicar turned on all the lights, needing to see the place fully illuminated for his final inspection.

He saw the boy immediately.

Up on the chancel, on his knees, one hand clasped to his forehead, apparently praying, oblivious to the vicar, and even to the lights that had been switched on.

For a moment, Thomas Pike stood still, silent.

And then he moved closer, and looked up at the altar.

The white cloth was stained the color of sacramental wine.

An animal – a cat – lay in the center of the cloth, its fur blood-soaked.

Anger rose sharply in the vicar, swiftly quelled by an admonition to be compassionate because clearly there had been an accident. The boy must have found the injured cat and, not knowing what else to do, brought it into the church to pray for its survival. An affront, certainly, but driven by distress and faith.

Pike took a few steps closer and recognized the boy, a member of his choir.

He took a breath, then cleared his throat.

The boy shuddered, but went on with his muttered prayers.

The cat, Pike saw now, was beyond help.

'Son,' he said, gently, 'you need to stop that now.'

The boy removed his hand from his forehead, turned his head and looked at the vicar, and Pike gasped because the animal's blood was on his face, smeared over his forehead and cheeks, on both his hands and all over his white shirt and tie.

His Sunday clothes.

Shock ousted compassion.

'In the name of God, what have you done?'

The boy's mouth opened, but no words came.

'Answer me,' Reverend Pike ordered.

'The Angel.' The boy's voice was a whisper. 'The Angel of the Lord came to me and told me to do it.'

Outrage flared in Thomas Pike's chest. Then, hard on its heels, fear.

Because he'd seen the knife tucked in the boy's belt, blood on its blade.

He steadied himself. 'Stand up.'

The boy's eyes were dark and unreadable. 'The Angel told me to put her on the altar. Like

7

Genesis, chapter twenty-two, verse nine. "*And Abraham built an altar there, and laid the wood in order, and bound Isaac . . .*" Only I don't have a son, obviously, so the Angel said it had to be something I loved, which meant it had to be Molly.' The eyes filled with tears. 'And I asked the Angel if I really had to burn her, but he said—'

'Enough!' Reverend Pike's face was scarlet, his spectacles misting with heat. 'This is sacrilege, and you will get that thing off my altar and out of my church.'

'It's God's church,' the boy said, softly. 'And I have to finish.'

Pike watched him turn back to the altar and fought a violent urge to take hold of him, clenched his fists, struggling to bring himself under control. This was a *choirboy*, he reminded himself, the son of one of the most devout women in his flock.

'All right,' he said. 'You can stay.'

The boy crossed himself, closed his eyes and went back to his prayers.

The vicar turned around, walked up the center aisle to the narthex, took a large key from his pocket, his hand shaking, and locked the main door, then walked slowly back through the nave, up the steps to the chancel without another glance at the boy, opened the door that led to the vestry and his parlor, went through, closed the door behind him and locked that too.

For a moment he leaned against the cool wall, and then he looked at his wristwatch.

Six-twenty on Holy Saturday and a choirboy had gone mad in his church with little over an hour to go before the commencement of the Vigil.

8

A dead cat and a pool of blood on the altar cloth.

'God help us all,' said Pike.

And then he went into his parlor, opened the side door that led to Elm Street, stepped out into the fresh and pleasant April air – and began to run.

And over the next few hours, during the long, anguished night and day that followed, a woman lost her life, and others conspired to blot out what had happened, and to change forever the course of the woman's son's life.

And his trinity of losses began.

Two right away.

Mother and home.

The third coming later, more gradually, perhaps the greatest loss of all.

Faith.

Because after that, he felt entirely alone.

And the boy who had spoken to angels began slowly crumbling to dust.

And flew down, into the dark.

Three

2014

Liza Plain was wandering around Copp's Hill Burying Ground in Boston's North End, browsing some of the seriously old tombstones, when she saw him.

Sitting on the grass by a gravestone about thirty feet away.

She *thought* it was him, though he was very changed.

But then, when he turned his head, noticed her and jumped to his feet, dumping a laptop into a bag, slinging it over his shoulder and wheeling his bicycle quickly away in the opposite direction, she *knew* it, for sure.

Michael Rider. Thirteen years older than when she'd last seen him, looking every day of it and then some. Still attractive, but thinner to the point of gauntness, and unshaven, his straight brown hair shorter than it had been, his clothes almost shabby.

Definitely not wanting contact with her.

Liza considered, momentarily, following him, wanting very much to speak to him, knowing of no valid reason why she should not. Yet still, she did have an idea, even some understanding, of what might have been behind that rapid departure.

There was a possibility that he might consider her guilty, by association, with the people who'd helped wreck his life. Because she'd let him down, even if that had been a long time ago and out of her control.

He'd told her, back then, that he'd never had much time for journalists. And her own grandfather always said that all journalists were scum.

Not that she was a real journalist these days, but still . . .

Something else struck her. The headstones she'd been looking at, not for the first time.

10

Belonging, she was fairly certain, to past generations of the Cromwell family.

His family.

He was almost out of sight now, turning right to exit the burying ground, and Liza considered again going after him, but that would be pursuit, she guessed, and gave it up. Reminded herself of what he must have been through, was perhaps still going through even now.

He did not want to talk to her.

She did not entirely blame him.

Their families both hailed from Shiloh, a village in Providence County, Rhode Island, nestled up against the town of the same name to its immediate north, east and south, with woods and farming land to the west, just a few miles from the Connecticut state line.

Not a picture-perfect New England village, more of a mongrel of a place, Federal architecture rubbing shoulders with Greek Revival, Queen Anne-style, a Gothic Revival church and a number of very ordinary twentieth-century houses. St Matthew's Episcopal Church at the east end of Main Street was rather fine, designed by a follower of Upjohn, and there was a grand house called Shiloh Oaks on the south-west corner of Oak Street built by the same architect, a run of small useful shops and a café that was pretty good; and finally, there was the Shiloh Inn at the west end of Main, a comfortable place with a decent dining room overlooking the elm-lined street.

All in all, especially by comparison to some of the old, now run-down villages in that part of the state, Liza guessed that Shiloh had kept up appearances pretty well, though its absence of 'pedigree' had kept it out of the majority of guide books or Trip Advisor.

There was little reason to pause in Shiloh.

Unless you were an aficionado of high-profile true crime stories.

Of murder, in particular.

Shiloh was Liza's 'home town', but not her home.

Had not been for a number of years, would not be again.

The occasional weekend break was OK, and either Thanksgiving or Christmas or New Year's – every other year and then only three nights max. Guilty as that often made her feel, any more time spent with her eighty-four-year-old, thoroughly disagreeable grandfather seemed almost intolerable to her.

It hadn't been easy even while her parents had still been there, but Andrew and Joanna Plain had died one icy February night five years ago after her father's car had skidded on Shiloh Road and hit a truck coming the other way. Three dead, Liza's greatest grief for her mom, an easy-going, generous person who'd never tried to change her daughter. Unlike Andrew Plain, forever disappointed in Liza for not following in the Plain tradition of doctoring, and his father, Stephen Plain, who was even more disapproving of the granddaughter who'd refused to fall in line, never appreciating that his own strong-willed gene had taken root in Liza.

She'd known from an early age that she wanted

to become a journalist, or at least to be involved with the *news*. The Plains had cable, and while most of her contemporaries were watching teen shows, Liza had been lapping up Dan Rather and Connie Chung on the *CBS Evening News*, Bernard Shaw on CNN and Katie Couric on *Today*. Unorganized ambition had become determination, her short-term target the Department of Journalism at URI. Kingston was less than an hour away, which meant that she might easily have commuted, but Liza had wanted to live as full a student life as possible, specifically away from Shiloh.

Hard to say, her own home aside, exactly what had made her so keen to escape. Village life, for sure, with its innate claustrophobia, its inhabitants permanently avid to know *everything* about each other's lives, yet paradoxically clutching secrets close with almost unnatural intensity. But there had been something more than that, something uncomfortable about Shiloh, Liza had always felt, even as a child.

Nothing at college came easily, neither good grades nor the right internships nor – with her father opposed – funding. She took out a student loan, shared lodgings, worked part-time jobs in a diner and bar, and her mom secretly helped out when possible. Though Liza had cherished her time at URI, especially her fifteen hours a week with CBS Boston, and her work for *The Good 5 Cent Cigar*, the student news organization, she knew she'd only just scraped through, completing her major but aware by then, alas, that she was no blazing natural talent.

13

All the more reason to work harder, she told herself, crawling reluctantly back to Shiloh, on the lookout for her real way out.

'Pipe dreams,' Stephen Plain said.

'Better than no dreams,' Liza told him.

He'd told her once that journalists were odious vermin.

'I should know,' he'd added. 'We had enough of them here during the case.'

The *case*. The big story that had spun Shiloh onto the front page of the *Providence Journal* and into the *Boston Globe* five years before Liza's birth. A shocking, tragic tale of murder and suicide that had fascinated her ever since she'd become aware that she was surrounded by people who'd been a living part of the *news*.

Something else she'd fallen out with her grandfather about, because the local doctor had to have known more than most about the Cromwell case, but Stephen Plain had not only refused to speak to her about it, he'd ordered his son and daughter-in-law to follow his line. Liza had heard whispers of the ugly basics early on at school, but little more because the head teacher had banned the subject and, outside school, too, no one seemed to like talking about it, even the meager library in Shiloh Town Hall's basement having no more than the scantiest record.

Talk about *asking* to light sparks under an aspiring journalist.

'You will not allow that child to become a vulture.'

14

Liza had heard Stephen Plain saying that to her mother.

The sparks had fanned, and become a fire.

Four

1975

The June day was warm and pleasant, Main Street almost deserted just after noon because people were lunching – many at home, a few at Ellie's, the café on North Maple Street, and some inside Tilden's, the only restaurant in Shiloh Village.

It was quiet, too, except for the sounds from the school playground. Shiloh Elementary and its adjoining house – home to head teacher, Betty Hackett – stood at the west end of Main, and though some people found the noise of small children at play cheery, others found it irritating, and there had long been talk of relocating the kindergarten and primary school to the town, where Shiloh High was located.

For now, they remained in the village, and the second- and third-grade boys and girls were letting off a little steam in the playground before their lunch. Ordinarily there would have been two teachers supervising, but Annie Stanley had the flu, so flame-headed Gwen Turner was on her own, and she was, at eight minutes after twelve, busy scooping eight-year-old Edie Jones off the ground after a spill, making sure she had no worse injuries than two scraped knees.

Which was why Miss Turner had her back turned to the side gate of the playground, the shadiest part, especially in summer, when the oak trees outside were in full leaf, and where Norman Clay was sitting with his back to the railings, his nose and attention buried in *The Adventures of Tom Sawyer*.

Alice Millicent was not naturally sociable, at least not when it came to other children. Seven years old and in the second grade, she liked her teachers well enough, and the other kids were OK, but she had no 'best' friend, nor had she ever found herself included in what she might, later in life – had she come to live that life – have known as a 'clique'.

She was, in some ways, a loner.

But she *loved* animals.

Dogs, especially.

The sight of an adorable golden puppy just outside the school gate was irresistible to Alice, especially since it was attached by a red leash to a man she knew, a man with a dark hat and shiny black shoes and a shiny black car, who was beckoning to her.

Alice looked back over her shoulder, wanting to ask Miss Turner if she could go play with the puppy, but the teacher was busy with one of the bigger girls who'd hurt herself, and she guessed that Miss Turner would have said yes because it was only strangers they weren't supposed to talk to, and everyone in Shiloh knew this man.

And the puppy was wiggling, its little tail wagging like crazy.

So she opened the gate, went through it and closed it again behind her, as they'd been taught.

The man with the puppy was standing under a big old oak tree beside his car.

'Hi there, Alice,' he said.

'Hi,' she answered. 'Can I pet him, please?'

'You most certainly can,' the man said.

'Thank you.' Alice ran forward, bent down and stroked the puppy's silky head, and the animal made the sweetest sounds, wagged its tail even harder and licked her, and Alice squealed with delight.

The man looked toward the playground. 'If you'd like,' he said, 'you can come play with her.'

'What's her name?' Alice asked.

The man hesitated, his cheeks flushing under the shade of his fedora.

Not that Alice noticed.

'Her name's Maggie,' he said. 'If you want to come play with her, I already cleared it with Miss Hackett. She said it's OK, just this once.'

Alice squealed again and tried to pick the puppy up, but the man quickly opened the passenger door of the black car, bent down, plucked the animal off the ground and put it inside.

'So what's it to be, Alice?' he said. 'And no more squealing, because I have a headache.'

'I'm sorry,' Alice said. 'Yes, please.'

'That's good,' the man said. 'Get in then, dear.'

And in she climbed.

Good as gold.

* * *

17

Edie Jones was inside the school now, her scrapes dabbed with iodine, Band-Aids administered, and Miss Turner was back in the playground, checking her watch, looking around.

Norman Clay was still reading.

All was well.

Only one man had seen.

Seth Glover, the owner of Glover's Food Market at the corner of Maple and Main, making his way to lunch at Ellie's Café. He'd noticed the pup and the little girl, knew who she was, that her family lived outside the village on the road to Chepachet.

He certainly knew the car she'd gotten into.

The only Cadillac in Shiloh.

He'd seen the child clamber into the front passenger seat, seen the door close, seen the man with his familiar fedora hat and elegant suit and shiny shoes get in on the other side, and then he'd seen the car glide away, wondering momentarily where they were going.

And then his stomach had growled.

An Ellie Burger was needed.

Right away, if not sooner.

They all came to help with the search. Adults of all ages, only those with disabilities, care-givers and locals with little children or dependent relatives staying away. Almost the whole of Shiloh Village had come, and some from the town itself, including its most prominent citizen, the president of the town council, Donald Cromwell, with his wife, Susan; and the vicar of St Matthew's, Thomas

Pike, was there, trying to comfort head teacher Betty Hackett, her heart heavy with guilt, the searchers fanning out now through the woods west of the village.

Denny Fosse, who bred German Shepherds, had brought Blaze, his own dog, a black-and-tan with a fine nose, Fosse told Cromwell, though he hoped to hell that Blaze would sniff out nothing more significant today than a rabbit or some old stinking pizza box.

'Sheriff Julliard told me they're going to be bringing in the real dogs,' Cromwell said. 'No offence intended, Denny.'

'None taken by me,' Fosse said. 'Though I can't speak for Blaze.'

Every available cop had been hunting since the school had broken the news to Mary-Anne Millicent that her daughter was missing, and they'd asked people to stay away at the outset, just to search their own properties and outhouses and land in case little Alice had wandered off and got herself lost. All the local shopkeepers here too now – except Seth Glover, who'd been called away to Sharon, Massachusetts, to tend to his sister, who'd taken a bad fall.

The only other people not actively involved in the search were Alice's mom and brother, and Gwen Turner, who had shut herself away in her house, too distraught to face anyone because that lovely child had gone missing on her watch, making it her responsibility, *her* fault, which meant she had no right to be falling apart now. But if anything bad had happened to Alice, Gwen couldn't imagine herself ever

19

going outside again, let alone going back to teaching . . .

It was Betty Hackett who found them.

A child's Clarks shoe first.

Then a pair of small pink underpants.

Then the golden puppy, its neck broken.

Then the child.

The head teacher thought she would faint, but managed to call out to the others, her voice cracked with horror.

They all came running. Dick Millicent, Alice's father, howling, being dragged off by two of Sheriff Julliard's deputies. Donald Cromwell coming forward to help, John Tilden (the local restaurant owner) alongside him with Eleanor Willard (of Ellie's Café); and Reverend Pike fell on his knees, praying, and Dick Millicent, struggling with the deputies, keening and kicking out, caught the vicar in his side, and Thomas Pike yelped with pain, but went on praying regardless.

A lot of people in the woods prayed, though it did no good.

A seven-year-old girl had still been strangled to death. No sexual assault, they learned later, despite the underwear that had been removed. The rest of her clothing all intact and nothing missing, her mother confirmed, except her pink hair ribbon.

Possibly, it was thought, the murder weapon.

Her killer at large.

Two days later, when Seth Glover, still at his sister's in Sharon, heard what had happened, his face blanched and rage and guilt filled him as he picked up the phone.

Seven hours after that, his statement secured and an arrest warrant issued, a suspect was picked up and taken in for questioning.

By morning, Donald Cromwell, President of the Shiloh town council, had been charged with the abduction and murder of Alice Millicent.

Less than a year later, two weeks into his trial, Cromwell hanged himself in his cell.

A good conclusion, many felt in Shiloh.

Hoping to put it all behind them.

Five

Tragedies have consequences. Some in the short term, others lasting a lifetime.

Some descending to future generations.

As it was for the Cromwells.

Four decades later, piecing the tale together, compiling notes and recollections, organizing them in chronological order to help her make more sense of the whole, Liza Plain came to think of it all as a kind of 'tragi-graph', with far more descending than ascending lines.

Cromwell's indictment and suicide. His wife Susan's subsequent nervous breakdown and, ultimately, permanent hospitalization.

Then a slow upward climb with their sixteen-year-old daughter Emily's escape to Boston. Facilitated by her father's decision, made before his disgrace,

21

to leave everything to her with the proviso that her mother be allowed to remain for her lifetime in their home, Shiloh Oaks, or in any home of her choosing, in the style and comfort he had created for her.

Lawyers in charge, given that Emily was a minor, the family's wealth dwindling steadily because of legal fees and Susan Cromwell's refusal to leave her comfortable nursing home, because of the slow recovery of the stock market after the disasters of previous years, because of the property slump in the region and, of course, because of the ongoing costs of the administration of Cromwell's estate.

Despite her age and the family's traumas, Emily had been clear about what she wanted. She could no longer bear to remain in that small Shiloh community with ghosts and pain, false sympathy and gossip encircling her daily. She met with the lawyers and agreed a modest advance from the estate, enough to get her away. Her parents had anticipated college for her, but what Emily now longed for was *real* life to immerse herself in; she didn't want to go to Harvard, but was attracted by the idea of living in Cambridge, rubbing shoulders with the young and brilliant while making her own way. Which she did by taking an apartment share and a job with the American Cleaning Company – good, honest toil to keep her going while she licked her wounds and tried to recover.

Her line ascended a little way, then leveled out until she met Thad Rider, a rock singer with a band called Tight. He had long gold-streaked hair, dark eyes made up with liner and mascara, a skinny guy with a voice like sandpaper laced with dark maple syrup and hands that could do what Emily Cromwell needed most back then. Make her forget.

She recognized the problems from the start, but tried to blot them out along with her own past. Thad was talented and sexy, but he drank and did drugs, everything to excess. Emily drowned herself in his chaos and pretended that it was the perfect, healing antidote to Cromwell history and Shiloh. She lost her job, drank too much, smoked marijuana – then discovered she was pregnant. They married, but seven months into the pregnancy, no longer enjoying this woman who now wanted to be clean, sober and a good mom, Thad packed his stuff and left her a note, wishing her and the kid luck.

Emily steeled herself for a visit to Shiloh, and found Susan Cromwell cocooned in her own protected, prescription-drugged world, beyond caring if her daughter showed up or not. Emily visited the lawyers, told them that all that she wanted now was to provide her child with a decent home and education – away from Shiloh. She relocated to Pawtucket, Rhode Island, bought a small house with a little backyard, transferred her health records to the obstetrics department of Memorial Hospital, terrified that her lifestyle with Thad might have harmed her baby, but gave birth to a slightly underweight yet otherwise healthy son in mid-January, 1979.

Michael Rider.

The line that had, for a while, descended again, began to rise.

Six

The man who had once been the boy who sang sweetly and heard angels, but who no longer sang, and tended, these days, to take his lead from a voice belonging to someone he called the Messenger, watched the woman as she stood on the chancel floor just below the sanctuary, regarding the high altar and her handiwork. She nodded, apparently satisfied that she had set all in readiness: the chalice – front center – properly vested, gospel book and missal on their stands. Two feet before her, forming a semicircle on the wood floor, pumpkins, squashes and gourds, all painstakingly polished for the Thanksgiving Eve service, after which, the man supposed, they would become offerings for the food bank detailed on the noticeboard outside.

St Luke's Episcopal Church on Burgess Road in North Foster. Rural territory, the road dark, the only light around coming from the church itself. A somewhat desolate spot, no sign anywhere close by of the preparations for feasting that had surely to be going on in homes all over. There should, he'd thought earlier, watching from inside the truck, be nice little houses close by, lights aglow, families getting set for the holiday, turkeys resting inside dark refrigerators, relatives in

24

distant places packing overnight bags before their journeys; or perhaps they'd already arrived and were sipping hot toddies or eggnog . . .

Here and now, inside the church, the lights at the sanctuary end were ablaze, bulbs and shades dusted, wood reasonably close to gleaming; but most of the nave was unlit, and he was seated on a pew beside the north wall, shrouded in semidarkness.

Very still. All but invisible.

He stared up, briefly, at the altar, then let his gaze travel around the whole interior, over the two stained-glass windows, their design scarcely discernible without sun or moon or electric light to show them off. He thought, for a few moments, of other intricate windows from his past, of choral music, of the glow that had once filled him.

And had been stolen from him. Together with his life.

Not that he'd been exactly *'right'* even back then.

'OK,' he said, inside his head. 'Speak.'

The Messenger spoke.

It was hard for him to be sure sometimes who was the obedient one: he or the Messenger. Both so different now, not at all the way they'd started out. He had believed in the Angel then with all his heart and soul, but he knew now that even back at the start of it the commanding voice had been in his head, part of his condition. And once he'd accepted that, it had become a matter of realizing that he could – at least some of the time – turn it on and off at will. Tricks he'd taught himself. Tricks no doctor or shrink would sanction, let alone condone.

Free will.

His will.

In the Bible, angels were messengers among other things, and the ancient Greek *angelos* meant messenger, depending on where you looked it up, and he'd appreciated learning that, felt that was good enough for him.

The Messenger was speaking now.

He closed his eyes, felt his heart contract, felt heat fill him, and then he cooled and his breathing slowed almost to a standstill, to nothingness, and he could concentrate entirely on listening – it was impossible to do anything *but* listen, because the voice filled his head, filled all of him, velvety gentle but galvanizing at the same time.

Commanding him.

She was kneeling.

An innocent, probably good woman, a godly person, most likely a member of the altar guild. A lay person, harmless—

'*Not* harmless,' the Messenger corrected him. 'Neither good nor innocent.'

And the man who had once been the boy who heard angels understood that it was neither a messenger nor an angel telling him these things, that they were simply the *truth*. For he knew who and what had stolen his life from him; and all through his hideous afterlife, his purgatorial existence, he had been keeping those truths carefully stored, locked inside the miniature sacristy in his brain, to be released only at *special* moments.

Released now.

Enabling him to see this woman for what she truly represented.

Hypocrisy. Cruelty. Wickedness.

One of his *visions* filled him, a terrible visualization of those things, a logjam of absolute inner ugliness, threatening to suffocate him. And with that came the *need* – and the Messenger was here to help him, urging him on, commanding him.

To emerge from the shadows, make himself known to her.

Do what he had to do.

What needed to be done.

By him.

Now.

Seven

Great childhood.

All Michael's early memories were happy ones.

His mom had cared for him twenty-four/seven until he was old enough to go to kindergarten, then taken part-time work in sales for a fashion store in Wayland Square in Providence. Michael could not recall a time when he had not felt proud to have her for his mother, simply accepting of the fact that his father was not in his life. Emily had told him when he was twelve that if he wanted to look his dad up when he was older, she would not stand in his way. Michael had looked into her blue eyes and doubted that he'd ever want any more parent than her.

She'd waited until he was fourteen before telling him about his Shiloh family history, and hearing that his grandfather had been accused of killing a child had packed quite a punch, though Emily had said she didn't think that Donald Cromwell had been guilty.

'My dad swore to me on my life that he was innocent, and I believed him. But no one else did, and there was no way of proving it either way, not once he'd died.'

'Killed himself,' Michael had said.

'Yes.'

'Why do you think he did that if he wasn't guilty?'

'I guess because no one believed him,' Emily had said.

'Except you,' Michael had reminded her.

'Yes,' she'd said.

When Michael had asked if she would take him to meet his grandmother, Emily said that it might be distressing, but Michael insisted he wanted to go.

The encounter had been sad and boring; just an old lady in a chair who didn't recognize his mom or care a damn who he was. And after, since they were near Shiloh, they'd gone together to the village, and Emily had shown him the house where she'd lived, and the site of the old school, the building now converted into an inn. He'd found her suddenly very bleak, which had troubled him, partly because the trip had been his idea.

She'd gotten drunk that night for the first time since her pregnancy.

The first time Michael had seen his mom in a less-than-perfect light.

Having the best mom in the world could give a kid unrealistic expectations.

Bound to crash sometime.

It had bothered him, for sure, even scared him, but Emily had been sober the next morning, and ashamed, and he'd told her he understood, even though he had not, at least not entirely, but then they'd both gotten over it and had gone on with their good, happy life.

No crash yet.

That was still to come.

Eight

1985

From *The Foster Weekly Post*
December 5
    Robbery Suspected in Case of
    Missing Foster Woman
The family of Margaret 'Peggy' Jerome, missing now for eight days, were persuaded yesterday by the Foster Police Department to make a Channel Five News appeal for urgent information into her disappearance. Mrs Jerome, fifty-two, a member of the Altar Guild of St Luke's Episcopal

Church, Burgess Road, North Foster, was last seen by her husband, Ray, on the morning of November 27, when, having made breakfast pancakes, she said that she was looking forward to preparing the High Altar for the Thanksgiving Eve service.

According to Reverend Anthony Rivera, all evidence pointed to Mrs Jerome having completed her tasks 'as beautifully as ever', though according to Deputy Police Chief Robert Cook, 'an item of value' was later discovered to be missing, presumed stolen. Robbery as a possible motive is now being considered by Foster PD, but with each passing day, deep concern is growing for the safety of this well-loved pillar of the local community.

Three graves here now, in the velvety dark, damp, beautiful place where Margaret 'Peggy' Jerome had been laid to rest, her grave previously dug, ready to receive her. The other two already occupied, the first by a dead lamb snatched from a field in Moosup Valley which he'd killed before burning it, a symbolic fulfillment of the first mission given him by the Angel. The second grave containing the body of a man he'd spied from the road in Chopmist one early evening, sitting in his kitchen with the door wide open, wearing a T-shirt and shorts and eating a bowl of cornflakes, the open door and absence of others seeming like an invitation.

Nothing to do with the Messenger, therefore,

that *first* one, just a case of sheer chance while he'd been driving around in his patron's truck looking for a place to rob, and there it was, this nice white Cape Cod house, and no one home but the cornflake-eater, which meant he'd been able to help himself to cash and the man's watch and wedding ring – all of which he would take back to his patron – and to a surprising stash of medication, which he'd keep for himself to sell on, and, finally, to a silver crucifix which he'd used down here to posthumously cut the dead man's throat.

Only he hadn't been able to stop there, had gone on and on, stabbing and pounding until his hunger was sated and he'd been fit to bury the man.

More than a hunger, he'd learned since then, for when it came, it crept through him as insidiously as the aura preceding a seizure, and then it grabbed hold, of his mind and hands, taking total possession. He'd heard men say that some things were better than sex, but he couldn't tell about that because he had never experienced a *true* act of sexual intercourse. Because the things that had been done to him, boy and man, had been acts of perversion and, loathing aside, he had always been able to detach from them, almost in the way that he'd been able to detach, at least partially, from what he'd done to the cornflake-eater and, more recently, to Peggy Jerome.

Dissociation, he had self-diagnosed, his learning coming from books. Possibly a result of his infant sickness. Possibly not.

He had read, too, that some psychotic killers

31

experienced powerful sexual gratification in their deeds. Not so in his case, his need simply overwhelming, the acts that followed giving him neither erection nor climactic explosion. Yet they were all-consuming, so perhaps it was death, he had wondered, the *creation* of death, in all its hideous magnificence, that was better than sex, better than anything.

'RIP,' he said, when he was ready, at last, to leave Margaret Jerome's grave.

Knowing it was time to go back.

Home, hideous home.

Nine

It had been during the late summer of 2001 when Liza, working on a feature for the *Cigar* about a special education school near West Concord, Massachusetts, had first met Michael Rider.

Walden Pond Campus School, she'd been told, was an extraordinary place staffed by inspirational people, all finding ways to draw the very best skills, confidence and happiness out of the children in their care. Rider, a year older than Liza, a graduate of Rhode Island College in Providence, had been chosen to show her around; a volunteer counselor at the school's summer camp, he was building up his own credits, a BA in early childhood education already achieved, striving toward his goal, which was to become a classroom teacher at this renowned school.

32

The attraction had been instantaneous for Liza.
Reciprocated, at least to an extent.
But she'd been there on assignment.
Priority for them both.

The school was as remarkable as anticipated, with a comfortable feel, sequestered yet outgoing, the summer camp's focus on the development of skills and fun, its approach relaxed, with plentiful laughter and almost tangible love. Liza had spent the day sitting in on various activities, after which she and Rider had gone for a working supper at a restaurant less than a half-mile away.

It was a relaxed family establishment, and when he'd excused himself for a few words with the owners about an upcoming event, Liza had taken a look around at the art on the walls – some well-executed charcoal drawings of musical instruments, all for sale – and had used the moments for a few covert glances at him. Truth was she'd spent the day liking the look of Michael Rider: his slim, wiry build, about five-eleven, his dark hair in a ponytail, his expressive, capable hands, friendly brown eyes, small sharp nose, mouth not quite straight, swerving from wryness to laughter in point two of a second.

What she'd liked most, though, had been his easy, gentle warmth with the kids, and he seemed much the same with these adults, demonstrating something now with those hands, laughing at some joke.

Nice guy, definitely, she decided as he turned toward her, and they sat down at a window table and Liza shut down those thoughts, remembered why she was there and switched on the recorder they'd agreed on earlier.

The owners, Rider explained, regularly provided picnics for school outings, had originally moved here to be close to their son while he was at The Pond – as it was known locally – and had loved it so much that they'd never left, though the son had long since gone to college and was doing great.

'I'm betraying no confidences telling you that,' he said. 'Apparently stories get shared around up here, positive and sad, and the kids get a welcome wherever they go.'

'Sounds like a special community,' Liza said.

'Lot of good people.' Rider glanced around at the drawings of musical instruments. 'The artist teaches arts and crafts at Walden Pond. Nice woman.'

'Talented,' Liza said.

'The cello's my personal favorite.' He smiled. 'Sparse lines but very female.'

Liza took another look. 'It's the violin for me.'

'Do you play?'

She laughed. 'I'm against cruelty to my fellow man.'

Their cheeseburgers arrived swiftly and they set to eating, both hungry, working easily through Liza's list of questions.

'You seem very invested in the place,' she said, midway through, 'considering you haven't been here long.'

'I think you'd have to have a damned cold heart not to feel that way,' Rider said. 'These kids deserve so much credit. I've never encountered such courage: the challenges they face on a daily basis, and the ways they find to tackle them. It's awe-inspiring.'

'I've been here less than a day,' Liza said, 'and I see what you mean. Though I think it's the school, the teachers and therapists – and the volunteers – who deserve as much credit.'

'Just please don't mention me in your feature,' Rider said. 'It's honestly a privilege to be allowed to work in that place.'

'Am I allowed to mention the impact The Pond has on its volunteers?'

'I guess,' he said.

'I'm looking forward to writing this,' she said. 'I hope I do it justice.'

'I have a feeling you will.' He finished his burger and drank some Coke. 'Off the record, I'm afraid I've never had much time for journalists.'

Liza smiled. 'I have a grandfather who loathes them, so if you feel like venting, I'm used to it, and I can always turn off the recorder.'

'I don't need to vent,' Rider said.

Something behind that perhaps, Liza had thought, but then he'd moved them back to the main subject, and his undoubted passion had gone on lighting up his answers while they ate apple cobbler and she finished her questions, and it had all added to her certainty that she really liked this man, was definitely attracted to him, though he probably had a girlfriend and it was unlikely, in any case, that her feelings might be reciprocated.

And then it had been over, he'd walked her back to her B&B and their handshake at the door had been warm but final, leaving her feeling flat.

'If it weren't inappropriate' – he'd waited till the last moment – 'I think I'd be asking if we could do this again.'

'Would it be inappropriate?'

'I'm here on behalf of the school.' Rider's mouth edged into wry mode. 'So yes, it feels that way.'

'I guess you're probably right,' Liza had said.

And that had been that.

Except that next morning, on checking out, she found that he'd come by earlier and had left an envelope for her containing a photograph of the violin drawing, signed by the artist (so maybe she was a girlfriend – maybe that was how he'd got it signed so fast), together with a note.

> *'The real work definitely would have been inappropriate, but I thought you might get a kick out of this. You can look at it and remember the kids. I know you'll do them proud.'*

She'd driven by the school but he'd been off somewhere with a group, so she'd scribbled a quick message of thanks and assurance that she'd be doing her very best and got back in her car, still warmed by the photo and his note.

But then, the first thing that had happened when she got back was that she'd caught the flu. The real McCoy, the kind that made you sick as hell and left you shaky for weeks.

The second thing, soon after the start of the fall semester, had changed everything for everyone.

9/11. Liza had written the piece by then, but now there was no space for it. She'd sent a letter of explanation and regret, addressing it to him c/o Walden Pond, but the response had come from the school because Rider was, of course, no longer there. She hoped he'd been sent a copy of her apology but didn't feel she could bother the school to ask about that, not at such a time, her feature so trivial a casualty she knew it would not be missed, probably not even by him. Massively greater things by far to be written about and wept over, people turning to those close at hand to share the horrors.

It would have been the same for Michael Rider.

Out of sight, out of mind.

Though it had not, in fact, been the last she'd heard about him.

Two years later, she'd spotted his name in a small article in the *Boston Globe*, and had read with dismay what had happened to him. Had learned, too, for the first time, about his connection with Shiloh and the Cromwell family. Having no other point of contact, she had mailed another letter c/o Walden Pond, marking it for forwarding, asking if there was anything she could do to help, because what he'd been accused of doing made no sense to her, but her letter had come back unopened with a note from the school's personnel department saying they had no forwarding address.

Nothing more she could do but remember, then put Michael Rider back into her mental lockbox and get on with her own life.

Some things just not meant to be.

Ten

The Messenger had spoken to him two evenings ago, just after lights out.

Clanging into his head suddenly, the way it often happened.

Issuing a command. Briefly and unequivocally.

So now he was here. Had found the place he was intended to find. Near Nooseneck, Kent County. Inside Grace Church. A simple house of worship, nothing fancy, yet still, a place obviously well-cared-for, smelling of polish. Ready for Sunday service.

This being Friday, though, there was no one here but the organist, practicing the *Te Deum Prelude* up front. Not much of an instrument, nor much of an organist. Playing badly, making the music ugly, the way *these* people were when their outer shells of piety were scraped away, the wickedness exposed.

He had a bad headache, and the music was hurting him, pounding in his skull. But the Messenger was back again, making himself heard. Louder, more powerful than any other sound could be.

The young man's hands and feet worked, his shoulders stooped, his eyes scanning the sheet music on its stand. Oblivious to anything else.

38

Unaware that an alms basin stored beneath a table in the narthex had been quietly removed, was gripped in the right hand of the man who had once been the boy who spoke to angels.

The basin, made of brass, ready to be swung.

As the Messenger directed.

Three hours later, the organist, whose name was Larry Kurtz, saw Death descending on him, saw its fizzing white heat in the pitch darkness, and understood only its absolute *strangeness*, because though he played organ part-time for Grace Church, he was not overly religious, and yet the instrument of his end appeared to be a cross.

'Oh, Jesus!' he cried out, his voice muffled by the material that had been bound around his lower face, covering his mouth . . .

The cross came down slowly, appearing disembodied, though Larry knew that there was a human being holding it, controlling it, and he squeezed his eyes shut, waiting for it, praying inside his head, because prayer was all he had now.

It touched down on his forehead gently, no force behind it.

'In the name of the Father,' his captor's voice said.

It took seconds for the pain to penetrate, along with the scorched smell and sizzle of his forehead's thin skin and the bone beneath it, and then, just as Larry began to scream, he realized that he was being *branded*.

He felt the light weight lift off, dared to open his eyes, saw it seem to fly away, heard soft footsteps, heard another small sound, saw a palely flickering bluish glow on the ceiling above, struggled to wonder where they were, how he'd gotten here trussed up, naked, on cold, damp ground, tethered to something invisible, something hard.

The darkness was impenetrable, but he heard breathing, movement, fabric rustling.

His tormentor struck a match. Larry smelled sulfur, saw another glimmer – of candlelight, he thought – and then there was another sound.

'Oh, God.'

It was a blowtorch, had to be, Larry recognizing it because his father used one for welding. And then the sound cut out and the footsteps came closer, and with them the hovering, burning cross.

It descended more swiftly this time.

'And of the son,' the voice said.

The cross landed on his naked chest, over his heart, and Larry screamed again, and the cross went away, and there was more blue light and the hiss and whoosh of the blowtorch, and he knew now that there would be two more brandings, that this was the Trinitarian formula, that he was being stamped with the Sign of the Cross, so two more, left shoulder, then right.

His next scream twisted into a howl . . .

'And of the Holy Spirit.'

Different sounds suddenly, *human*. Breathing, growing more and more rapid, like a sobbing sound, and it sounded almost like the monster was masturbating, for Christ's sake, and he was *saying* something . . .

'He that speaketh lies shall not escape.' The voice was breathless and low, but clear. 'He that speaketh lies shall perish.'

He was not going to survive, Larry realized. Except those words made no sense, because he hadn't spoken lies so far as he could recall, at least no more than most people did now and then. But the blue fire was burning again, and his abductor, his torturer, was working himself up into a frenzy.

'Put on the whole armor of God.'

Larry stopped listening, felt his soul shrivel with terror.

'I'm sorry,' he whispered in his mind to his father.

'I love you,' he told his mother.

And then, finally: 'Please help me, God.'

No help coming. Only the white-hot cross.

Coming down real hard this time, smashing down on his Adam's apple, cutting off his scream. Cutting off his breath.

'Amen,' the voice said. 'Amen.'

And the cross rose up and came down again and again, no longer branding Larry Kurtz, church organist and pleasant, happy human being. Bludgeoning now, stabbing, pulverizing flesh and bone, over and over and over.

'Amen, amen, amen . . .'

Eleven

In the summer of 2002, Michael had returned to Walden Pond Campus School to volunteer again. One year after the journalist major with the direct blue eyes and short, wavy blonde hair had wasted his and the children's time on the so-called 'feature' which had never materialized; Liza Plain, who'd claimed – who'd really seemed – to be so genuinely interested, who hadn't even possessed the common courtesy to write or call, and Emily had warned him long ago about journalists, but Liza had seemed different. He'd felt more than a little attracted to her, had really felt they'd *connected* . . .

That disappointment in the past a year ago, his reconnection with those remarkable kids much more important; another summer in which to build up his experience and hope to make a difference. Besides which, he'd met Louise Lawson. Mom of eight-year-old Jessica, a bright, sweet child with cerebral palsy, mother and daughter both dark-haired with soft eyes and a great, positive attitude. Louise, single since her husband had walked out six years back, had invited Michael to a barbecue at her parents' house in Concord where she lived, and the spark between them had ignited into something stronger. They'd begun getting together every chance they had, Michael driving up regularly, Edward and Julie Parks, Louise's parents, more than welcoming.

And then, just before Thanksgiving, Michael had decided it was time to share his family history with Louise, and she had repeated the tale to her parents.

Beginning of the end.

The old story: sins of the grandfather.

'There's *evil* in his blood,' an appalled Edward Parks had told Louise.

'If you don't have the sense to think of your own safety,' Julie Parks had said, 'can't you at least consider Jessica's?'

Louise had been outraged, had told them that Michael's mother had been sure of Cromwell's innocence, and that anyway, it had nothing to do with Michael.

'The bastard committed suicide,' Parks said flatly. 'Guilty as hell.'

'And it's not as if Cromwell's daughter came out of it *normal*,' Julie Parks had added.

The fact was, they said, Michael Rider was the grandson of a child-killer and a woman in a mental institution. The son of a degenerate alcoholic druggie.

Parks had gone to the local press. Parents needed to know the kind of man who had the daily care of their vulnerable children. The papers had bitten, and in the space of a few low-news days, the story had made its way into the *Providence Journal*, even scoring a few lines in the *Boston Globe*.

Hard to know who Michael despised more: Louise's parents or the journalists who'd picked up their poison and run with it. Louise had wanted to stick by him, but, shocked and depressed and hating to put her or Jess through any more, he'd ended it and dropped out of college.

Within a month, Emily had begun drinking again and then, staggeringly swiftly, all the wheels had come off. First, she'd lost her job, then the house, and soon mother and son had crashed to earth in a South Boston one-bed.

* * *

43

It might, up to that point, have been reparable. But one afternoon the following February, a journalist had approached Michael in the street, getting right in his face, refusing to take no for an answer, asking intrusive questions.

One too many.

Michael had lost it, smashed the guy's camera, busted his nose and ended up in court.

It had been a first offense and the judge had been lenient, but Emily, distraught and blaming herself, had tried to drown her guilt in vodka, taken too many sleeping pills and choked to death on her vomit.

That same night, shattered, grieving and guilty, Michael had gone back to their old Pawtucket house, climbed up onto the roof with a bottle of whiskey and had fallen off into the backyard. He'd woken up in the ER with minor injuries, people telling him how *lucky* he was.

He had not felt lucky.

He'd been on his way to the men's room when, still half out of his mind, he'd spotted an unattended instrument cart and grabbed a small scalpel so he could finish the job that he guessed he'd been starting up on the roof. But a nurse had seen him and tried to take it off him, and the *last* thing Michael had wanted was to hurt her, but she was tough, had really wrestled him for it, and her arm had gotten badly cut, an artery sliced.

Major injury. Her attacker deemed a danger to himself and the public, and sent to the psychiatric wing at the Garthville House of Corrections.

Infamous place back then, where bad things happened.

All the same to Michael Rider, who'd given up.

The *real* start of a long downward line on the 'tragigraph' that Liza Plain would come to trace thirteen or so years later.

Descent almost vertical.

To his personal ground zero.

His hatred for journalists had grown during his time at Garthville.

He blamed them for *everything*, had made the mistake of telling that to one of the shrinks, whose subsequent report had stated that Rider was a potential risk to all newspaper and media-related people, that until he could properly address this and come to terms with it, he needed to remain in custody.

Another reason to hate them.

It was a while before he scrabbled back enough logic to realize that honesty was no way to go. Better to take meds as prescribed, not to speak of blaming others for his own weakness, to tell them instead that he was remorseful and learning about acceptance and renewal of optimism.

Michael had not been brought up to lie.

Scary how a man could change in five years.

It was true that he hated himself even more than the journalists. All that love and care and money wasted on him by Emily. And in the end, he'd let her down.

He'd as good as killed her.

He had still been on antidepressants upon his release, had tried several times to quit, but the bleakness always returned, a growing reluctance to face every dawning day, and sometimes he forced himself to think back to the brave kids at Walden Pond, but all that did was bring him memories of Louise and Jess, and greater shame. So he'd continued on the meds, had done his best to get work, but no job lasted for long because he was too consumed by bitterness and self-loathing.

For a while, he went all the way under, really let himself go. Drank too much, got in fights, his self-destructive behavior getting him locked up again. In Quidnick Correctional Center, a *real* prison this time.

For the very first time, he was glad that his mother was not alive to see him.

'Are you proud?' he asked his warped reflection one day, staring into one of the battered steel sheets that passed for mirrors in such places.

He got no answer, had to look away again.

Let himself go again.

In 2010, life took an upturn after his parole officer, a good guy, kicked Michael's butt until he got his act together. He attended a One-Stop Career Center for ex-offenders, went to counseling sessions, bought a laptop from a pawnshop so he could put together a résumé; and then a counselor set up an interview with the manager of a Quincy Market café, an open-minded man named Jake Bollino.

Michael landed a job waiting tables, serving happy, *normal* people, and just having pleasant work to do, having customers thank him when he brought their good food or coffee or fresh-squeezed

46

juice made him feel that he might, after all, have a future.

'You have any ambitions?' Bollino asked him one afternoon.

'Just one right now,' Michael answered. 'To stay here.'

He meant it, felt as close to content as he needed to be, having the café, a nice sublet in Allston and an old black Giant bike that Jake swore no one needed.

Some people were just *good*.

And then, one spring day in 2013, off his meds, promoted to assistant manager and considering applying for the vacant manager's job in the café's other branch, he took a late lunch break and spotted Louise sitting alone at a window table in Anthem Kitchen picking at a salad.

Michael stopped, his heart lurching, unsure what to do.

And then Louise saw him. A smile lit up her face, and that was it, he had to go inside, and she stood up and they hugged, and she began to cry and told him that Jess had succumbed to pneumonia in February, had passed away. And for a while after that they sat quietly together, Michael shedding tears too for Jess and her mother, telling Louise about his new life, staying gently upbeat, until he realized that he had to get back to the café.

'Can I call you?' he asked.

'The sooner the better,' she said.

Two days later, she came to meet him at the end of his shift.

They embraced, and Michael introduced her to Jake, and then he turned around.

And saw Edward Parks.

Nearly a decade older, but still colder than frost to Michael.

Julie Parks had spotted his name on an email on Louise's laptop, it quickly transpired, and Louise was furious with both her parents, but it was plain that the Parks machine had already ground into motion. In front of paying customers, Parks informed Jake that he'd told the proprietor that Michael Rider was a convicted felon and a danger to the public, had been in a psychiatric institution as well as prison and could not be trusted around sharp objects.

The proprietor had assured Parks that Michael was *out*.

He saw right away in Louise's devastated eyes that she wasn't up to the fight, watched her leave with her father, saw her angry body language, but doubted that she'd be back in touch. And if he did hear from her, he would push her away, because this was how it would always be. No second chance for them.

Jake was deeply upset, but in no position to fight his boss.

'I'll give you a good reference,' he said.

'Better not make it on company stationery,' Michael said, 'or you might be out too.'

'It'll be a great reference,' Jake said quietly. 'But if Parks tries this the next place you work, you might be advised to get yourself a lawyer.'

Pointless advice, they both realized, because Michael couldn't afford an attorney, and even if he could, he wouldn't stand a chance against a man like Parks. Deep pockets plus enmity. No chance.

Down he went again, really spiraling this time, doing it hard. No money to speak of coming in, the Allston sublet lost, his laptop and the bike – which Jake had insisted he keep – his only significant possessions. Living in a shithole of a room on one of Roxbury's bad streets, he began drinking again, not really caring what came next. Jake's reference helped him find a breakfast shift job, but three hung-over late starts saw him fired.

What he deserved.

He'd had his chances and he'd screwed up.

Louise had never gotten back in touch and he couldn't blame her.

It was what he deserved.

End of.

Twelve

2014

It had been more than a week since Michael had seen Liza Plain in Copp's Hill and bolted. He'd gone back twice, because he liked the place, had hung around for a while in case the journalist was there again, but with no sign of her, he guessed it was OK to return.

He felt as comfortable here as anyplace, and today was a pretty fall day and the birds were singing, so he decided he'd sit for a while, maybe even take a look at a psychology essay he'd begun when he'd worked at the café. He hadn't realized that he was hungry until he smelled the hot dog cart pulling up outside the Hull Street entrance, and on impulse he hid his laptop and book under his old, cracked leather jacket, jogged over to the vendor, bought his dog and a Coke, turned around and saw, immediately, that though his bicycle was where he'd left it, the jacket had been moved.

'Fuck,' he said, and sprinted back.

Book still there. Laptop gone.

His link to the world, to a semblance of sanity, stolen.

'*Fuck*.'

His stomach clenched, anger flaring in his chest, scanned around, saw no one.

Just graves.

He sank down on the grass next to his bike and jacket, and then he glanced down and saw that he'd been squeezing the dog in its napkin with his clenched right hand, that it had leaked ketchup and mustard down his sweatshirt and old Levis.

Not that he had any appetite left. And he didn't know who he was angrier at: the thief or himself for his sheer stupidity for *leaving* the computer.

'Fuck,' he said again, quietly.

And, oh Christ, he felt so goddamned *finished*, and he wanted out, almost as badly as the last time, but he didn't think he had the guts.

Thirty-five and useless.

Finished.

Back in Roxbury, he dragged himself and his bike up the stairs – and saw it.

A brown paper package leaning against his cruddy front door.

He never got packages.

It had no label. Weighed a few pounds.

Heart beating faster, he stuck it under his arm, opened his door, wheeled the bike inside, kicked the door shut behind him, then tore open the paper and the corrugated stuff within it.

'Hey,' he said.

His laptop.

His, for sure, knowing its scratches well.

There was no note.

He opened it up and turned it on, rested it on the table, got himself a glass of water, downed it in one, then pulled up his only chair and looked at it.

His personal, familiar desktop was gone.

Just three big, bold words in the center of the screen.

YOURS, I BELIEVE

Anger surged again.

'Son of a bitch,' he said.

The thief had stolen his property and then messed with it.

And then he'd given it back.

For another moment, Michael regarded the words almost warily, and then he tried the startup. It worked, so he started checking over his stuff, making sure that his essay was still there, seeing if his emails were working, his free downloads there . . .

Everything seemed in place except the desktop. Nothing but new junk in the emails, his Word files apparently unmodified.

51

He ought to be grateful to have it back, and he *was*.

But still, this was weird and more than a little creepy.

Then again, this was Boston, and Michael had taken to hanging out in a cemetery, for fuck's sake, so maybe someone had been watching him. Maybe this was their idea of a joke. Or who knew, maybe some Good Samaritan had witnessed the theft and gotten it back for Michael, then followed him so he could return it without fuss.

Impossible, since the package had gotten here before him.

More probably the thief/finder had found his address inside the PC. Not hard, since Michael didn't bother with passwords, and he'd created a letterhead for job applications. His address was on his résumé too, so there was no mystery about where he lived, and maybe, after all, someone had done him a kindness.

Bottom line, there seemed to be no harm done, and he had it *back*.

And the fact was a real dark day had ended on an almost sunny, if quirky, note.

So, room for hope, maybe.

Not that he was any better off than he had been this morning. Worse, in fact, since he'd had a shitload of stress, plus he'd never even gotten to eat the dog he'd paid good bucks for.

Life still stank.

Like they said, it was shit, and then you died.

And, looking around his pisshole of a 'home', hopelessness already weighing back down on him, that last part couldn't come a day too soon.

Thirteen

With Thanksgiving just two days away, after which Christmas would inexorably power down on them, Liza was busy writing website updates for the season's hard sell in between copyediting a novel for a Providence-based publisher and helping with the clean-up of the recently flooded office of a local children's charity.

So much for her ambitions.

By 2003, sucked back home after her college freedom, she'd taken a reporting job with the *Shiloh Weekly*, while always staying on the lookout for a permanent exit. Meantime, there was local news, such as it was, to help hone her basic skills, and also access, finally, to the files on the old murder case stored in editor-proprietor Thomas Osborn's archives. Which seemed anticlimactic after so long, because Liza had, of course, moved on. The cold truth was that people like her – borderline-mediocre journalist majors – had to grab anything they could, and there were websites paying fees to writers good enough to help them snare clients, and Liza had discovered a knack for advertorial and press release writing, so by the end of 2004 she'd been working for five websites and two Boston businesses.

And then the Boxing Day tsunami had swept away almost a quarter of a million human beings, and yet again, Liza had reeled and wept along with the rest of the world, feeling shame, not just for the inadequacy of the words she'd written about the catastrophe, but for the fact that she could be inspired by the hideous nightmares of others.

'Scum.' Stephen Plain had resurrected his tired old insult, watching TV interviews with survivors and relatives.

Not for the first time, Liza had wondered if he might have a point.

It was Ben Kaminski, her best friend at college, who had saved her, telling her in 2006 about the room in his Boston apartment on Snow Hill Street that had become available. Thanks to his generously low rent, her prolific website work, plus a copyediting sideline and a dog-walking job, she'd finally been in a position to leave home for real. And since then, on the personal front, there had been plenty of dating and two long relationships with nice men – neither of them the 'one' – both ultimately fizzing out. Now and then, a glance up at the framed photograph of the charcoal-drawn violin on her bedroom wall caused a small dig of regret and fresh concern about what had happened to Michael Rider. Once, she'd taken the photo down and put it in a drawer, but the next day she'd hung it back up again because the fact was she liked it, and those twenty-four hours at Walden Pond were a good memory.

She'd had enough money coming in to pay bills and shrink her outstanding loan. Occasional income from writing features for free dailies, a happy period with a trainee investigative reporting job at WHDH-TV, followed by a short-term job at NBC Universal, working out of Hartford. But then everything had ground to a shattering halt in early 2009 with her parents' death, after which Liza had attempted for a few months to see if some kind of existence with her grandfather might work out.

It had not, unsurprisingly and not least because, with his son gone, Stephen Plain had taken to openly blaming Joanna Plain for indulging Liza's ambitions, for being an inadequate wife and even for the fact that, with Andrew Plain dead, the office in their house would stand forever empty, the village left without a doctor, and he left without a single caring relative.

'Which will suit me well enough for the time remaining to me,' he had told Liza. 'And far better a housekeeper, a stranger, than the granddaughter who probably wishes I'd been in the car with my son.'

Ben had suggested that the old man might be pushing her away for her sake, but though Liza had seriously doubted that, it had still added extra guilt and self-reproach to her grief. Both emotions self-indulgent and pointless, she'd decided after a while, impatient with herself, especially since Stephen seemed to be thriving under the care of the housekeeper in question, a local woman named Ethel Murrow, who still called her employer 'Doctor' and took pride in caring for him.

Five years later, with her life back in Boston at Ben's, her income still coming from diverse sources, journalism rather depressingly near the bottom of the heap, Liza's brief sighting of Michael Rider in the graveyard had triggered a new impulse to write a Shiloh-based feature: the real story *behind* the murder case, the stuff that people had been reluctant to talk about with a young person. The story, perhaps, behind Rider and his family.

'I thought you'd moved on,' Ben said this Tuesday evening.

It was cold outside and raining, and they were eating chowder.

'It isn't actually the murder I want to write about now,' she said. 'I understood Cromwell's wife cracking up and their daughter turning to drink, obviously. But what happened to Emily's son, to Michael, seems so crazily out of keeping with the man he seemed to be when we met.' She shook her head. 'I know bad things can change people, but I just can't forget how great he was with those kids, Ben.'

'I still find it hard to believe you didn't know he was Cromwell's grandson.' Ben spooned out the remains of his chowder.

Liza shrugged. 'I guess we were both distancing ourselves from Shiloh.'

'He clearly doesn't want to talk to you now.'

'Maybe if I could get him to listen, he might change his mind.'

'You'll have to find him first.'

'I know where he went to college, I know he volunteered at Walden Pond, I know where he served his jail time. If I can't dig up some point of contact, then I'm even more of a failure as a journalist than I thought.'

56

Ben picked up both bowls, took them to the sink.

'Maybe this is telling you it's time to go home, visit with your granddad.'

He was right, Liza knew, her last visit two Thanksgivings ago.

'I was thinking next year,' she said.

'He's an old man. He might not still be around next year.'

'He's a curmudgeon, and he's never cared about Christmas.'

'He's your only family,' Ben persisted. 'Besides, if you want to write about Rider . . .'

'I don't have to go to Shiloh to do that.'

'If you wait much longer, Stephen might get Alzheimer's.'

'At least if he forgets who I am, he might like me.'

'Not nice, Liza,' Ben said.

'I'm not sure that I am very nice,' Liza said.

Fourteen

Michael was home when the email arrived.

It was Wednesday, the day before Thanksgiving, just another lousy late November afternoon so far as he was concerned. He'd started out the day quite upbeat, checking websites for paid work, then lowering his sights for volunteer ushering opportunities at a couple of theaters, failing on all fronts; and then he'd figured that a bike ride alongside the Charles River might give his soul a boost.

And so it might have, had a white van not cut across his lane near the Harvard Bridge. No real physical damage to him, just scratches and bruises, but his bike, that precious gift and possession, had been wrecked. Totaled. Kaput. The end.

Bad, bad day.

And now, a new piece of weirdness on his PC, in his mail inbox.

> From: Reaper at Whirlwind
> Are anger, hatred or bitterness destroying your life, Michael Rider? Are any or all of these emotions eating away at you, sapping your energy, ruining your personal relationships, making it hard for you to love or work successfully? Does no one understand your feelings? Has counseling failed you? Join Whirlwind in the security of anonymity, and share your problems. Lean on us and help others in similar situations. Join us in finding a way to channel negative emotions and impulses into a worthwhile, lucrative cause.
> *'They have sown the wind, and they shall reap the whirlwind.'* Hosea, chapter 8, verse 7.

Bizarrely apt, but just another piece of junk mail.

Michael consigned it to trash.

Even if it did pretty much fit his crappy life.

* * *

No luck yet locating Michael Rider, though Liza felt she might be getting closer.

She'd learned nothing either from his college or from Walden Pond, and then she'd run a logic trail leading from the Quidnick Correctional Center to Boston's North End, trying to follow the route of a fundamentally decent ex-offender via the substantial supply of organizations set up to help former prisoners get back on their feet.

In the process, she'd encountered mostly busy people with better things to do than talk to dubious strangers; but then she'd found a nice guy at a career center who remembered Rider, who said he knew the counselor who'd gotten him a job two or so years back – though Liza surely realized, he'd added, that no counselor would give her personal information about a client, present or past.

'The thing is,' Liza had said, 'when I caught that glimpse of him a couple of weeks ago he didn't look great, and all I'm hoping for is a chance to talk to him again, and most people need all the friends they can get, don't you think?'

'Some do,' the career center man had said.

'So all I'm asking is that if this counselor knows how to get hold of Michael, he could just tell him that Liza Plain would really like to speak to him.'

Career man had seen no problem with her just leaving her phone number.

No calls yet.

Fifteen

The motel room was more than adequate. The location vaguely interesting, the town of Danvers, Massachusetts having once been known as Salem Village and, a couple of centuries later, as the site of a psychiatric hospital known by some as the Danvers Lunatic Asylum. To him, though, at this point in his life, to the man known to a very few chosen people as 'Reaper', it was simply a place to sleep and work.

His goal finally beginning to come into view.

His own end in sight, too, for which he was grateful, the pain of his metastatic cancer becoming harder to tolerate as the weeks wore on, the limited medication that he permitted himself no longer really adequate. In a hospital, or certainly in a hospice, he would probably by now be heading into a blur, pain gradually dulled until at last . . .

No real rest for him. Not yet. Not until his work was complete.

Much to do.

Reaper sat in the lumpy armchair, set his open MacBook on his knees and regarded the item frozen on its twelve-inch screen, downloaded courtesy of the Vanderbilt Television News Archive and a minor miracle, considering that, to the world at large, this little piece of news history was of zero interest.

Not to him.

Or to a number of others. Not all of them appearing in this video, which he had already played many times.

He pressed Play again now, and there was grim-faced CBS reporter Dick Rosworth again, standing outside the perimeter of RIDOC Maximum Security Prison back in 1976, microphone in hand, addressing the camera.

'The trial of Donald Cromwell at the Providence County Superior Court, that has gripped the citizens of New England for more than two weeks, came to a premature end yesterday when the former president of the Shiloh town council – a man tipped for higher office until horror and scandal rocked his life – was found dead in his cell at the maximum security prison known as "steel city".'

The video cut to an image of Cromwell in happier times, presiding over a summer lunch in a handsome backyard, his wife, young daughter and two friends smiling at the table.

'Full details have still to emerge, but sources suggest that Cromwell – who stood accused of the abduction and murder of seven-year-old Alice Millicent in the village of Shiloh, Rhode Island—'

The report cut to a moving shot of the village.

'—took his own life.'

The camera focused on Cromwell's home, Shiloh Oaks.

'Witnesses present during the last days in court have said that Cromwell had appeared progressively more depressed as the prosecution laid out

61

its case. It seems ironic that Mr Cromwell's own lawyers had not yet begun the case for the defense.'

Another shot of Cromwell with wife, Susan, vacationing in Newport.

'His death leaves many unanswered questions. Was this perhaps an innocent man wanting to spare his family more pain? Or a guilty man unable to endure the shame? We may never learn the truth.'

Now a photograph of the victim, seven candles on her cake at her last birthday party.

'Just as we may now never know, beyond reasonable doubt, who brutally murdered little Alice last summer.' Dick Rosworth paused. 'Mr Cromwell leaves a wife and daughter. Alice Millicent left a brother and two still-grieving parents.'

Reaper pressed the stop button, leaned back with a sigh, and closed his eyes.

Rest first.

Then to work.

Sixteen

On December 2, Liza was home, working on her favorite part-time job, a blog she ghost-wrote for the website of a Boston-based crime writer, a man at ease with creating his characters' worlds but unwilling to write about his own life. When the phone rang, she picked up absently.

'Liza Plain.'

'What is it you want?'

The hostility in the voice startled her, yet she knew instantly who it was.

'Michael.' She sounded calm. 'I'm so glad you've called.'

'For one reason only,' he said flat out. 'To make sure you never play a stroke like that again. That you leave me alone.'

The words stung, but she stayed even. 'I know it might have seemed a little sneaky.'

'To hell with sneaky,' Michael Rider said. 'It was intrusive and low.'

'And I'm sorry for that, but I couldn't think of another way to speak to you.'

'It takes two to make a conversation.'

'You didn't have to call me.' Liza took a breath. 'Michael, I didn't know, when I came to Walden Pond, who you were. I didn't even know you were from Shiloh.'

'Would you actually have written your "feature" if you had known?'

'I did write it,' Liza said. 'But then 9/11 happened, and—'

'I'm aware of what happened,' Rider said. 'And you're obviously more interested in me now because you've found out some things about me, but I stopped talking to journalists a long time ago.' His voice was flat, hard. 'Please don't try to contact me again.'

'When I read about what happened to—'

He was gone.

Caller's number withheld.

Liza stared at the phone, a heap of conflicting emotions stirring. Annoyance, upset, confusion, embarrassment, even shame.

'Shit,' she said.

And went back to the blog.

A lot to be said for fiction.

Michael didn't much like the way he'd spoken to her.

Because maybe – only *maybe* – Liza Plain might just be what she'd seemed way back then.

Too long ago to think about. Different times. Different world to him.

And she was a journalist. One of *them*. And he hadn't asked her to get in touch. He'd made it plain enough when he'd turned his back on her in Copp's Hill that day that he didn't want to talk to her, and only the most insensitive person could have failed to read that clear message.

Only a reporter. With a nose for a story. Which had to have been what she was after when she'd persuaded his former counselor to pass on her message.

'No way,' he said now, deleting her number.

No *way* was he ever going to help anyone write another word about him and demolish what little was left of his life.

The beep of new mail on his laptop cut off his bitter thoughts.

He opened it.

From: Reaper at Whirlwind
We know all about pain and bitterness.
We understand isolation.
But the time has come for us to help
one another.

Wouldn't you like friends to lean on, Michael Rider?
Whirlwind wants you to join us.
Whirlwind needs you.
'*They have sown the wind, and they shall reap the whirlwind.*' Hosea, chapter 8, verse 7.

He went on staring at the message for a while.

Other words abruptly coming back to him – those he'd found on his desktop after his stolen laptop had been returned. *Yours, I believe.*

That possible connection had not occurred to him when he'd received the first of these emails from 'Reaper at Whirlwind', but suddenly it seemed more than probable.

'Fuck,' he said angrily.

He stabbed at the junk key, and the message vanished.

But its words lingered.

Along with that intrusive use of his name again. Right after Liza Plain digging into his privacy – and might she be the sender?

'No way.'

He might have been pissed at her for letting him down years ago and later for just being a journalist, and he was mad at her again now for hunting him down, but if he was honest, he still remembered how much he'd liked her, that he'd been intensely attracted to those clear blue eyes and petite, curvy body – and most of all her ease with the kids. She'd been relaxed around them, there'd been no fakery.

Whatever this was had nothing to do with her.

65

'*Reaper.*'

Maybe – probably – it was the same person who'd stolen his computer, trying to get into his head for fuck-knew what reason, and he'd had enough of jerks screwing around with him.

Only one way to try and find out who this was.

He went into his junk folder and opened the email up again.

Clicked Reply, and typed: I'm interested in learning more about Whirlwind.

He held back one more moment, then clicked Send.

Gone.

Seventeen

At around eleven a.m. on December 3, the man known by some as Reaper emerged from the walk-in doctor's office in the strip mall on Shiloh Road and went next door into the drugstore. It was cold and damp, and he moved slowly, a little shakily, needing his cane badly, his face gray with pain.

Inside, the store was quiet, the pharmacist obliging and kindly, directing Reaper to a chair, dispensing two pills within minutes along with a plastic cup of water, advising him to rest until the remainder of the drugs were ready.

'You should eat something,' the man said after Reaper had paid him. 'You need to keep up your strength.'

'That I do,' Reaper said.

'Jack's, two doors away, is pretty good,' the pharmacist told him. 'The special's always the best, if you've the appetite, but most things are fine.'

Reaper thanked him, took his advice, found a table near the back of the small diner and ordered a turkey sandwich, because that usually seemed to sit well with him, and because the pharmacist had been correct.

No time for weakness now.

Places to go.

Shiloh, to be precise.

Where, having parked his rented Ford Focus on Elm Street, he was now taking a walk, and the medication and food had helped, or perhaps, it occurred to him, he felt stronger, almost invigorated, simply by being here at last.

Before long, dusk would fall and lamps indoors would be turned on, but for now, on this early December afternoon, the sun still shone out of an almost clear sky, and there was an air of relaxation about the place.

It never changed much. The shops changed hands now and then, and parking restrictions grew tougher, same as in most places. The Shiloh Inn stood, part white clapboard, part old red stone, on the site where, as attested to by a plaque on a side wall, the elementary school had once stood, a handful of people sitting out in the inn's pretty yard despite the cold, smoking. A few tourists roamed up and down Main Street, snapping each other with their phones, and Reaper walked too, taking it slowly, glancing in at an antique store, looking at the pastel-painted narrow town houses, moving toward the far end of Main Street, to St Matthew's Church.

Nothing special about him to attract attention. Just a tall, thin, gray-haired man with a slight stoop and a polished black cane, walking up the steps to the church's main entrance, holding the heavy door open to allow a woman to enter before him.

And going inside.

Eighteen

1995

The woman he'd abducted earlier from Christ's Church on Farnum Pike, a pretty green road near the village of Primrose, close to the town of North Smithfield in Providence County, had worn a clergy blouse, and was more than probably the Reverend Laura Farrow, associate rector of the church, though there had been no opportunity for introduction before he had choked her into unconsciousness with the black tippet he'd spied hanging in the vestry, where she had been engrossed in writing what might have become her next sermon.

She should, by now, have been dead, ready to join the others below, her grave already dug, but she was not quite gone, and he found himself glad of that.

Glad she was not yet quite extinguished.

Because it meant he had to finish her.

Do it again.

Kill her again.

The hunger was already rising, a beast devouring him from the inside.

No beast, he knew that, even now, in the heat of it. All him.

The woman was watching him through her one undamaged eye, the rest of her face too destroyed to allow speech, though grotesque, bubbling sounds were emerging through the bloodied, swollen flesh and splintered bones. Sounds of suffering and of appeal.

The eye, glinting in the light of the candles that he had lit to see the grave, knew that there would be no help, no stay of execution, and maybe, he thought, the appeal was not her plea for life, but for death.

'Finish me,' the eye said.

So he did.

Nineteen

2014

There were times when it was hard not to believe in fate.

If Liza had brought a cup of coffee to Nancy Schön's *Make Way for Ducklings* bronze statues on a warm summer's day, it would have seemed far less coincidental, because so many people were drawn to that popular spot in the Boston Public Garden each year. But this was December 4, and the weather had turned cloudy, threatening rain, and Liza had come here simply because she felt in need of something to boost her spirits.

And there he was. Michael Rider sitting cross-legged on the grass nearby, apparently lost in thought, looking at the sculptures but not really seeing, she thought.

Not seeing her either, which was presumably how she'd managed to get so close.

'Michael?'

He looked up, startled, brown eyes dark with anger. 'Liza.'

'I'm not stalking you,' she said quickly, lightly.

'Just a lucky strike, right?' He stood up. 'Goodbye.'

'Couldn't we talk?' she asked.

He was already moving away but she wasn't letting him go, walking beside him.

'We have nothing to talk about.' He increased his pace. 'Please leave me alone.'

'I'd really like to talk about what happened to you in 2003.'

He made an impatient sound then carried on walking, and at closer quarters than last time he didn't look exactly shabby, just worn down and mad at the world, certainly at her.

'After I read about that, I wrote to you,' she said, 'but the letter came back, so I gave up.'

'I didn't receive a letter.'

'I wanted to help.'

'You couldn't have.' He kept moving. 'Would you please stop following me.'

'I will.' Liza was still alongside him. 'Only I was just so sorry, hearing that your mother had died.'

He stopped abruptly, wheeled around, his face

70

furious. 'Write one word about my mother, and I'll—' He stopped and turned, strode away.

Momentarily thrown, Liza stood still, then hurried after him.

'Is that what you wanted?' Michael asked. 'More violence from the killer's psycho grandson?' He ground to a halt again. 'You know, I did like you back then, up at Walden Pond, and I really believed you were going to write something worthwhile. And maybe it wasn't your fault that you didn't, but it doesn't mean I'm going to start talking to you now, any more than I would to any other journalist.'

He began walking again, a little more slowly, and Liza stayed with him.

'I don't work for gutter press, Michael,' she said. 'I don't actually work for any newspaper right now.'

'And you figure a story about a loser like me might help you change that.'

'I don't see you that way.'

'I don't give a damn how you see me.'

'I just want to understand what really happened to you.'

'And I just want to be left in peace,' Michael said. 'Is that so hard for you to comprehend? Is your skin really so thick?'

'I don't think so, but—'

He stopped again. 'No buts. No more talk. Not one more word.'

Finally, she knew she'd lost him. Had never had him.

'Got that?' he said, wearily.

She nodded.

'*Got* it?' he repeated.

'Loud and clear,' she said.

Without another word, Michael walked on.

This time, Liza stayed put.

Twenty

2005

It had been a long time.

The hiatus not by choice.

The Messenger had been very patient. Opportunities hard – impossible – to come by.

Patience finally rewarded.

Hope Church near Harmony was small, yet aesthetically pleasing, white and clean, with three attractive stained-glass windows of contemporary design, a triptych worthy of a grander church.

One of the windows was under repair of some kind this evening.

Someone up a ladder inside, visible through the cross in the center section.

Lights already out, he killed the engine, coasted down the slope to the rear of the church, quietly pulled up the handbrake, got out and opened the tailgate, then walked around to the front and went silently inside.

Not so much as a squeak from the door.

And no one else in there.

No need for the Messenger to tell him what to do.

It had been so long, and he was hungry for it, and here it was, like an invitation.

He approached the foot of the ladder.

The man at work on the stained glass was young, listening to music through ear phones, immersed in his intricate labor.

'*As the shaking of an olive tree,*' the Messenger quoted from Isaiah inside the head of the man standing below.

Not one to tolerate being left out, the Messenger.

No tree here, just a ladder.

So he shook that instead.

Twenty-One

2014

Until today, seven days after his last encounter with Liza Plain, Michael had been having a fair week. Volunteer ushering at the Harvard Film Archive one evening, same gig at the Tate Museum of Fine Art for three, and *that* was the one he'd been hoping for, because the TMFA liked long-term commitment, so maybe it might lead someplace, and though Michael was the oldest usher in the museum, his line manager seemed to like him, and he guessed he'd been rubbing along pretty well with the visitors. And so, yes, this week he had been almost *happy* . . .

And then there they were.

Edward and Julie Parks.

The architects of the beginning of his ruin, and the wreckers of his last attempt at rehab. Here again now, eighteen months later, their stares furious enough to make him aware that he was finished at the Tate before he'd really begun.

His line manager was embarrassed and apologetic.

'They're generous patrons, Michael,' he told him. 'I know it's unfair, but we have no choice but to let you go.'

'There's always a choice,' Michael told him.

Beyond disconsolate, he left the museum and walked home, hoping the exercise might help him burn off some of the anger, considering stopping at a bar and getting hammered, knowing it wouldn't really help his blues; besides which, he couldn't afford it.

'Oh, Christ,' he muttered, still walking, wishing his mind would just stop, wishing *he* would stop, because he'd been screwed yet again, and how much more could a man take?

Back in his room, legs aching, he put the kettle on the stove to make coffee, then turned on the laptop.

And there it was.

From: Reaper at Whirlwind
If there was a way of proving to the world that Donald Cromwell did not murder Alice Millicent, would you take it? If there was a way to avenge the destruction of your family and the theft of your personal happiness, would you take that?
'*They have sown the wind, and they shall*

74

reap the whirlwind.' Hosea, chapter 8, verse 7.

The shock was profound. Anger flaring first, familiar and sickening, before it dissipated and his legs turned to jelly and he had to sit down, trying to make sense of the new, unanticipated burst of *longing* suddenly overwhelming him.

This was insane. He needed to delete it, from the PC and from his mind.

But Emily's face was suddenly right there, and his awareness of the ruination of her childhood, about *her* struggles rather than his own, and none of that would have happened if it hadn't been for the murder, and what if his grandfather *had* been innocent – as she'd believed – and what if this 'Reaper' was someone who really could help him prove that?

His hand moved to the trackball and hovered.

'Crazy,' he said.

Don't go there, his rational mind told him.

Michael ignored it.

He moved the cursor onto Reply and tapped out his answer.

One word.

Yes.

Twenty-Two

Seated in the comfortable armchair in his wood-paneled room at the Red Door Inn in Woonsocket, Reaper nodded, satisfied.

75

This place was a gift to himself. A night or two of real comfort while preparations continued. There'd been too many nights of discomfort and ugliness, years of endurance, then of making ends meet while he worked things out. Life in a trailer, for a time, though that had made his chest worse, and he'd known he had to survive a while longer.

The Ford rental had been exchanged for a Volvo XC70. The right car for the job, whatever the weather, he'd been assured.

His short home movie already prerecorded, only his voiceover to add.

No script needed. Just a tumbler of malt whisky – strictly *pro*scribed by the last doctor he'd seen before the man on Shiloh Road a week ago.

No more doctors for him now, ever, if he had his way.

The movie was on his screen, ready to run, first clip selected, voiceover primed.

Shiloh Village in the fall. Nature rendering it pretty as a picture.

As deceptive as some of its inhabitants.

He began to speak into the built-in microphone.

'I present you with some of the citizens of Shiloh. All of them witnesses for the prosecution against the then town council president, Donald T. Cromwell.'

Second clip of a white-haired elderly man emerging from a clapboard house.

'Seth Glover. Owner of the local food market at the time, and the only eye witness to the abduction, who testified to having seen Alice Millicent climbing into Cromwell's Cadillac Seville. Glover's retired now, but his son Adam has expanded the old business . . .'

A shot of a store on a busy main street: Glover's of Greenville.

'. . . into one of the finest markets in Providence County.'

Cut back to Seth Glover, walking down his pathway.

'Seth's a grandfather, but he still lives in his old Shiloh house, in an add-on built by Adam and Claire, his daughter-in-law.'

The next clip was of another man of similar years, well-dressed, gray-haired and paunchy, walking into the Shiloh Inn, once the school.

'John Tilden, formerly of Tilden's restaurant, now the proprietor of the village inn, who made remarks during the trial about the councilor's womanizing habits. The defense objected and the judge sustained. Tilden's eighty now, but doesn't he look fit and prosperous? He lost his first two wives, but then he married Eleanor.'

The movie cut to the bar at the Shiloh Inn, to a strong, vigorous-looking blonde woman in her mid-sixties, pouring drinks for customers.

'Ellie used to run her own café, but now she pretty much rules the inn and their marriage, and I've heard it said that she's cut her husband's drink tab in half.'

Reaper froze the frame and reached for his own glass. The whisky burned as it went down, but he relished it anyway, wanted it – and other motivations aside, wasn't all this ultimately about what he wanted?

He replaced the glass, began to cough, and opened the small bottle of water standing beside the whisky, drank a little, fought to try to prevent the cough from having its way, felt it settle, then threaten again.

'No,' he told it, and it subsided.

He restarted the movie.

Another clip: a third elderly, tall man climbing slowly out of the passenger seat of a Chevy.

'Dr Stephen Plain. Answers given by the now-retired doctor to the prosecution's loaded questions concerning Cromwell's "inappropriate closeness" to Emily, his own daughter, raised furious objections by the defense. They were the last pieces of testimony heard by the accused before he took his own life.'

Reaper paused to cough again, took another sip of water, then forged on.

Two women in their sixties now on the screen, sweeping leaves off a driveway, both energetic, laughing.

'The redhead is Gwen Turner.' Reaper's voice was a little huskier. 'The teacher on duty in the playground at the time of Alice Millicent's disappearance. She wept on the stand because of her sense of guilt, but admitted, under duress, that she had once told a colleague that during an official school visit by Cromwell he'd seemed to pay more attention to the girls than the boys.' Reaper paused. 'Turner left Shiloh soon after, but returned to her parents' house after their deaths ten years later. She lives there still, with her partner, Jill Barrow.'

Next, a signpost reading *Jackson Farm*, and

another old couple, sitting on a porch drinking out of mugs.

'That's Mark Jackson with his wife, Ann. Jackson told the court that they'd once seen the councilor in a Providence department store buying women's underwear and joking about it. The prosecutor was chastised, Jackson's remarks stricken from the record, and in any event, though Alice's underpants had been removed, there was never any allegation of sexual molestation, but the jury had heard the remarks. Damage done.'

Two clips followed in swift succession, the first a shot of the *Shiloh Weekly* building on Shiloh Road, cutting away to film of another elderly man, portly and balding, with a silver-haired woman, the couple wearing matching green Barbour jackets – the film taken through trees as they walked two black Labrador retrievers in a sprawling landscaped backyard, the woman throwing sticks for the dogs.

'William Osborn, proprietor and editor of the local paper at the time, who went on vilifying Cromwell after his death. Shiloh's richest, fattest cat, rumored to have stashed away a fortune made from loan sharking, though nothing ever stuck, and so William and his wife, Freya, ten years his junior, seem likely to live out their days in Shiloh Oaks, the home they took over when all the Cromwells were gone.'

Reaper reached for the whisky glass, watched as the screen cut to that house, after which the shot pulled back on to Main Street, finally encompassing the whole village once again.

He went on, still holding the glass, not drinking.

'Shiloh Oaks. St Matthew's Church. The Shiloh Inn. The inhabitants, most of them respectable, some veritable pillars of their community, as Donald Cromwell once was.' A pause. 'Shiloh Village. A New England postcard. Not quite Norman Rockwell material, but almost grand by Little Rhodie standards.' Another brief pause. 'But, oh, the deceit, the hypocrisy, the *lies*.'

His voice had weakened a little.

'Not long now,' he said, 'till they rise to the surface at last.'

Another pause.

'Not long.'

He stopped speaking. Stared at the screen, not really looking now, gazing at nothing at all.

Not wholly aware of the frozen shot.

Or of the glass falling from his hand.

Which was trembling.

He was aware, though, of the tremor, knew in the cognizant part of his brain what it might be heralding.

It came, sometimes, at moments of great fatigue, but it also came, paradoxically, at times of intense psychological stimulus.

He regarded the hand.

Waited for what he knew would come.

It had been a long time since he had heard it, and he welcomed it now.

He nodded.

Closed his eyes.

And listened.

Twenty-Three

On Thursday, a week before Christmas, Liza was working in her room when a Google Alert caught her eye.

She'd set Shiloh, Rhode Island, as one of her subjects because, though nothing significant ever happened there, at least she got to find out who in the neighborhood had died.

She peered idly at the piece, then sat up a little straighter.

This from the *Shiloh Weekly*:

> Thomas Pike, the eighty-five-year-old former vicar of St Matthew's Church, disappeared a week ago and has not been located since. Despite the absence of any evidence of foul play, Mr James Pike, 48, the reverend's son, who lives in Providence, is deeply concerned. The elderly man has lived alone in his Shiloh home since the passing of his wife eight years ago, but has remained a devoted member of St Matthew's congregation. The incumbent vicar, Reverend Simon Keenan, says that he and all of Mr Pike's many friends are hopeful that the gentleman has been traveling and will soon return safely.
>
> When asked by the *Weekly* if any connection was being made with a series of

unsolved Rhode Island church-linked disappearances between 1985 and 1995, a spokesman at the Scituate-based headquarters of the Rhode Island State Police commented that almost twenty years had passed since the disappearance of Reverend Laura Farrow, associate rector of a church near Primrose, Providence County, and that as yet there is no reason to connect the two cases. Both the RISP and the Shiloh Sheriff's Office say that they are, however, taking this latest matter seriously, their focus on finding Mr Pike and bringing him home to Shiloh safe and sound.

Probably nothing, Liza thought. Almost certainly nothing if the RISP – with a rep for being one of the sharpest police forces in the country – believed that, so this would likely turn out to be no more than an old man getting himself lost or taking an unannounced vacation.

But something was niggling at her. She remembered that during her time working at the *Weekly* there had been another 'church-linked' case in the early winter of 2005. An artist fixing a stained-glass window that he'd previously made for a little church north of Harmony had apparently fallen off his ladder, blood found on the floor of the nave, but no sign of him. There had been varying hypotheses as to what might have happened to the poor guy, including amnesia following a blow to his head. Liza remembered that Glocester PD had been involved in investigating, but not long after that she'd relocated to Boston, and she was almost certain that the guy hadn't turned up by then.

No mention of that case in today's *Weekly*, nor had the RISP included it in their 'series' of disappearances, which presumably meant either that the artist had surfaced since then, or that the investigators had ruled out any link. Though if neither of those reasons applied, that changed the time frame somewhat radically: people disappearing over *two* decades, not one – and less than ten years having passed since the last case.

'OK.' Liza stretched, got up and went over to the window, gazing into the night, mulling it over.

Whatever the updated facts about the Harmony man, this new case was an actual Shiloh news story, and as such, maybe she could take it as a minor sign encouraging her to visit her grandfather. Though when she'd called him last week, Ethel Murrow had told her that Dr Plain couldn't come to the phone, and he had not called her back, so Liza wasn't quite sure why she was bothering.

Except, of course, that the housekeeper always spent holidays with her own family, which meant that if Liza did not visit, her grandfather would be alone.

And then again, this might actually be a story, and even if Reverend Pike turned up safe and well, she might still try to interview him, find out where he'd been, maybe take a look at elderly care services in their part of the state. And if the old vicar was *not* found before Christmas, and if she discovered that the Harmony artist hadn't ever shown up, then she'd definitely have something to look into.

Something more worthwhile, perhaps, than Michael Rider.

So, arrival on December 23, then all of Christmas with her grandfather, and something legitimate to work on to absent herself for some of the time . . .

And duty done for a while.

Twenty-Four

Early Thursday evening, Michael had been to the Mini-Mart around the corner for provisions and was carrying a six-pack of Narragansett Lager and some sandwich makings, and he was in no mood for anything tonight but his shitty little TV and a couple of 'Gansetts.

Two weeks had passed since he'd replied to that email, and nothing, not another word. No work either, no volunteer gigs, his old jacket was no match for the icy wind *and* it was starting to snow.

Happy days.

It was dark, several lights broken, and the street looked deserted as he approached his building and heard a sound behind him.

He paused, started to turn and was grabbed from behind, something – a bag or maybe a sack – pulled down hard over his head, and Michael freaked, his shopping hitting the sidewalk as his arms were pinioned behind him.

'Help!' he yelled and kicked out, but his voice

was muffled by the thing over his head, and he was being dragged, struggling like crazy, hauled up into some kind of vehicle – a van, maybe, his voice echoing, the floor beneath him hard – and his wrists were being tied with something, and he kept on yelling, but his jackhammer heart sounded louder to him now than his voice, and he doubted that anyone would hear him, or that they'd take much notice if they did.

'You're OK,' a voice said.

A deep, rough voice, belonging to a strong man.

'I'm a friend.'

Friend.

'If you're a friend, let me the fuck go,' Michael said through the bag.

'Soon,' the voice said.

And suddenly Michael knew – he just *knew* – that this had something to do with those goddamned emails, with him having said *yes.*

That probability made him no less afraid.

The man pulled Michael out of the van, cautioned him to watch his step and told him again that he was a friend.

'If we're friends,' Michael repeated, 'take this fucking thing off my head.'

'It's for your protection,' the voice said.

He heard a door open, creaking loudly, and then they were inside, out of the icy wind, though it was still cold and damp, and Michael figured they were in a warehouse, maybe a workshop, and he could smell gasoline, so maybe a garage.

'Sit,' the deep voice said, and hands pressed him down.

Not on to a chair – something hard, wooden, maybe a crate.

The bag was pulled up off his head and he saw a cone of brightness coming from a flashlight on the ground ahead of him, started to get up.

'Please stay where you are,' someone said.

Another male voice, lower, quieter, coming from a shadowy figure sitting dead ahead, a few feet past the light.

'What the hell is this?' Michael said, shakily.

'Welcome to Whirlwind, Isaiah,' the new voice said.

Isaiah?

What the fuck?

Twenty-Five

The old man had been mortally afraid from the beginning, had felt certain that he was about to die.

Yet though he had by now lost all track of how long he'd been here, had no way of knowing even if it was night or day, he was still alive, despite his injuries and his age and his intense fear.

Despite the bone-chilling cold and damp.

He had drunk thirstily the water he'd been given – a while ago, maybe hours, maybe a day, maybe more – peering up at his tormentor with bafflement as well as terror, because the man who had first battered him unconscious, then brought him to this hideous place, the man who so clearly had

86

wanted him dead, had suddenly brought him water and bread.

The Staff of Life.

The crumbs had stuck in his throat, made him cough, and he'd longed for more water to wash them down, but the other man had just smiled, had waited until he'd stopped choking, then tied back the material around his face, gagging him. Had turned, blown out the single candle he had brought with him and had left him again in the unrelieved darkness, surrounded by sounds that might have been rats or cockroaches or bats or multitudes of worms.

The old man had asked him, once: '*Why?*'

The answer had come simply.

'Don't you know?'

But he did *not* know. He had been a good man, he hoped.

Except for one particular lapse a long time ago. Of judgment at the very least, perhaps even of humanity.

A long time ago.

He had never felt particularly troubled by it, had always slept the peaceful sleep of a just man, had chosen to blot it out.

Now, though, he remembered it with an abruptness so strong that he jolted, the movement tearing at his already intensely painful joints and limbs.

He remembered the boy who had brought sacrilege into his church.

A boy with blood on his hands and face, and madness in his eyes.

Could it be?

He would ask him, next time he came.

If he did come.
If he found the courage to ask.
If death had not claimed him by then.
He had thought he wanted to live.
He was no longer sure of that.

Twenty-Six

'I regret the manner in which we brought you here, Isaiah,' the softer voice said out of the dark, 'but it was necessary.'

'That's not my name.' Michael's heart was still pumping hard. 'You've made a mistake.'

'I know your real name,' the voice said. 'Isaiah will be your codename until the end of our operation. If you agree to it.'

'What operation?' Michael was sweating. 'What the fuck?'

'Isaiah was a great prophet who brought messages of vengeance,' the man said. 'Fitting, wouldn't you say?'

'I wouldn't say anything because I don't know what the hell this is *about*.'

'I think you have an idea. It's about righting wrongs.'

The voice was Rhodie-accented, Michael thought, but there was something almost cultured about it, reminding him of a teacher from way back.

'So if this is "Whirlwind"' – he fought to think straight – 'that probably makes you "Reaper", right? The bastard who stole my laptop and started sending me weird emails.'

'Your laptop was borrowed,' the other man said. 'To facilitate contact.'

'What for? Why me?' Michael's panic was rising. 'What *is* this? Why am I tied up in the dark? Where the fuck *are* we?'

'The darkness is for your benefit, Isaiah. To give you time to make up your mind. Because once you see us, there can be no going back.'

'So does that mean I'm free to leave?' Michael asked.

'Would you like to leave, Isaiah?'

'I'd like you to quit calling me that. I'd *like* you to untie me.'

'Of course,' the man said. 'Amos?'

'You sure?' The rougher voice, belonging to the man who'd grabbed him.

'Certainly.'

Michael felt the big man close in again and free his wrists, and he flexed his hands, felt a little relief, tried to figure out where the door was, doubted he'd make it out if he found it, and he didn't know how many others were here, and for all he knew they were armed.

'So would you like to leave now, Isaiah?'

'Damn right.'

'We'll have to hood you again until you're back home.' The man paused. 'Aren't you even a little curious, since you're here?'

Michael hated the fact that now he'd been untied, he *was* curious.

'Why don't I tell you about the team?'

'I haven't said I'm staying.'

'Just codenames, don't be alarmed.'

'Codenames.' Michael shook his head. 'This is so nuts.'

'But necessary, and in a fine cause.'

'If you say so.'

'I do. First, I am Reaper, as you surmised. I'm very glad to finally meet you, Isaiah.'

'Can't say the same,' Michael said.

'Hopefully, that will change,' Reaper said.

The 'team': four other men and one woman, all with hard-luck tales, related briskly by the man called Reaper. A guy codenamed Jeremiah whose daughter had died and who'd lost everything trying to lay blame. A woman named Nemesis, who'd gotten herself in trouble struggling to pay hospital bills for a disabled kid brother. An ex-Marine named Luke who'd lost half his face to a roadside bomb in Iraq and who couldn't bear being a burden to his elderly parents. And a guy codenamed Joel who'd been an MD in the nineties until he'd gone to help a victim of a car wreck, cut himself and contracted HIV; enlightened times since then not making up for his losses.

Michael's unease intensified with each story. All those biblical names, for one thing, religious nuts rarely being good news in his book; besides which, this was sounding like some off-the-wall support group with *money* presumably its members' primary aim. Which meant that Whirlwind was probably a criminal gang, and maybe Reaper had picked on him at least partly because of his record, in which case Michael wanted out before it went any farther.

'All of them bitter, angry and isolated until they joined Whirlwind,' Reaper said. 'Sound familiar, Isaiah?'

Sounded like a bunch of sad-sack losers.

Familiar as hell.

Michael took a breath. 'What about Amos?'

'Amos chooses not to share his story with Whirlwind, but his codename sums him up pretty well. Amos, the prophet, pronounced judgment on those who perverted justice. Amos is a man you want to have on your side.'

Not a man to pick a fight with, for sure.

'All the team know your background, Isaiah, and they're all committed to helping you. As you would need to be for them.'

'Helping with *what*, for Christ's sake?'

'That's not for today,' Reaper said.

Impatience stoked Michael's anger. 'And what's your story?'

'It's a long one. Not for today either.'

'But I'm supposed to join your little gang, no questions asked?'

'I prefer "team", but yes, that is what we're hoping for.'

'This is crap,' Michael said. 'I want out of here.'

'To what end?' Reaper asked. 'What exactly will you be going back to?'

'That's my business.'

'Of course it is.' Reaper paused. 'I've known about your history for a long time, Isaiah.'

The short hairs on the back of Michael's neck rose and he was still filled with anger, but now intrigue was mixing with that and the fear, and there was something about this man that was

threatening to suck him in, he could almost *feel* it.

'You wrote something about proving Donald Cromwell's innocence. Which is ancient history.'

'Not to your mother.'

Anger surged again. 'What do you know about my mother?'

'That she was a good person who died too young. That her troubles might not have existed but for that history.' He paused. 'Even now, you're still suffering its consequences.'

'So what are you claiming? You can't change the past. If you have evidence, why not take it to the cops?'

'They wouldn't help,' the other man said. 'Whirlwind could.'

'Even if that's true, what's in it for you and your *team*?'

'Whirlwind would benefit us all,' Reaper said. 'You need to have faith, Isaiah.'

'I stopped having faith a long time ago.'

'As we all did. Until Whirlwind.' Reaper paused.

'Jesus,' Michael said, frustrated because they were going around in circles, and because he wasn't certain what he was more afraid of now: getting dragged into whatever the hell this was or shrinking back into his own darkness. And even that familiar bleakness seemed suddenly muddied, and he had *questions* to ask, all of which would stay unanswered if he left.

If they even intended to let him go.

'You want me to jump off a cliff because you say it's going to be good for me.'

'And for your family name,' Reaper said.

'My family is dead,' Michael said.

'Your grandmother isn't dead.'

'Shit.' Michael's fists clenched.

'Isn't posthumous justice better than none? Take a leap of faith, Isaiah.'

Michael was silent.

'After all, what else do you have left?'

Nothing.

Suddenly, the same longing that had hit Michael after he'd received that last email shook him again, its intensity shocking. Because the truth was he did want what this stranger seemed to be holding out to him.

Faith. In the possibility of justice.

And wasn't *anything* better than the non-life he'd been living?

There was something on offer here, an alternative, perhaps a way forward. And all he needed, it seemed, was to grab hold.

His head was spinning.

Grab hold, or go back into the dark.

'I'm offering you my hand, Isaiah,' Reaper said softly. 'I'm offering you friendship and justice.'

Michael felt a deep, jagged shudder of need pass through him.

He had nothing left to lose.

He sighed.

'It has to be now, Isaiah,' Reaper said. 'Are you in or out?'

Michael swallowed hard and took the leap.

'In,' he said.

Twenty-Seven

Four days after Whirlwind had pulled him off the street, on the evening of Monday, December 22, Michael was lying on his bed, his right forearm across his eyes, when his cell phone rang.

'Yes?'

'Revelation' – the codename for Whirlwind's 'D-Day' – minus two days, and it seemed that his heart had hardly stopped hammering since Thursday night, and this was all happening too damned fast.

He and Reaper had met twice since then. First on Saturday evening in a bar less than a half-mile from Michael's room. Second time yesterday in a busy Starbucks – kids' noise keeping their conversation private – where Reaper had bought him a ham-and-Swiss.

The man was tall and thin, his hair iron-gray, short and sparse, his eyes gray too, couched in wrinkles behind small oval spectacles. His nose was small and mottled, his mouth narrow, his face lined. He wore an old tailored topcoat and black wool scarf, and he walked with a black cane, and Michael thought he might have arthritis, had noticed flickers of discomfort, though the other man had not complained. His age was hard to determine, probably mid-sixties, and he appeared stoic and sane.

Despite the 'mission' he'd outlined on Saturday,

94

which had sounded totally crazy to Michael and scared him half to death.

Now only four days since he'd jumped off that cliff, and no question he was being pulled head-first into a major crime. If it actually came to pass, which, right now, Michael hoped it would not.

Two all-too-real items had been delivered by courier on Sunday morning before he'd left to meet Reaper – both seeming to confirm that, in criminal terms, Whirlwind was the real deal. A credit card and driver's license, both in the name of Michael Rees (maybe a real person someplace, maybe deceased, he didn't want to know) complete with signature and PIN to enable him to purchase anything he might need in the run-up to Revelation.

He'd already learned a good deal about the 'mission' in that bar. More than enough to ensure his close attention. More to follow on Sunday and, finally, at the chosen time.

During Revelation itself.

'So,' Reaper had said in Starbucks after outlining the plan. 'What do you think?'

That he wanted *out*.

'Are you saying I still have a choice?'

'There are always choices.'

'You'd let me walk away?'

'Of course.' The older man had smiled. 'I'm not sure how far.'

A threat, plainly. No great surprise given how much Michael now knew.

He'd asked when he would meet with the team.

'Probably not until D-Day.'

They'd had a brief conversation about justice. Nearly forty years overdue.

Except there had to be better ways, *had* to be.

'Why not just go to the cops?' Michael had asked again.

Reaper had smiled. 'First, if I went near the cops, that would be the end. Second, your cause is not the only one crucial to Whirlwind.'

'What if I'd refused?'

'You'd have missed out. The operation would still have gone ahead.'

'I still don't know what exactly is in this for you,' Michael had said. 'I'm taking it that yours is the other "cause" that's crucial to Whirlwind?'

'I won't answer that yet,' Reaper had said. 'Other than to say that our causes – yours and mine – are much more closely linked than you could possibly imagine.'

Tantalizing as that answer had been, it had still not felt like enough to Michael, not *nearly* enough, leaving him with the certainty that he needed to get out, run, maybe catch a Greyhound someplace – just get *lost*.

Though the old loneliness and bleakness would travel with him.

And then, later, back in his shitty room, the sense of isolation had become *so* intense again, the grindingly relentless absence of motivation . . .

Whirlwind was dangling its promise of *something*.

Reaper had been totally straight with him about one thing.

'It may all go wrong,' he'd said. 'Badly wrong.'

'That seems like a given.'

96

Reaper had said nothing.

'So a good chance of prison,' Michael had said. 'Or worse.'

The man called Reaper had smiled his thin smile.

'Depends on your outlook,' he'd said.

By Monday evening, two more things had arrived. A padded envelope containing keys and a note informing him that a gray Toyota Corolla was waiting for him around the corner, a bag in the trunk. A car, delivered by persons unknown – maybe in the team, maybe not.

Hell, this was no team, this was a *gang*, and he was a part of it now.

A criminal.

And nothing trivial.

Hard to believe he'd come to this, because he'd thought of himself, in the distant past, as a decent person. Had still harbored a hope that he might, some day, be able to return to feeling that way about himself.

It would never happen now. Not after this.

Which was painful to bear.

The bag in the trunk had contained clothing, scale drawings, a flashlight and a MacBook. And something else in the padded envelope: a USB flash drive containing a kind of home movie 'Who's Who in Shiloh, Rhode Island?' narrated by Reaper.

Michael had played it with deep interest.

No one there he actually knew, though there were names he was familiar with. His grand-father's name repeated several times.

And now, this phone call.

'Isaiah?' Reaper's voice said.

Michael was getting almost accustomed to being called that, though the other alias worried the hell out of him: initials the same, but having to practice forging the signature on the license and credit card, knowing he'd have to turn around when someone called him 'Rees'.

Major Felony 101.

'Did you find the car and contents?'

'I did.'

'Computer work OK?'

'Fine,' Michael said.

'Clothes fit?'

'Yes.'

'And you've watched my little movie.'

'Yes.'

'Feeling all right?' Reaper asked.

'I guess.'

'Questions?'

'A thousand, but not right now.'

'So you're all set?'

Michael shut his eyes.

'As I'll ever be,' he said.

In the armchair in his room at the Red Door Inn, Reaper keyed in another number on his phone, and waited.

'Yes,' the voice at the other end answered.

Its tone keen and sharp.

'Jeremiah?'

'Yes.'

'Ready to go?'

'You bet,' Jeremiah said.

Reaper cut off the call, made another, then waited briefly.

'Luke?' he said.

'Why did you talk me into going?' Liza asked Ben just before he left that evening on his way to pick up Gina, his girlfriend, to drive to her parents' in New Jersey for the holidays.

'I didn't. That was your conscience speaking.'

'They're forecasting snow,' Liza told him. 'Be careful.'

'You too. Leave early, allow extra time.'

'Maybe I should stay here.' Liza flopped onto the couch.

'Don't start again.' Ben bent, pulled out a gift-wrapped package from under his desk and tossed it to her. 'Not to be opened till Christmas morning.'

Liza felt it. 'Soft. Yours is by the front door.' She squished her gift. 'What is it?'

'Something you might need in Shiloh,' Ben said.

'It's too big to be Valium,' Liza said.

Twenty-Eight

Michael had received only two Christmas cards: one from Jake Bollino, the other from his former parole officer. The latter stood on his windowsill, the former packed in his duffel bag. For luck, he'd figured, but now, abruptly, he changed his mind and took it out, put it on the table. Last thing he wanted was to bring trouble to Jake.

Ready to go. Tuesday, December 23, six a.m. Revelation minus one day.

He was leaving earlier than necessary. It was still dark outside but he hadn't really slept, and if he hung around here any longer he was afraid he might chicken out.

He'd left his cell phone as instructed, pulled on comfortable clothes – turtleneck sweater, jeans, old boots – but he was already jangling with tension.

'Time to go,' he said, picked up his jacket and walked slowly toward the front door, passing the small square mirror on the wall, where he paused, took a long look.

A goodbye kind of a look.

And then he shrugged on the jacket, picked up the duffel and the bag he'd found in the trunk of the Toyota, checked his keys, turned out the light, let himself quietly out and walked down the stairs to the street.

It was snowing.

The gray car was common and pretty nondescript, though white, Michael thought now, if the snow forecast was accurate, might have been a better choice.

He got in the car, organized himself, felt his pulse speed up.

Told himself to settle down.

Started the engine.

Liza could have chosen to leave Snow Hill Street at dawn and beaten the holiday rush, but then she'd have arrived in Shiloh at breakfast time, and comparing the prospect of a little bad-tempered

100

gridlock on the highways with another *whole* day around her grandfather . . .

No contest.

Which was why she'd waited until noon, and it was good to be getting out of the city in her little blue Honda, even if it was a shame about the destination.

'You're such a drama queen,' Ben had said last night. 'Your granddad's probably just a sweet old guy.'

'More like Dr Seuss's inspiration for the Grinch,' she'd said.

'That's getting tired,' Ben had said.

Light snow was already falling as she got in the car, but nothing disruptive yet, so Shiloh here she came, and she reminded herself that there might just be a decent story in the trip. Not that anyone in the village was likely to want to talk to her about missing persons until Friday or Saturday, which meant she could have waited till tomorrow to go.

'Change the script, Liza,' she told herself.

And edged out of her space.

Twenty-Nine

There were only two people inside St Matthew's just after half-past noon: Patty Jackson, the cleaner, polishing pews, and the vicar himself, Reverend Simon Keenan, sitting in his small office in the undercroft – the vaulted chamber

101

beneath the church which also housed archives, restrooms and a basement parish hall.

Upstairs, the church was looking festive, had been decorated the previous Sunday by volunteer parishioners; and come Christmas Eve, with candles aglow, incense burning, voices raised in carols and hymns and the kind of atmosphere that usually made the hairs on the back of Keenan's neck prickle, St Matthew's would be, he hoped, at its absolute best.

All it needed now, he thought, still struggling with sermons for the coming days, was a vicar to do it justice – and perhaps some good news, too: the safe reappearance of Thomas Pike to share with the congregation.

Just in time for tomorrow evening would be perfect.

Something extra to lift the soul and give thanks for.

Snow was falling steadily on Glocester, Rhode Island as a rented gray Honda Accord pulled off Putnam Pike and parked outside the Casey Motel, the driver getting out of the vehicle, looking up at the sky, then over at the motel.

The man known by Whirlwind as Luke was thirty-two years old, five-nine, stocky, with short dark hair, and the scarring on his face was the kind that some people shrank from while others openly stared or occasionally jeered at.

'Looks OK,' he said as his passenger opened her door.

The woman codenamed Nemesis was forty-one, slim, her face lean with high cheekbones and a

102

mouth taut with tension. Her brunette hair was cut in a bob, and in her dark straight slacks, stone-colored parka and ankle boots she looked like a sales rep or manager, the picture of convention.

She regarded the entrance, its Christmas wreath hung on the door, and nodded.

'Let's go,' she said.

He popped the trunk and they unloaded together, Luke taking his own backpack and a long, bulky bag, Nemesis taking out two backpacks and closing the lid.

They went to check in.

In his second-floor room at the Shiloh Inn, the man called Reaper stood at the window, leaning on his cane, looking down at the snow-covered garden, at its prettily decorated fir tree and at Main Street itself.

Not many more people around than when he'd walked the street almost three weeks ago. A pair of tourists at the far end photographing St Matthew's, the shops seeming quiet, most last-minute Christmas shoppers presumably doing battle in the big malls closer to the cities.

A figure was moving slowly along the street, coming this way. An old woman planting her boots carefully, using a carved wooden cane, wary of slipping. Reaper knew who she was, was aware that he was standing in the very building that she had once ruled as head teacher of Shiloh Elementary School. Betty Hackett, who, once upon a time, many years before, had found the body of a young murdered child.

The soft sound from the open MacBook on the

103

table behind him announced that he had new mail. He turned, picked up the computer, sat down on the chintz-covered armchair, placed the laptop on his knees and saw that it was one of those he'd been waiting for.

Opened it and nodded.

Minimal words, as arranged.

LUKE AND NEMESIS CHECKED IN.

He opened another window, exposing a Google Earth map.

Shiloh Village at the heart of the predominantly green map.

Glocester to the north.

Using the touch pad, he moved a yellow pushpin to the approximate location of the Casey Motel, then typed 'Luke and Nemesis', clicked it and their names appeared on the map.

He smiled at the magic of it, then sighed.

'Small things,' he said.

Outside the Foster Inn near the town of the same name, the man codenamed Joel took a moment before getting slowly out of the white Ford Focus allocated to him by Whirlwind.

The former doctor was five-ten, aged fifty-four, his silver-gray hair cut very short, twenty pounds lighter than he had been prior to getting himself in shape for Reaper and their mission: all that Joel was living for now.

Which was not to say that he did not fear it.

He'd have given a lot to turn and run.

If he'd had anyplace or anyone worth running to.

He reached into the well behind his seat for his bag and coat, looked up briefly into the iron-gray sky, felt big cool flakes land on his cheeks and melt.

He shivered, pulled on the coat, and then, head down, he walked toward the inn.

At the Shiloh Inn, Reaper read the new email, saw that Joel had checked in, brought up the map, located Foster, south-east of Shiloh, found the yellow pushpin, slid it down to the location, typed 'Joel', clicked, then sat back again.

His hand trembled a little and he clenched it.

'Not now,' he told it, and willed it away.

The tremor ceased.

It was snowing steadily too now over the state line in Putnam, Connecticut, as the men known as Amos and Jeremiah retrieved their bags from the rear of a white Ford Explorer (leaving three more bags concealed beneath the lining in the cargo space), locked up and headed into the Five Mile Inn. Amos was middle-aged, heavy set, shaven-headed and intimidating looking, Jeremiah a decade younger, tall, fit and trim with buzz-cut dark hair and brown, darting, suspicious eyes.

'Hey,' Jeremiah said at check-in. 'Wasn't this where that nuclear thing happened?'

'That was Three Mile Island.' Amos grinned. 'And it was nowhere near here.'

'Pennsylvania.' The clerk smiled. 'You'd be surprised how many people remember that when they see our name.'

'Maybe they should change it then,' Jeremiah said grimly.

'This inn is named after a river near here,' the

young man said. 'Its original Native American name is—'

'Are we done?' Jeremiah cut in.

'I'm sorry,' Amos told the clerk. 'My friend has a headache.'

They picked up their bags and followed an arrow to their rooms.

'Do me a favor,' Jeremiah said quietly as they walked. 'Don't apologize for me.'

'Don't be a jerk,' Amos said, 'and I won't have to.'

Another click on Reaper's touchpad. Another pushpin in place, south-east of Putnam.

Amos and Jeremiah

Only one more to come.

The one.

Thirty

Michael had decided on a detour, rationalizing that had he gone straight to Woonsocket, his room would not be ready.

Going instead to a place he'd vowed never to go near again.

Just looking, he'd told himself.

Only a section was visible from his vantage point just off Route 6. A small part of the behemoth collection of buildings that made up the Garthville House of Corrections, but enough to bring back the memory of his first glimpse through the window bars of the bus transporting him to the psych wing eleven years ago. The old structures still irredeemably ugly, redbrick long since turned nicotine brown, massive walls and fences topped with coils of vicious barbed wire.

A jagged fragment of one of Michael's still-recurring nightmares.

Worse inside. Bad, bad place.

Today, he'd sat for a long while in the Toyota, staring back into the pit, wondering why exactly he'd done that to himself, driven *there*, of all places.

Not so difficult to answer, he guessed.

He'd wanted a reminder of what had brought him to Whirlwind.

His own failings, for sure, but this place was symbolic of his lowest times.

Fresh, real, sharp fear pierced him suddenly.

Of returning here, in another prison bus, in shackles.

'Never,' he said.

Not that he could be sure of that, since what he was about to embark on might well lead him to exactly such a place. And there was only one way to evade that possibility: turn around *now*, ditch the car and credit card and driver's license and flash drive and clothing and MacBook, and get himself the hell as far away from New England as he could.

Renege on the deal, in other words. Forget about Reaper and the others. Forget about long-overdue justice, because who would that really help now? Not that he knew how to ditch a car that might end up being linked to a major crime: a vehicle that already had his prints all over it, because he'd taken off his gloves earlier, and he'd sneezed twice, so his DNA was spread around liberally too.

No point kidding himself.

Too late to cut and run.

And anyway, he wasn't entirely certain that he wanted to. Because he was, when all was said and done, a man of his word, and even if all this was sheerest madness, then he was already an integral part of it.

Had been from the moment he'd said he was 'in'.

Hard to believe that was only six days ago, but he was *in*, and that was that.

Done deal. No backing out.

So he'd taken one last look at Garthville, and then he'd closed his mind to it again, turned the car around and gotten back on the road.

And now, just before two o'clock, he was outside the Red Door Inn in Woonsocket, his mood lifting, because this looked like a seriously nice place.

An act of generosity by the man leading this operation.

Reaper, man of mystery.

Check-in straightforward. No one seeming to hear the pounding of his heart; no one querying his identity as Michael Rees, and now, all alone in his comfortable room, he made up his mind to do something he hadn't managed since he'd landed the Boston café job.

He was going to try to enjoy this for as long as it lasted.

First, though, he had an instruction to follow.

He pulled his laptop from his bag.

The last email had arrived.

Isaiah had checked in.

108

A second line tacked onto this message.

The only one who had not adhered *absolutely* to directions.

No harm in it, though. On the contrary.

THANK YOU

Reaper leaned back in the armchair in his room at the Shiloh Inn, and closed his eyes.

'I thank you, Michael Rider,' he said quietly.

And then, a moment or two later, he opened his eyes, shut down the computer, then rose and moved back to the window, looked out again at the snow falling ever more heavily.

The plan ultimately strengthened by the weather, though if the new forecasts of a massive snow-storm likely to hit sometime on Christmas Eve were accurate, some vital preliminary changes would need to be made.

Time in hand to wait and see, forecasts being frequently unreliable.

He turned, picked up his overcoat from the bed, put it on with a grimace of the pain that seemed to be spreading further through his body, looked over at his pills on the bedside table, thought better of taking one now, picked up his cane and let himself out of the room.

Thirty-One

I-95 had been gridlocked for miles. News Radio 920 were reporting a major accident up ahead, and Liza, aware that she'd been expected for lunch and knowing that her grandfather liked meals on time, called the house.

Ethel Murrow answered tersely. 'We were wondering where you were. Your grandfather's getting very hungry.'

'I'm stuck in traffic, Ethel,' Liza said, though she could see it clearing up ahead. 'Please don't wait lunch for me.'

'There's a good spread waiting for you.' Ethel was having none of it. 'I'll be leaving soon, but I'll let the doctor know you won't be long.'

'Maybe we could keep it till dinner?' Liza suggested.

'I've laid the table,' Ethel Murrow said with finality. 'I wouldn't like it to spoil.'

Guilt-tripping as thick as fudge icing.

Something she'd probably learned from the guilt-master himself.

The snow was falling more heavily and the radio was declaring yet another huge snowstorm on its way to the Northeast, which might turn out to be an all-time record breaker, *maybe* due to arrive over Rhode Island some time tomorrow, though there was a chance that Massachusetts might bear the brunt instead.

'Shit,' Liza said.

Screwed either way, the prospect of being snowbound in Shiloh a hellish one.

She left that station behind and tuned into Magic.

Sam Smith asking her to 'Stay With Me'.

'If only,' she said.

At two-fifteen, Simon Keenan, having given up on his sermons again, was on his knees on the chancel, praying for inspiration.

Unaware of being watched.

By the man who called himself Reaper, seated on a pew halfway back in the nave, sitting very still.

Keenan rose, crossed himself and bowed, then turned and began to walk up the center aisle, until, noticing the stranger, he paused. 'Are you all right, sir?'

'Why wouldn't I be?' Reaper's voice was soft. 'Sitting here in this good place.'

Keenan smiled. 'I'll leave you in peace.'

Reaper made no reply, and Keenan, inexplicably discomfited, turned back toward the chancel.

'Weren't you going the other way, Reverend?' Reaper's voice echoed slightly in the empty church.

'I forgot something.' Keenan walked on.

He climbed the three steps up onto the chancel, turned to the vestry door, then heard small sounds behind him: soft squeaks of rubber on wood.

He turned again.

The stranger had gone.

Thirty-Two

The Plain family house on South Maple Street, right around the corner from St Matthew's on Main, was a pre-World War Two Colonial with pale blue wood siding and a blue and white porch.

A handsome, welcoming kind of a house.

The Honda had no sooner turned left into Maple, then left again halfway up the street onto the old, familiar uphill driveway, than the front

111

door opened and Ethel Murrow appeared, boots already on and pulling on her down coat.

'You're still here,' Liza said, getting out of the car. 'How nice.'

'I didn't like to leave the doctor. You might have had an accident and then who would have taken care of him?'

'He's not sick, is he?'

'Not as such.'

Nothing more forthcoming, and Liza put out her hand, but the other woman made no move to take it. 'The roads were pretty bad,' she said lamely. 'I should have left earlier.'

'You're here now,' Ethel said. 'But I do have to be leaving.'

'I'm so sorry to have held you up.'

'Better late than never, I suppose.'

Liza popped the hatchback, pulled out her bag and banged it shut. 'Where is my grandfather?'

'Upstairs. Complaining of hunger.'

'I did say not to wait, Ethel.'

'It's a special occasion. He didn't want to start without you.' She stood back to let Liza through the doorway, then eyed her boots. 'If you wouldn't mind. The floors are clean and polished, and I washed you a pair of socks.' She nodded at a pair of grayish socks on the hall table.

'That's very kind of you,' Liza said.

Ethel Murrow turned toward the staircase.

'Dr Plain,' she called. 'Your granddaughter's here.'

No response.

'Perhaps he's sleeping,' Liza said.

'Perhaps.' Ethel pulled gloves from her pocket. 'I'll be leaving now.'

'Merry Christmas,' Liza said.

'And to you,' the other woman said.

She set off without a backward glance.

Liza shut the door.

One down, one to go.

She took a breath.

'Granddad,' she called. 'I'm here.'

Thirty-Three

At almost three o'clock, the bar of the Shiloh Inn was still hectic when he walked in. Log fire burning, people eating, drinking, talking loudly, laughing.

Conviviality unconfined. Happy days.

He made his way slowly to the bar, leaned on his cane, waiting, and when his turn came the woman behind the bar told him she'd bring his Balvenie malt over to the just-vacated table by the window.

Eleanor Tilden not recognizing him, and no reason why she should.

Several others he could name, he noted, taking his seat. Gwen Turner and Jill Barrow, her lover, tucking into quiche. William and Freya Osborn, seated at what Reaper supposed was the best table in the house, perhaps the proprietor's table when he was dining; the boss himself not present, and maybe that was as well. Not that Tilden would be likely to recognize him either, yet still, it might have been one roll of the dice too many.

It felt strange. Being here, among these people, in this place.

His drink came, nicely served with a dish of pretzels, water on the side, and Reaper thanked Mrs Tilden, who smiled back down at him.

'Will you be wanting to eat?' she asked. 'The kitchen's about to close but we can still offer sandwiches and chowder.'

'I don't think so,' he said. 'But thank you. I won't keep the table long. I know it's a busy time.'

'Don't you worry about that,' Eleanor Tilden told him. 'Take your time.'

He thanked her again, picked up his drink, took a swallow and found it painful, making it hard, momentarily, to breathe. But he wanted the whisky and managed it, followed it with a little water to douse the discomfort.

He sat back for a moment, looking around.

Taking it in.

And then he put down enough cash to cover the check, and stood again.

Time to go.

Thirty-Four

Still alive.

Not living, but not quite dead.

Longing for that now, after what *he* had come back and done to him.

Longing for death with every struggling fiber of his being, which was sinful, of course, but he no longer cared, was past that.

Past everything but suffering, it seemed.

He still wondered, in moments of cruel semi-clarity, how long it was possible to survive without sustenance.

In the beginning, there had been the bread and water. Then just water.

And then his tormentor had come that one last time.

Had removed his gag – and then done *this* to him. Had perpetrated perhaps the most blasphemous crime possible. And had not come again.

He had tried, a few times, to cry out, but such pitifully thin, painful sounds had emerged that he had given it up, yet the loss of the gag was a small blessing, because he could breathe the foul air more easily, could, now and then, catch in his mouth the drips of filthy water that landed on his head from above and rolled downward. And though he yearned for death, he could not reject the water.

Survival instincts, he supposed.

Yet still, only one hope remained in him.

For an ending.

Not much longer now, surely.

Thirty-Five

Ethel had decorated the dining table with winter-berries, and a deep red amaryllis stood on the sideboard, probably a gift, but Liza could not recall seeing a Christmas tree in the house since her parents' death. Not that Stephen Plain had ever spoken to Liza of the grief and pain he must have felt, at least for the loss of his son. Yet it was still here, she felt, in this room, in the unnatural silence forming its usual invisible barrier between old man and granddaughter.

'Mrs Murrow made a great effort.' His glance at her clothes was an accusation.

'I didn't want to make you wait any longer while I changed,' Liza said.

Not that she'd planned to change at all, and this was even worse than she'd anticipated, and if this single meal felt like an endurance test, how on earth would she survive the next few days?

'I was very pleased when I heard that you were coming, Liza,' Stephen said. 'How long has it been?'

'Too long,' Liza said.

'I don't suppose you can just drop your noble work at a moment's notice.'

'Don't start, Granddad, please,' she said, and cut them both slices of pork pie. 'This looks almost as good as Mom's.'

'I prefer it. Less rich.'

'I thought we'd be eating in the kitchen,' Liza said.

'Mrs Murrow thought this a special occasion.'

Liza took some crabmeat salad, and wondered if the housekeeper had made this or ordered it from Glover's. 'This is very good. I must remember to leave her a thank-you note.'

'Making leaving plans already, Liza?' Stephen said dryly.

'Of course not.' Liza glanced at him, thought she saw some humor in his eyes.

'Then perhaps you could try not to look so

116

thoroughly bored,' he said. 'I know that coming home is a painful duty for you, but you needn't think you have to spend every minute with me. If I were you, I'd get yourself out to the inn this evening. I gather there's always something going on there.'

'We could both go,' she said.

'Not me,' he said. 'Can't bear the place.'

'Then I'll stay here with you.' Liza drank some of the red wine her grandfather had poured when they'd sat down. 'So, any village gossip for me, Granddad?'

'For you to pass on to your avid readers?'

'For my ears only,' Liza said. 'Any news of Reverend Pike?'

'The missing vicar stays missing,' Stephen said.

'What's the new one like?' Liza asked.

'Young, golden-haired, popular with the ladies, pleasant wife. Can't say what his sermons are like because, as you know, I do my best to avoid church.' He wiped the corner of his mouth with a napkin. 'I don't imagine he'll be much duller than Pike used to be.'

'When did he disappear?'

'Is this why you've come? The sniff of a story?'

'I'm here to spend Christmas with you, Granddad.' She changed the subject to avoid a barefaced lie. 'You will be coming to the Christmas Eve service, won't you?'

'I can hardly avoid it since you are here,' he said.

Liza smiled. 'Maybe you'll come with me to the inn this evening too.'

'Too much of a good thing,' Stephen said. 'Never sensible.'

Thirty-Six

At two minutes before five p.m. Michael sat at the small table in his room at the Red Door Inn, laptop open, flash drive beside it. The lights were out, and though it was already dark outside, the falling snow seemed to draw in its own soft, eerie light.

Michael glanced at his watch, waited another minute, then inserted the flash drive into the port on the side of the computer, located it, clicked, found the file titled 'Dec 23, 5 p.m.', and clicked again.

An image appeared.

Shiloh Village in the snow at night. The place looking pretty, lamps casting a glow, St Matthew's the star of the show.

The kind of picture taken to attract tourists.

'Welcome,' Reaper's voice said. 'If you're right on schedule, there should now be less than thirty hours to go before Whirlwind goes into action. Some of us have tasks to complete before that; some, with too much time on their hands, may be tempted to give in to doubts. But we all know it's too late for doubting now.'

The lighter mood that Michael had felt on arrival had long since been overtaken by bleakness, but suddenly that too was gone.

Fear in its place, again, for sure. But something else, too.

Motivation.

And clarity of a kind.

In the Casey Motel in Glocester, Luke and Nemesis were in her unit, listening via her laptop. The man in the chair, the woman on the edge of the bed.

Both absorbed in their leader's words.

'Too late for doubting now.'

Luke's own doubts were burning ulcers in his gut. As a marine, he'd been trained for far more dangerous missions than this, but he'd never come to terms with the trauma of risking innocent lives.

Mostly innocents on the line in this 'mission', no getting away from that.

Nemesis was fighting with all she had to blot out her own misgivings, listening so hard to Reaper's voice that she thought her ears might bleed.

'We all know what to do,' he said. 'What's expected of us.'

She closed her eyes, kept her brother's dear face in her mind.

For him. All for him.

At the Foster Inn, feeling his isolation keenly, Joel lay on top of the bed, dressed in a roll-neck and jeans, feet bare, listening to Reaper's voice but remembering the life he'd loved before it had been snatched from him.

He'd only felt fully alive as a doctor, felt that he'd ceased to matter since then. Not dead but not living either. Yet right now, he did matter again, could be of *use* again, and not only to Whirlwind but, if things went to plan, to others suffering out there in the world.

'We've checked and triple-checked the details,' Reaper said from the MacBook resting on his legs. 'We know exactly how Revelation will begin.'

Jeremiah was in Amos's room at the Five Mile Inn listening to the voice coming from the reconditioned MacBook Pro standing open on top of the chest. Amos leaning against the windowsill, Jeremiah on the other side of the room beside the door.

The less time they spent together, the better.

Nobody except Reaper knew anything about Amos. Which meant, Jeremiah figured, that Amos had more to hide than the others, which probably meant that he was some kind of career criminal. Unlike the rest of them, who were, however well Reaper and Amos had primed them, still beginners.

And the new guy, Isaiah, had had no time at all to prepare, for fuck's sake, which made Jeremiah edgy.

Everything making him edgier by the minute.

'What we have no way of knowing, of course,' Reaper's voice went on, 'is exactly how things will move on from that point. Or how it will end. We know our aims, our individual and collective goals.'

The man called Amos listened to the boss and watched Jeremiah.

Jittery as shit, though he guessed they all were; and he had high regard for Reaper, but there were too many amateurs on this job.

Always a dangerous thing.

Worth it, though, if it went according to plan.

He never did anything that wasn't worthwhile.

Not planning to start now.

In Woonsocket, Michael had not moved since Reaper's first words.

'No one with quite as much reason to be here as Isaiah,' the man said now.

Michael shut his eyes.

'We all know what his goal is,' Reaper went on. 'It's the same in many ways as yours and mine. It's why you were chosen. We all want to right wrongs. We all want justice.'

Michael's eyes opened in more ways than one.

There was hypocrisy in those words and no way of denying that to himself, however much he might have been longing to do so.

Reaper had not chosen them because they wanted justice. He had selected them – with the possible exception of Amos – because they were all *losers*. Because they saw no legitimate or sane way left to get themselves back on course.

They had been *lured* here because of their weakness. And though he had no way of knowing how Reaper had gone about snaring the others, Michael suddenly had little doubt remaining that he was using them to some personal end.

His cause and Reaper's, according to the older man, were closely linked.

Whether that was true or false was yet to be seen.

Still apparently only one way to find out.

Revelation.

Thirty-Seven

Less than an hour later, the man himself came to call.

Reaper wore his overcoat but no hat, his scalp shining wet through his hair. 'I hope I'm not disturbing you.'

'Of course not.' Michael stepped back.

Reaper glanced around, then nodded. 'Good.'

'It's a wonderful room. Very generous.' Whether against his will or not, Michael felt his hostility melt away in the older man's presence. 'Can I take your coat?'

'I'm not staying.' Reaper paused. 'I've made some changes because of the weather forecast. ETA any time from noon tomorrow.'

Michael moved his leather jacket off the armchair.

Reaper sat, removed his gloves, unbuttoned his coat, took an envelope from an inside pocket and handed it to Michael. 'This shows your new approximate time of arrival, the secure parking place for your vehicle and the location where you'll have to wait between then and the appointed hour.'

Michael opened the envelope, unfolded a sheet of paper, regarded it.

'I wish you could have stayed here till then, as planned,' Reaper said. 'That place won't be nearly as comfortable.'

'Will we all be there?'

'You'll wait there with Joel, then walk together.'

Reaper paused. 'I think you'll be a good match. Joel is a pacifist by nature, like yourself.'

'And the others?'

'No need to concern yourself with them now, and there are no other changes from your perspective.' He paused. 'So, how do you feel, Isaiah? Doubting me, I imagine. And your decision to be here. How could you not?'

Michael didn't answer.

'Yet you seem calm enough. I expected to find you pacing, more agitated.'

'Pacing in my head.'

Reaper studied him for another moment. 'You're almost looking forward to it.'

'In a way.' Michael realized it was true. 'I never expected to feel any kind of drive again. I'd begun to think it was all over.'

'As it may be, all too soon.' Reaper's gray eyes remained on his face. 'You're much too intelligent a man not to know that, Michael Rider.'

It was the first time this man had used his real name since the emails, and the use of it now felt oddly significant, as if a real connection had been forged between them.

The man was a *user*, Michael reminded himself. He scraped dregs from the bottom of the pile and set them to work for him.

And yet, old and arthritic as he was, Reaper did possess magnetism, a fascinating knack of persuading people to do his bidding.

The kind of power that equaled danger.

Then again, that was what Revelation was all about, wasn't it?

Danger. Risk. Bad, *crazy* stuff.

123

He'd been put away years ago because they'd said he was crazy.

Michael guessed he could see now why they'd done it.

They'd been right.

Thirty-Eight

Liza had prepared Stephen's supper of pot roast and vegetables, following Ethel's precise written instructions, then she'd put on a little extra makeup to boost her festive spirit and pulled on her boots for the walk to the Shiloh Inn.

'Are you sure you won't come, Granddad?' she asked as he began his meal in the kitchen. 'I'll be happy to wait.'

'I think not. Old man, snow and false geniality – not my idea of pleasure.'

'And you're sure you don't mind if I go?'

'As I recall, I suggested it.' He regarded her as she zipped up her parka. 'I'm trying to decide if you look more like a clown or a whore.'

Liza managed a smile.

'How I've missed that silver tongue of yours,' she said.

Reaching the inn, she almost turned right around because a private party was being thrown, but then Gwen Turner spotted her and called her name, told her to stay because she wanted to catch up.

'I can't just gatecrash a party,' Liza said. 'I don't even know whose party it is.'

'A banker and his wife from Shiloh Town called Mack and Mabel Sutter.' Gwen laughed. 'Really their names. Very nice people and they won't mind.'

Liza hesitated but gave in, buying a decent bottle at the bar for the hosts, who were as welcoming as Gwen had described, and soon she was enjoying miniature smoked salmon blinis while being introduced to Rosie and Simon Keenan, the new vicar and his wife, both of whom seemed like fun. And Liza had not meant to stay long because of Stephen, but then she noticed the Osborns arriving; Freya in absurdly high-heeled boots, arm-in-arm with William. Liza had never much liked Osborn when she'd worked for him at the paper, but it always seemed to her that his younger wife genuinely loved the plump old millionaire.

So, good food, pleasant company and maybe even an opportunity to get the lowdown on Thomas Pike and those other missing Rhode Islanders.

Alone again, almost two hours after Reaper had left, and Michael had asked for a tray of sandwiches and beer, neither yet touched.

The drawings and addendum were spread over the bed, though he'd memorized everything, knew as well as he could where and when each stage of Revelation was to take place, knew how it was going to kick off.

Though still not much more than that.

Uncertain whether that was a good or a bad thing.

Reaper had commented on his stillness, but now Michael was really pacing. Back and forth between the window – pausing there each time to stare out into the snowy night – and the bed, where the sheets of paper lay like a challenge.

Or maybe a reproach.

At eight o'clock, the party was buzzing. Liza had just eaten a sweet chili-glazed chipolata and was drinking her second glass of champagne when she decided to dive in with her first question.

'Do you know much about the missing vicar?' she asked Jill Barrow, Gwen's partner.

'Afraid not,' Jill said. 'I'm not much of a churchgoer.'

'Bill Osborn's your best bet.' Gwen had over-heard. 'He may be retired, but I'm guessing he's still the person in Shiloh with the most information about just about anyone.'

'Is this for a story?' Jill asked.

'Possibly,' Liza said. 'What about the new vicar?'

'Worth a try, I guess,' Gwen said.

'Though I heard him say he couldn't stay long,' Jill said. 'Stressing over his first Christmas service, poor man. I suggested he give sermons a miss, said I wouldn't mind.'

'Will you be going?' Liza asked.

'Tomorrow night? Oh, sure.'

'We like the music,' Gwen said.

'And vexing the upstanding villagers who consider us deeply sinful,' Jill added.

'Really?' Liza said. 'Still?'

'Lord, yes,' Gwen said. 'Not to our faces, of course, and not the majority.'

'A righteous handful,' Jill said.

Thirty-Nine

At a quarter to nine, the man codenamed Amos was in the Explorer, alone, driving slowly south on Oak Street in Shiloh Village.

He'd finished his calls to the guys only he and Reaper knew about.

Four men, hired by him for an essential part of the mission.

Efficient types, not high-flyers in their field, but cold and sufficiently skilled to do what was needed to get the job done.

Reliable because, bottom line, they wanted what he was going to give them.

Oak Street was quiet, no one out, not even a dog being walked.

A party happening inside the Shiloh Inn – lights, music, movement, laughter.

Seven out of the eight rooms on the first and second floors booked through to Monday, Reaper had informed him. Most of the third floor permanently occupied by the proprietor and his wife.

Amos had a list of Shiloh Village residents pretty much memorized, his near-photographic memory always useful in his profession.

The only fulltime lawbreaker inside Whirlwind.

Unless you counted Reaper, though he couldn't really be categorized, and Amos, having come to know him at least a little over time, had no wish to know more, knew when and where to draw the line.

What he felt most for the old, sick guy was respect.

No higher compliment in Amos's book.

The snow was light this evening, the sidewalks well-covered by late December standards, though nothing – if this mega-storm came their way – compared with how it might look this time tomorrow.

He went on driving slowly, peering at houses, passing St Matthew's on Main, then taking a look at the homes on Elm Street, and moving on to South Maple. Lights were on in most houses and apartments, drapes, blinds or shutters keeping many private.

Just checking the place out. Reconnoitering. Liking to be prepared, not feeling any significant anxiety about Reaper's plan because he understood worst-case scenarios, was as ready for them as he could be in this mission.

Being a loner suited Amos. No wife or kids, no one to give a damn. A life of pleasing himself and getting through tough times without the guilt of having someone else weeping into their pillow.

Reaper's 'team' his biggest concern now.

Jeremiah still too damned uptight, and Amos was sure he wasn't the only one.

Nothing to be done about them.

For now, all was quiet.

'Ghost town,' Amos said quietly.

He found his way back onto Main and headed west on Shiloh Road.

Forty

'Not much to tell you, dear.' William Osborn put a miniature steak pie into his mouth, chewed, swallowed and smiled at her. 'A retired cleric living alone in our midst, yet I can't say that I knew him.' He shrugged. 'Not being a regular at Saint Matthew's or anywhere else – tomorrow evening and possibly Easter, you know how it is.'

'You said 'knew" him,' Liza said. 'Past tense.'

'I did, yes,' Osborn said. 'Though naturally I hope to be wrong.' He picked up a bite-size rib, tore meat and sauce off the bone with his teeth, then licked his lips. 'Food's fine, don't you agree? Not Tilden's own. Private caterers.'

'It's delicious.' Liza looked around and saw Eleanor Tilden behind the bar, serving, her husband John holding a large glass of red, working the room.

'So how have things worked out for you since you were with us, Liza?'

'Ups and downs,' she said. 'You know.'

He nodded. 'Keep looking for the ups and you'll be fine.'

'Last week's *Weekly* mentioned other church-related disappearances,' she said.

'Glad you're still a reader.'

'It brought back a memory of a man going missing from a church near Harmony while I was working for you. It wasn't mentioned in the article.'

'I daresay the new editor had good reason to omit it. Maybe the man came back and all was rosy.'

'Maybe,' Liza said, and suddenly, with Osborn right beside her, it seemed idiotic not to raise the older topic. 'The Cromwell family used to live in your house, didn't they?'

'You know very well that they did,' Osborn said, a little testily. '*Our* house now, as you rightly say, for a very long time. Freya and I like to think we've expunged all traces of that man, Miss Plain.' Osborn gave a small wave to his wife, presently in conversation with Mabel Sutter, the banker's wife. 'Donald Cromwell was a disgrace to this community and to his family.'

'It's actually the family I'm interested in,' Liza said.

'Destroyed.' Osborn stood up. 'Wife lost her mind, daughter too, finally, and who could blame either of them?'

'I saw Emily's son in Boston a few weeks ago.'

'I'm surprised you'd know him,' Osborn said.

'Our paths crossed a long time ago. His name's Michael Rider.'

'I know his name.'

And with that, he moved away.

Subject closed.

130

Forty-One

At nine-seventeen, one mile west of Shiloh Village, the Explorer made a left off Lark Road onto a track leading to a long-abandoned fruit farm, its old signpost and the narrow access road itself covered in the steadily thickening blanket of white, no vehicles having passed this way for a long while. Amos might have missed the barn altogether if it hadn't been for its snow-clad rooftop visible from a couple of hundred yards away. The landscape was like a photographic negative tonight, outlines of every tree, bush or structure showing up clear and sharp.

No sign of the Volvo yet.

Amos killed the Explorer's lights and waited. Heard, after about twenty seconds, the engine, then the door and, finally, the sound of boots tramping slowly through snow, coming his way.

The rear offside door opened and Reaper climbed in, leaning his cane beside him against the seat. 'All well?'

'All good. Damned quiet,' Amos said. 'Where'd you leave the car?'

'On the road, a little way,' Reaper said. 'Can you get this around to the back of the barn?'

'Got the right tires. Should be fine.'

Amos put the Explorer into gear and nudged it forward, his touch confident, giving the barn a wide berth in case of a skid, making it smoothly to the rear.

'I'd say we're invisible from the road now,' he said. 'Can't speak for anyone out that way.' He nodded toward the old farm and the desolate-looking white space beyond. 'Looks deserted, but you can never tell.'

'Hardly the only risk we're going to be taking,' Reaper said. 'Good job, Amos.'

He opened his door, stepped down into the snow and used his cane to steady himself, the other man not offering assistance, aware he disliked help.

At the rear of the vehicle, Reaper took a small Maglite from his coat pocket and nodded to Amos to open it up, saw two tarps, one gray, the other white, nodded approval.

'Leave you to it?'

Amos took a cloth, spray and canister from the right-hand corner of the rear. 'I'll clean first, then cover her.'

Reaper watched for a few moments, his breath steaming as the big man began the business of wiping clean every reachable surface, because even though gloves had been worn since the SUV had been picked up, there were no guarantees that any of them would be back to drive the vehicle away, and they both knew how much debris humans could leave behind. Scratch an ear and skin cells could land anyplace, though if a person sneezed or coughed, this level of cleansing would never be enough.

Risks, as Reaper had said, now moving away, treading carefully around to the front of the barn. The snow that had drifted up against the door

132

was soft, easy to move with his boots and cane, though when he'd cleared enough away, his breathlessness was audible.

He waited for his breathing to settle.

And then he opened the barn door and disappeared into the dark interior.

'I wish I could help you more with Pike,' Gwen told Liza. 'But so far as the Cromwells go, you'll know that's a time I've done my damnedest to forget.'

'I'm sorry,' Liza said. 'I should have thought.'

'It's OK. I still remember Alice most days anyway, guess I always will.' She thought. 'If you want to talk to people who'll give you halfway honest answers . . .' She shook her head. 'Actually, I don't really know who to suggest. Except your grandfather. Though I'm assuming he hasn't been too forthcoming, or you wouldn't be asking me.'

'Sadly true,' Liza said.

'Still, the fact is Stephen must have known just about everyone back then. And as I recall, he gave evidence at the trial.'

'He won't discuss it. Never has.'

'Forgive me for being blunt,' Gwen said, 'but for a journalist, you're sounding awfully lily-livered.'

And Liza laughed.

Reaper emerged from the barn, closed the door, used his cane and boots to heap back enough snow to disguise the fact that anyone had been inside, and walked back around to the rear.

Amos was waiting beside the covered Explorer.

'You left the key?' Reaper asked.

133

'As agreed,' Amos said. 'Want me to cover your boot prints?'

Reaper glanced up at the sky, flakes settling on his cheeks. 'No need. Let's go.'

Silently, they began the walk back to the road and to the Volvo, parked just beyond a bend, shrouded in fresh snow.

Everything hushed. A peaceful world.

'Would you mind driving, Amos?' Reaper said. 'I'm a little tired.'

'Sure. Where to?'

Reaper got in on the passenger side. 'Back to the inn. Then you can drive this back to Putnam, get some rest.'

'There's a party at the inn. Best not go inside till it's over.'

Reaper nodded. 'Park up nearby. I'll catch a nap till you wake me.'

'Sure you don't want to keep the car?' Amos asked.

'Perfectly,' Reaper said.

'Anything changes, just call,' Amos said.

Reaper nodded again.

And shut his eyes.

'You left Shiloh for years, didn't you?' Liza asked Gwen.

They were sharing the window seat in the bar, Jill perched on the arm of a chair close by, popping a mini chocolate soufflé, the last of her desserts, into her mouth.

'I escaped for a whole decade,' Gwen said, 'but then my parents died and left me the house, so I came back. I was going to stay just long enough to sell up.'

'Then I came along,' Jill said.

Gwen smiled. 'It was always a nice house, but suddenly it felt like home.'

'And I guess they're no more bigoted in Shiloh than in a lot of small places,' Jill said.

'I don't think we actually mind anymore,' Gwen said.

'Most people have got used to us.' Jill glanced around.

'Big of them,' Liza said.

'It's the whisperers that annoy me,' Gwen said.

'Plenty of those,' Jill agreed. 'They like their secrets here.'

'What kind of secrets?' Liza asked, still living in hope, having failed to extricate anything of use from anyone, including the Keenans, both too new to the village to know much about the past, and probably too discreet anyway.

'How would I know?' Jill grinned. 'They're too busy hugging them close.'

'Don't encourage her,' Gwen said to Liza. 'It's one of her things.'

'"The Secrets of Shiloh",' Jill said.

'Oh, stop,' Gwen said.

In Woonsocket, in his room, Michael's restlessness had become unbearable.

The deal had been that, dinner or a stroll aside, they should all stay put, and until now he hadn't wanted to go anyplace else because his room was comfortable and secure, and because tonight was still *before* . . .

Now, suddenly, he felt he had to get out.

Not out of Whirlwind. Totally committed now,

to Reaper and the others, even if he had not yet met them and still didn't know their real names – probably never would. And maybe what was coming might turn out to be some kind of closure for him.

Or another nightmare.

As for post-Revelation, who knew?

And who was there to care?

Now was all he had.

And now, right this minute, before he lost his mind altogether, Michael Rider, aka Michael Rees, aka Isaiah, was going *out*.

Forty-Two

'Good of you to come back,' Stephen said.

He was in the kitchen, wearing an old, wine-colored dressing gown, nursing a mug of tea at the table.

'I'm sorry, Granddad. I didn't mean to be so late but there was a party at the inn, and Gwen and Jill were there and asked me to stay.'

'Was it their party?'

'No. A couple from Shiloh Town called Sutter were throwing the party, and they were very nice, said I must stay.'

'Sounds like bad manners to me,' Stephen said.

'It probably was, but they didn't seem to mind, and I did enjoy it.' Liza pulled out another chair and sat down. 'The Osborns were there, and the Keenans, who I liked a lot.'

'I'm sure they're happy to have your seal of approval.'

Liza sighed, then reached out to touch his mug. 'That's cold. Can I make you a fresh cup?'

'No.' He moved the mug away from her. 'Thank you.'

'How about a snack?'

'Too late for me to eat now,' Stephen said. 'I might have liked something an hour or so ago.'

'I saw ham in the fridge, and cheese.'

'You think I should have made my own sandwich.'

'Since you're able, and were hungry,' Liza said evenly.

'As a matter of fact,' her grandfather said, 'my right hand is very arthritic.'

'I didn't realize,' she said. 'I wish you'd mentioned it.'

'Would you have given up your party?'

'Of course. I certainly would have come back earlier.'

'Not too busy trying to pump the locals for scandal?'

'I don't write scandal, Granddad.'

'How could I know that, when you never send me anything to read?'

'It didn't occur to me you'd be interested.'

Stephen Plain said nothing.

Liza debated, then decided she might as well be hung for a sheep.

'Gwen and Jill and I were talking about Reverend Pike, and one thing led to another, and Gwen said she thought you were probably the best person to ask about village history.'

137

'*This* again.' Stephen's anger flared. He leaned closer and took hold of her right wrist, startling her, squeezing it hard. 'You come here after all this time and five minutes later you're going round upsetting people.'

'I haven't upset anyone.' She had to wrench her wrist away. 'That hurt.'

'How many times do you have to be told?' His voice shook. 'Leave the past alone.'

Liza stared at him for a moment and felt a pang of confusion, the solid ground of almost a lifetime of dislike shifting to something more like concern.

'Are you OK, Granddad?' she asked him.

'As if you care,' he said. 'Get out of my sight, you stupid girl.'

Silently, she left the room.

The air outside the inn was bracing, the surroundings lovely, the lights tossing small rainbows into the softly falling snow, sounds muffled, the kind of atmosphere that might have brought tranquility to a man not doing battle with conflicting emotions.

On one hand, Michael wished that tomorrow was already here, and on the other that it would never come. He was afraid and excited, ashamed and exhilarated, and right now, even out here, his greatest problem still seemed to be how to find a way to get through this night.

He walked slowly for a while, found no pleasure even in the fresh snow beneath his boots, upped his pace, picking up his feet, hoping some physical challenge might help suppress the unbearable tension building in him, but it wasn't *enough*, and maybe if he could have gone for a run, but clearly that wasn't possible . . .

Suddenly he knew where he wanted to go.

Bad idea.

Going anyway.

He found the Toyota, brushed snow from the door, got it open, leaned in to start the engine and turn on the heater and demists, then began clearing the snow from the windshield.

'The party's over,' Amos said quietly, and saw Reaper open his eyes. 'Just the night staff left on duty.'

'Good.' Reaper stretched a little and winced. 'I'll be going in then.' He reached for his cane and this time the pain made him grimace.

'Need a hand?'

'No, thank you, Amos.' He opened the door. 'You get back safely.'

'Till tomorrow then,' the big man said.

'Any problems, I know where to find you.'

'Me too.'

Reaper turned in his seat. 'Nearly there, Amos.'

'Go get some rest,' Amos said. 'Long day coming.'

'For you too,' Reaper said. 'Last one for us.'

'Maybe not,' Amos said.

'Not for you,' Reaper said.

Amos didn't answer, just waited as he got out of the car, then leaned across to pull the door shut and watched as the old, thin man walked slowly along the pathway to the front door of the inn, where he rang the bell and waited to be admitted.

A moment later he was inside.

The bravest and strangest man Amos had ever known, and he'd known plenty.

Many things he didn't know about him.

Something in his gut figured that was probably just as well.

The signpost to the right was barely readable beneath the snow.

Not that Michael needed a sign.

He knew exactly where he was.

On Shiloh Road, about to enter the village of that name.

He'd been fourteen the last time he'd come, with his mother.

Just coming here had done Emily harm.

Some places you never forgot.

Never forgave.

He parked the Toyota halfway along Oak Street, off the main track and with enough space front and back for an easy departure. The last thing Whirlwind needed was him causing any kind of disruption tonight, here of all places.

He should not have come. Yet suddenly it had felt as if he had to, and he thought now that he'd known all along that he would.

He wanted to see it as Emily must have as a child, still happy, enjoying snowy winters and Christmas, before . . .

He'd wanted to come before tomorrow.

At the west end of Main Street, the Shiloh Inn looked inviting, lights shining through some windows on the upper floors, and the white fairy lights strung across the street from lamp to lamp were pretty, but at twenty past ten there wasn't another soul to be seen.

Michael looked up into the snowy sky for a moment, closed his eyes and took a deep breath. And then he opened them again and started walking.

Toward St Matthew's.

Forty-Three

Liza was much too restless to consider sleep any time soon.

She'd thought of going back to the inn for a couple of quiet drinks, or maybe jumping in her Honda and going for a drive, but neither really appealed, nor was she ready yet to pack her bag and walk out on her grandfather.

Besides, there was something about that anger of his, that physical roughness of the way he'd grabbed her wrist, that had really troubled her, making her wonder if she ought to speak to Ethel Murrow after the holidays, ask her if she'd noticed any early warning signs of some kind of dementia. And even though Stephen had always been something of a bully, it distressed her to think that he might be coming to that, especially living alone . . .

Reading too much into just one incident, she told herself.

And heaven help her if he found out she'd been discussing his mental health with anyone else.

For tonight, anyway, she thought he'd gone to bed; she'd gone to the bathroom a while ago and had seen no light, heard no sounds from his bedroom.

She had the house to herself, but found she wanted no part of it.

Different when her parents had been here, though even then she'd wanted out.

She remembered, suddenly, where she'd sometimes gone, seeking privacy, thought that going there now might help her.

For the second time that night, she pulled on her boots and parka and crept down the stairs. Snow still falling steadily as she shut the front door quietly behind her and started down the driveway onto Maple, heading for Main Street.

In his bedroom at the Shiloh Inn, Reaper, as comfortable as he ever was these days in pajamas and a gray dressing gown, stood at the window, staring out into the night.

A young woman was just turning onto Main from South Maple.

Hard to see from this distance, but he thought he knew who she was.

Unable to sleep, perhaps, maybe not certain why. If she but knew.

She was walking toward St Matthew's.

This time tomorrow, the church would be crowded.

His thoughts turned back to Whirlwind, hoped the others were getting some rest, that nerves were not getting the better of them.

He stared into the still-slowly-tumbling flakes

a few moments longer, and then he blinked,
turned away and drew his drapes.

'Take care,' he said.

Not entirely sure to whom he had said it. To
those five men and one woman, on the verge of
something each of them only partially understood. Or to himself.

The pain was bad again. Not unbearably so,
but he wanted to rest.

He sighed, walked slowly to the bed, took a
pill and lay down.

Closed his eyes, then opened them again.

Not liking what he saw when they were closed.

Forty-Four

Liza had come to the churchyard in her teens
when she'd felt like getting away but had not had
the means to get much farther. The bus schedule
had always been sparse, Shiloh Town not worth
the walk and worthwhile places too far away.
She'd wandered west sometimes onto rural
pathways, or she'd taken the bus to Chepachet,
stopping by the Brown and Hopkins Country Store
to buy candy before strolling out to the woods,
sometimes to the walkers' bridge that crossed into
Connecticut.

But St Matthew's churchyard, far more accessible,
had always felt to her somehow other-worldly,
detached from the rest of the village. Now, she
took a breath of the frigid night air and felt

instantly better, leaned against one of the taller stones, shivered and wrapped her arms around herself.

The creak of boots on the snow behind her startled her, and she whipped around.

'My God,' she said. 'Now who's stalking who?'

'What the *hell* are you doing here?' asked Michael Rider, in a battered tan leather jacket, hatless in the snow, clean-shaven, looking better, sharper than the last time she'd seen him, but thrown nonetheless.

'I'd have thought that was obvious,' she said. 'Christmas?'

'I meant here.' He gestured to the gravestones.

'Just getting away from it all,' Liza said. 'What's your excuse?'

'Visiting family.' He pointed to a large stone ten feet away, snow partially brushed away from its face, the name Cromwell exposed. 'Not all here, of course.'

'Some in Copp's Hill.'

'Generations back,' Michael said. 'Was that what you were doing there that day?'

'Not really. I like it there and I live close by.' She paused, took a chance. 'Your grandfather's not buried here.'

'Not buried anywhere, so far as I know. Scattered someplace private. No gravestone to desecrate.'

She sensed another opening and took that too. 'I really am sorry. For having been so intrusive in Boston.'

'And I'm sorry for overreacting.' He looked at her curiously. 'So if you're home for Christmas, why do you need to get away before it's even begun?'

'Because I hardly ever do come here, and this visit's already reminded me of why that is.' She looked up into the sky. 'That's why I'm standing here getting hypothermia.'

'You could have gone to the Shiloh Inn.'

Liza shook her head. 'I think they close the bar at night. Anyway, I was there earlier.'

'So just go back home,' Michael said. 'Better than getting pneumonia.'

'Not ready to go back yet.' Liza wondered at this apparent ceasefire, was glad of it.

'If it's that bad,' he said lightly, 'maybe you should go back to Boston. I hear there's nothing much worse than the holidays with relatives you don't get along with.'

'I used to get on with my mother. Now it's just my grandfather, and we've always clashed.'

'Christmas. Pressures to be jolly.' He looked away from her, up at St Matthew's. 'You should leave, come back at a normal time.'

'Trying to get rid of me again?' Liza said wryly.

Michael said nothing.

'Anyway, I can't leave. My grandfather's housekeeper's gone to her family. He'd be alone.' She looked up at the sky. 'Would you want to drive to Boston in this?'

'They say it's going to get much worse tomorrow.'

Liza shrugged.

'Maybe we should go somewhere, get a drink?' he said. 'I'm staying in Woonsocket, at the Red Door.'

'Bit far for a drink.' Liza wondered briefly why he'd chosen to come to Shiloh late on a snowy night rather than in daytime, then realized that

145

he probably had good reason for wanting to avoid locals.

'Where then?'

She thought. 'Cady's Tavern in Pascoag? It's a biker place and it can get noisy, but at least it isn't Shiloh.' She shivered, and glanced over in the direction of South Maple.

'You could call home,' Michael said. 'Stop your grandfather worrying, say you've met up with a friend. Probably best not to tell him who.'

'Best not,' Liza agreed. 'Though he won't be worrying. He's asleep.'

He'd referred to himself as a friend.

Big improvement on threatening to break her neck.

Though the night was still young.

Cady's wasn't too crowded, the snow already keeping people off the roads, but the chicken wings were good, they served Sam Adams beer, and Michael was sure that this was the last thing Reaper would want him doing; but back there in the churchyard, running into her yet again, he had experienced a violent need for human company. And maybe this was more than meaningless co-incidence, and illogical as it was, having unfairly singled her out for blame on behalf of every lousy journalist, what he actually wanted now, more than anything, was to risk spending an hour with Liza Plain.

And if not now, when?

'I can't believe I'm eating again,' Liza said, 'but this is so good, and I feel—'

'What?'

146

'I feel relaxed.' She shrugged. 'Which is un-expected.'

'I guess so,' Michael said, and drank some beer.

'You seem very different tonight,' Liza said.

Guilt rose up and he shoved it away.

He knew why he'd asked her for a drink. Not just for company, nor because she looked so great, but because he wanted, suddenly, to talk. Not about tomorrow – Whirlwind was the *last* thing he wanted to talk about. He wanted to talk about himself, and it was dawning on him, here, tonight, that maybe he'd been right about her all those years ago at Walden Pond, that maybe Liza Plain was what she had seemed back then. A good person.

'Being in Shiloh,' he began, 'made me think about my mother.' His voice was anger-edged but soft. 'About how she started out with every-thing and ended up with less than nothing.'

'She had you,' Liza said.

'Much good I did her,' Michael said.

'What was she like?'

'Fragile,' he said. 'Brave. Disconnected, some-times, she told me. I think she meant from herself.' He paused. 'She was just sixteen when she left Shiloh. She called it escaping, said she couldn't stand another day in the place that had destroyed her world.'

He took another drink from his bottle.

Began sharing.

Emily's story first. Then his own.

Told it all the way to 2001 and their meeting at the school, and what had come afterward. About Louise and her daughter and the events that had ultimately led to Emily's death and his dark descent.

147

Cady's was emptying out but they'd ordered coffee, and Michael found that he was not yet ready to stop, finding release in the telling, knowing, at the same time, that he was perhaps just keeping tomorrow at bay for a little while longer.

And not much more he could tell her without betraying Whirlwind.

He looked at her face. 'Don't look so sad. It could have been worse.'

'I guess,' she said. 'If you'd managed to kill yourself.'

'It was what I wanted,' he said, and abruptly stood, picking up the check.

'Please.' Liza got up too. 'Let me.'

'No way,' Michael said. 'This one's on me.'

She didn't argue.

He took out Michael Rees's credit card, then put it away again, feeling sick.

Paid cash.

Outside, the snow had eased off, but it took time to clear the fresh snow off the windows and to demist.

They sat in the car with the fan blowing, waiting.

'I have another question,' Liza said.

Michael didn't answer.

'What's changed? How come you've talked to me tonight?'

'Nothing's changed,' Michael said.

'I'd say something must have.'

He saw her confusion and felt a sudden intense urge to take care of one more thing.

'Will you do something for me, Liza?' he said.

'If I can.'

'Go back to Boston.' He paused. 'Not right

148

now, not after you've been drinking, but in the morning.'

'Why should I do that?' she asked, mystified.

He hesitated, because, oh, Christ, he wanted to tell her this too now, and maybe, with his world so totally upside down, maybe after all these years Liza Plain was the one person who might be able to help him, show him the way out of this.

Except she wouldn't *want* to help him if he did tell her, and anyway, he couldn't. It was too late.

'I can't tell you why,' he said.

'Because I'm a journalist?'

'No. It has nothing to do with that.'

'Why then? Why do you want me to go? I don't understand.'

Michael understood very well. He wanted her to leave because maybe, if they hadn't lost touch, if he hadn't met Louise, if his life hadn't imploded, then everything might have gone a very different route for them both.

No point thinking like that now. Too late.

He saw that she was watching him, troubled and uncomprehending, searched for something to say that might make sense.

'Shiloh's a rotten place, Liza,' he said.

'I'm not sure I believe that,' she said.

'Believe what you want,' Michael said brusquely, then gave the windshield a rough wipe with his gloved hand. 'I'd better get you back to your grandfather.'

Harshness the only way then.

'I could get a cab,' Liza said, deflated.

'Yeah, they'll be lining up.'

'I don't get this, Michael. It was so good talking.'

149

'Good,' he repeated. 'Maybe so, from a journo's viewpoint.'

'For God's sake,' she said quietly. 'I thought we'd got past that.'

'We had,' Michael said coldly, put the car into gear and slid them back onto the road.

The village was sleeping when they arrived back, street lights out, and even up at the Shiloh Inn only a single lamp showed through a divide in the drapes of a second-floor room. St Matthew's, at the opposite end of Main Street, was in darkness, drifted snow settled up against its stone walls.

Michael pulled up at the corner of South Maple.

'Better for you if I leave you here,' he said. 'Will you be OK?'

'Of course.' Liza could barely manage a smile. 'You might hate Shiloh but it's hardly filled with muggers.'

'Just the occasional child killer.'

'Oh, Michael,' she said, exasperated and sad.

'Emily was always certain that he hadn't done it,' he said.

Liza looked at him. 'Is that why you're here?'

The question surprising her, springing from instinct.

He reached out and touched her left arm. 'Liza, please just listen to me, and don't ask any more questions because I can't answer them.' His eyes were more intense than ever. 'You *have* to go back to Boston in the morning. Get out before the storm hits.'

She stared at him, and knew that what he

was telling her had nothing to do with the weather. 'I can't leave.'

'I can't tell you why, only that you really need to go.' He took a breath. 'And one more thing.'

'What?' She was growing more bewildered by the second.

'Don't tell anyone you've seen me.'

'Is that now, tonight?' She was sharp now, ironic. 'Or ever?'

'Ever doesn't matter,' he said. 'Just till after Christmas. Can you promise me that?'

'Will you even believe me if I do promise? I'm a journalist, after all.'

'You're Liza Plain,' he said. 'I'll believe you.'

She stared at him again, glimpsed, for an instant, the young man she'd first met, and saw that he meant what he said. 'Then I promise.'

'Thank you,' Michael said.

'Who would I tell, anyway?' she said.

Out of nowhere, he put out his hand and touched her cheek.

And then he leaned in and kissed her.

She hadn't seen it coming, but knew, instantly, that it was what she wanted too, more than anything, and the kiss was fast, shocking, almost violent, filled with some kind of desperation, his face hot to the touch, his arms pulling her tightly closer.

She broke away first, *had* to, because suddenly it felt wrong, too desperate, and what he'd just asked of her was crazy and she was too thrown by it all.

'I'm sorry.' He sat back, looking shaken. 'I shouldn't have done that.'

151

'Michael, I don't understand what's happening.'

'And I can't explain it to you,' he said, tightly. 'You need to trust me and you need to leave in the morning.'

'You can't just kiss me like that and tell me to leave.'

'That's all I can do,' he said harshly. 'Please. Now go. Just *go*.'

Liza stared at him again, and then she turned and opened the door, got out, pushed the door shut behind her and walked quickly along Maple, not looking back, knowing he was still there, that he was watching her all the way.

It was only when she reached her grandfather's driveway that she turned.

And saw him drive away.

Forty-Five

Michael sat in the car back outside the Red Door Inn.

The jangling in his mind so loud that it hurt.

Any number of ways this Christmas could unfold for him now.

One a brand-new option, the most tempting by a million miles. Drive straight back to Shiloh, figure out which was Liza's window and throw snow up at it, then persuade her to drive back to Boston with him, and to hell with Christmas.

And to hell with Whirlwind.

This evening had changed everything. And nothing.

He might feel differently, but he should have recognized that back at the start of the month when she'd tried approaching him and he'd rejected her so violently.

And he should, of course, have realized that she might be here – though would knowing that have made any difference to his decision-making? He doubted it, still hiding as he had been behind his irrational shield of anger.

Too late now.

Blaming Liza Plain had been unfair, disproportionate and unfounded. She had yearned to become a journalist as he'd striven to become a teacher. Good and bad in both professions. And zero justification for his behavior toward her.

Not as wrong, though, as what he'd done to her tonight.

Spending time with her, opening up to her about the past.

Kissing her.

Unforgivable on so many levels.

There'd been no one since Louise, and Lord knew he'd had little enough to offer her, but even if he could get out of this mess now, he had *less* than nothing to offer Liza.

Nothing but bleakness with a screwed-up ex-con with suicidal tendencies.

Though maybe life might not be nearly as bleak with a woman like Liza.

'It would be,' he said.

Because he was the same man he had been a few hours ago.

A loser.

Besides which, he was not going to run out on Whirlwind. Not now.

Not that Reaper would let him if he tried.

So, depending on how things panned out, he might be back in prison before New Year's.

Or maybe the morgue.

Until tonight, he'd have figured the latter the best option.

Now he wasn't quite as certain.

Liza was in bed. She hadn't closed the drapes and it was snowing lightly again, casting patterns on the closet door opposite the window, flakes settling whole on the glass like small design miracles before they dissolved.

Like the promise of the evening just past.

Michael Rider was keeping Liza awake.

His history, so much of it tragic and disturbing.

And the kiss, which had set off something she hadn't felt in a long time, perhaps ever. And even before that, in the bar, she'd definitely been feeling that *connection* again.

Though it wasn't really that or even the kiss preying on her mind now.

It was his asking her, repeatedly, to leave the village.

It was the *intensity* of that, its oddness, with no explanation given except: 'Shiloh's a rotten place, Liza.'

She might understand that from his perspective, but it was most certainly not enough to make her abandon her grandfather for the holidays now that she was actually here; besides which, Michael's past hardly qualified him as the most reliable man in Rhode Island.

154

Liza sighed, turned on her side, closed her eyes. 'Merry Christmas,' she said.

The drapes in Reaper's room at the Shiloh Inn were three-quarters closed, the bedside lamp still on, the occupant of the bed lying tidily, as was his habit, in the center of the mattress, arms straight down by his sides.

He wished that Isaiah had not come to Shiloh tonight. Had not made contact with that young woman.

He knew a little about Liza Plain – knew something about every person present in the village tonight.

His head ached, and his chest, but his pain level in general was nowhere near its worst. His medication working for now, and no sense in mulling over tomorrow.

On the bedside table, four bottles of tablets and a water glass.

Beside them, a gold cross on a long chain. A substantial thing.

Not his. Something borrowed.

For a special occasion.

Revelation.

Reaper's eyes closed, but his lips moved as he murmured something.

The same word over and over.

'Soon.'

In Woonsocket, Michael was tossing and turning.

No sleep for him this night. Perhaps no sleep ever again, he thought, not even eternal rest. Damnation more probable.

155

The kiss still warming him, its folly still goading him, fear uppermost in his mind.

Of tomorrow.

He closed his eyes again, sick with fatigue.

Emily's face appeared, laughing, happy, then disappeared, Liza there instead, her lovely blue eyes filled with confusion.

Another face blotted her out, of a man he'd found hanging at Garthville.

Worst thing he'd ever seen.

Michael opened his eyes, shuddering, tilted his head toward the window and stared out into the night.

Thought about Revelation.

'Not long now,' he said.

Forty-Six

Liza had waited until eight to get the phone number from Directory and call the Red Door Inn, but when she'd asked for Michael Rider she'd been told they had no guest of that name.

She had thought briefly. 'Michael Cromwell?'

Negative, and why would he?

Nothing to be done but get on with the day.

Christmas Eve.

Long day.

She'd made Stephen breakfast and then she'd driven to Greenville to pick up some shopping from Glover's, including a couple of bottles of wine for herself, and when she'd got back, her grandfather had dressed himself neatly: well-pressed slacks and crisp white shirt, navy wool cardigan, polished shoes, his white hair tidily combed and clean-shaven, all of which he'd clearly managed himself.

Clearly no dementia to blame for his roughness last night. Just an unpleasant old man with anger issues.

'Someone called several times,' Stephen had said as she was putting food in the refrigerator. 'Hung up when they heard my voice.'

'Any caller ID?' Liza had asked.

'I'm not senile, Liza,' Stephen had said sharply. 'No number. Just a time-waster.' He'd looked at her intently. 'Someone for you, perhaps.'

'Why should it be for me?' Liza had said.

Michael flying straight into her head.

Her lips humming suddenly with the memory.

She had shaken that off, wondering nonetheless if it might have been him, had made lunch, forcing herself to be nicer, to make allowances. Best way to survive Christmas, and then she could go back to her real life.

The long day had gone on.

Michael was cursing himself.

He'd found Dr Stephen Plain's number in the phone book that morning, had tried it twice, hesitating when the old man had picked up, then hanging up because Christ knew he'd done more than enough harm talking to Liza last night without inviting her grouchy grandfather to ask questions about him.

His own bad temper having made him delete

Liza's personal details after he'd told her in early December to leave him the hell alone, he had no other means now of asking her one last time to get out of Shiloh while she still could.

Not that she'd listen anyway, not without the truth. And even then, she'd probably refuse to leave her family, might even call the cops.

So, nothing more to be done.

Except follow directions.

Long, long day ahead.

For Reaper too.

A longer one to come.

Perhaps his last.

Hard for his team too, soon to be leaving comfort and safety behind and getting themselves to their new waiting posts because of what the weather experts were now calling 'The Blizzard to End All Blizzards'; and with plenty of derelict farm buildings in walking distance of Shiloh, it had not been hard for Amos to pinpoint the temporary shelters needed.

For now, Reaper opened up his MacBook and looked at the image on the screen.

At the text: *They have sown the wind, and they shall reap the whirlwind.*

And below that, photographs of his six chosen ones.

This the first time that they'd all be able to see each other.

Too risky earlier, in case one of them had decided to quit.

Now, however, it was vital that they would be able to recognize one another.

He felt, at that moment, immense fondness for all of them.

And then he returned to his comfortable armchair, sat down and listened to his final recorded message to them, knowing that they'd all be listening now as he talked, once more, about justice and fear and courage.

Another of his 'leader of men' moments.

Still listening, he felt his right hand begin to tremble.

Felt the flutter in his head, the precursor to dissociation.

He understood his sickness, the one that had begun decades before his cancer, a relic, almost certainly in part, of infantile meningitis. Controllable to a point, but untamable without medication, without restraint.

He had, over time, become its master, as it, paradoxically, remained his.

'No,' he told it now. 'Not yet. You'll have to wait.'

And here it was again, the proof of his monstrous guilt.

The ability to control. Making his childhood sickness his excuse for evil.

The tremor ceased; the flutter in his head subsided.

His calm, benevolent voice still speaking from his computer.

'So. Shall we go through it one last time?'

Reaper went on listening along with the others.

'At around a quarter before ten this night, as the fine people of Shiloh Village and their dear ones file into church for their favorite service of the year, as the prerecorded bells of Saint Matthew's ring out, the old house of worship brilliant with light, four of our number will take their place with them . . .'

Forty-Seven

They hurried through the big open doorway, brushing snow from their hats and coats and faces, for the promised blizzard had stormed in about three hours ago, the National Weather Service warning of dangerous winds and life-threatening conditions. Advice statewide, in Rhode Island and Massachusetts, to stay home, some meteorologists estimating five feet of snow in the next several hours.

Liza walked alongside Stephen Plain through St Matthew's narthex at the west end of the church, moving farther into the nave, greeting Gwen and Jill on their right, waving at Betty Hackett and old Denny Fosse, Stephen taking time to give season's greetings to Steve Julliard, once the local sheriff, now wheelchair-bound and mute after a stroke; her grandfather far more cordial with the villagers, Liza thought, than he'd ever been with her or her mother.

His choice of seating in the fifth row of pews, halfway along, wasn't too bad, she decided, Stephen taking the second place in, leaving her the aisle seat, which she liked, church services sometimes making her a little claustrophobic. Not that she ever attended out of choice; a christening in Boston her last visit, and that over a year ago.

'Good turnout, considering the weather,' Stephen said.

'Very.' Liza watched people, some bowing and crossing themselves before taking their places, all ruddy-faced, shedding hats and coats, exposing Sunday-best suits and dresses, Santa ties and snowmen sweaters, this service still clearly a big event for most.

'A rotten place,' Michael had said about Shiloh last night.

Taking in the festive, cheerful atmosphere now, she decided he'd definitely been wrong about that. She unzipped her parka and stood up again to arrange herself more comfortably, cozy for now in her long red sweater, thick black leggings tucked inside her snow boots. She became aware of her grandfather's disapproving glance, smiled back at him regardless, saw him shake his head but smile back anyway.

Pleased by that hint of Christmas spirit, she remained standing and looking around, saw the Glover family up front, supposed that the child beside old Seth Glover was Grace, his granddaughter. Saw Norman Clay, another lifelong Shiloh resident who owned a pharmacy in the town, then Rosie Keenan, who waved at her; noted that people were moving forward from the rear pews as it became clear that the church was never going to fill tonight, and glancing back, there weren't too many people she recognized, which was hardly surprising . . .

And then, there he was.

161

Michael Rider.

Just walking in, a snow-covered black wool beanie in one gloved hand, clearing snow off the shoulders of his jacket with the other – not the old beaten-up leather jacket he'd worn last night, this one a black padded, zip-up waterproof over a black turtleneck sweater, and he looked pretty spruce, dark hair damp but neat.

He sat in the rear pew aisle seat, and she wondered if he'd move forward with the rest. He'd said nothing to her last night about coming to the service, and it made no *sense* after badgering her to leave, and was it possible that in the end he'd come because of her? And maybe that had been him calling when she'd been out shopping, maybe he'd been wanting to tell her . . .

She looked straight at him, but he seemed not to see her, or maybe he was avoiding her, in which case, why was he here?

The kiss came back to her again, heated her cheeks, flustering her.

'Sit down, Liza,' Stephen told her. 'They're starting.'

The organ began its familiar opening chords, and the choir – down to eight voices – began to sing 'O Come, all ye Faithful', and the congregation rose and joined in. The processional at St Matthew's had never been grandiose, as Liza recalled, but all the elements were present: a female deacon and one altar server, incense being swung in a censer, the Gospel Book held high by the deacon – and of all those now moving up the center aisle with crosses and candles and incense,

162

the only one Liza recognized was Simon Keenan, white-robed tonight with a narrow cincture around his waist, no head covering, a modest man for the job, she felt, and all the better for it.

She shifted and turned her head, trying not to be too obvious, but Janet Yore, the elderly village dressmaker, had moved into the pew directly behind her, was smiling at her, blocking her view, so Liza did the only thing she could: smile back and face the front again.

And go on singing.

At the other end of Main Street, inside the Shiloh Inn, all was quiet except for the soft, muffled sounds of terrified weeping.

Eleven traumatized guests, the duty manager and his wife, all on the floor of the bar, bound and gagged. Window shutters and drapes closed. Telephone system disabled, cell phones, tablets and one Kindle Fire confiscated. The inn's wireless router disconnected. Entrances and exits secured.

Two of the four men hired by Amos were standing guard. Halloween masks covering their faces, dark gray point-forty-caliber Sig Sauers in their black-gloved hands.

The other two men back out in the village, calling on anyone who'd stayed home tonight, including seniors, infants, small children, the sick and their caregivers.

Amos's organized 'cleanup' being aided by the blizzard.

'Keep it simple,' he'd instructed the men.

As at the inn, phone lines had been cut, cell

phones removed, along with computers and readers, even Xboxes and any other smart devices.

The rest taken care of by simple, credible threats from men in white Scream masks bearing deadly handguns:

'Stay home and keep your mouths shut, and you live to see Christmas Day. Step outside, try to go for help or alert anyone, anyplace, and you die.'

Not that anyone would get far out there.

Whiteout and howling winds.

No one coming in or out of Shiloh any time soon.

Forty-Eight

The waiting nearly over now for the team.

If all was going to plan inside the church, four members would already be in their pre-action positions. Isaiah in the back pew, north side of the aisle. The man named Luke at the end of the front pew if possible, taking the seat closest to the Stars and Stripes and the north-east fire exit. The man called Joel one row back on the opposite side, near the door that led to the undercroft.

The woman named Nemesis down there, still concealed and waiting.

As was Reaper.

Ten rows of pews in the nave, room for six, comfortably, on both sides of the center aisle. St

Matthew's official capacity one hundred and twenty – no more than half-full tonight.

The Whirlwind members all dressed in black, though not identically. Not a uniform, but a means of helping them to identify one another.

Amos and Jeremiah were still outside in the white, wild night, sitting in the Volvo parked at the corner of Main and South Maple, keeping watch for latecomers, two in particular.

Both men silent, Jeremiah's tension palpable.

'And here they come,' Amos said, softly.

The old Bentley bearing William and Freya Osborn pulled up close to the main entrance of the church, parking only a little askew, narrowly avoiding the buried fire hydrant behind the vehicle.

Parking tickets the least of Osborn's problems tonight, Amos thought.

'OK.' Jeremiah could feel blood pulsing in his ears.

They watched the stout old man in his lambskin coat and hat get his door open and struggle out of the car, his boots useless, sinking beneath the piling snow, fighting the whipping wind to get his door closed, then holding on to the Bentley's body as he worked around to the passenger side and hauled that door open, his wife pushing from her side, dressed in mink and equally useless, too-dainty snow boots.

Amos sat still as the couple laughed, battling their way inside.

'How much longer now?' Jeremiah dug his gloved fingers into his right thigh.

'Not long,' Amos said.

* * *

The two gunmen on the street, having completed their own tasks and having witnessed the two late arrivals, waited another minute, as previously instructed, and then, masks removed, began to walk, wind- and snow-buffeted every inch of the way, toward the Volvo.

Amos opened his door, felt it almost flung out of his hand.

One of the men bent to speak to him, but his voice was drowned by the wind, so he raised his right thumb, and Amos nodded in response.

'I owe you,' he shouted, with no risk of being overheard.

'Believe it,' the other man shouted back.

Amos dragged his door shut again.

'Ever see anything like this weather?' Jeremiah said. 'It's like the fucking end of the world.'

'It's our best buddy tonight,' Amos said. 'Except we can't hear the service. Makes it harder to time.'

He watched the two gunmen, shoulders hunched, staggering back to their waiting four-by-four across the street. A good position from which they would keep watch on the church entrance, ensure that no one else tried to go inside once Revelation had begun.

'They going to stay right through?' Jeremiah asked.

'They stay till they leave,' Amos said.

'So that's it now? We go in?'

'Another minute,' Amos said, 'and then we unload the bags and get ourselves to the door, and then we listen hard.'

'What the hell are we listening for?'

Amos threw him a look.

'For the end of the fucking singing,' he said.

166

Forty-Nine

Inside, as the processional moved slowly around for the third and final time, Reverend Keenan stepped onto the chancel, bowed and crossed himself before the altar, then turned and moved to the pulpit.

The voices stilled, the organ's last notes faded to nothing, and the vicar took a breath.

'The Lord be with you,' he said.

'And also with you,' the congregation said.

The sounds were the first discordant sign, and with them, the shock of freezing wind and snow blowing in and through the nave.

Doors being opened. The main and north-east fire exit door simultaneously; that one being opened from the inside by a man in black with a badly-scarred face, fighting the elements to push the door wide, allowing a second man, also in black, to enter, his head and face snow-coated, stepping inside bearing a large bag.

'Close the door!' someone yelled.

The door shut with a loud clang behind the stranger. Then another bang as the front door was closed.

Simon Keenan collected himself.

'Lift up your hearts,' he said to the congregation.

'We lift them up to the Lord,' they responded.

Gasps rose suddenly from congregants near the fire door.

'Oh, dear God!' Eleanor Tilden cried from the south front pew, right of the aisle.

'It's OK,' John Tilden said beside her.

Liza, rising from the fifth row, looked front left toward the fire door and saw that it was *not* OK. That the man who'd opened the door was now pulling things out of the other man's bag – what looked like *wires* – and was fastening them, sticking them, she thought, to the fire exit.

Wires and white cables and something wrapped in plastic.

The second man's gloved hands were shaking.

'Oh my God,' Liza said, very quietly, and sat down.

'What's happening?' Stephen asked.

'I don't know, Granddad.'

Alarm spread quickly, a great wave of fright all around the nave, and Liza stood up again, turned and saw that something else was happening back in the narthex.

She looked for Michael and found him two rows from the rear, still on the aisle.

This time he looked back at her, very briefly and grimly, then averted his gaze.

He seemed, Liza felt with a great thump of fear, to be waiting for something.

Dressed in black.

'What the hell?' Stephen Plain said suddenly.

Liza swung around, saw that a third man was coming up the center aisle, black-clad like the other two, but much bigger, tall and heavyset and very intimidating, hatless and shaven-headed, gripping another large bag.

He halted less than three feet behind Liza.

Bent and pulled something from the bag.

'Oh my God, he's got a *gun*!' a man yelled, sparking a jagged chorus of terror.

Simon Keenan looked down at his wife, Rosie, in the front row beside the Tildens, then back at his congregation.

Then at the big man in black, now holding some kind of a shotgun.

'I don't know what you want, sir' – Keenan's voice shook only slightly – 'but I would remind you of where you are, and what tonight is.'

The man did not answer.

'They've *all* got guns!' Janet Yore cried out from behind Liza.

And people all over the nave of St Matthew's Church began screaming.

Heart pumping hard, body quivering with adrenalin, Michael stood up.

He checked swiftly around, locating the other Whirlwind members, and saw Luke first – easy to identify because of his scars – being handed a shotgun by a man with close-cut brown hair and a lean physique – Jeremiah. Watched Luke, a shotgun now in each hand, quickly cross the nave and give one of the weapons to the man Michael already knew to be Joel, having spent the final waiting hours with him, and all credit to the silver-haired former doctor for not letting his fear show now, when it counted.

Jeremiah had turned, was climbing the chancel steps, taking a position a few feet behind the pulpit, the best spot to survey most of the nave.

Michael knew that Amos's work at the entrance had to be complete.

169

No going back.

He moved out of his pew and began walking forward.

Felt Liza's eyes on him.

Don't look at her.

He reached Amos – no doubting him, big shaven-headed thug of a man, the one who'd grabbed him that night and brought him to Whirlwind – and saw that his eyes were cold but calm, green irises speckled with brown. Nodding at Michael now, drawing another shotgun from his bag and handing it to him.

Do not look at her.

Heart pounding even faster, Michael carried on walking, turned right at the front of the nave, passed Joel and reached the door that he knew, from the scale drawings, led to the undercroft.

Opened it.

Liza stared in horrified disbelief as yet another man emerged.

Much older, thin, gray-haired, bespectacled, also wearing black.

The same kind of jacket as Michael's and the other gunmen, she saw, every vestige of hope dying, their jackets all combat-style waterproofs, with multiple zipped pockets.

This man's jacket was open, revealing a roll-neck and a large gold cross on a long chain around his neck, and he was not carrying a shotgun, only a black cane.

The screaming lowered to fearful hushed layers of weeping, whispering, praying.

'Thank you, Isaiah,' the older man said to Michael.

Who closed the door to the undercroft and took up a position before it.

Sentry duty.

Liza knew now why he had wanted her to leave Shiloh.

His wanting her gone making this no better.

Isaiah.

'I know him,' Eleanor Tilden, in the front row right of the aisle, whispered loudly to her husband, clutching his arm. 'He was in the bar yesterday.'

'Quiet,' John Tilden hissed back. 'Not now.'

'He ordered Balvenie,' she whispered.

'Ellie, shut up,' Tilden said.

Walking slowly toward the chancel steps, Reaper heard them and smiled, climbed the steps and stopped, two feet away from the vicar, who was staring at him.

'Apologies for the intrusion, Reverend,' Reaper said.

'You were here yesterday,' Keenan said, fighting for calm.

'Correct. You were kind, asked me if I was all right.'

'Then in the name of God, what *is* this? This, of all nights, here, of all places.'

'The perfect place,' Reaper said. 'Now I'd like you to go take a seat, Vicar.'

'I'm not leaving this pulpit,' Keenan said.

'I don't wish to threaten you,' Reaper said, 'but in case you haven't noticed, there are five men in this church perfectly prepared to use their weapons if need be.'

'Oh, dear God!' a woman cried – Norman Clay's

wife, Liza thought – and a fresh billow of fear rippled around the church, and in the north-east front pew, young Grace Glover began to weep and her mother, Clare, wrapped a protective arm around her.

'Please, Reverend.' Reaper remained courteous. 'I'm simply asking you to go sit down there.' He gestured toward the pews. 'For the sake of your congregation.' He looked down and picked out a young man sitting beside Rosie Keenan. 'You. Give your place to the vicar.'

'Me?' The young man – a church volunteer from Shiloh Town named Luther Brown who'd stayed the night with the Keenans because of the weather – sat still, frozen with fear.

'Now, if you please.' Reaper's voice sharpened.

'Go on, Luther,' Rosie said gently.

Brown stepped unsteadily into the aisle, stared helplessly at the people in the second row, who quickly made space for him, and huddled down, trying to make himself invisible.

'Thank you,' Reaper said.

With no alternative, Keenan moved aside, descended the steps, reached the seat beside his wife and took her hand, then looked up at the stranger with the cane now taking over the pulpit.

For the moment, the man in charge.

Reaper laid his hand on the open Book of the Gospel.

Regarded the congregation, taking his time.

This night years in the planning, his strategy vague, not fully formed until he had found and enticed his team to join him.

He looked down over the sea of faces, some ashen, many clutching hands with their neighbors, some with their eyes shut, praying. Waiting.

'People of Shiloh.' Reaper's voice rose to the occasion, became resonant. 'I am here to tell you that you have all been taken hostage by a group named Whirlwind.'

New alarm flew around the nave, people repeating the word *hostage*, quickly hushing each other, afraid of being singled out for any reason.

'Not only are we armed,' Reaper went on, 'but I must advise you that every exit from Saint Matthew's Church, above and below ground, has been wired with plastic explosives.'

Patty Jackson, the church cleaner, sitting in the sixth row with her elderly parents, let out a terrified cry.

'So long as you all keep your places and remain calm,' Reaper said, 'there's no immediate danger to any of you. Stay well clear of the doors, people of Shiloh.' He paused. 'All will become clear quite soon.'

'What do you *want* with us?' William Osborn asked from his front row place, left of the aisle.

'For you all to be *quiet*,' Reaper said sharply. 'Speak only when you're spoken to. That includes you, Mr Osborn.'

The old newspaper man's face grew red with anger, but Freya Osborn grasped his hand, squeezed it urgently, and he nodded, kept silent.

Reaper looked around the church, smiled and took a breath.

'A happy and a holy Christmas to you all.'

Liza stared at Michael Rider, standing at the

undercroft door, looking back at her again now, his eyes dark and unfathomable.

'May you all live to enjoy it,' Reaper said.

Fifty

As the Blizzard-to-End-All-Blizzards continued to render highways impassable, bringing down trees, fences, barns and smaller manmade structures and bridges in rural districts, Whirlwind was at work inside St Matthew's.

Nemesis the only member not yet up in the nave, and she'd been wavering earlier in the day, until she'd called her brother and been refused a conversation by some bitch at his care home, and anger had refueled her commitment, made it easier to push on.

Busy now, downstairs in the vicar's office.

Reaper had instructed the deacon, altar server, the choir and Stan Nowak, the organist, to move back to the eighth row, after which Jeremiah, Luke and Joel had collected every cell phone in the church, those claiming not to have brought one being subjected to bag and body searches.

Now, at eleven-fifteen, the team were back in position. Clergy and worshipers sitting in angry, strained silence, many leaning on others for support, a few unable to stop weeping, the atmosphere shifting constantly as pockets of panic rose, then fell again into uneasy quiet.

'Isaiah.' Reaper turned to the man still standing

at the undercroft door. 'A short introduction and explanation from you, if you please.'

Sitting beside her grandfather, Liza froze.

Watched Michael hesitate before moving to the steps and up to the chancel, where he gave Reaper his shotgun, and Reaper moved to a carved chair beside the pulpit so that the younger man could address the congregation.

'My real name is Michael Rider,' he began. 'I expect that few of you, if any, have heard it before, though some of you have most definitely heard of my grandfather, whose life and death have come to form a small, but significant part of Shiloh's history.' He paused. 'His name was Donald Cromwell.'

'Oh, dear Lord,' Betty Hackett said.

'Cromwell,' Stephen Plain said disgustedly. 'We might have known.'

Liza saw Michael waver, thought she saw his eyes find her again, then veer quickly away as he waited for the murmurs to die down.

'Emily Cromwell Rider, my late mother,' he went on, 'left Shiloh soon after my grandfather's death, and I was born three years later. Her hope was that the past might have no impact on my life, but that was not to be.' He paused. 'My life, however, is not my reason for standing here tonight. My reason for being here, for wrecking your Christmas Eve, is that I recently learned that nearly forty years ago a miscarriage of justice took place here in Shiloh, continuing at Providence County Superior Court and ending in a prison cell at the Rhode Island maximum security prison.'

175

'Where a child killer committed suicide,' William Osborn said loudly.

'I asked for silence,' Reaper said.

'We don't kowtow to bullies with guns,' Stephen Plain said.

'That's very noble, Dr Plain,' Reaper said. 'But ill-advised.'

Liza looked at her grandfather, saw anger and distaste, hated that the man with the cane knew him by name, and wondered with a chill what was coming.

'Several of you here tonight' – Michael was continuing – 'were key witnesses at that long-ago trial, people whose testimony led Donald Cromwell to conclude that he had no hope.' He paused. 'Don't be afraid. We're not here to punish you, just to get to the truth.'

'The truth' – this time, Osborn got to his feet – 'is that Cromwell was guilty as sin and hanged himself because of it.'

'He hanged himself, in good part,' Michael said, 'because of the biased reporting of the case in your newspaper, Mr Osborn.'

'I'd write it all the same way again,' Osborn said, 'and be proud of what little I was able to do for poor Alice Millicent.'

'But not interested, apparently, in doing the same for Donald Cromwell, when I now know that you were in possession of a letter that might, at the very least, have cast doubt on his guilt. A letter from my grandmother.'

'A piece of paper scribbled on by an unstable wife,' Osborn said. 'A woman later proven to be mentally ill. Hardly a document worth raising as

176

evidence in a case where the accused was so patently guilty.'

Reaper got to his feet, handed Michael back the shotgun, changed places with him and focused on the congregation.

'Most of you weren't here in Shiloh back then, many not yet born, but there is a great deal at stake here tonight, so I have to ask you to bear with us.'

'Or you could let us all go home,' Denny Fosse – whose German shepherd had helped in the search for the missing child back in 1975 – said from the seventh row.

'Not until we're done, I'm afraid,' Reaper said.

'This is a *church*.' Simon Keenan was unable to stay silent any longer. 'This is the night we celebrate the birth of our Lord Jesus Christ, and you've come in here with *guns*.'

'And now' – Reaper ignored him – 'I'm going to ask that anyone present who feels they may have something to contribute in the way of long-belated testimony, should take some time to search their conscience.' He paused. 'And in the meantime, while our further arrangements are put in place—'

'What arrangements?' Keenan asked.

'They're going to *kill* someone.' Mark Jackson, a retired local farmer whose testimony at Cromwell's trial had been ordered stricken from the record, spoke loudly now. 'They're going to have some kind of terrorist-type trial and then they're going to lynch someone.'

'For heaven's sake.' His wife, Ann, stared at him, appalled. 'Are you trying to scare everyone to death?'

'They're already scared to death,' Jackson said.

'Dad, *please*.' Patty Jackson's face was scarlet.

A woman three rows ahead began to sob – Annie Stanley, a teacher who'd been off sick the day of Alice Millicent's abduction – and Betty Hackett put her arm around her. An angry sound escaped old Steve Julliard, who'd been sheriff back at the time, and a child near the back was crying too, and some of those who'd struggled for a semblance of calm since the initial terror began weeping again.

'See what you've done?' Ann Jackson accused her husband.

'While our arrangements are put in place' – Reaper overrode them – 'we would simply ask that you continue your Christmas Eve service as you intended.'

'You've got to be *kidding*,' a man said.

'For God's sake,' Gwen Turner said.

'Precisely why we want you to have your service, Ms Turner.' Reaper stepped away from the pulpit, leaned on his cane and motioned to the vicar. 'Reverend Keenan, please return to your rightful place, and Mr Nowak' – he pointed to the man in the eighth row – 'go back to the organ.'

'What about us?' one of the choristers called out.

'The choir can sing from back there,' Reaper said.

'So now we're supposed to just sit here and sing carols?' Stephen Plain demanded. 'This is an *outrage*.'

'Take it easy, Granddad,' Liza said.

'You think those explosives are real?' Janet Yore whispered from behind her.

Liza turned around. 'Probably safest to assume they are.'

'I can't believe what's happening,' Janet said. 'It doesn't feel *real*.'

'What's he doing now?' Stephen said.

Liza turned back and saw that Michael Rider was coming down the aisle.

'He's looking at you, Liza,' her grandfather said quietly.

Michael stopped, stooped beside her. 'Liza, I'd appreciate it if you'd come with me,' he said quietly.

She looked at him. A total stranger now, shotgun in one hand.

'Where to?' she asked, coldly.

Stephen stood up. 'What do you want with my granddaughter?'

'It's OK, Granddad.' Liza's heart was thumping. 'We know each other.'

'You know this man?' Stephen sat down again. 'Things just get better.'

'Liza?' Michael said.

'Do I have a choice?' she asked.

'Of course,' he said. 'Though I think this is something you might be interested in.'

'You're holding us *prisoner*.' Liza was incredulous. 'You have guns and explosives. Are you out of your *mind*?'

'They're terrorists,' Stephen said.

'No one's going to be hurt, Dr Plain,' Michael said to him.

'Then put away your guns and defuse your bombs,' Stephen said, 'and let us go.'

'We will,' Michael told him, 'when we're through.'

'Through with what?' Liza asked.

'Justice,' Michael answered.

'*Terrorists*,' Stephen said again.

The bizarreness of her own situation hit Liza suddenly, made her dizzy.

'Are you OK?' Michael asked.

Liza took a deep breath, steadied herself. 'What is it you want from me?'

'Come with me, and you'll see it's in the interests of the whole congregation.'

'You're not going anywhere with him,' Stephen said.

Liza looked up at Rider, searching for the man she'd been with last night, the man she'd *kissed*, trying to remind herself of all he'd been through.

No excuse for this. There could never be any excuse for *this*.

She heard the organ, and then the singing, first from the displaced choir, altar server and deacon, then a few members of the congregation following, faltering at first, then seeming to strengthen.

'*Gloria in Excelsis Deo*,' they sang, sounding almost defiant.

Surreal.

Liza stood up.

Her grandfather's hand gripped at her sweater. 'No, Liza.'

'I'll be OK,' she said, and gently extricated his fingers.

And began to walk, just ahead of Michael Rider, down the aisle.

The singing wavered a little as Liza felt people

180

staring, knew they had to be wondering about her, maybe even asking themselves if she had some part in this. Not being visibly forced, after all, so far as they could see, even if Rider did have a gun.

Liza looked up momentarily and saw Simon Keenan looking down at her from the pulpit.

He caught her gaze, held it, then nodded and smiled.

The vicar on her side.

That was something.

Fifty-One

The woman in the office down in the undercroft was also dressed in black; sweater, slacks and boots, zippered waterproof jacket over the back of a chair, latex gloves covering her hands.

Liza had only been down here once, to some event in the parish hall, found this section of the church a strange mix with its vaulted ceiling and ugly partitioned rooms.

Nothing overtly threatening about the Whirlwind woman. No shotgun in sight. Brown bobbed hair, slim figure, fortyish, Liza guessed. She had been working at the vicar's desk when Michael and Liza had entered. The desktop PC was switched on, an open MacBook Pro and small backpack beside it.

'Isaiah feels you might be interested in what we're doing,' she said.

'Isaiah,' Liza repeated wryly. 'And you are?'

'My Whirlwind name is Nemesis.' The woman offered her hand.

Liza didn't take it. 'My name is Liza Plain. It's my real name.'

'We're going to be broadcasting from the nave,' Nemesis said, 'using a lightweight streaming pack – I'm guessing you might know what that is.'

'I'm beginning to *guess* you know what I know and what I don't,' Liza said.

'I don't know anything about you,' Nemesis said. 'Didn't know you existed until Reaper asked Isaiah to bring you in.'

'"Bring me in"?' Liza turned to Michael. 'I'm not *in* on any of this.'

'So.' Reaper had come down behind them, stood in the office doorway. 'I gather you're a journalist, Ms Plain.'

Close up, he looked old and lined, a million miles from any kind of gang leader or hard man Liza had ever imagined, though energy emanated from him like electricity.

'Your name, Reaper,' she said. 'Is that as in "Grim" or as in reaping and sowing?'

'The latter,' Reaper said. '"They have sown the wind, and they shall reap the whirlwind."'

'Biblical,' Liza said.

'Readers interpret it differently,' Reaper said. 'My take is that those who've sinned and not repented will finally suffer the consequences.'

'What does that make this?' Liza felt nauseous, knew she was trembling, only anger holding her together for now. 'The Day of Judgment?'

'I hope so.' Reaper paused. 'Which we're hoping to broadcast to as many people as possible,

182

with the aid of Nemesis's remarkable bag of tricks.'

'Not mine,' Nemesis said. 'On loan. A professional-grade lightweight field unit. Everything needed to broadcast live.'

'All in a nifty little backpack,' Liza said. 'Good for you.'

'Maybe for you too, Ms Plain,' Reaper said. 'If you'd like to report this.'

She stared at him, then turned on Michael. 'How could you be with me all those hours and not *tell* me?'

'I tried to tell you to leave,' he said. 'I wish I could have done more.'

'But he'd sworn to be loyal to Whirlwind,' Reaper said. 'An honorable man, your friend.'

'He's no friend of mine. And if you thought all this' – she waved her hand at the equipment – 'was going to tempt me to help you, you're crazy.'

'The original plan was for me to handle the broadcast,' Nemesis said. 'But it's not my field. You'd be better.'

'I'm not a reporter,' Liza said. 'And even if I was, I'm not doing anything for you.'

'Am I wrong about you being a journalist?' Reaper asked. 'Presently wasting your talents on retail websites and the like?'

She stared at him. 'You've been spying on me?'

'I know you spent time with Isaiah last night, so I did a little research early today, and it occurred to me that this might be the perfect opportunity for you.'

'My big break.' Liza was caustic. 'You really are crazy.'

'I do believe it would be exactly that,' Reaper said. 'Your big break.'

'You've been wanting to write about this,' Michael said. 'You told me as much weeks ago.'

'When you accused me of stalking you.' Liza shook her head. 'And here we are, down your mad rabbit hole.'

'I hadn't heard of Whirlwind back then,' Michael said. 'For the record.'

'But you damn well had last night,' she said.

'I'm not asking you to report this from our viewpoint, Ms Plain.' Reaper got back on-subject. 'You could handle this entirely your way, be totally unbiased, just report it from your on-the-spot vantage point.'

'Why would you want me to do that?' Confusion muddied Liza's thinking.

'To get the truth out.'

'But meantime, we're all your hostages, right?'

'Yes,' Reaper said.

'And what is it you're hoping to get for our release?' She was still shaking, fighting to stay clearheaded because this exchange might be crucial to getting out of here.

'There's no ransom,' Reaper said. 'We just want the truth to be seen and heard.'

'About this alleged miscarriage of justice.'

'Correct.'

'I don't buy it. There has to be more at stake for you.'

'See? You're perfect for the job,' Reaper said. 'Looking for what lies beneath.'

'And you're a walking cliché,' Liza said. 'This is insane.'

184

'You're more likely to find that out for sure if you accept the assignment.'

'I'd be grateful if you'd take over the reporting,' Nemesis said.

'I don't want your gratitude,' Liza snapped. 'What are you getting out of this?'

'Nemesis has solid reasons for joining Whirlwind,' Reaper said.

'Maybe you could explain them to Liza?' Michael said. 'If you want her to help us.'

'I am not going to help you,' Liza said flatly.

'I don't want Nemesis to tell Ms Plain anything,' Reaper answered Michael, 'because it might affect her impartiality.'

'I wouldn't be impartial,' Liza said. 'I would be one hundred per cent *partial*.'

'Good,' Reaper said. 'Report to the outside world what's happening here as you see it – true breaking news.' He paused again. 'I don't want to be too crass, Ms Plain, but consider the aftermath. Features, interviews, maybe a book deal, even a movie.'

'That's not crass,' she said. 'It's obscene.'

Except despite that, she was recognizing – God help her – a buzz of something too like excitement. Because her situation was *extraordinary*. Standing here speaking to hostage takers: people probably prepared to go to deadly extremes to achieve their goals. Yet at this instant she was not feeling as afraid as she ought to be, could even picture herself in some kind of fantasy bubble becoming caught up in this *news* story.

What did that make her?

A journalist.

Scum, as her grandfather said.

'So, have you ever used anything like this?' Nemesis touched the backpack.

'I've never even seen one,' Liza said.

'It's remarkably straightforward. I can take you through it.'

'Did you hear me say yes?' Liza asked.

'Consider this, Ms Plain,' Reaper said. 'The longer you take to decide, the longer the ordeal of all those people up in the nave. Your grandfather included.'

'If you're so concerned about their ordeal, go ahead without me,' she said. 'Better yet, let them go.'

'That's not going to happen,' Reaper told her. 'And there's something else to consider. As you realize, not every resident of Shiloh has come to church tonight. We've done our best to ensure that no one inside or outside Saint Matthew's comes to harm, and the blizzard's helping to keep people away, but if someone does show up and try to open a door, I can't guarantee anyone's safety.'

Liza's skin prickled. 'So those are real explosives?'

'Very real.' Reaper paused. 'Won't you agree to do this, Ms Plain?'

She was wavering and he knew it.

'You have to know that the first thing I'll do is ask people to call the cops?'

'You're being held prisoner in church during the Christmas Eve service,' Reaper said. 'Calling the cops sounds perfectly reasonable to me.'

* * *

186

'You can't seriously be considering doing this,' Stephen Plain said after Liza had been allowed to return to their pew to consider her dilemma.

The service was still continuing as ordered, the captive congregation having latched on to it as something halfway *normal*, if illusory, to distract them, their prayers less about the birth of Jesus now than for their safe deliverance from this nightmare.

Liza was conscious again of people watching her, and everyone had seen her returning from the undercroft, coming back from wherever she'd been with *them*, still safe and unharmed and, therefore, a person of suspicion.

'I suppose I'm wasting my breath,' Stephen said, 'this being any journalist's dream.'

'At least I'd be letting people know what's happening to us,' Liza whispered. 'I'll be doing everything I can to make sure we get help.'

'They won't let you do that,' Stephen said.

'They say they will.'

'Who's said that? Your *friend*?'

'I hardly know him, Granddad,' she said. 'And he's one of *them*.'

'You could be putting yourself in terrible danger.'

'This "Reaper" claims they don't want to harm anyone,' Liza tried to reassure him. 'But he says the explosives are real, and I believe him, so no one should take any chances.'

'Delightful company you keep,' Stephen said.

'You're not wrong there,' Liza said.

Fifty-Two

'You're almost up and running,' Nemesis said to Liza, less than forty minutes later back down in the undercroft.

It was already Christmas Day.

Running late, Nemesis had said when Michael had brought Liza back, her decision made. Punctuality vital for the scheduled event, formal booking necessary to ensure guaranteed live streaming.

The event's title: Christmas Eve Midnight Service from St Matthew's Episcopal Church, Shiloh, Rhode Island.

That was a mistake by them, Liza had registered, because the service was never held at midnight, and if any of this was genuine, if they were really going to broadcast what was going to happen, then surely locals would be the only people remotely interested in viewing, and someone might realize right away that something was amiss.

She'd kept the vain hope to herself, had asked instead why anyone should want to watch an insignificant church service.

'You'd be surprised. And for our purposes, it may only take one person to turn it into news,' Nemesis had said. 'They see what's happening, call it in to their local news station or the cops or maybe CNN, and bingo.'

'So that's really what you want? To publicize this crime?'

188

'That's what Reaper wants,' Michael had said.

'What if no one sees it or calls it in?' Liza asked.

'Reaper says they will,' Nemesis said.

Was that blind belief in her leader, Liza wondered, or did they have viewers out there, part of the gang, ready and waiting to set the publicity ball rolling?

Surreal not a strong enough word for this.

Just her and Nemesis down here now. And a small fortune's worth of equipment set up and ready for her to use. 4G LTE courtesy of Verizon Wireless; hard-wired connection courtesy of the apparently technically-minded vicar; a professional camcorder plus a tripod plus a fluid video head to facilitate wide shots and panning, said the other woman—

Terrorist, Liza corrected herself, remembered the FBI's definition of terrorism, and this was ticking enough boxes to make her grandfather's assessment correct. And it ought to have set her screaming, she thought, but her brain was swimming with details about multi-cellular cards and battery hot-swapping and embedded video and audio media compression processors . . .

'Though pretty much all you really have to know,' Nemesis said, 'is how to start and stop recording, and which microphone to use.'

One when Liza was speaking, the other for picking up what was going on around her, though if that became too confusing, Nemesis said, she could just cancel out her own voice and still pick up both her subject and herself. And she didn't have to concern herself with bandwidth issues because they were going to be storing and forwarding, so everything Liza recorded would be saved.

'This is mad,' Liza said. 'Clearly you should be doing this.'

'You're the reporter,' Nemesis said.

'So how come you know so much about it?'

'I'm a quick study.'

Not giving anything more away, though Reaper had at least given her the codenames which the Whirlwind team would use for the duration, and Nemesis had shown her a page on the MacBook Pro with photographs and names.

Isaiah. Amos. Jeremiah. Luke. Joel. Nemesis.

'You want me to use those names in the broadcast?' Liza had asked.

'I do,' Reaper had answered. 'So remember them, please.'

Afraid to argue, she had stared at the screen, wanting to ingrain the faces on her memory, not in order to do this man's bidding, but to be able to identify them later to the cops, and it seemed vital for her to believe that would happen.

Vital to her sanity.

'I need some kind of script,' Liza said now, to Nemesis.

'Just tell them what's going on. Be yourself and let the events speak for themselves.'

'Live events,' Liza said, bitterly, 'are generally very well-planned by broadcasters.'

'This is living news,' Nemesis said. 'It's different.'

She rechecked settings, connected cable, then loaded the backpack and held it out. 'I'll help you put this on.'

'I've changed my mind,' Liza said.

'It's amazingly light.' Nemesis ignored her panic, slipped a strap over her right arm and Liza reacted automatically, numbly held out her left arm, allowed the pack to be securely placed, felt it against her back.

'God,' she said, quietly.

'I'm pulling a small cable out of the top of the backpack, and routing it over your shoulder.' Nemesis did so, plugging it into the camera, which she handed to Liza.

'I'll take the tripod and the rest.'

She picked them up.

'All set,' she said.

Fifty-Three

It felt as if she'd been beamed down into an insane nightmare.

One minute, a lousy, all-but failed journalist scrabbling for stories. The next, *the* exclusive on-the-spot reporter of a major terrorist crime, armed with a totally unfamiliar set of equipment which seemed, so far as she could tell, to be real. And she still had no idea who Nemesis was, who *any* of them were?

Except Michael Rider.

Panic set in again. She couldn't *do* this.

But if she changed her mind and refused, what might Reaper do to her?

She had been taken to a position less than halfway

along the aisle, just ahead of her grandfather's row, thankful not to be able to see his disapproval.

She could see herself now though, earphones on her head, in the viewfinder.

Could hear the storm howling outside.

People all around were staring at her again.

All too obvious what they had to be thinking.

One of *them*.

The service had ended. The vicar was back beside his wife in the front pew, the organist back with the choir in the eighth row. The big man – Amos – was patrolling, ensuring that the hostages stayed put. The man with buzz-cut brown hair – Jeremiah – was up on the chancel to the right of the altar. The scarred gunman – Luke – stood between the front pew and the north-east door; and Joel, the older one with silver hair, paced near the south-east exit. Nemesis had positioned herself on the aisle two rows back – close enough, she'd told Liza, to help with equipment glitches.

Reaper was at the pulpit. Michael – Isaiah – standing to his right.

'Are you ready, Ms Plain?'

Last chance to back out, to return to being clearly defined again as a hostage.

Yet this still had to be her best chance of helping to *end* this.

And her 'big break', she reminded herself wryly.

All trussed up and loaded with equipment and massively, horribly confused.

And, oh Lord, she would be grateful for *ever* just to get back to Boston and the mundane January updates for her websites.

* * *

Something was happening.

Some of the gang members were pulling on black balaclavas – and *that*, at least, made sense, if this live stream was for real.

No balaclavas for Reaper or Michael. Or for Luke, over near the Stars and Stripes.

'Are you ready?' Reaper repeated the question.

Ready or not.

'Ready,' she said.

Pressed the red button on the camera.

Go.

She took a breath.

'To whoever is watching and listening to this live stream broadcast, this is Liza Plain in the village of Shiloh, Rhode Island, reporting on a major breaking news story and calling for urgent help.'

Liza paused, felt panic surge, summoned up the courage to continue.

'I'm in Saint Matthew's Episcopal Church in Shiloh where, almost three hours ago, the Christmas Eve service, one of the most sacred services of the year, was hijacked by gunmen.'

She'd been taught to get it *out* there. Start with a bang – hit the key words, hit the *point*, especially when you weren't sure how long you might have.

'So please, if you're watching, this is no prank, this is very real, and there are approximately' – oh, Lord, she hadn't done a headcount – 'approximately fifty to sixty innocent people here – hostages now – who need you to call the Rhode Island State Police or the FBI.'

She took another breath, remembered Nemesis's brief tutorial and panned around the church, hands shaking, glad of the tripod and fluid video

193

head, and found the focal point she was after: the chancel, the altar, the crucifix up behind it.

When you have their attention, flesh it out.

'Just before ten o'clock tonight, Eastern Standard Time, this old church was filled with people who'd braved the Blizzard-to-End-All-Blizzards, all anticipating a traditional, inspiring night, when, moments after Reverend Simon Keenan had begun his first Christmas Eve service at Saint Matthew's, an armed gang of six males and one female – collectively naming themselves "Whirlwind" and led by a man calling himself "Reaper" – entered the church, wired up all the exits with explosives and declared us their prisoners.'

Liza panned unsteadily around, paused at the north-east fire exit, zoomed in on the wires and explosives, then on Luke, his shotgun clearly identifying him as a gang member, then zoomed out again, moving on slowly around the nave.

'I came here with family as a member of this congregation – now a fellow hostage – and then, apparently because of my background in journalism, I was *asked* to do this job, and I can report to you now that just after one a.m. this Christmas morning, we've been told very little about why we find ourselves victims in an armed siege.'

She brought the lens back to herself.

'For the record, my name is Liza Plain, and though I was born in Shiloh, I live in Boston, and I am neither an experienced journalist nor a reporter, though that still seems to be why our captors have given me the job of reporting these events to the outside world.'

She heard murmurs. Damning her, probably.

Concentrate.

'As you've seen, they have shotguns, so I didn't feel I had much choice, and I felt it better that one of us did the reporting, not one of the gang.'

She gulped a breath and told them what they had been told about a connection with a forty-year-old child murder and subsequent events.

'They claim that there was a miscarriage of justice back then, and that *justice* is what they're here for, and that's all we know for now, but it's clear that something big is about to happen. Meanwhile, the great blizzard is pounding us . . .'

Liza panned to one of the stained-glass windows, zoomed in on the whiteout beyond it then came around slowly, back to the chancel.

'. . . so I'm guessing it won't be easy for help to reach us here in Shiloh Village, Rhode Island.' Her pace grew more urgent. 'But believe me when I say we need *help*, and we need it *fast*. We are being held by an armed gang of six males and one female, all using aliases.'

You know Michael's name.

'Four of the Whirlwind gang – they call themselves a "team", but I'm sticking with "gang", or maybe they're hostage takers—'

'Terrorists!' Denny Fosse called out.

'Or terrorists.' Liza wasn't arguing. 'Whichever, four of them pulled on balaclavas to cover their faces just before this broadcast began.'

She panned around, and held the camera tight on each of them in turn.

'I believe that's the man they name "Jeremiah" up near the altar.' She moved over to the south-east fire door, also wired. 'That's Joel.' She found the big man near the back. 'That's Amos.' The panning made her dizzy. 'And sitting by the aisle there is a female named Nemesis, the one who helped set up this equipment and who claimed it was on *loan*.'

Her voice grew husky, and she cleared her throat, went on.

'And then there are three men who've chosen, for whatever reasons, not to disguise themselves. That's the man named "Luke".'

She panned away from the scarred man up to the pulpit.

Focused on Michael.

'This man has been called "Isaiah" but he's the only gang member who's actually told us his real name – and here's the thing, which clearly I have to mention: I knew this man before tonight. I do not know him well, but I met him briefly thirteen years ago and again only last night, believing it to be a coincidental meeting. He has openly stated that his name is Michael Rider, and that it was his grandfather, Donald Cromwell, who was accused of murdering Alice Millicent four decades ago.'

Michael was standing, shotgun gripped in his right hand, barrel resting on his left forearm. Unblinking as Liza focused on him.

'Finally' – she swiveled to the man holding center stage – 'we come to the leader of "Whirlwind". The man who calls himself "Reaper".'

She zoomed in on him.

'He doesn't look dangerous, and he's holding a cane rather than a shotgun. But he's the *mind* behind what's happening here tonight, which may make him the most dangerous criminal here. So please, whoever's watching this, take a good look at "Reaper". Whether or not you recognize him, please call the Rhode Island State Police or the FBI, because there are *children* here, and we need your help *now*. It may be the middle of the night on Christmas morning and the blizzard must be creating havoc outside, but there are about fifty innocent people in here all relying on you to get here.'

'Fifty-six,' Reaper interjected. 'Fifty-six, *mostly* innocent, people.'

'Did you hear that?' Liza's voice shook a little. 'Reaper clarified that there are fifty-six people here. "*Mostly* innocent", he said, whatever that means.'

Remember the explosives.

'But – and this is terribly important – whoever arrives here first will need to be very careful' – Liza panned back to the fire exit – 'because all the doors are wired, and I've been assured that those explosives are *real*, and I don't know much about weapons . . .'

She swiveled the camera across to Joel, zoomed in first on his balaclava-covered face, then on the gun in his hands.

'But those shotguns look real to me.'

Up at the pulpit, Reaper raised his hand.

'It looks as if something's about to start happening, because Reaper has just signaled to me to stop.' She took a swift breath. 'This is Saint Matthew's Church in the village of Shiloh, Rhode Island, where the Christmas Eve service was hijacked by gunmen over three hours ago. My name is Liza Plain, and I'm hoping that this

197

live streaming is being picked up by the New England news stations and CNN, because this is breaking news, and we need your help *now*.'

Fifty-Four

Her legs were shaking, adrenalin coursing through her, sweat trickling between her breasts, and she longed to sit down, shut down before she had to return to the drama – and that was how it felt, as if she were playing the *part* of a journalist caught up in this.

Not playing a part. The real thing.

Reaper was speaking, and she'd missed the beginning of it.

Concentrate, Liza.

'We have no demands,' Reaper said, 'other than to ask you to listen. Two members of Whirlwind are here mainly because that's what they need, to be *heard*, because no one has listened to them.'

All through the church, people shifted uncomfortably, William Osborn's grunt of disgust audible, and Liza thought she heard Stephen grumbling, but did not allow herself to look at him. The general level of fear had subsided, she felt, at least temporarily, a greater awareness of discomfort taking over after more than three hours of sitting on hard pews under constant threat.

The man called Jeremiah moved to the pulpit and Reaper stepped aside, sat down, Michael standing just a few feet away.

'I guess you could call me the warm-up act,' Jeremiah said.

No one laughed.

'Put down your gun and take off that mask,' Eleanor Tilden called out boldly, 'and maybe we'll listen to you.'

'It's been ten years since this thing happened to me,' Jeremiah told her, 'and I never resorted to any kind of violence in all that time. I was just an ordinary man trying to get some simple justice for his dead daughter, but that didn't work because, as Reaper said, no one was listening.'

'For God's sake,' John Tilden said, 'get on with it then, so we can all go home.'

'Hear, hear,' Betty Hackett said from the third row.

Jeremiah told his tale of loss and grievance, and in other circumstances, people might have been moved, Liza thought, but this was a man holding them prisoner, hiding his face from the outside world with a balaclava, and anyway, how could he imagine that his obsession with laying blame gave him the right to do *this*?

No compassion being felt either for the next man, she thought, the one called Joel, a former MD with HIV contracted in the line of duty, his life fallen apart ever since.

Hard luck stories not going to wash with this captive audience.

'So what do you get out of taking us hostage?' a man in the fourth row demanded as Joel stepped down from the chancel. 'We all know life can stink – we don't need to be threatened with bombs and guns to be told that.'

'It'll be money,' Osborn said from the front. 'It always is.'

'They just wanted to be heard, one last time, Mr Osborn,' Reaper said.

And introduced Isaiah.

Liza, chilled by the finality of 'one last time', watched Michael moving back to the pulpit.

'Real name Michael Rider,' she said into the mike. 'The man who told us before we began this broadcast about that so-called miscarriage of justice. Rider told us there were people here tonight who were key witnesses, and Reaper asked those people, whoever they may be, to search their consciences.'

'And now it's time' – Michael took over – 'to ask if anyone here, whether they gave testimony or not back then, has remembered anything else relating to Alice Millicent's murder. Anything significant enough to cast new light on the case?'

'Last chance for honesty,' Reaper said.

And sat down.

Last chance.

Before what? Liza wondered.

Chilled again.

'Anyone?' Reaper said, ironically, from his seat beside the pulpit.

'Why can't you let the dead rest in peace?' Ann Jackson cried out.

'Or at least let the younger people go,' Jill Barrow called, 'since they can't have anything to do with this?'

'Let the children out,' Simon Keenan said. 'Show some compassion.'

'Can't be done,' Reaper said, implacably.

'I was one of your so-called "key witnesses".'

The voice came from the front pew, on the north side of the aisle, and old Seth Glover was getting to his feet, and though Liza's angle was poor, as he turned toward the pulpit she found a partial view of his craggy face.

'And let me tell you I *still* know what I saw and why I gave evidence in court. I *saw* that poor child' – his right forefinger stabbed the air – 'climbing into Donald Cromwell's Cadillac. It may be a long time ago, and I may be an old man now, but there's nothing wrong with my mind, and if I close my eyes right now I can still see Alice as clearly as if it happened yesterday, and I still blame myself too, every single day, for not stopping her.'

'You couldn't have known,' Osborn said, two seats away. 'None of us could.'

'That's William Osborn,' Liza said quickly, her voice low, 'former editor, still proprietor, of the local newspaper. And the gentleman before that was Seth Glover, a Shiloh storekeeper at the time.'

'Thank you, Mr Glover,' Michael said.

'You're not welcome,' Glover said, and sat down.

'Mr Osborn,' Michael said. 'The letter that Susan Cromwell, my grandmother, wrote to you.'

'That *again*?' Osborn shook his head impatiently. 'Ramblings of an unstable woman, as I said.'

'Did you really expect my husband to help a man he knew had murdered a little child?' Freya Osborn demanded.

'I've had enough of this.' Stephen Plain got to his feet.

Liza panned back to the fifth row. 'For the record, Dr Stephen Plain is my grandfather, and was Shiloh's MD back at that time.'

'And for your *record*'– Stephen was scathing – 'Susan Cromwell wrote to me, too. After her husband's suicide, in the midst of her appalling grief, and like Bill Osborn, I placed little credence in what she said, not least because Susan was on heavy medication.'

'What did she say in her letter, Dr Plain?' Michael asked.

'I wouldn't tell you even if I could,' Stephen said. 'I'm sure even you must have heard of patient confidentiality. Which still applies, especially given that your grandmother is still living.'

'I can tell you what *my* letter said,' Osborn said. 'Anything to put an end to this. Susan got it into her head that the murder was *her* fault, that she felt she might have driven her husband to do such a terrible thing. I knew that was demented nonsense, so I took no notice.'

'Do you know why she might have thought such a thing?' Michael asked.

'Because she'd lost her mind,' Osborn said. 'Maybe it runs in your family.'

'Actually,' Janet Yore said from the sixth row, 'I think I might know.'

Michael asked her name, and she gave it, her cheeks hot.

'Though I'm not *really* sure,' she said. 'Oh, Lord, I shouldn't have said anything.'

'It could be crucial,' Michael persisted. 'I don't want to push you, but—'

'The hell you don't,' John Tilden erupted from

the front row, south side of the aisle. 'Any minute now you'll be apologizing for the *inconvenience*. Am I the only person here who remembers that this is the night before Christmas, and we're all being held against our will by a bunch of *terrorists*?'

'But isn't that what they always do?' Mark Jackson said. 'Get all buddy-buddy with hostages, make them think they're on the same side.'

'Stockholm Syndrome,' Patty Jackson supplied.

'I don't care what they call it,' Jackson said. 'All I care about is getting out of here and home in time for my Christmas dinner.'

'You'll have a long wait,' Ann Jackson said dryly, 'since it's still in the freezer.'

The sound of laughter rippling through the church was like balm.

Then the screaming started.

Everyone froze, staring around.

And then Liza saw.

Young Grace Glover – no more than six or seven – was up on her feet at the front, clutching at her reindeer-embroidered green sweater, her face white.

'I can't breathe!' she shrieked, and gasped for air. 'I have to get *out* of here!'

'It's OK, honey.' Adam Glover, her father, put his arms around her, pulled her close. 'It's going to be fine, sweetheart.'

'But I can't *breathe*!' she sobbed.

'Grace, calm down, baby,' Claire Glover told her. 'Come sit back down.'

Liza's eyes flicked to Michael, caught his upset, saw Reaper signal to Joel, the former doctor, already on his way, tracked him approaching the Glovers.

'You stay away from us,' Adam Glover told him.

'I'd like to help,' Joel said. 'Does she have asthma?'

'You're making her *worse*,' Claire Glover cried. 'That mask's terrifying her!'

Joel stood stock-still for a second, and then he pulled off the balaclava and dropped it on the floor.

'I can't breathe, Mommy!'

'We need a real doctor!' Adam Glover shouted.

Stephen Plain got up again, began to move.

'Doc Plain's coming,' Glover told the child. 'He'll help you.'

'*No!*' Grace pulled away, panic overwhelming her. 'I need to get *out*!'

Liza saw, with horror, where she was heading.

The fire exit left of the Stars and Stripes. The wired door.

'*Stop* her!' Michael yelled from the pulpit.

Liza kept on recording, lifted the tripod with one hand, moving forward, working on automatic even while her heart was slamming in her chest, because this was all she *could* do, go on filming Grace Glover's outstretched arms, her mother's open-mouthed scream drowned in the shrieking mayhem all around her, Stephen Plain and Joel both stopped in their tracks, rigid with alarm—

Adam Glover going after his daughter.

'*No!*' Michael bellowed. 'The door's going to *blow*!'

The gunman named Luke stepped forward,

204

right into the child's path, but she evaded him, and he threw himself at her, brought her down less than three inches from the wired door.

Shock silenced Grace for about two seconds, and then she began to struggle.

'Let me go! Let me *go*!'

'You're OK, sweetheart,' Luke told her. 'Calm down so I can let you go.'

'But I have to get *out*!' she shrieked.

'Oh, my God,' Claire Glover whispered, aghast. 'The gun.'

Liza zoomed closer, realized what the anguished mother had seen.

The shotgun was wedged between the scarred man and the child.

'Grace, you have to stop this now, honey.' Adam Glover, right behind Luke, bent down, started to reach for her.

Liza saw the unthinkable through the viewfinder.

Grace Glover's small right hand clutching at the shotgun.

Heard Luke's low sound of horror. 'Honey, no – don't touch that.'

Liza saw the little fingers hook around the trigger, felt her heart stop.

Saw which way the barrel was pointing.

'*No!*' the mother screamed. 'Grace, *no!*'

'Jesus,' Luke cried, grappling for the weapon. 'Honey, let *go*!'

The shot reverberated all the way up to the vaulted ceiling, echoed around the nave.

Liza ripped off her earphones and others covered their ears, deafened and disbelieving as the child collapsed back onto the floor, motionless, blood spreading over the embroidered reindeer on her sweater.

Liza forgot about commentary, about the camera, her heart a sledgehammer now, her mind scarcely able to register the horror.

Claire Glover screamed again. A drawn-out, piercing, heartbreaking sound.

And the man called Luke stared down at the child, gave a long howl of purest anguish, extricated the shotgun from Grace's limp grasp, released the trigger, turned the muzzle to his own scarred temple.

And fired.

Fifty-Five

Moments passed.

Outside, the storm still pounded.

Inside, the longest, most terrible silence Liza had ever known.

And then the sounds began again, the stunned congregation returning to life. Awful sounds of loud sobbing and soft weeping, a sense of utmost shock and renewed terror, pockets of intense anger rolling like waves from pew to pew, swiftly suppressed by fear, because what might rage achieve except more bloodshed?

Around Grace Glover there was quiet, frantic activity, Stephen Plain on his knees, Rosie Keenan giving first-aid assistance. The retired doctor alternating chest compressions with mouth-to-mouth rescue breaths, the vicar's wife fighting to stem the blood flow with pressure from clean handker-chiefs folded beneath her right hand.

'You get *away* from her,' Adam Glover snarled at Joel, the ashen-faced Whirlwind man standing by helplessly.

Liza watched the gunman step away, shaking his head over and over, staring down at Luke's body, and then, finally able to react, she averted the lens from the huddle on the floor, looked up at the chancel, saw that Reaper was back in the pulpit and that Michael was sitting on the floor, his face in his hands.

She realized, abruptly, that she had not spoken since the first gunshot, knew that if there was anyone watching, they'd have seen and heard what had happened, but still, she had to make sure they had fully comprehended it.

She put the earphones back on, checked her settings.

'Two people have been shot,' she said. 'A child panicked and ran toward one of the wired exits. One of the gang members tried to stop her and she struggled and grabbed at his shotgun, which went off. She is critically injured, and two people are working on her right now.' Liza's voice choked and she cleared her throat. 'The shooter, who was trying to help the child, then shot himself in the head and is almost certainly dead.' She paused. 'To anyone who's listening to this, *please*, we're in Saint Matthew's Church, Shiloh Village, Rhode Island, and a child needs urgent medical attention *now*.'

Stephen and Rosie Keenan were still working

on Grace Glover, the vicar there too now, one arm around Claire Glover, who was rocking back and forth, both hands clasped over her mouth.

'But please remember,' Liza went on, and panned to the door, zoomed in on the cables and wiring, 'if anyone is already outside, that all the exits have been booby-trapped with explosives and—'

'*No!*' Claire Glover's cry was agonized. 'You can't just *stop!*'

Liza's heart turned over.

Because Adam Glover had turned away from the group on the floor, his face contorted with grief, and Liza realized that he was making a move toward the shotgun still lying on the floor beside Luke's body.

The man called Joel saw too, got to it first.

No violence in him, Liza saw that clearly, just common sense, and was grateful to him, because if Glover had reached the gun, what could he have done except maybe get himself shot?

Keep talking.

She did so, quietly but clearly.

'And to the best of our knowledge, that means that as of' – she checked the time – 'two-twenty this Christmas morning, there are still at least six armed gang members inside this church.'

'You're doing great,' Nemesis said, behind her. 'Are you OK?'

Liza wanted to hit her.

'Get back in your position, Nemesis,' Reaper said. 'You too, please, Ms Plain.'

The big man named Amos passed both women on his way to the front, retrieved Luke's shotgun from Joel, directed him back to the south-east exit, then walked up the chancel steps and handed the spare weapon to Reaper.

Liza panned across, canceled out her own voice on the mike switch and listened intently to Amos's low, harsh voice.

'How in *hell* could that have happened? The guy was a marine, for fuck's sake.'

'He's paid the price,' Reaper said. 'And now we have to go on.' He began to cough, then mastered it. 'The girl's dead?'

Liza caught the question, stared at them in the viewfinder, saw Amos nod, felt the thump of the tragedy deep inside herself.

'Bad scene,' Amos said. 'A fucking mess.'

'Nonetheless,' Reaper said, 'we go on.'

Cold as stone, Liza knew now, for sure.

No chance of reprieve for any of them.

'Sir.' Simon Keenan was facing the pulpit. 'Do you have any objection to our moving this child into my parlor?'

'By all means.' Reaper turned around and found Jeremiah. 'Go with them.'

'Surely you can grant her family privacy now?' Keenan's face was hot with outrage.

'I'm afraid not,' Reaper said. 'For their own safety.'

'Bastard,' someone said.

'*Bastards*.' The word was repeated around the nave, and Liza watched in silence, recording as Adam Glover lifted his dead daughter in his arms, as his wife and old Seth Glover rose to accompany them.

And then, as they climbed the chancel steps, guided by Keenan to the door that led to the vestry and parlor, Liza cut away again, back to the pulpit, and switched the mike back.

'If Reaper won't allow them privacy, we can,' she said. 'But I do have to confirm the tragic news that a young child named Grace Glover has died as a result of her gunshot wound. Her parents and grandfather are moving her into the vicar's parlor, accompanied by Reverend Keenan and the gunman codenamed Jeremiah.'

She caught movement from the left, saw that Michael had come down from the chancel and was covering Luke's face with the dead man's jacket.

Liza turned off the microphone.

'Michael,' she called to him.

Someone nearby hissed with contempt.

He turned, hesitated briefly, then walked up the aisle towards her. Close up, she saw intense pain in his eyes.

'You must realize now that it's over,' she said softly. 'I've reported that her death was accidental, that Luke was trying to stop her from getting hurt.'

'We brought guns into church,' Michael said. 'We all knew the risks.'

'If you defuse the doors now,' Liza said, 'at least no one else need be hurt.'

'Ms Plain.' Reaper's voice from the pulpit was sharp. 'Please switch your microphone back on and do your job.' He paused. 'Isaiah, time is passing.'

Michael closed his eyes briefly, then opened them and looked at Liza.

'I don't know what to say to you.'

'I'd say we're beyond words, wouldn't you?'

He turned, made his way slowly back to the chancel.

Liza switched the mike back on, hating herself for doing Reaper's bidding.

And wasn't that just what Michael was doing? *Not the same.*

'Apologies for the silence, people out there. I hope you're still with us. From CNN to News Radio 920. FBI, Rhode Island State Police, Glocester PD. According to the man in charge of this nightmare, the man calling himself Reaper, they're going to carry on.'

'Tell them to bring a SWAT team,' the man from the choir behind her said loudly.

'I'm sure they will,' Liza said.

From above came a fearsome, groaning noise.

Everyone looked up.

Just the pitched roof doing its job, allowing gravity to slide some of the overloaded snow down over the filled gutters, then onto the packed white stuff below.

Someone laughed and then, promptly, began to cry.

Liza took a breath, spoke into the microphone again.

'What next?' she said.

Michael didn't know exactly what was coming next. He'd arrived in Shiloh with a little more knowledge than the others about Revelation, but nowhere near all. Only the tidbits, he realized now: the bait that Reaper had used to reel him in. And he *was* in, way over his head, and he hadn't imagined that his soul could grow any bleaker than it

211

had been before Whirlwind. But with that child's blood right there before him, soaked into the timber floor, his conscience felt more heavily burdened than even after his mother's death.

Everyone was back in position, Reaper in the seat beside the pulpit, Luke's shotgun across his knees, and Michael was at the pulpit again, silent . . .

'Isaiah,' Reaper prompted. 'The dressmaker.'

Michael took a breath, looked straight ahead, saw Liza recording.

And began again.

'Mrs Yore. What did you mean when you said you might have known what Susan Cromwell meant in her letter to Dr Plain?'

'How *can* you?' Eleanor Tilden was on her feet. 'Another child is dead, and—'

'Ellie, sit down.' John Tilden tugged at her hand, pulled her down.

'Mrs Yore,' Reaper said. 'Please answer the question.'

'I don't know anything for sure.' The woman's cheeks were red again. 'But I did believe back then that Susan was in love with another man. And I don't know who, so I can't tell you, but she once let slip to me – when she'd had a few drinks – that she was in love with somebody else and was thinking of leaving Donald.'

'Was that all she said?' Michael asked.

'No.' Janet Yore sighed. 'Susan told me that Donald had tried just about everything to stop her. He'd forbidden her, begged her, she said. He'd even made threats against the other man.'

'It wasn't another man,' someone said.

212

Heads turned to stare at Gwen Turner.

'Susan was having an affair with a woman,' she said.

A collective gasp rose and was swiftly suppressed.

'Who was she?' Michael asked.

Numbness in him, nothing surprising him.

'I'd remind you, Rider,' Stephen Plain broke in, 'that your grandmother's still alive.'

'And long past caring, from what I've heard,' Osborn said dryly.

'Come on, Gwen,' Eleanor Tilden encouraged. 'Spill.'

'Ellie, don't,' John Tilden said. 'Let's not get involved in this.'

'We're all pretty *involved*, I'd say,' she said.

Tilden made an exasperated sound and sat back.

'Was it you, Gwen Turner?' Ann Jackson asked loudly.

'No, as a matter of fact,' Gwen answered.

'So who was it?' asked a young man, probably about sixteen, Michael estimated, with dyed black hair and an ear stud, seated in the eighth row with the choir. 'Come on, lady.'

'Don't let them bully you, Gwen,' John Tilden said.

'I won't, John,' she said. 'I'm sorry. I shouldn't have said anything.'

'I'm sure you should,' Jill said beside her, clearly fascinated.

'Everybody except Gwen Turner be quiet,' Reaper ordered loudly. 'Miss Turner, do you know the identity of the other woman in Susan Cromwell's life?'

'You might as well tell them, Gwen,' Eleanor

213

Tilden spoke up again. 'They're obviously not going to let this go.'

'For the love of God, Ellie, will you shut *up*!' her husband snapped.

'I will not.' She glared at him. 'I think that if Gwen knows who Susan was sleeping with and has already said as much, then she should tell them, especially if it's going to help put us all out of our misery.'

'Jesus Christ, Ellie, your mouth.' Tilden's cheeks were scarlet.

Eleanor looked at him. 'John? What's wrong?'

'It was Lynne.' The words were stark. 'OK?'

'Lynne?' Eleanor stared at him. 'Your Lynne?'

'My Lynne, yes. Till that bitch got hold of her.' Tilden looked up at Michael, hate in his eyes. 'My late wife was being *bedded* by Susan Cromwell, and there isn't a day goes by when I don't still damn your grandmother to hell for it.' He glared at his wife. 'Satisfied?'

Silence fell for a second or two, quickly over-taken by murmurings, even a little reined-in laughter, because *scandal* was suddenly rocking the church, allowing the captive congregation, however briefly, to blank out their fear and focus instead on something older than many of them.

'I'm sorry, John,' Gwen called to Tilden. 'I wish I'd kept my mouth shut.'

'Not alone there,' he said.

'Surely it was all a very long time ago,' Jill Barrow said lightly. 'I wouldn't worry about it now.'

'No,' Tilden said. 'I guess you wouldn't.'

'I had no idea,' Eleanor said softly. 'I'm so sorry. If I'd known—'

'You never know when to keep quiet,' he said.

'You know I hate church. You know I didn't want to come tonight.'

'Hey,' she said. 'Let's settle down and let them get on with their nonsense. It has nothing to do with us.'

'Hasn't it?' Tilden stared up at Michael.

'Something to say?' Reaper said. 'John Tilden?'

Eleanor watched her husband close his eyes, heard his breath quicken, saw his fists clench, their liver-stained knuckles whitening.

'Please leave him alone,' she said to Reaper. 'He's an old man.'

'Plenty of old people here,' Reaper said. 'Minds filled with things they'd sooner forget. Running out of time to let them out.'

'God,' Tilden muttered.

'Do you have something to say, John Tilden?' Reaper asked, his tone mild.

'*God.*' Tilden's face had reddened again.

'Calm down, John.' Eleanor reached for his hand, but he jerked away from her. 'You're going to make yourself ill.'

'Wouldn't want to do that, John Tilden,' Reaper said.

Michael stared at him, perplexed, then transferred his gaze back to the man in the front pew, still trying to process what he'd just learned about his grandmother.

'Oh, Christ.' Tilden's voice was duller, flatter.

'Hey,' Eleanor said. 'It's all in the past. It's OK.'

'No,' he said. 'It isn't OK.'

'Sure it is,' she said kindly, comfortingly.

'It was. Not any more.' Tilden looked back at her. 'I'd blotted it all out, you know.'

'Why wouldn't you?' she said. 'It's history.'

'Lord knows I've been so happy with you, Ellie.'

'We've both been happy.' She looked around, embarrassed and confused.

'But these people . . .' He shook his head. 'And you just had to push.'

'I'm sorry,' she said again. 'But it's forty years ago.'

'It's forty years, and it's yesterday,' Tilden said softly. 'And it was all his fault.'

'Whose fault?' Eleanor was mystified. 'His?' She looked up at Reaper.

Tilden shook his head.

'Whose fault, John Tilden?' Reaper asked, more loudly.

Michael heard Reaper's resolve, the curious inflection behind the multiple repetitions of Tilden's full name, and he felt a great longing suddenly to go sit down with the other people, just to watch and listen and not be a part of this . . .

'Please.' Eleanor was suddenly afraid. 'Leave him alone.'

'Cromwell's,' Tilden said, and sat up straighter. 'It was all Donald Cromwell's fault.'

'John, you have to *stop* this,' Eleanor hissed. 'Let them get on with it and keep us out, like you said before.'

'Too late now.' Tilden looked up at Michael. 'It was your grandfather's fault that Lynne went to Susan Cromwell. She'd never have gone that way if they'd let us have kids.'

'They?' Michael said.

In the midst of his confusion, he saw Liza tilting the camera lens, knew she was probably focused

216

on him now, supposing that he knew what lay beyond this, but he didn't know, didn't understand, was just a man now with questions.

'Who wouldn't let you have kids?' he asked.

'The *council*, may they rot in hell.' Tilden pushed his wife's restraining hand away again. 'And their president, Lord High and Mighty Donald Cromwell, keeper of all our morals.'

'Stop this now, John.' Eleanor was sharper. 'Stop and think.'

'I can't stop, Ellie,' Tilden said. 'It's too late for that. I have to let it out.'

'No,' his wife said. 'You don't.'

'Lynne couldn't get pregnant'– Tilden went on, words and history suddenly tumbling out – 'so we decided to adopt, but Cromwell said we weren't good parent material – except he meant *me*, not Lynne, but he didn't care that he'd just broken her heart, because children were what she wanted more than anything in life.'

'For God's sake, John,' Eleanor begged. 'This is your business. You don't have to tell them any of it.'

'I'd say he does, Mrs Tilden,' Reaper said.

'It's *private*,' Eleanor said.

'Cromwell ate in my restaurant every day,' Tilden went on. 'Took every free drink on offer, knew how much I loved my wife, *knew* what having a family meant to her. Big-shot Cromwell, always bragging about how much he could do for the people of Shiloh, how much *influence* he had, but when it came to us, he wouldn't lift a finger. And *that* was what turned Lynne, because she couldn't face it.' Tilden stood up, swung around,

217

found Stephen Plain five rows back. 'You know how she was, Doctor.'

'She was depressed,' the old doctor admitted. 'It was a bad time for her.'

'What about *me*?'

'For you, too,' Plain agreed. 'But it was harder for your wife.'

'It changed her, drove her half crazy.' Tilden's face was still red, his eyes bloodshot too now. 'And Susan Cromwell took advantage of her, evil bitch that she was.'

'Hey.' Eleanor had grown pale. 'That's enough, John.'

'More than enough, I'd say.' The vicar had come through from the parlor and shut the vestry door quietly behind him. 'So is this your great aim?' Keenan asked Reaper. 'To turn Christmas into this *travesty*?'

'A good time for confession, surely?' Reaper turned toward him. 'You said it earlier, over and over. "Lord have mercy."'

Keenan's cheeks grew hot. 'You'd do well to ask for that yourself.'

'No mercy for me, Vicar.' Reaper turned back to the man in the front row. 'But maybe for you, John Tilden. Think confession might be worth trying? "O Lamb of God, that takest away the sins of the world . . ."' He stopped. 'So what was it that Cromwell knew about you? What was it he knew that made him say you shouldn't be allowed to adopt a child?'

'For pity's sake!' Eleanor burst.

'Have you ever considered confessing, John Tilden?' Reaper's cough started up, but he forced himself on. '"O Lamb of God, have mercy on us."' His voice rasped, but he controlled the cough, relentless now. 'Do you think you *deserve* His mercy, John Tilden?'

Silence fell all across the nave.

'Well, John Tilden?' Reaper took the shotgun in his right hand, his cane in the other, stood up and took a step forward, leaning on the cane, no other sign of weakness in him.

Tilden was staring up at him.

'*Well*, John Tilden?' Reaper's voice was stronger, more compelling.

The color in the other man's face drained away.

'You know,' he said, quietly. 'You *know*, don't you, you son of a bitch?'

'John.' Eleanor Tilden's voice shook. 'Please, whatever this is, stop now.'

'It's OK,' he told her, then gave a short, brittle laugh. 'Or rather, it isn't. It never will be again.' He gave her a weak smile. 'I'm so sorry, Ellie. More than you'll ever know.'

'Well, John Tilden?' Reaper said for the third time.

'What is this?' a young man said, halfway back on the other side of the nave. 'The fucking day of reckoning?'

'Remember where you are,' another man said.

'In the middle of a fucking siege is where we are.' The younger man's voice trembled. 'A little kid dead, and who knows what comes next? I'd say I'm allowed to curse, don't you think?'

And the hush came again.

Fifty-Six

Liza watched in fascination as John Tilden got back on his feet, saw that his whole body was trembling and zoomed in as well as she could manage.

'All right.' The innkeeper's face was pasty now. 'I'm ready.' He stared up at Reaper. 'I always knew this day would come. I don't know who the hell you are, but you've won, you son-of-a-bitch.'

They waited. Captive audience and captors alike.

'Come along then, John Tilden.' Reaper's tone was colder. 'Get it out. Spill, as your own wife said a while ago. The vicar would probably say you'll feel better, though I'm not sure that's true.'

'If you know,' Tilden said, 'why don't you tell them?'

'We need your words,' Reaper said. 'For the record.'

Liza stirred, and checked the equipment again. Nemesis had told her that everything she recorded would be stored, and suddenly that seemed more vital than ever.

Tilden was staring up at Reaper again. 'But you can't know. How could you?'

'Your words, please,' Reaper repeated. '*Now.*'

The 'now' seemed to crack right through the nave.

Tilden remained silent for a long moment.

'I blamed them all.' He still trembled, but his

tone was bitter, defiant. 'I think most men would have in my position. I'd loved Lynne so much, but I blamed her for betraying me, for letting herself be corrupted, and I certainly blamed Susan Cromwell for her wickedness. I'm no churchgoer, as the new vicar already knows, but I'm sure I remember something in the Bible that calls that wicked.'

'I'm surprised you'd know that, John Tilden,' Reaper said, 'since you never thought much of the Bible. Though your first wife, Naomi, was certainly a devout woman.'

'What does Naomi have to do with anything?' Tilden looked thrown.

'She was your first wife, was she not?' Reaper asked. 'First of three, am I right? Eleanor being the third. Lynne the second, after Naomi died.' He looked down at Tilden, then smiled. 'You were saying that you blamed Susan Cromwell.'

'Of course I did, but most of all, I blamed her husband. For being a sanctimonious bastard and for not having any control over his wife. It was fine for him to say that other people didn't deserve to have children – he had his little Emily, after all.' Sudden tears threatened and his voice shook violently. 'Oh, I blamed Donald Cromwell all right. And I hated everyone who had what I couldn't have – a clean, normal family.'

'Ms Plain.'

Reaper's voice startled Liza.

'Time for you to move your equipment,' he said.

'Where to?' she asked.

'To the front, below the chancel. Nemesis will assist you.'

The move was swift, Liza transferring to a place near the undercroft door from where she could see the men on the chancel and the Tildens in the front pew. She glanced quickly up at Michael, saw his stillness and incredible tension, told herself to focus, and turned her lens back onto the man of the moment, who'd sat down during the break.

'Go on, John Tilden,' Reaper said. 'Stand up, if you're able, and tell us about those people you blamed and hated.'

Tilden rose, looked down momentarily at Eleanor's frightened face, then stared into space. 'I was crazy at the time,' he said. 'I know that now. I just wanted to punish them all so *badly*.' He took a breath. 'I didn't really know the little girl at all.'

'By "little girl", do you mean Alice Millicent?' Reaper interrupted.

In the third row, Betty Hackett drew a sharp, audible breath.

'Yes,' Tilden said.

The case, Liza realized. Finally, after four decades, this church had become a courtroom, with that man as prosecutor.

Maybe judge too.

She remembered what Mark Jackson had said earlier about lynching someone, and felt sick.

'I'd seen her now and then, going to school,' John Tilden said. 'She was a pretty little thing, and her family lived outside the village. My troubles had nothing to do with them, but I was crazy, wasn't I?'

'Oh, dear God, no,' Eleanor Tilden said, and covered her face with her hands.

'I'm sorry, Ellie,' he said. 'Sorrier than you'll ever know. But from the moment I met Lynne Rigby over near Greenville – we were both buying blueberries at an orchard – she called it "serendipitous". I'd never have come up with a word like that, would I, Ellie?'

'John, please stop this.' Eleanor's voice came from behind her hands.

'I can't. Can't hold it in any longer. She was so beautiful, and she *wanted* me, which seemed like a miracle. She wanted to move to Shiloh and bear my children.' His old mouth quirked. 'That's what she said: "I want to bear your children."' He looked down at his present wife, her face still covered. 'You've been the best wife any man could ask for, Ellie, but you're a strong woman, you're tough. You'll get over this.'

'What did you do?' Michael asked, horror in his voice.

'Yes, John Tilden,' Reaper said, quietly. 'What did you do?'

'I set him up.' Tilden's voice was starting to crack. 'I went to a rental company and hired a black Cadillac Seville, same model as Cromwell's, and I sprayed the license plates with paint I could clean off later. I went to Providence and bought an expensive suit and panama hat just like his, even the kind of shiny black leather shoes he wore.'

Beside him, Eleanor groaned, dropped her hands from her face, looked briefly at the pulpit, then stared straight ahead, her gaze on a split piece of grain in a wood panel, best place as any to stare at while her life cracked wide open.

'The puppy wasn't so easy – you need luck

223

on your side to find golden retriever pups just when you need one. But I was lucky. I don't know if she was the spit of the one Cromwell had bought for his daughter, but it was good enough.'

A spasm of cramp in her right leg hit Liza, and her back and shoulders had begun to ache too, from the backpack and from sheer strain, but she didn't dare move, panned to Eleanor briefly, then to Reaper, then Michael, wanting the outside world to see his stunned expression. No way had he known of this when he'd joined forces with Whirlwind, and she didn't know if that made him less or even more guilty.

She moved back to Tilden, the lens tight on him now.

'I'd picked my day well.' Tilden sounded as if he was reciting. 'It was a good week, because one of the teachers was off sick, so there was only one teacher – Gwen Turner – supervising in the playground.'

Liza saw the vestry door open, saw old Seth Glover step onto the chancel, saw him stop, realizing that something was happening, but she didn't pan to him, kept her lens on Tilden.

'I parked the Cadillac under an oak tree just to the side of Main in a shady spot so that Alice would see the puppy, focus on that, not me, and my plan was that anyone else who saw me would assume they were seeing Cromwell.' He licked his dry lips. 'I was counting on someone seeing. It was a gamble, but that was the whole point, after all. I don't know what I would have done if they hadn't.'

'Oh, dear Jesus.' Glover stood frozen with

horror, his lined face already gray with the tragedy of his family's loss, and now, hearing *this* . . .

'It was me you saw, Seth,' Tilden told him. 'You mustn't blame yourself. You thought I was Cromwell, just like I meant you to.'

'How could you *do* that?' Eleanor's voice was soft, incredulous.

'Yes, John Tilden,' Reaper echoed. 'Tell us all. How could you do that?'

'Honestly? I don't know.' Tilden sank down onto the pew.

'Get up,' Reaper told him.

'I can't,' Tilden said. 'And the truth is—'

'What would you know about truth?' Gwen Turner called out bitterly.

'I don't expect anyone to understand – I can't understand now how I could have done those terrible things to that poor child. I just remember being so consumed with hate, with such a need to destroy, to ruin, to *punish* – not her, not Alice – but I don't actually remember doing any of it, not after getting her into the car. I know what I did, but I can't picture it.'

'Convenient,' Reaper said.

'Maybe.' He looked up again at the man in the pulpit, his expression puzzled, and then he glanced sideways at his wife, and then he looked back down, focused on his knees. 'I do remember the moment she went quiet. And then, God forgive me – and I know he won't . . .' He began to weep. 'Then there was such a sense of relief, because it was out of me, all that terrible destructive hate.'

'So you felt better,' Reaper said.

'I'm telling the truth,' Tilden said.

'Which is what, exactly?' Reaper asked. 'You say you know what you did, John Tilden. What did you do to Alice Millicent?'

'I can't,' Tilden said again.

'Did you strangle her?' Reaper asked.

'Don't make me tell you,' Tilden said.

'Did you strangle Alice Millicent to death?' Reaper was relentless again.

'Yes.' Tilden's voice was low.

'Louder,' Reaper said.

'Yes,' Tilden said again.

'And then you felt better.'

'Yes,' Tilden said.

A sound emerged from Michael Rider, an exhalation of revulsion so profound it sounded close to sickness, and finally Liza risked moving her cramping leg, let her own soft grunt of pain mingle with the collective damning mutterings of people all around the nave, and she looked up at Michael, saw him gripping the pulpit's edge.

'I know how that sounds,' Tilden went on. 'But I was crazy. I don't excuse what I did, I'm just trying to explain. And it was almost easy after that, watching Cromwell getting what was coming to him. I think I almost managed to blot out what I'd done, to believe that he was a murderer.' He shook his head. 'There was no real shame in me back then.' His tears were flowing again now. 'But I can honestly say that I'm finding this even more of a relief. Now that it's out, after so . . .'

His voice tailed away, and for several more moments everyone sat very still, the nave filled

226

with sounds of dismay and nervous coughing, and of Eleanor Tilden's quiet, anguished moaning.

'You're Cromwell's grandson, do I have that right?' Seth Glover was still near the vestry door, Keenan beside him.

'Yes, sir. You do.' Michael's voice was quiet.

'Then in other circumstances, I guess I'd be telling you how sorry I am for that terrible mistake. And may God forgive me for it.' Glover took a breath, and a wrenching sob escaped, ran into his next words. 'But given that you just helped to kill my own sweet, innocent granddaughter, I'm sure you'll understand if I don't feel inclined to apologize to you.'

'Amen,' someone said.

The old man turned and went back through the vestry door, the vicar following.

Michael didn't speak, just moved away from the pulpit, sank down on the chancel floor and put his head in his hands, as he had after the shootings, and Reaper, too, turned and sat in the chair beside the pulpit.

Everyone silent now.

And still no new sounds from outside, Liza registered numbly, only the howl of the wind and the creaking of snow on the roof. No sirens or motors. No helicopters.

And maybe no one was even hearing this, let alone seeing it.

The camera was real enough, she thought, but maybe the box of tricks on her back was a fake, who the hell *knew*?

She looked back up at the stained glass, now totally opaque with snow, and knew that for as

long as the blizzard kept up, neither law enforcement nor even the hardiest news breakers would
be putting choppers or crews at risk.

Many against a few in here, but no fight-back
likely. All too exhausted and scared and cold and
hungry after more than five hours of fear and
shock upon shock, no one equipped to do more
than sit and brood.

St Matthew's, to all intents and purposes,
cut off.

Fifty-Seven

An hour or so ago, Doris Clayton had still been
sitting at her living-room table trying to work
out if this was real, or maybe some bad taste
drama or just a prank.

Whichever, it was coming from Shiloh, her
former home, from her own church – and it *was*
St Matthew's, she was certain of that by now, had
seen enough, despite the poor picture, and one
thing was for sure: it was doing nothing to alleviate
her insomnia. She'd been happy in Shiloh Town
as long as she'd remained in ignorance of her
husband Wiley's longstanding affair, but once she
knew, she'd just had to get out. She'd come to
Saugerties, New York, because her brother lived
here, and she liked the place well enough, had
made friends, but however easily she napped in
front of the TV, as soon as she went to bed, she
was always wide awake.

That was why she'd bought a computer, and these nights she emailed, tweeted and played games, and since she'd learned about 'live streaming' last year, she'd watched tennis matches and other sports from different time zones, and she'd even tried NASA's live link to the International Space Station – that *had* sent her off to sleep for a while because nothing ever seemed to happen.

Still, it had become a habit to check to see if anything fun was happening someplace, and she'd been wrapping gifts ready for tomorrow when she'd spotted the name Shiloh, because some bright spark (maybe the new young vicar she'd heard about) had organized live streaming of the 'Christmas Eve Midnight Service from St Matthew's Episcopal Church, Shiloh, Rhode Island'.

'Midnight' had puzzled Doris somewhat, because she was pretty sure that it had always started at ten – though maybe this was another of the new vicar's ideas, and it suited her perfectly, because she'd always loved that service, so come midnight she'd been ready and waiting, a little pot of hot chocolate and saucer of Oreo cookies beside her.

Nothing.

She'd waited a while longer, double-checked her settings, then dropped off in the chair, waking to find the chocolate cold and still no service, figuring the blizzard was messing with the link. And she was wide awake again, so she'd gone to heat up more milk, and when she'd come back into the room, it was connected.

Live from St Matthew's.

Except it wasn't a church service at all.

A woman was speaking, and the picture – as shaky as Wiley's hands during a hangover – was of a fire exit with cables strung across it, and Doris thought she'd heard the woman say something about *explosives*, so this was probably some kind of movie. And then the camera had moved dizzyingly across what did look like a church nave, coming to rest on a man with a black mask over his face, holding a shotgun.

'What the heck?' Doris said out loud.

She stared at the screen as the focus turned to an elderly man at the pulpit – not the young vicar, for sure, but it certainly *looked* like a real church pulpit – and she leaned forward, trying to see if it might, after all, be St Matthew's.

The man had raised his hand, and the woman was still speaking. She sounded unsteady too, not a bit like a professional . . .

Doris had stopped trying to see if it was her old church or not, listening instead to what the woman was saying.

'This is St Matthew's Church in the village of Shiloh, Rhode Island, where the Christmas Eve service was hijacked by gunmen over three hours ago. My name is Liza Plain, and I'm hoping that this live streaming is being picked up by the New England news stations and CNN, because this is breaking news, and we need your help *now*.'

'Dear God,' Doris had said.

Had begun to get up to go to the phone.

Then sat down again.

Not prepared to be made a fool of. Because this

had to be a hoax. You read about such things all the time, and she was not going to be the one to call the cops for a bad joke, certainly not in the middle of the night on Christmas Day, and in such terrible weather.

She'd turned on the TV because if this was real it would be on the news, but found nothing on any channel, which meant it had to be a prank, or maybe some kind of amateur movie.

She'd gone back to the computer.

Actually, when you got used to the lousy picture, it was pretty convincing for an amateur movie.

But then, a while later, something terrible had happened.

Something very sick, if it was a part of a movie.

Except right then, just after two twenty-five on Christmas morning, Doris had suddenly felt much less sure that it was either a movie or a joke, and goose bumps had sprung up on her arms. Because just supposing it was real, supposing what that woman had just told them about a child having been shot was true . . .

It meant that St Matthew's had actually been hijacked.

That a real-life little girl had been *killed.*

'Oh, dear God, forgive me,' she had said.

Had stood up, trembling, and gone to pick up the phone.

'Oh, my dear God, please forgive me.'

She'd been wearing the wrong glasses, but she made out the numbers.

Nine. One. One.

Fifty-Eight

Michael was still sitting on the chancel floor when Reaper stepped back into the pulpit.

'John Tilden, please stand up,' he said.

Like a judge about to pass sentence.

'Told you,' Mark Jackson said to his wife. 'They're going to hang him.'

'Be quiet,' Ann Jackson told him.

'Dad, please, shut up,' Patty Jackson said.

John Tilden did not move.

Michael got slowly to his feet, looked at Liza, saw that she was too absorbed to look back at him.

'John Tilden, get *up*,' Reaper commanded.

Tilden sighed and stood, and a wave of trepidation rippled around the church.

'What now?' Eleanor Tilden asked, bitterly.

'A little more truth to come, Mrs Tilden,' Reaper answered.

'I've made my confession,' Tilden said. 'What more do you want?'

'I want you to look at me, John Tilden,' Reaper said.

'I'm looking,' the child killer said. 'We've all been looking for hours.'

'Look more closely.' Reaper paused. 'No recognition?'

Tilden shook his head, his expression confused.

'That's not so surprising,' Reaper said.

232

'Are you saying we've met before?' Tilden asked.

'I am saying that,' Reaper said. 'Though it has been a very long time. Stretching back even farther than your crimes against Alice Millicent and the Cromwells. It all links up, of course. If we go back to the *reason* Donald Cromwell considered you unfit to adopt.'

Watching Tilden, Michael saw his eyes narrow, confusion seeming to waver.

'Almost ten years before that,' Reaper went on. 'So, a half-century ago, give or take.' He paused, then spoke with great clarity. 'Since you put me away.'

Tilden went chalky-white, shock seeming to hit like a punch to the solar plexus.

'Remember now, do you?' Reaper's voice was loaded with irony.

'Oh dear Christ,' Tilden said. 'Oh dear, fucking Christ.'

He sat down again, hard, and stared.

'Remember now, do you?' Reaper said. 'Remember your own *son*?'

Reaction rumbled around the nave, sounds of disbelief and doubt, people shaking their heads, craning their necks to see better, everyone wondering if they'd misheard.

Michael saw Liza look up at him then, and shook his head in bewilderment.

Tilden was saying something, his voice too soft to carry.

'I'm sorry, John Tilden,' Reaper said, 'but I don't think everyone heard that. Perhaps you'll repeat it for them and for the record.'

233

Tilden shook his head.

'I'll repeat it then,' Reaper said. '"Always mad." That's what my father just said about me. About his *son*. That I was always mad.'

'But you can't be.' Eleanor spoke for everyone.

'It seems impossible, doesn't it? But your husband is seventy-nine years old, Mrs Tilden, and I'm twenty years younger. Born in 1955 to Naomi and John Tilden.'

'Dear God,' Stephen Plain said quietly.

'I know I look much older,' Reaper went on, 'but that's what suffering does to a person. If it starts early enough, goes on long enough.' His hands were on the pulpit, his cane hooked over his left wrist, the shotgun leaning beside him. 'I'm not here to argue John Tilden's point about my sanity. But I was just ten years old when he had me shut away. And I was mad about one thing back then, that is true enough. About the church. This church. About God.'

'He was *insane*.' Tilden was rallying, sitting up straighter, his expression wild. 'He was a young boy, but he killed animals and—'

'One animal,' Reaper corrected calmly. 'An intended sacrifice, by a naïve boy.'

'It was his mother's fault,' Tilden said frantically. 'Naomi filled his head with the Bible, read him scriptures instead of fairy tales, and he swallowed everything she told him.'

'Good Lord,' William Osborn said. 'Is there to be no *end* to this?'

'At eight, he knew all about hell and purgatory and all the Commandments. And when he was ten, he killed his own cat and brought it here, to this church, and he put it on the altar, dripping blood – right up there—' Tilden pointed. 'And when the vicar came in and found him – it was the day before Easter—'

'It was Holy Saturday,' Reaper said.

'And you told the vicar that an angel had made you do it,' Tilden said. 'A goddamned *angel*, for Christ's sake, and you were covered in blood, and poor Thomas Pike didn't know what the hell to do, so he locked you in here and came to find me, and he agreed you were sick in the mind, and we came back here together and got you home.'

Reaper leaned forward, over the pulpit, his eyes boring through his spectacles into the man now floundering before him like an ugly fish on a hook.

'And after Pike had scurried back to clean up his church – "*his*" church was what he called it – my poor, sweet mother tried to stand up for me, and you did what you always did, John Tilden. You lost your temper, and you shoved me and I stumbled against my mother, and she fell over and hit her head on our fireplace, and she *died*.'

Her blood still so vivid in Reaper's mind after nearly fifty years that the tears of boyhood sprang, hot and fresh, into his old, sore, still rage-filled eyes.

'And what did you do then, John Tilden? Did you grieve for Naomi, your wife? Did you comfort me, her son, *your* son?'

Reaper moved suddenly, left the pulpit and the shotgun and walked down the chancel steps, barely needing his cane now, his old fury enough support for him as he closed in on Tilden, who was cringing now, not daring to look up at the man who was his son.

'You did neither, did you, old man,' Reaper went on. 'What you did instead was call Pike back.'

Liza stopped listening.

The first two mentions of that name had done no more than snap at her overloaded brain, but that third time . . .

Thomas Pike. The missing Shiloh man.

The retired vicar of St Matthew's.

A small shudder ran through her, but she made herself go on with the job, her 'assignment', Reaper had called it, and if there was a break any time soon, she would share that connection with whoever was listening out there, but for now . . .

'You told him I'd been hysterical,' Reaper was saying, 'that I'd caused Naomi's fall, that it was obvious that I badly needed "help", but before you called Dr Plain, you wanted to be sure you had Pike's understanding.'

Liza's eyes flicked to her grandfather and saw him shake his head, nothing more.

'You'd always be in Pike's debt, you told him, if he helped you with this *problem*,' Reaper said. 'But Pike said that however much he wanted to help, he was only a vicar, he didn't have the contacts, and besides, it was Holy Saturday, and he had to get back and lead the Vigil, and the only person who could help you work this out for the best was Donald Cromwell.'

Liza looked at Michael, saw that this, too, was as new to him as to her.

'So I assume it was Cromwell who made it all

happen so fast,' Reaper said, 'who helped have me taken away. And looking back at it all over time – and I had a lot of time to do that – I came to see how that must have irked you, Father. Owing so much to a powerful man like Cromwell.'

He turned away from Tilden again, tiring suddenly, moving back toward the chancel, pausing to lean against the platform.

'I was admitted the very next morning,' he told the congregation, 'to the Ames Residential Home for Emotionally Disturbed Children and Adolescents.' He looked up at Michael. 'So you see, Isaiah, this man's grievance against Cromwell started long before his second wife turned to your grandmother for comfort.' He saw that Simon Keenan had come back through the vestry door. 'As for me, bereft boy that I was, my greatest confusion was not that my own father had turned against me, but that the *church* had.' His lips tugged in a thin smile. 'All I wanted, age ten, was to serve the Lord. But they wouldn't let me. They wouldn't even let me go to my own mother's funeral.' He paused. 'There are people here tonight who must have been there, who must have wondered where I was.'

Liza kept the camera on Reaper, but her eyes traveled back to her grandfather again.

If the words caused him discomfort, there was no sign.

'Any of you care to stand up?' Reaper asked. 'Make yourself known?'

No one moved.

'I thought not,' Reaper said.

Liza watched as Michael Rider stirred, walked

237

slowly down the chancel steps and stopped a few feet from the man he had till now known only as Reaper.

'I still don't know your real name,' he said.

Fifty-Nine

'I was born Joshua Tilden,' Reaper said.

'Yes, indeed,' Stephen Plain said quietly.

Liza heard through her earphones, cast another questioning glance, but received no response.

'Is it true?' Gwen Turner leaned across the aisle.

'It could be,' Stephen Plain said. 'I have no way of being certain.'

'I've used a number of names over the years,' Reaper went on. 'Tilden as infrequently as—'

A commotion in the nave halted him.

'Don't even *think* about it.' Amos, in the aisle, was pointing his shotgun at two young men in the eighth row, halfway out of their places, frozen now. 'OK, *you*—' The big gunman motioned to one of them, a choir member named Eddie Leary, red-haired, angry-eyed but scared rigid by the gun. 'Move back a row – climb over the damned pew and sit down.'

He waited while the young guy clambered cautiously across and sat.

'And your little *pal*—'

Liza, trying to focus, saw it was the young guy with the dyed hair and the ear stud who'd goaded Gwen earlier when she'd hesitated about naming

Susan Cromwell, wondered what they'd been doing to get Amos so worked up.

'Same deal for you,' the gunman ordered, 'but stay halfway along, OK?'

'OK, man.' The teenager, whose name was Mitch Roper, vaulted the pew with ease. 'Jeez,' he said.

'I got my eye on you,' Amos said.

'All done, Amos?' Reaper called, returning to the pulpit.

'That's up to them,' Amos said.

'Excuse me,' Janet Yore called out warily. 'I don't know about the rest of you, but I need the bathroom.'

'Me too,' Gwen Turner said. 'It's been over five hours, for God's sake.'

Voices erupted all over the nave.

'Everyone shut the fuck *up*!' Amos yelled, shotgun raised.

Silencing everyone.

'Thank you, Amos,' Reaper said. 'Ms Plain? Are you recording?'

'Yes,' Liza said.

'I have a little more to say, and I want it heard.'

'He's going to pass sentence,' Mark Jackson said. 'Betcha.'

Amos spun around, found the farmer in the sixth row, leaned across and aimed the gun right at his head. 'You want a goddamned bullet?'

'No.' Jackson was ashen, his wife and daughter both crying.

'Then shut your mouth,' Amos said. 'One more word.'

'Thank you, Amos,' Reaper repeated.

Amos backed off, positioned himself two rows back.

Reaper began to speak again.

'I was in that place for eight years, and at the end of that, I was told there was no place for me in Shiloh, that arrangements had been made for me to go into a group home. I didn't much care for that idea, so I left the Ames, walked to a church about four miles away and told the vicar I was seeking shelter in exchange for work. I told him where I'd been, but that it was still my hope to study, to work towards a Masters in Divinity, told him that I'd been called by God to serve. The man got edgy and told me to leave, said that if I didn't, he'd call the cops, and having another vicar treat me that way made me mad, so I punched him as hard as I could, knocked him down and ran.'

Everyone waited.

'And then?' Michael broke the silence.

'*Then* is another story,' Reaper said. 'Suffice it to say, I was caught and sent to the Garthville House of Corrections for assessment, and, given my history, they deemed me a danger to myself and others, so there I stayed.'

'In the psych wing?' Michael asked softly.

Liza remembered the name, realized that had to be their link, saw Reaper's nod.

'How long?' Michael asked.

'Most of my life.' Reaper paused. 'Long enough for it to become my world, and once I was used to the hell of it, I learned how to make things work for me.'

'When did you get out?' Michael asked.

'When they knew I was dying.'

240

'So you were there while I was.'

No one moved or spoke, most newly unsettled by what had just become an almost private conversation.

'It's a big place, as you know,' Reaper said. 'But I'd read about you, felt bad for you. And being a person who appreciates coincidences, I kept tabs on you after you were out.'

'So you could use me,' Michael said.

'Definitely,' Reaper said. 'And try righting a few wrongs at the same time.'

'Am I allowed a question?' John Tilden said.

'It's a free country,' Reaper said. 'So I'm told.'

'How did you know what I'd done?' Tilden said.

'Let's be good and clear for these people, and for Ms Plain's record,' Reaper said. 'You're asking how I knew that you'd set up Donald Cromwell and murdered a little child. Not forgetting the puppy.'

Tilden flushed. 'That's what I'm asking, yes.'

'I found that out in several ways,' Reaper said. 'But one piece of evidence will suffice for now. The hair ribbon.'

Tilden was ashen again, dots of heat on his cheek.

'That's right, John Tilden. The ribbon that Alice Millicent's mother probably tied around her daughter's hair on the last morning of her life. It was, when I saw it, long and pink and horribly twisted from having been used to strangle her.' Reaper raised his voice. 'Whichever law enforcement agency with jurisdiction is hearing me, either live or later, on Ms Plain's recording, I'd suggest you visit the Shiloh Inn when this is over – not before, since the doors to that place have been wired with explosives too.'

'Dear God,' Eleanor Tilden said.

'So when all this is finished, go to Tilden's office and take a look in the locked bottom drawer of his wooden file cabinet, in a dinky little trinket box, also locked. I can't say I know where the keys are now, but when I let myself in one night a good long while ago, they were in John Tilden's coat pocket hanging on the hat rack in his office.'

'How in hell . . .?' Tilden stopped.

'How did I come to be in your office? Walking around your inn?' Reaper smiled again. 'That's not for you to know. I may yet share that information, but not with you. You can just twist in the wind, John Tilden.'

This was her chance, Liza realized, as Reaper fell silent. She'd waited, galvanized along with the rest, but for all she knew, time might be running out, and she had to ask.

'I have a question, too.'

Her voice carried, loud and clear, across the nave.

She felt all eyes turning to her.

'It's about Thomas Pike,' she said.

Sixty

Reaper shifted his gaze from John Tilden to Liza.

'What about Thomas Pike?' he said.

'We all know that he's been missing for nearly

two weeks.' She faltered, took a breath, pushed on. 'So I'm wondering now, in view of the part you say he played in helping your father "put you away", if you might—'

A sound intruded.

From outside the church.

Just a distant siren heard through a brief lull in the gale. Too far away to imagine it might be coming to Shiloh on a night like this when all kinds of emergencies had to be devouring resources, yet still . . .

Liza spoke quickly into the mike. 'We just heard a siren,' she said. 'So in case that's the police or FBI coming to our aid, we urge you again to be very careful. Do not attempt to enter Saint Matthew's or the Shiloh Inn through any door. And for all we know, there may be other booby trap devices elsewhere.'

'Ms Plain,' Reaper said. 'You were wondering.'

She looked at him through the viewfinder, tried and failed to read his gray eyes.

'I was,' she said. 'About Thomas Pike?'

'A missing person, as you said. And no time for that now.' Reaper cleared his throat. 'Whirlwind's mission being far from over.'

He stood very still for a moment, then raised his voice again.

'We've reached the next stage of our operation. Joel, please fetch Jeremiah and bring the Glovers back into the nave.'

'You can't ask them to leave their daughter,' Keenan said.

'They can't stay there unguarded, Vicar,' Reaper said. 'The exit near your parlor has been wired, and I wouldn't want to place them in further danger.'

He nodded at Joel, who left his position at the south-east door, moved swiftly up to the chancel and out through the vestry door, and seconds later, angry voices were heard, but then the Glovers were back as ordered, the two gunmen behind them on the chancel, Jeremiah's face still masked.

'You really have no shame at all, do you?' Adam Glover asked Reaper.

'Please take your seats again,' Reaper told him.

'What about Tilden?' Seth Glover said.

'For now,' Reaper said, 'he waits.'

'For *what*?' Tilden burst out.

'Be quiet,' Reaper told him.

'If you're going to kill me, why don't you just get it *over* with?'

'Nothing so swift,' Reaper said. 'Everyone please sit down.'

He watched, Liza continuing to record as the shattered family returned to their pew, only feet from the darkening stains left by Grace Glover's fatal wound, as Jeremiah moved to the north-east door, and Joel back to the exit on the opposite side of the nave.

'William Osborn, would you please stand?' Reaper said.

'I think not,' Osborn said.

'Amos, please *escort* Mr Osborn to the undercroft.'

Osborn looked around, saw the powerful gang member heading his way, and stood up quickly. 'No need for assistance,' he said.

'What do they want with you?' Freya Osborn whispered, agitated.

'One distinct possibility comes to mind,' her husband told her gently. 'Don't worry yourself, Freya, and do as they tell you. I want us both home safe by Christmas night.'

Freya grasped his hand and Osborn stooped to kiss her forehead, then turned to face Amos and walked ahead of him to the undercroft door, casting a look of distaste at John Tilden as he passed.

'Please be careful, Bill,' Freya called out as Amos opened the door.

'Always.' Osborn raised a hand, went through ahead of the gunman and the door closed behind them.

'Now then, Ms Plain.' Reaper was brisk. 'I need you to bring your equipment and follow them in order that you may bear witness to the next part of the proceedings. Nemesis will accompany you.'

'Don't go with them, Liza,' Stephen Plain called out sharply.

Surprised by his urgency, she turned, and managed a smile. 'Seems like I have to, Granddad.'

'Proud of you, Liza,' Gwen Turner called. 'You're doing an amazing job.'

'Just please be careful,' Jill Barrow shouted after her.

'You too,' Liza said. 'Everyone.'

'You can leave the tripod,' Reaper told her. 'Just take the camera and backpack, and make sure they stay connected.'

Liza busied herself, trying to suppress the new surge of fear engulfing her, because who *knew* what she was heading toward now, and glancing

245

at Michael, she saw that his eyes were on her too, their expression anxious.

'Will I be coming back?' she asked Reaper.

'I certainly hope so,' he said.

She looked up at him again, at this man, so old before his time, and she hoped that someone out there had picked up on the fact that Reaper was dying, because it almost certainly made him a man with nothing to lose.

'Come on.'

Liza turned, saw that Nemesis, still masked, was behind her, holding out Liza's parka.

'To whoever's out there,' Liza spoke rapidly into the microphone, still connected, 'you'll know that I'm leaving the nave. I'll continue broadcasting if I can, though we're apparently heading down into Saint Matthew's undercroft, so I can only hope the signal will carry. If not, I'll get back on air just as soon as I can.'

The woman called Nemesis leaned over her shoulder.

'For now,' she said sharply, 'that was Liza Plain signing off.'

Liza realized abruptly that she hadn't mentioned the parka and the possibility that it might mean they were going outside, which might mean an exit being defused, which the police or the FBI needed to know.

Nemesis leaned forward, put her hand over the microphone.

'No more,' she said.

Raised her shotgun a little, as a warning.

Sixty-One

Special Agent Clem Carson was always snow-ready. It was a big issue with him, a skill gleaned from his former life in Buffalo, New York, and a modest source of personal pride. His old Jeep Wrangler, complete with snow tires and emergency kit, was safely garaged, and he'd been out shoveling, snow-blowing and salting the driveway, sidewalk and road outside his Spragueville house at regular intervals since the snow had begun, even though he'd been laid up with the flu for a week and was now officially on leave.

Always on call, though, in his line of work, always good to go, even in a blizzard, and he'd gotten a reputation for that in the Providence satellite office, where they called him The Snowman. Which was part of why he'd gotten a call, five minutes ago, from Assistant Special Agent-in-Charge David Balfour, and why he was already warming up the Wrangler, his laptop open on the passenger seat, earphone in his right ear, listening to the terrifying nightmare apparently breaking loose in a church over in Shiloh Village.

An act of terrorism, it was being deemed, not of the jihadist kind, but damn well fitting the FBI's definition, and Carson was beginning to feel that if conditions were halfway normal, a Joint Terrorism Task Force and Lord-knew-who-else might already be at the scene, but as things were, so far as he could make out, for the moment it was just him, which was downright bizarre.

The ASAC had told him not to do anything until the HRT or a Crisis Negotiation Unit or JTTF team got there. And that even then, no one was going anywhere near the church till the Bomb Techs had it all nailed down.

'Orders?' Clem Carson had asked.

'Just get there,' Balfour had answered.

Clem Carson hadn't wasted time asking why him, because he knew the answer. In normal conditions it would have taken the State Police, headquartered in Scituate, around fifteen to twenty to reach Shiloh, and not much longer for a Hostage Rescue Team from Providence. But these were horrendous conditions, and Clem Carson was, in practical terms, closest to the scene, added to which, he lived alone and had no one to argue with about going out in the Blizzard-to-End-All-Blizzards with the remnants of the flu and no chance of being home for Christmas morning.

And he was, when all was said and done, The Snowman.

'What now?' William Osborn asked the big gunman as Liza and Nemesis came down the steps after them.

'You'll see,' Amos said.

The vaulted underground chamber felt cold to Liza after the relative warmth of the nave. She looked down the corridor, past closed doors on either side to the Emergency Exit at the end, saw wires and cables and plastic-wrapped *something* – same as upstairs.

248

What now indeed?

Amos picked up one of two large backpacks ready and waiting on the floor in the corridor, pulled it on and handed the second one to Nemesis as she put on the black zippered jacket she'd left in the vicar's office. 'Anyone wants to use the john, speak now, but the door stays open.'

'I'm not proud.' Osborn looked at Liza. 'Mind if I go first? Age before beauty.'

Liza smiled at him, respecting his courage, then turned away, waited till he was done, handed the camera to Nemesis and took her own turn, the relief exquisite.

'Why can't the others come down here, a few at a time?' she said.

'Not your problem,' Amos told her.

'You need to put your jacket on.' Carefully, Nemesis removed Liza's backpack.

And Lord, that felt almost as good as peeing had.

Except that as soon as she'd zipped up the parka, she realized that Nemesis had put all the camera equipment back on the desk in Keenan's office.

'You need to help me get rigged up again,' she said.

'You won't be needing it till we get back,' Amos said.

'But Reaper said I was to "bear witness".'

'And you will,' Amos said.

'But I thought he meant—'

Liza stopped, her mind shooting into overdrive, because this had to be bad news. Had Reaper said she should bring the camera just as a means to persuade her down here, or was this the big gunman playing his own side game? Clearly Amos didn't want this next episode recorded, in which case why take her along at all, and was she even going to *get* back?

She cut off the scary thoughts, and asked the obvious: 'Are we going outside, and if you don't want me to record, why am I coming?'

'You're coming because that's what Reaper wants,' Nemesis said.

'Come on,' Amos said.

He went ahead down the corridor, Osborn behind him, then Liza, Nemesis bringing up the rear, passing the storeroom and a door leading to the parish hall, stopping outside another door bearing a small brass plaque engraved 'Archive'.

Amos opened it, leaned in and turned on the light. 'Come on.' He led the way between two rows of shelving with library-style ladders, then stopped again, crouched and pulled back a rug on the floor, exposing a trapdoor.

Liza saw the round hole in the ground and felt a clutch of icy new fear.

Going down, not out.

'I see,' Osborn said grimly.

'I'm getting a very bad feeling,' Liza said, feeling for the gloves in her pockets and putting them on.

'No need.' Osborn was comfortingly matter-of-fact. 'There's a tunnel system under the village, commissioned by the original owner of my house, long before the Cromwells' time. I was told that the gentleman fancied a direct link to church, though I was also led to believe it had been bricked up long ago. Lot of tunnels in New England.'

'Mostly smuggler tunnels, I thought,' Liza said. 'Near the ocean, like the Salem system.'

'My sources said these were dug for different purposes,' Osborn said. 'A fear of being cut off by snow, and a rather more paranoid need for an escape route in case of attack.'

'Let's go,' Amos said.

Osborn smiled at Liza. 'I don't think I'm being paranoid in assuming that the intention right now is to get to my house and rob me, hence the decision about your camera.'

'Move it,' Amos said.

'Steps or a ladder?' Osborn eyed the hole. 'I'm not sure I'll fit.' He patted his stomach. 'Too much good food.'

'It's a ladder, and you'll fit.' Amos gestured with his shotgun. 'Now.'

'Does this young lady really have to be put through this?' Osborn said.

'*Move*,' Amos said.

'I tried,' Osborn said to Liza.

'And I'm grateful,' she said.

She watched him start his descent, the gunman shining an LED flashlight down into the hole for him, felt admiration and compassion for the overweight old man, heard him wheezing as he went, found it hard to listen to, but was glad they had each other for support.

'Your turn,' Nemesis said, as Amos climbed down after Osborn.

Liza moved to the edge, looked down into blackness.

251

'I'm not keen on tunnels,' she said.

'Too bad,' Nemesis said, and shone her own flashlight into the void.

Liza lowered herself, found the first rung of the ladder.

'Why isn't Reaper coming with us?' she asked, trying to keep her mind off what was happening.

'That's his business,' Amos said.

'How sick is he?' Liza asked, still descending. 'How long does he have?'

'Like Amos said, that's nobody's business but his,' Nemesis said.

Outside the church, Shiloh was deserted, the wind's incessant wail and the groaning of roofs under pressure blotting out any other sounds, the snow still blowing into white dunes, the houses and the inn at the far end of Main Street in darkness.

The four-by-four parked hours ago on North Maple by Amos's hired guns had all but disappeared, nothing but perfectly smooth white humps showing now.

No one inside the vehicle.

Reaper's Volvo opposite buried too.

Likewise, Osborn's Bentley outside St Matthew's.

Amos had called it a ghost town when he'd driven through on Tuesday evening.

More like a moonscape now.

A village imprisoned and snowbound.

Helpless.

Sixty-Two

If they had been able to walk above ground, even in snow with the old man, the hike between St Matthew's and Shiloh Oaks would probably have taken no more than ten to fifteen minutes, but in this tunnel, with the ground uneven, slippery and barely visible despite the two flashlights, the path littered with stray bricks and broken boards, the journey seemed interminable.

Pitch-dark, narrow, damp, foul-smelling and claustrophobic, and the only halfway good news from Liza's perspective was that Amos and Nemesis seemed in a hurry, which hopefully meant that the plan was to get there and back as fast as possible.

Reaper had said she'd be coming back.

But then, Reaper had told her to take the camera and backpack.

She cut back on thinking, kept her head down and followed.

The most disturbing features, to her, were the gaping black holes to left and right – an awful, foul stink coming from one as they passed, probably from some old cracked sewage pipe. All those black holes leading *someplace*, she supposed, though she couldn't picture where, had already lost her bearings, only Osborn's company keeping her from full-blown panic.

She could hear his labored breathing up ahead,

and she was finding this tough at age thirty-four, but that poor man had to be around eighty.

'You OK, Mr Osborn?' she called.

'As well as can be expected,' he called back. 'Though I think, in the circumstances, Liza, perhaps you might call me Bill.'

'Oh my *God*,' Liza exclaimed. 'A rat!'

'With or without a shotgun?' Osborn asked.

Liza laughed. Which felt good, despite everything.

And a moment later, Osborn said, 'So much for bricking up our end of the tunnel.'

She saw what he meant, saw in the beam from Nemesis's flashlight the remains of a wall, stepped carefully over scattered, crumbling old bricks, saw a big sewage pipe to their right, wondered suddenly if there were tunnels below their own house on Maple, though no one had ever mentioned them, and surely, when her great-grandfather had bought the place, he would have been told of their existence . . .

'Nearly there, I'd say,' Osborn said, gasping with effort.

'Can we take a break?' Liza said.

'No time,' Amos said, up ahead.

'Mr Osborn's really out of breath.'

'No break,' Amos said. 'Not even for *Mister* Osborn.'

'Thanks for the consideration,' Liza said, loathing him.

'The sooner we get there,' Nemesis said, 'the sooner we'll be above ground.'

'You do realize,' Osborn said, 'that my house won't be empty?'

'As a matter of fact' – Nemesis raised her voice – 'it's as good as empty.'

'Your housekeeper's gone to her son's, remember?' Amos said. 'And if you're thinking about your dogs, they won't be bothering us.'

Osborn stopped dead. 'What have you done to them?'

'Keep walking,' the gunman said.

'What did you do to my dogs?' Osborn didn't move.

'They're fine,' Nemesis said. 'Locked in your bedroom, sound asleep.'

'You doped my dogs?' For the first time, the old man sounded frightened. 'What did you give them?'

'Reaper organized it,' Nemesis said. 'He likes animals. He won't have done anything to harm them.'

'Likes animals so much he cut his own cat's throat,' Osborn said bitterly. 'Children who kill animals often turn into psychos, you know.'

Amos walked back to where the old man had stopped and prodded him with the barrel of his shotgun. 'Move.'

They began walking again.

'So.' Osborn panted after another minute. 'I'm presuming it's cash you're after. In which case, I should warn you there isn't much. We never keep more than five hundred dollars in the house.'

'Save your lying breath,' Amos told him.

'If your Reaper thinks there's more' – Osborn was puffing with effort – 'he's been misinformed. But don't worry, I'll give you what there is. I have a wife I love and no aspirations to heroism.'

Amos halted so abruptly that they all almost collided.

Spiral steps to their right. Narrow, but better than a ladder.

Shiloh Oaks, Liza presumed.

Carson was well on his way, though it was no day at the beach, visibility so poor at times that he'd had to stop, but even if the biggest problem was that too few roads had yet been cleared, the upside of that was the absence of other cars for him to run into. For one thing, they'd issued a travel ban, plus it was still the middle of the night, and most people traveled ahead of Christmas Day – and hey, maybe next year he might buy himself a sleigh and a couple of reindeer, he thought, lifting his foot off the gas as the Wrangler went into another skid.

Snowman or not, however, Clem wasn't too happy not knowing how things were going to play out when he did reach Shiloh, because it was going to take a while longer for the CNU or JTTF to get through, let alone the Bomb Techs. And it was all well and good Balfour telling him not to do a damned thing till backup arrived, but sitting on his backside doing nothing while fifty-six hostages were inside scared out of their minds – one already dead, a little *girl*, for crying out loud – was not the reason he'd joined the FBI.

Not that Balfour wasn't one hundred per cent right.

Nothing one guy could do if those church doors really were booby-trapped.

Another way in was what they needed.

There were guys in Providence right now trying to get hold of architectural plans.

Not the easiest thing to do in the middle of the night on Christmas morning.

Carson not holding his breath.

The spiral steps up to Shiloh Oaks were dizzying, Amos moving fast, Osborn painfully slow now, stopping a couple of times, and the gunman yelled at him twice, then reversed down a few steps and took hold of the old man's left arm.

'I've got no time for this,' he said harshly.

'For God's sake,' Liza protested. 'You think this is easy for him?'

'He's not some nice old man,' Amos said. 'He's a bastard.'

'I may not be nice,' Osborn said weakly, 'but I'm definitely old.'

'A fucking loan shark is what you are,' Amos said. 'Worst kind.'

'You have proof of that?' Liza said. 'Or is that another Reaper story?'

'You questioning what Reaper's been through?' Amos was cold as ice.

'I guess I'd better not.'

'Can we just get up there?' Nemesis said from behind her.

Amos started up again and they followed.

'Not a loan shark at all, Liza,' Osborn's voice carried down to her. 'I helped some people who needed it. Not a charity.'

'And I don't need to know about that,' Liza told him.

'You're a journalist,' Osborn panted. 'You need to know everything.'

Finally there was a door and Amos got it open

257

easily, as if he'd done it before, and they all sped up, even the old man, and Liza's heart rate accelerated with the anticipation of light and air.

More darkness.

'Our cellar,' Osborn gasped. 'Light switch somewhere. Lost my bearings.'

Amos went on ahead, found it, came back and hauled the old man up.

A wine cellar, Liza saw, when she'd stopped being dazzled by the brightness. Racks of bottles, rows of them.

'A decent collection.' Osborn, breathless and wheezing, leaned on a wall for support. 'Not worth a fortune, but by all means help yourselves.'

Amos took a bottle from a rack and dropped it on the tiled floor.

'Wasteful,' Osborn said. 'And ignorant.'

'You think?' Amos used his shotgun to sweep about a dozen bottles of red off a rack.

'Wasting time,' Nemesis said.

The masked man nodded. 'Care to lead the way?' he asked Osborn.

'I'm sure you've worked out where you want to go,' Osborn said.

'We disabled your alarm system same time as we doped your dogs, old man,' Amos told him. 'So if you were hoping we're going to set it off, forget it.'

'Let's *go*,' Nemesis said.

In more of a hurry than Amos, Liza noted, wondered why, guessed she'd probably find out soon enough.

'You'll be wanting the safe, then,' Osborn said, wearily. 'First floor. Library.'

Sixty-Three

'They're getting very restless,' Michael told Reaper, up on the chancel. 'If this goes on too much longer, someone's going to blow.'

'They're fine for now,' Reaper said. 'Half of them are asleep.'

There had been some heated discussion a while back, after Eddie Leary, the redheaded young guy ordered by Amos to the ninth row, had suggested they tie up John Tilden, and several others had agreed. Tilden had taken fright, protesting, and Mark Jackson had asked Simon Keenan if he'd loan them his cincture, his narrow rope belt, which had angered the vicar, but Reaper had pointed out that Tilden was not about to escape, and everyone had subsided.

'How much longer?' Jeremiah asked, passing by just below.

He and Joel patrolling now, checking every pew, every hostage.

'As long as it takes,' Reaper answered steadily.

Michael regarded Joel, presently near the back of the nave. He looked exhausted and unhappy, the shotgun suiting him no better than it had at the outset. No balaclava, no real sense of threat about him, and if he thought that, then one of those younger guys had to be similarly aware – and come to that, if this blew up into some open act of defiance, what the hell would *he* do? he wondered, gripping his own shotgun. He had limited knowledge of what was going on now, what they were waiting for, was seriously worried about the fact that Liza had become involved in that too, and Revelation might finally be wholly clear to him – the link between their two stories, as Reaper had promised – but at what cost?

Another thing seemed clear to him now. That Reaper – Joshua Tilden – had only really been using him to help in the slow, painful exposing of his father's guilt. Which surely he could have done without bringing Michael along for the ride – and maybe he'd just been the icing on Reaper's cake?

Or maybe there was worse to come.

'Waiting's always hard, Isaiah.' Reaper was watching him.

'Why are you still calling me that?' Michael asked quietly.

'It's your Whirlwind name,' Reaper said.

'I need the bathroom, and I need it *now*!'

Janet Yore again, her voice high and sharp with distress.

'Not the only one,' another woman agreed.

Keenan stood up. 'Couldn't you organize for us to use the restrooms in the undercroft? We could be escorted, a few at a time.'

'Not yet,' Reaper said. 'Sorry for the discomfort.'

'I'm going to pee my pants,' a teenager halfway back said.

'I already did,' another male voice said from somewhere.

'Oh, what the fuck,' a third man said.

'Language,' Stephen Plain said.

And almost everyone laughed.

And then, a moment or two later, a few more of them began to cry.

Michael looked at Reaper, wondered how Liza was coping.

Wished, for at least the hundredth time, that he'd never answered that email.

The house was as handsome as Liza had expected. She'd seen photographs at school, Shiloh Oaks being a building of local historic interest and, after St Matthew's, the most important structure in the village, but she'd never been inside.

They were in the library now. The drapes were closed, only one desk lamp lit, but the room was nothing short of gorgeous. Money beautifully spent over a long time, not just on antiques and old leather furniture, but on the books themselves.

'Where?' Amos asked tersely.

'I wonder,' Osborn asked politely, 'if I might be permitted to visit my bathroom?'

'You went in church,' Amos said. 'Where's the safe?'

'Open it, Mr Osborn,' Nemesis said, 'and I'll take you to the bathroom.'

'Good of you,' Osborn said. 'I need to fetch some medication from there, for myself and my wife.'

'Where's the fucking safe?' Amos demanded.

'No need to get tetchy.' Osborn pointed. 'There. In that base cabinet. Open the door, you'll see.'

Amos crossed the room in two strides, bent to open the cabinet, and for just one insane instant, Liza wondered if she had any hope of disarming Nemesis while the big man was occupied . . .

261

No chance. The masked woman totally focused, shotgun firmly gripped.

The contents of the safe clearly as vital to her as the big man.

'Numbers.' Amos stared at the steel box, its electronic keypad.

'Digits,' Osborn corrected. 'Let me see my dogs first.'

'Your dogs are fine,' Nemesis said. 'Give Amos the numbers.'

Osborn glanced at Liza, and she nodded, hoped he'd give them what they wanted before things got out of hand, and no prizes now for guessing why they'd made her leave the camera behind.

'Give me the fucking *numbers*,' Amos said.

Osborn hesitated.

Nemesis turned swiftly, jammed her shotgun up against his neck. 'Now.'

'For God's sake, Bill,' Liza said. 'Tell them.'

Osborn's smile was grim. 'Six digits. Three, nine, one, four, one, eight.'

The masked gunman keyed the numbers in, and Liza held her breath.

Heard the door open. Exhaled in relief.

'This isn't it,' Amos said.

'Sure it is,' Osborn said. 'Just as I told you. Go ahead, take the money.'

Amos stood up, holding a bundle of what looked like fifty-dollar bills. 'Where's the real safe, you bastard?' He came at Osborn, thrust the money in his face, then threw it on the floor. 'Where's the real cash?'

'Nonexistent.' Osborn turned to Nemesis. 'Will you take me to the bathroom now?'

'Where's the money, Osborn?' she said. 'You don't want to jerk us around any more, believe me.'

Liza looked at the telephone on the writing desk, thought that maybe if she said she needed to sit down . . .

'Don't even think about it,' Amos snapped.

'Why not?' Liza said. 'Would you shoot me?'

That wasn't brave, she told herself, just *idiotic*, because she wanted to survive this whole thing, not bleed to death on some Persian rug.

'I'd rather not,' Amos answered. 'But I wouldn't mind shooting this scum.'

'Where's the real money, Mr Osborn?' Nemesis asked again.

Amos returned to the safe, took out a flat leather box and opened it.

'That's my wife's,' Osborn said.

'Not any more.' Amos took out a diamond and emerald necklace, tossed the box onto the rug, stepped over to Nemesis, stuffed it in one of her jacket pockets and zipped it up. 'You'll need to be careful how you sell it, but it might help.'

Definitely for profit then, in Nemesis's case, Liza registered.

'It'll be money,' Osborn had said hours ago.

Not necessarily money in Michael's case, Tilden's confession surely more important to him. Though she couldn't be sure, not of that, not of anything, especially as he'd seemed shocked by Tilden's guilt.

'Unzip another pocket, Nemesis.' Amos was back down at the safe, pulling out more boxes – Cartier, red and unmistakable.

'Please,' Osborn said, pleading for the first time.

'Not that one.' He pointed to a small square box. 'Take the rest if you must, but not that one.'

'Sentimental value?' Amos was sarcastic.

'I'm not explaining myself to you, you piece of *filth*,' Osborn said.

Amos stood up, moved fast, sideswiped him on the side of his head with the butt of his shotgun, and the old man fell onto his knees.

'Jesus.' Liza got down and put her arm around Osborn's shoulders. 'Bill, are you OK?'

He seemed unable to answer, his eyes glazed, blood trickling down from his right temple, his breathing too shallow.

'My God, what have you *done*?' Liza's heart was pumping hard again, that single brutal act removing any hope that this might still end well. 'Bill, try to stay awake. I'm going to help you.'

'Bill's going to help himself by telling us where the cash is.' Amos took a diamond ring out of the red box that had caused Osborn such distress, tucked it into another of Nemesis's pockets and zipped it up. 'Aren't you, Bill?'

'Can't you see he's *hurt*?' Liza said.

'He doesn't look good.' Nemesis sounded uncertain.

'He's old and he's a son of a bitch,' Amos said. 'There's different ways of hurting people, and this bastard's done plenty.'

'Even if that's true, please just leave him alone now.' Liza kept her arm around the injured man's shoulders. 'Take what you've got – the jewelry's obviously valuable. Go back to Reaper and tell him that's all there is.'

'But it isn't.' Amos hunkered down in front of

264

Osborn. 'Here's a deal for you, fuckface. You tell me right now where the *real* money is, and I won't go back into church and cut your wife's throat. How about that?'

'He won't do that,' Liza said softly to Osborn.

'I think you know by now that I would,' Amos said. 'Because there's a fortune somewhere in this house, and Whirlwind has plans for it.'

'Just tell him, Osborn,' Nemesis said. 'Please.'

Osborn said something unintelligible.

'What?' Amos leaned in closer. '*What?*'

'He can't speak,' Liza said, afraid the old man might be having a stroke.

'The hell he can't.' Amos pulled a folded knife from his pocket. 'Tell me now, or this is for your Freya.'

William Osborn's eyes were suddenly less glazed, clear with loathing.

'Cellar,' he said, slurred but intelligible. 'You were looking right at it.'

'Where in the cellar?' Nemesis asked.

'Floor. Near the champagne.'

'Come on.' Amos put away the knife, grabbed Osborn's right arm, hauled him up off his knees and the injured man cried out.

'Stop it!' Liza protested. 'You'll kill him.'

'She's right,' Nemesis said. 'We don't need another death.'

Amos let go of his arm, and Osborn crumpled to the floor. 'Then think of your wife now, old man, while you still can, and tell me what kind of safe it is.'

'Not a safe,' Osborn whispered. 'Locked hatch.'

'Where's the fucking key?'

265

'In this safe,' Osborn told him weakly, giving up. 'Over there.'

Amos was there in an instant, and for such a big man, Liza thought, he moved nimbly, and in another moment he had two keys in his hand. 'One of these?'

Osborn didn't answer.

'Which one?' Amos yelled.

'He's passed out,' Nemesis said.

'Oh, God.' Liza ripped off her gloves, felt for a pulse in his neck. 'He's alive, but he needs help.'

'Leave him.' Amos bent and pulled her up.

'He has to have help,' she told him.

'Not from you,' he said. 'You're coming with us.'

'At least let me dial nine-one-one,' she said. 'We'll be gone before they get in.'

'They'll be blown to fuckdom if they try.'

'You wired this house too?' Liza stared at him.

'So come *on*.' Nemesis took her arm.

'If he's been lying,' Amos said quietly, 'I'll do what I told him I would.'

'No, you won't,' Nemesis said.

'I don't think he was lying,' Liza said.

'Who the fuck asked you?' Amos said.

'I'll get you help, Bill,' Liza said at the door, urgently. 'Soon as I can. You just hang in there.'

There was no answer.

'What have you done with my husband?' Freya Osborn was on her feet. 'They've been gone for over an hour.'

'They've been gone for fifty-two minutes,' Reaper said. 'Please sit down, Mrs Osborn. I've done nothing to him.'

266

'Not you, maybe, but I don't trust that big brute.'
She stood her ground in her dark mink, gloved
fists clenched, makeup smudged, exhausted but
furious. 'Where have they taken him? He's an old
man and he's sick. He needs his medication.'

'So long as your husband is cooperating, you
have nothing to worry about.'

Freya Osborn turned to the vicar on the other
side of the aisle, back beside his wife. 'There are
offices down there, aren't there?'

'My office, yes,' Keenan said.

'So there's a computer?'

'Yes.'

'That's what they'll be using,' Osborn's wife said.
'It's money, just as Bill said, and the rest of it's
hogwash. Some kind of computer fraud. They're
here to steal.'

'Sit down, Mrs Osborn,' Reaper told her again.

She sank down, leaned back, shivered, pulled
her fur around her, closed her eyes.

'Try not to worry too much, Freya,' Stephen Plain
called to her. 'Bill's tough.'

'He's brave,' Freya said. Then, close to tears, added:
'That's what's frightening the hell out of me.'

Sixty-Four

Osborn had told the truth about the cash in the cellar.

It took them a while to find it, and Amos was
ready to smash every tile, but then Nemesis spotted
a square of grouting that looked different from the

rest, and there was the hatch, well-concealed and rectangular, and Liza held her breath, desperate for the money to be there, fearing for Osborn and Freya if it was not.

Amos knelt, opened it with the first key, and a neatly carved lid of six floor tiles came away easily.

He set it aside and stared down into a crawlspace.

'Fuck,' he said, awed.

'My God,' Nemesis said, and pulled off her balaclava, her cheeks flushed red.

'Put that back on,' Amos snapped at her.

'She's already seen my face.'

'There might be security cameras.'

Nemesis quickly pulled it back on, and looked around.

'Too late if there are,' Amos said. 'Shall we?'

They got down to business, Liza ordered to help as they began heaving out the money, and there was more cash down there than she'd ever seen in *real* life, vast quantities of what looked like mostly hundred-dollar bills, some in bundles, some loose, as if it had been carelessly stuffed into the void – and maybe, she thought now, on her knees, this was why they'd brought her down here, just to lend a hand with this robbery?

Definitely no question now as to why they'd taken the camera from her, and clearly this had been the real motivation for the rest of the gang too. Money. Filthy lucre. Those words from the Bible, Liza thought. Right up Reaper's alley.

Watching Nemesis now, she wondered if she'd ever been a bank teller, because she handled the cash so deftly, and they'd come equipped with plastic bags and rubber bands to separate the bundles and facilitate counting, and their back-packs were on the floor now, waiting, Liza guessed, to be filled.

They worked in silence, lips moving as they counted.

'You see now,' Amos said to Liza, sitting back for a moment. 'Only a loan shark – a thief – would have this kind of money. Black, dirty money.'

'Takes one to know one, as they say,' she said.

'You want a smack?'

'Hey,' Nemesis said. 'None of this is her fault.'

He shrugged and went back to work.

'I get now why you stopped me broadcasting,' Liza said.

And then a new kick of fear hit her hard, the sudden realization that if Osborn was dead, that would make her the only witness to this.

'You'll be able to start again soon enough,' Nemesis said easily.

Liza nodded at the mounting piles of plastic bags. 'How much do you all need? There must be well over a million in those bags already.'

'Lot of good causes out there,' Amos said wryly.

'I'm taking a cut,' Nemesis told Liza, 'and I don't mind you knowing why.'

'Not in the plan,' Amos said.

'What difference?' Nemesis said. 'I've made big mistakes in my life, got in all kinds of trouble, all my own doing. But my brother has spina bifida, and I swore that I'd always take care of him, but he's stuck in an institution and he needs surgery, which he's not going to get without a shitload of money. I'm here to see that he gets it.'

'And this was really the only way?' Liza asked.

269

'I tried everything else, believe me, but nobody gives a damn, and why would they? I thought it was game over until Reaper found me, and here I am.' Nemesis snapped a rubber band around another cash bundle. 'I feel terrible about that little kid, and for Luke, and even for Osborn.' She regarded Liza through the balaclava's slits. 'I should have known we couldn't pull this off without anyone getting hurt, and yes, I'm ashamed, but I'm just going to have to live with it.'

'Are you done?' Amos enquired scathingly.

'I wanted her to know,' Nemesis said. 'So sue me.'

At ten after four, Clem Carson was right outside the village, the Wrangler parked up on Shiloh Road, staring through night-vision goggles at Elm Street and the rear of St Matthew's.

Still alone, and likely to remain so for a while. The go-ahead given for all kinds of help: CNU (motto *Pax Per Conloquium*, which meant Resolution through Dialog) and some kind of task force being organized now *stat*, but the blizzard still preventing choppers from flying any time soon.

Carson's orders until a few minutes ago: watch, listen and report back. And though the link with the reporter-on-the-spot was still down, Providence was feeding him info, and they knew a little more now about Joshua Tilden, aka Reaper, the most crucial detail being confirmation from Garthville, where he'd been a long-term psychiatric inmate, that the bastard was dying of cancer.

Which made it all the more probable that he planned to finish what they'd started inside the church, no matter what. Which gave Clem Carson a sick feeling, because he doubted that these people were simply going to defuse their bomb-rigged doors and let their hostages walk free. That just wasn't the kind of decision a dying, deranged bastard was likely to come to at crunch time.

His latest order was, he guessed, good news. To try to establish communication, to be *damned* careful, and if he managed to speak to Reaper/ Tilden or any of his gang, then Carson was to procrastinate until the real negotiators arrived.

'Just get them talking,' Balfour had said. 'Find out what they want to bring this thing to a safe conclusion. Then tell them you can't guarantee anything, but you'll pass on their demands.'

And Clem was ready to start calling, but, since he didn't remember ever hearing a landline phone ringing in any church nave, chances were it would ring in the office, which they knew was down below, and that was fine, so long as someone heard it, but if no one was in that office, then with this banshee wind still shrieking they probably wouldn't be hearing much of anything.

Still, Clem kept an assortment of useful stuff in the back of the Wrangler.

Including a fully-charged megaphone – his own property, a thing he used now and then when he was coaching his rowing team.

Hard to be sure, with those heavy walls of snow covering up the high windows of St Matthew's, if they'd even hear him calling on that.

But if no one picked up the damned phone, he'd made up his mind to try.

Happy Christmas, Snowman.

271

Sixty-Five

Inside St Matthew's, Michael, having listened to Reaper coughing for a while now, had offered to bring him water from the undercroft, but Reaper had shaken his head, had pointed, instead, to a veiled chalice of wine on the altar table, and in the front pew, the vicar had suppressed his anger and given his wife a rueful smile.

'Perhaps Dr Plain could help?' Rosie Keenan suggested moments later.

'No help needed,' Reaper said.

'None offered,' Stephen Plain called. 'I'm not a doctor anymore anyway.'

'Good for you, Doc,' Mark Jackson said from the sixth row. 'With a bit of luck, he'll choke to death and we can all go home.'

A few sips of sacramental wine, and Reaper's cough first grew more rasping, then faded away, but Michael felt it had tired him, and thought about whatever he might be dying of, wondered how long he could keep this up.

Wondered, too, if it would be better for everyone if he just keeled over now.

Felt guilt for thinking that way.

Guilt now whichever way this went.

The voice, booming in from outside the church, startled everyone.

'This is the FBI.'

272

A male voice, strong, rational, uncompromising.

Michael heard gasps, saw the light of hope in some eyes, new fear in others, and he understood that, felt it himself, because who knew what would happen if some SWAT team stormed the church?

Or what Reaper might decide to do before that.

'That's it. All we can carry.' Amos kicked at a pile of the loose green stuff around his boots. 'Time to organize you, Nemesis.'

The other woman removed her jacket, pulled off her sweater and the vest beneath, keeping the balaclava in place, then raised her arms while Amos began taping bundles of cash to her bra and her skin, and Liza tried to keep a tally but lost count, thought it was maybe as much as seventy thousand, perhaps even a hundred grand, being concealed on her person.

'How does that feel?' Amos asked.

'Warm.'

Amos turned to Liza. 'Help her put her clothes back on.'

'I'd rather not.'

He jerked the shotgun her way. 'Do it.'

Liza struggled to get the black vest down over the other woman's cash-fattened body. 'Not sure this is going to fit.'

'Make it fit,' Amos said.

Liza stretched it, succeeded, and Nemesis tucked the bottom of the vest into her waistband, then motioned for the sweater.

'Don't you think people might ask questions when you pay your brother's hospital bills with amazing stacks of cash?' Liza asked.

'I'm not a moron,' Nemesis said.

'Speed it up,' Amos said.

Liza dragged the sweater down over the bala-clava, helped Nemesis get her arms through the sleeves, then turned to the gunman. 'What's your cut for? Sick mom? Dogs' home?'

'Mind your fucking business, smart mouth,' Amos said.

'None of us knows his story.' Nemesis picked up her jacket.

'Help her with it,' Amos rapped.

'I'm OK,' Nemesis said, and grunted as she tried zipping it up.

'Any connection with Osborn?' Liza dared to go on probing. 'You seemed so angry with him.'

Amos stepped forward, fastened the jacket for Nemesis. 'Can you bend?'

Nemesis tried. 'Well enough.' She turned to Liza. 'Don't push him.'

'I'm just interested in motivation,' Liza said.

Amos turned around and came so close that she could feel his sour breath. 'How'd you like to get left in one of those tunnels we passed on the way in?'

'Not one bit,' Liza said, feeling sick.

'Then keep it zipped.'

He hoisted the largest bag onto his own back, then helped Nemesis with hers.

'Do you want me to carry some?' Liza said.

'Little Christmas bonus for you?' Amos said. 'I don't think so.'

'I just thought it might help us get back quicker,' she said. 'Less time in the tunnel.'

Nemesis turned to Amos. 'All set?'

'One request,' Liza said. 'I'd like to check on Mr Osborn.'

'No requests,' Amos said.

The telephone in Simon Keenan's office was ringing off the hook.

Michael could hear it, had been tuned in to it ever since the FBI had first appealed for someone to pick up. Special Agent Clement Carson, the man calling through a megaphone, telling Reaper that he wanted to speak to him, wanted to help any way he could.

No sign from Reaper as yet that he was remotely interested in talking to Carson.

Everyone growing edgier as time passed, Michael felt.

'Wouldn't hurt to talk to the man,' Nowak, the organist, had called out a while back.

'Just answer the damned phone,' Adam Glover had added.

Reaper had told them to be quiet.

'Making a noise won't help you,' he'd said.

'If you don't want to leave the nave' – Simon Keenan tried now – 'I could just go down and pick up.' He stood up from his seat beside Rosie. 'You could tell me what to say.'

Jeremiah moved across the nave, and pointed his shotgun at the vicar.

'Or maybe not,' Keenan said.

Michael just kept silent.

Thinking about Liza, hoping she was OK, not understanding why Reaper had wanted her down there with Amos and Nemesis.

Her continuing absence more troubling by the minute.

275

Sixty-Six

Liza had been aware, since just after they'd reentered the tunnel, that a few feet behind her Nemesis had been softly counting the black holes to right and left along the way.

'Five,' she heard her say, passing one – the worst of the foul-smelling black holes. And then, 'Lord, that's disgusting.'

'Why are you counting?' Liza's curiosity got the better of her.

'Shut up,' Nemesis said.

Then, a little later: 'Six.'

Liza couldn't remember her doing that on their first journey, but then again, maybe she'd been too scared to notice.

And then, abruptly, Liza heard the other woman stop.

'Seven.'

Up ahead, Amos had stopped too, and turned around.

'Guess this is it,' Nemesis said.

Liza's heart rate shot up again, because she was sandwiched between them, and because maybe they *were* going to leave her down here, take her down one of those holes, and if that happened, she would lose her mind for sure . . .

'Guess so,' Amos said.

Nemesis heaved off her cash-loaded backpack,

pushed past Liza and gave it to the big man, who threw it easily across his left shoulder.

'Hope it goes well for you and your brother,' he said.

'Hope you all get out with what you need.' Nemesis's voice was husky.

She stepped forward, leaned against him in an awkward kind of hug.

'You're leaving?' Liza stared into the smaller tunnel to her left, not so much as a pinpoint of light visible anywhere. 'Through that? Where does it lead?'

'That would be telling,' Nemesis said. 'You clear on working the gizmo when you get back up top? Just plug in the cable from the backpack to the camera and—'

'She'll work it out,' Amos said. 'You worry about yourself.'

'You too.'

'Weapon,' Amos said.

Nemesis handed him her shotgun, which he slid easily into a side pocket of the backpack she'd just given him.

'I am sorry,' Nemesis said to Liza. 'For all of it.' She pulled off her balaclava again, rubbed the perspiration off her face with it, then gave that to Amos too. 'I didn't really get to know Luke, but I think he was a good guy.'

'Go,' Amos said.

Nemesis nodded, and then, without another word, she took her flashlight from another pocket and slipped into the tunnel.

For several seconds, the sounds of her breathing

and the swish of her clothes and the tread of her feet were audible, and then it all faded to nothing.

Amos shone his own flashlight onto the ground, and, with his own rubber soles, roughly obliterated Nemesis's boot prints.

'Let's go,' he said.

The Snowman was no longer alone. Law enforcement was arriving piecemeal, State Police first, and the word was that Shiloh Road was being made passable. No sign yet of the task force, and Clem Carson was not sorry about that, in no rush to see innocent blood spilled.

The CNU was not far away, but though he'd been ordered to move the Wrangler farther away from St Matthew's, Carson was still, for now, the agent on the phone, still getting no response. Shiloh Village had been cordoned off, only key Bureau personnel, cops and Fire Rescue being allowed anywhere near. The walls of snow were, he'd learned, rendering the use of remote or laser listening devices impossible, with no time for covert preparation. News trucks had apparently started showing up too, but were being kept well away, major players still obstructed by the blizzard.

Liza Plain's earlier warning about explosive devices at the Shiloh Inn and possibly elsewhere in the village had curtailed for now any door-to-door calling, let alone evacuation of those village residents not inside the church.

Clem watched as more experienced men and women, helmeted and plumped up by Kevlar vests and cold weather jackets, joined the situation.

All quiet, no sirens, no lights, car doors being quietly shut, minimal conversation, radio silence ordered.

Not long now until he was off the hook as would-be negotiator, and he would be heartily relieved to return to being one of a team – and even more relieved when the Bomb Techs arrived.

Not long now, he told himself, and redialed the church number.

It was time, Reaper decided, to answer the phone.

He told Michael to stay at the pulpit, walked down the chancel steps and out through the under-croft door, descending those narrower steps carefully, using his cane, opening the door below, then walking unhurriedly to Keenan's office.

He sat down at the vicar's desk, took a breath and picked up the phone.

'This is Reaper,' he said.

'Yes.' The voice sounded as startled as a bunny in headlights. 'Thank you for picking up, sir. My name's Clem Carson, and—'

'I thought I should do you this courtesy since you've been very patient, Agent Carson,' Reaper said, 'but you should know that there'll be no further communication from this end.'

He heard sounds on the line, figured it was the agent trying to get someone else's attention, maybe rapping on a car window, and went on regardless.

'In case you didn't fully comprehend the situation from Ms Plain's excellent reportage, all entrances and exits to St Matthew's have been wired with explosive devices. Likewise the Shiloh

Inn. Likewise Shiloh Oaks on South Oak Street. Likewise *some* other residential properties on Main Street and beyond. I caution you, therefore, to be careful. I regret the loss of life that came about earlier, and though it was entirely accidental, I do, of course, accept all responsibility for it.'

Reaper felt his chest tighten and his throat constricting, but continued.

'So long as no one tries anything foolhardy, everyone inside the church will be released unharmed when Whirlwind's mission is complete.'

'That's very good to hear,' the agent came in quickly.

'Please don't interrupt,' Reaper told him. 'For your further information, John Tilden, the man who earlier confessed, among other crimes, to the forty-year-old murder of Alice Millicent, is presently seated in the center of the front southeast pew of the nave, and I trust you will see to it that he is placed under arrest and charged.'

'Sir – Mr Tilden – can you tell me—?'

'Tilden is not a name I use,' Reaper rapped. 'And please do not interrupt again.'

His cough erupted then, infuriatingly, and for several moments he could hear nothing over the sounds of his own spasms.

'Sir, are you OK?' he did hear when it finally let up.

'When our mission is complete,' Reaper went on hoarsely, 'we'll contact you.'

'Are you sick, sir? Do you need a doctor?'

Reaper put down the phone.

Sat for several more moments in Simon Keenan's chair.

280

Regarded his hand, its tremor.

'Get thee gone,' he said, to the tremor and to the threatening sensation in his head, and to the Messenger, long since banished.

And then he inhaled as deeply as his damaged lungs would allow, took a pain pill from an inside pocket of his jacket, swallowed it dry, then stood up and made his way out of the vicar's office, back to the steps that led up to the nave.

Sixty-Seven

'Where is he?'

Freya Osborn jumped to her feet the instant she saw Amos emerge alone from the undercroft shortly after six a.m.

'What have you done to my husband?'

'Your husband's fine,' Amos told her, looked at Reaper, back at the pulpit again, and gave him a nod. 'All under control,' he said, and then his sharp ears caught sounds from outside.

Reaper smiled. 'The FBI arrived a while back. All still well. I'll see you shortly.'

'Where's my granddaughter?' Stephen was up now too.

'Ms Plain is in the vicar's office,' Reaper said as Amos turned and disappeared back through the door. 'Settle down, people. This will all be over soon. Be patient just a while longer, and then you'll be free to leave.'

'Fuck patience,' Mitch Roper, the young man with the ear stud, said.

Adam Glover stood up. 'We'd like to go back to the parlor, to be with our daughter.'

'Not yet,' Reaper told them.

'Rot in hell,' Adam Glover said, and sat down.

'Amen!' Annie Stanley shouted.

'I daresay,' Reaper said. 'But for now, I'd ask you all to be quiet and wait.'

'I won't be quiet until you bring my husband back to me.' Freya Osborn was still standing. 'If he's safe and sound, just let me see him.'

'All in good time,' Reaper said. 'Now, please sit down.'

'I've told you he needs his medication.'

'The sooner you sit down,' Reaper told her, 'the sooner he'll get it.'

'How?' Freya wasn't budging. 'If he's in the vicar's office with Liza Plain, then surely—'

'Mrs Osborn, for the last time, sit *down*.'

Right on cue, Jeremiah was on his way across.

'I want to see my *husband*,' Freya insisted.

The masked gunman was right in front of her, shotgun leveled at her chest, and Claire Glover began to cry, and all over the nave anger and fear erupted again.

'Hey.' Michael, patrolling halfway up the aisle, turned quickly and moved back to the front. 'No need for that, Jeremiah.'

The elderly woman had still not given in, but Jeremiah shook his head, moved away, and some of the cries subsided, only sounds of exhausted weeping continuing.

'I understand you're afraid for your husband,

Mrs Osborn,' Michael said to her. 'But this won't help him, and as you've heard, there shouldn't be long to go now.'

'Has something happened to Bill?' Freya's blue eyes locked on Michael's face.

'Amos said he's fine.'

'Do you believe him?'

'I have no reason not to,' Michael said. 'But if you sit down, Mrs Osborn, I'll do my best to get your husband back to you as quickly as possible.'

'I'll be holding you to that,' Freya said.

At last she sat down, and Jeremiah went back to patrolling.

Reaper beckoned to Michael, who came to the foot of the chancel steps.

'That was well handled,' the older man told him quietly. 'I have business to take care of now. Can you look after things up here till we're done?'

'Won't the others mind?' Michael said.

'All in their interests, as you know.'

Reaper stepped away from the pulpit again, and moved to the steps.

'Is Liza really OK?' Michael asked.

'Definitely.'

'I need her to stay that way.' Michael's tone was soft, urgent.

'We all have needs,' Reaper said.

In the brief time that she had been left alone, Liza had considered her options and realized that, for the moment at least, she had none.

As soon as they'd climbed the ladder and come through the trapdoor back into the undercroft,

Amos had closed the hatch, replaced the rug, and then he'd set down the cash-loaded backpacks, fetched her camera and the gizmo from the office, locked the archive door behind them and pocketed the key. After which, he'd ordered her into the store room and locked her in.

'Won't be long.'

No way she could break out, get to the office phone with nothing to use as a tool.

And anyway, minutes later, he'd been back.

He'd let her out, retrieved the backpacks, leaving the camera and equipment, and had gone with her into the office, where he'd begun unloading the packs and, with his shotgun leaning against his right thigh, had started building tidy stacks of cash on Keenan's desk and the floor behind it.

He'd raised no objection when Liza had taken off her parka, and minutes later, when she'd asked to use the bathroom again, the gunman had agreed, waiting impatiently at the half-open door until she was done, and then he'd used the vicar's kettle to make himself a mug of coffee, offering her the same, which she'd refused.

'Everyone up there could use some hot drinks,' she'd said.

'They weren't in that tunnel,' Amos had pointed out, slugging down some coffee and returning to his task, and Liza had sat down on the vicar's couch and rested her aching back and legs.

The phone on the desk began to ring, her heart racing faster with it.

Amos looked at her, knew she was itching to answer.

'You pick that up,' he said, 'and I'll shoot your grandpa.'

Reaper came down soon after Amos had finished.

The phone was still ringing, jangling in Liza's head.

'Marks for persistence.' He sat in Keenan's chair, vacated by Amos. 'The FBI are outside, Ms Plain, you'll be pleased to know.'

Her broadcast *heard* then, or maybe just someone somewhere realizing something was badly wrong, but either way, it was the greatest news. Then fear struck again, harder than ever, wiping out the relief, because what if they stormed St Matthew's? What if she *hadn't* been heard and they didn't know about the explosives?

Reaper was watching her. 'They know about the doors.'

Liza looked back at him, uncertain whether to believe him or not.

'We're all set here,' Amos told him.

'William Osborn was badly injured at his house,' she said. 'He needs help.'

Reaper ignored her, regarded the piles of cash. 'Let's have Jeremiah down then.'

'I'd say Joel first,' Amos said. 'Jeremiah's better at keeping control.'

Reaper shrugged, then winced.

'You OK?' Amos asked.

'As ever,' Reaper said.

'She should go up before we start,' Amos said, looking at Liza.

Liza started to rise.

'Sit down,' Reaper told her.

'Is that a good idea?' Amos asked.

'Ms Plain is my chosen witness. She may as well stay for this.'

'Can I start broadcasting again?' Liza asked. 'He took away the camera and backpack.'

'Not just yet.' Reaper turned to Amos. 'I have no concerns about her cooperation. Not with all those hostages upstairs.'

Another threat hitting home.

No one safe yet.

And clearly no surprise to Reaper that Amos had confiscated the equipment before the robbery, which really begged the question as to why she'd been taken along, though maybe just having a hostage along made for additional insurance in case of trouble . . .

'I'll go get Joel,' Amos said.

The phone was still ringing as he left.

'What about Mr Osborn?' Liza said.

'Enough,' Reaper said.

And took the phone off the hook.

Joel came down alone, and Liza was able to study his face more closely, saw lines and contours probably driven south by disappointment and bitterness, saw bleak eyes, showing no hint of pleasure on seeing the money.

A doctor unfairly robbed of his career in the AIDS-fearful years.

Not a good enough reason for *this*, Liza thought again now. Nothing a good enough reason.

Not even Michael's car crash of a life.

She watched Reaper organize his share, place a huge amount of cash in a buff-colored envelope

and hand it over, remembered Joel, clearly distraught, trying to help after the Grace Glover
tragedy. Yet after that, he'd gone on doing Reaper's
bidding, and now, hours later, he was taking a large
chunk of what had been stolen from Bill Osborn
– and she was trying not to think about him because
there was nothing she could do, and he might
already be beyond help.

'It's been a pleasure.' Reaper shook Joel's hand.
'Time for you to go now.'

'I'm not leaving,' Joel said.

'Sure you are.'

'Once the others go, there'll just be you and
Isaiah, and if the hostages get the upper hand and
try storming the doors, I don't like anyone's
chances, so I'm staying.'

'The deal was you get out safely with your cut,'
Reaper said.

'I don't care any more if I get out or not,' Joel
said. 'I'd like it if the cash could reach the right
people, but I care more about Whirlwind. About
you.'

Reaper said nothing.

'I've written down the charities' names.' Joel
opened one of his zip pockets, took out a piece
of paper and held it out.

Reaper didn't take it.

'You're sure about this?' he asked. 'You understand what might happen?'

'Death or prison,' the other man said flatly. 'But
I'd still be grateful if my cut could get through,
help a few people.'

Reaper took the piece of paper. 'I'll do my best
for you.'

'I know you will,' Joel said. 'I trust you, sir.'

Sir.

The word hung in the air, seeming to Liza to embody the power that this man still held over those he'd dragged into this nightmare.

Joel started out of the office, then stopped.

'I'll see you up there,' he said, 'when the others have gone.'

'When we're all done,' Reaper said.

'And then we'll make the doors safe, and let them go,' Joel said.

Craving reassurance, Liza thought.

'As planned,' Reaper said.

The man lingered in the doorway.

'Anything more I can do for you?' he asked Reaper.

'Nothing. Thank you, Joel.'

Jeremiah, next one down, had no qualms about leaving. He accepted his cut, secured it beneath his clothes, removed his balaclava, stared at Liza as if daring her to identify him later at her peril. Which she would, she decided, no matter what, certain that she'd always recognize those darting, resentful eyes.

He left the way she and the others had earlier, Liza hearing the trapdoor open and close in the archive room, and she guessed that Jeremiah would be heading to the intersecting tunnel down which Nemesis had disappeared, taking his chances along with his blood money.

'Interesting group, don't you think?' Reaper asked Liza after he'd gone.

She didn't answer.

Another matter having just sprung forcefully back into her mind.

The unanswered question she'd asked twice earlier.

'Thomas Pike,' she said again now, knowing she was crazy to raise this again, but unable to stop herself.

Her mind flipped back to something she'd been taught about using journalism to help people in jeopardy. About deciding whether to simply report or, in certain circumstances, to get involved. Probably the best way for her to deal with her suspicion that Reaper might have taken some kind of revenge on the retired vicar (maybe even on those other missing people, which was quite a stretch and one she *really* didn't want to contemplate) was to keep herself safe and pass on her thoughts to the FBI at the first opportunity.

Except, what if she did not make it out?

Get the facts.

'Are you behind Pike's disappearance?' she asked.

He smiled. 'You have guts, Ms Plain. I admire that.'

'Did you do something to him?'

She heard the door at the foot of the stairs open and close.

'She being a nuisance again?' Amos asked.

Reaper smiled again. 'Just doing her job.'

'Want me to deal with her?' Amos asked.

Liza's mouth was suddenly dry as dust.

'No need for that,' Reaper said.

Amos shrugged. 'Your call.'

* * *

289

He received more than the other two men had, she noted. Double, she estimated. Probably his reward for the robbery, or maybe Amos had helped with more than that, maybe there was some other connection between him and Reaper.

Unlike Jeremiah, Amos did not remove his balaclava in Liza's presence.

She thought she'd know him though, if it ever came to that, would not quickly forget what she'd seen of him before he'd donned the mask. The shaven head, the intimidating expression, the strange green-brown eyes which she'd seen close-up before, during and since their visit to Shiloh Oaks.

'If you need me again,' Amos said to Reaper, just before he left, 'you know where to find me.'

'I won't trouble you again,' Reaper told him. 'But I thank you, Amos. It couldn't have happened without you.'

'It's been a pleasure.' Amos turned to the door.

'Are you going the same route as Nemesis?' Liza asked.

'How many more times?' Amos said. 'Mind your own fucking business.'

'Manners, Amos,' Reaper rebuked mildly. 'Just doing her job, remember.'

The big man shrugged again and went without another word.

Now what?

Clem Carson, relieved from phone duty but still in Shiloh, awaiting updated orders, had learned that an off-duty patrolman in the Glocester PD had called in some info that might turn out to be gold dust.

Seemed the guy had read someplace that there were tunnels under the village. He didn't know where they began or ended, but he was pretty sure that the tunnels were seriously old – as, of course, was St Matthew's. So Providence and the State Police were on the case, kicking people out of their beds, urgently seeking survey reports, zoning plans or old maps.

Not easy before sunrise on December 25.

And even if the right people were found and ordered to open up their offices, even if the worst of the blizzard had given way to heavy snow, the forecast for it to become lighter, the fact was that the son of a bitch running this show had stayed true to his word about not answering the phone again. No negotiation never good news.

Which left a church filled with exhausted, terrorized, possibly sick hostages, one family grieving for their child and everyone at the mercy of Whirlwind, a name that had not shown up on a single Bureau database.

Four key players inside St Matthew's unofficially identified.

The leader, Joshua Tilden, the man Carson had spoken to.

A second man, also self-identified as Michael Rider, who had a rap sheet and had been in the same psychiatric wing of Garthville as Tilden.

Liza Plain, a former Shiloh resident, who claimed that she'd been reporting at the insistence of the gang, using equipment provided by them.

And then there was John Tilden, apparently Reaper's father, who had, before the congregation

291

and anyone watching or hearing Plain's broadcast, confessed to a forty-year-old child murder.

Snipers in place now, tunnel plans awaited.

Not much else that could be safely done to end this thing till then.

Unless Whirlwind defused the explosives and came out with their hands up.

Clem Carson, for one, not anticipating that outcome.

Sixty-Eight

Now what?

Liza got her answer to that within seconds of hearing the trapdoor closing after Amos.

'I have a big favor to ask of you, Ms Plain.'

She looked at Reaper across the desk, said nothing.

'There's little likelihood of my leaving this place a free man. Death or prison, as Joel said.' He picked up the single sheet of paper from the desk, and held it out to her. 'His preferred charities.'

Liza took it, saw through eyes suddenly so tired that they hurt, the former doctor's shortlist: *American Foundation for Children with AIDS. Bailey House. Keep A Child Alive.*

'Fine choices.' She tried to hand it back, but Reaper held up his hands, palms out, so she placed it back on the desk. 'What's the favor?'

Though she already knew.

'It seems to me you're the only person here who could get Joel's cash out to the right places. Luke's cut too, if possible, which I know he wanted split between his parents and other Iraq veterans.'

'This money belongs to William Osborn.'

'This money actually belongs to a great many other people, none of whom are ever going to be identified or even looking for it,' Reaper said. 'I'd hate to think that Luke gave his life for nothing, and we both know what Joel wants.'

'They made their choices when they joined you.'

'Still,' Reaper said. 'Good causes.'

'An old man was *bludgeoned* to get that cash,' Liza said.

'Regrettable, but necessary.'

'It was not necessary, it was brutal, and is it *necessary* to refuse to get him help now?'

'He'll get help when this is over.'

Anger was making her shake. 'I'm not doing one more damned thing for you – other than transmitting again, telling people out there what's happening.' Frustration goaded her on. 'And you still haven't answered my question about Thomas Pike.'

'This is your last chance to help decent people.' Reaper was cooler. 'This money is tainted, Ms Plain. Whatever happens, it won't go to any kind of worthy recipient unless you say yes.'

'I've given my answer.'

'Because we're criminals,' Reaper said.

Liza's laugh was short and bitter. 'Understatement.'

'You heard my story. Don't you feel sympathy for me?'

She looked him in the eye. 'I feel sympathy for the boy you were back then.'

'Don't you think I've had a hard life?'

She didn't answer, too busy asking herself why she felt this need to keep on pushing when she knew how potentially dangerous it might be.

But the fact was she had to know.

'Where is he?' she asked. 'Where is Reverend Pike?'

Moments passed, and Liza noticed the tremor in his right hand.

'Are you OK?' she asked.

His eyes looked different, the pupils larger.

'You want to know about Pike,' he said.

'Yes,' she said.

Though she was suddenly intensely unsure if she did want to know.

Reaper rose, slowly.

'Put on your jacket, Ms Plain, and wait here.'

He turned left outside the office and Liza heard the sound of keys.

Stared at the phone, still off the hook.

She put out her hand – but heard him coming back.

Quickly, she put on her parka, zipped it up, felt for her gloves, then remembered that she'd dropped them in Osborn's library.

He was holding the backpack and camera, held them out. 'You need help?'

'Only connecting the cable to the camera.' Liza slipped her arms through the straps. 'Feels tight with the parka.'

Reaper adjusted the straps. 'Better?'

She hated his closeness. 'Yes.'

He handed her the camera, made the cable connection, and then he bent, reached beneath Keenan's desk and, with some effort, brought out another backpack and put it on, and Liza could see now that he was in pain.

'Can I help?' she asked.

He smiled, picked up his cane with his left hand and the shotgun with his right.

Liza saw that the tremor had ceased.

'You're about to,' he said.

'Where are we going?'

Though she thought she already knew, the prospect terrifying.

'Is my grandfather OK?' she asked, playing for time.

'Perfectly,' Reaper said.

'And Michael?'

'Don't worry about Isaiah,' Reaper said. 'You go first, Ms Plain.' He gave her a gentle nudge with the shotgun. 'You know the way. Back to the archive room.'

'I don't want to go down there again,' she said.

'If you want to record, you should probably use the shoulder strap for the camera.'

'You really want me to report this?' She allowed herself a tiny surge of hope.

'You're the journalist.'

'You think it'll work down there?'

'Time will tell,' Reaper said.

In the nave, Michael paced, watched, waited and listened.

The telephone below had ceased ringing, was probably off the hook since he doubted that the FBI would have stopped calling.

Only two of them up here now, though Joel's return a while back had touched him, but still, he was beginning to feel overwhelmed by tiredness and lack of food. And fear.

Less for himself than for everyone else here, and, increasingly, for Liza.

His shame piling ever higher, his personal motivation for this crime no longer remotely comprehensible to him.

He thought that something was going on, back in the eighth and ninth rows, something to do with the two kids Amos had dealt with earlier. The one with red hair and the one with the ear stud were sitting closer together now than they had been, the general sense of listlessness apparently not affecting them, and Michael had noticed too that, while the choir, deacon and altar server were all sleeping, Nowak, the organist, had become jumpier.

Those three planning something, he was almost certain, making him very apprehensive. Because if they did try jumping him or Joel any time soon, Michael was as certain as he could be that neither he nor Joel would fire a single shot. Which meant that the kids and Nowak would probably seize their weapons, and then Christ only knew what might happen, because next step, they'd be looking for a way out, which meant they'd probably head down below.

Reaper was armed too, would not let them leave without a fight.

And Liza was with him.

He walked down the aisle, scanning left and right, reached the front, saw that John Tilden, the murderer, was asleep, his wife's back to him, her eyes following Michael's every move.

He wondered what Eleanor Tilden saw, found

it hard to imagine her pain, her world shattered, learning that she was married to a monster. Not that the Tildens or the wrongs perpetrated against his family were at the forefront of Michael's thoughts right now. Not even the uprising he felt might be coming.

Almost all his thoughts were for Liza.

His fear for her growing with every passing quarter-hour, because though he'd been deeply uneasy about Reaper's apparently last-minute decision to use her as reporter-cum-witness for everything, right down to the robbery and division of spoils, all that had to have been done with by now.

So what the hell was *happening* down there with her and Reaper?

An interview, perhaps. Liza's first major exclusive. Not impossible.

Michael had been trying to remember what she'd asked Reaper before he'd dispatched her to the undercroft, and now it came back to him. Something about the missing former vicar, her implication seeming to be that Reaper might know something about that disappearance.

Good question, perhaps, and one which Reaper had chosen not to answer, and Michael hoped to Christ she hadn't persisted with that.

Alone down there with an armed, sick man.

A man capable of organizing this madness.

Michael wanted to go down to the undercroft, to check on them.

On *her*.

But he could not leave the nave, could not leave Joel.

He looked at Liza's grandfather and saw that the old man was staring back at him.

Accusation in his eyes.

Michael didn't blame him.

Sixty-Nine

Back in the dark, Liza's teeth were chattering with cold and fear.

Going somewhere.

Not allowing herself to think where or to what.

She'd tried to start recording again once she'd climbed down, Reaper behind her, but her fingers were icy and she'd been shaking too badly to hold the camera still, so she'd stuffed it into her parka's right-hand pocket, and it wasn't so much a case of reporting now rather than of trying to alert someone to her whereabouts.

Please come find me.

Send help.

The only light was coming from behind her, from Reaper's flashlight, tucked into his belt, the man with the shotgun slow, but keeping her moving, with no chance of retreat, and it occurred to her that if she suddenly accelerated, ran ahead of him to Shiloh Oaks, where Osborn might still be alive, maybe they could lie in wait together for the sick man lagging behind . . .

Though if she left Reaper too far behind, she'd be in absolute darkness, so the odds of her finding the spiral steps up to the big house were worse than poor, and if she got lost down here, fell down, hurt herself – just the *thought* made her want to scream.

Besides which, if she ran, Reaper would probably shoot her.

'Where are we going?' Her voice sounded scared, hollow.

'To Pike,' he answered.

Her heart seemed to flip over in her chest.

'You took him.'

'Obviously,' he said. 'Keep on walking.'

He was breathless, and she could hear a wheezing, different from Osborn's, almost a creaking sound in this man's throat and chest, and maybe, if she was incredibly lucky, he might collapse, might *die*. She wished for that suddenly, had never wished for anyone's death before, though collapse would be enough, would be *better*, because then he'd have to answer for what he'd done . . .

'I know these tunnels very well.' His voice echoed spookily. 'I've known them most of my life.'

'When you were a boy?' she asked.

'When I was a boy who believed that the Angel of the Lord was speaking to me.'

She thought she heard a dreamier quality in his tone, and maybe she should try keeping him there, in the past . . .

'You came down here then?' she asked.

'As often as I could.'

She waited, but he didn't elaborate.

'How come?' she asked.

'You have to realize that I wasn't the same person then, Ms Plain. I'd say that I was probably a rather sweet, deeply religious boy who adored his mother and had good reason to dislike and fear his father. That boy loved Bible stories, but John Tilden disapproved, made the boy's mother's life wretched over it, so the boy needed a place of his own, where he felt safe, could be himself.'

The switch to third person was fascinating, even in these circumstances, and Liza realized abruptly that she should be recording this, and as smoothly as she could, she put her numb right hand into her pocket, felt for the camera's red button and pressed it, could only hope that the built-in mike would pick up his voice, because for one thing, this was evidence, and for another, it was the most extraordinary interview she was ever likely to undertake.

'How did you know about the tunnels?' she asked.

'Stop a moment, please.' Reaper's breathlessness was worse. 'I need to rest.'

She stopped, turned. 'Are you OK?'

'Never better.' He leaned heavily on his cane, went on talking. 'The boy was in Saint Matthew's one day when his mother was praying – she'd pray for hours sometimes, and though he was religious, he was still just a boy, so he got bored, went exploring. He knew about the undercroft – everyone did – and that day he went down there, and no one was around, and he was inquisitive as well as bored, so he wandered into the archive room, kicked at a rug, discovered a trapdoor and opened it.'

'And went down? Just like that?'

'Not that day, but once he knew it was there,

he felt drawn by it. And one afternoon, not long after, he went into church with his pocket flashlight, hid until the vicar had gone out, opened the trapdoor, used a wedge of paper to keep the hatch open, found the ladder and climbed down.'

'Wasn't he scared?'

'Only once, when he thought he was lost, but he prayed for help and found his way back, and after that he knew why he'd been sent there. It was his place to pray and read the Bible without John Tilden knowing, without his mother getting yelled at or slapped. So next time, he went back with two candles and matches, and that was when he found his actual *place*. It made him think of the tomb, the sepulcher that Christ had lain in before his resurrection. It was perfect.'

He took a breath, and his cough came.

'Damn it.' He coughed harder, then cleared his throat and straightened up. 'Onward, Ms Plain.'

They began moving again, and Liza wondered if he could hear the faint sound of the camera working in her pocket, maybe even see its red light.

'He had to stop coming down for a very long time, after they put him away,' he went on. 'But he never forgot it, and so, when he got out of the Ames, and after he attacked the vicar at that other church and went on the run, he came to the obvious place.'

'Back here.'

'I think he hoped it might give him peace, help to restore his faith, and briefly he even wondered if the Angel had sent him on a long detour via the

301

Ames. But he had to be practical, had to eat, find a way to survive, so after he'd rested a while, when he knew it was the middle of the night, he went back up to the street and helped himself to food from the garbage outside his father's restaurant. And a dog started barking, and the vicar had reported the assault, and the Ames had alerted John Tilden, so when the dog woke him, he called the cops.'

Reaper paused again.

'And that was the very end of the boy who believed in angels.'

Above ground, in the nave, limbo was continuing to take its toll.

Eddie Leary, Mitch Roper and Stan Nowak were side by side now in the ninth row, had made their latest move after Stephen Plain had finally joined forces with Keenan, organizing makeshift 'bathroom' arrangements, utilizing basins and vessels stored beneath a cloth-covered table in the narthex; and neither Michael nor Joel had raised objections, and people were now waiting in line in the south-west corner, those nearing the front turning their backs to give an illusion of privacy.

Michael had noted the young men's move, had decided that splitting them up again might lead to altercation, perhaps even to another tragedy, so he was just leaving them be, keeping an eye on them, and had advised Joel to do the same.

Limbo wearing thin now all over.

Seventy

'I didn't come back down here again for years,' Reaper told Liza.

'Till you got out of Garthville,' Liza said.

'It was long before that,' he said.

She realized then that he'd moved back to first person, had left young Joshua Tilden behind, and if she weren't so afraid, Liza knew she would be riveted.

'Stop, please,' he said.

She turned, saw that he was leaning more heavily on his cane.

'I carved myself a quite bearable existence in Garthville,' he went on. 'I toughened up physically, earned myself a job working for the gardener. They grew vegetables at the prison and sold them to the public. We never got to taste them.'

Liza longed to sit down, the weird light making her unsteady.

'Film me, if you like,' Reaper said. 'I know you've been recording my voice.'

'Are you sure?'

'Just while we're taking this break.'

She organized the camera and he tilted his flashlight helpfully upward, lighting his face from below so that he resembled some Halloween creature.

'The gardener was lazy and greedy, very easy to play. It started out with him letting me fetch and carry, pick up heavy stuff outside. He'd give me his wheelbarrow and the keys to his truck, even the code for the entrance gate he used. He'd have been fired or worse if he'd been found out, but he thought I was naïve and liked having a dumb, unpaid helper. He sent me for compost, plants, bricks, pizza, whatever he wanted. If I got caught or gave him up, he said he'd deny everything, say I'd stolen his keys and the truck and the code, and no one would believe me.'

'So you got to go out,' Liza said after a moment.

'I started running my own little errands, got myself a thieving sideline. Money's important in places like Garthville. I always brought him gifts: cash, a few cigars, something for his wife, left them under the spare tire in the truck. It kept him on side and left me enough to buy what I needed, even to save a little. He got nervous the first time I was gone a little longer, but we worked things out so I just had to be back for room checks. Security was lax back then, some of the guards bribable, but I always took care to make it back on time.'

He paused for breath.

'So did you ever come back here while you were out?' Liza asked.

'Oh, yes.'

She waited.

'I earned access to the library, mapped out my missions there, calculated how long I'd need to reach a destination, then get here – to my place, which you'll get to see for yourself soon – then get back to base before the gardener gave me up or had a stroke.'

304

'What kind of destinations?'

'Churches, mostly. Houses, sometimes.'

'To steal from?'

'Mostly.'

She saw his smile curve meanly, felt a terrible, creeping sensation.

'What else?' she asked.

'You'll see,' he said. 'Stop recording now, please.'

'I'd like to hear more,' she said.

'Don't be selfish, Ms Plain. Think of your grandfather and the others, waiting.'

She held onto that, told herself it meant they would, ultimately, be going back, and he waited and watched while she turned off the camera, and on they went.

Not very far this time.

She knew before they stopped again where he was taking her.

The tunnel Nemesis had counted as fifth from Shiloh Oaks.

The tunnel with the worst stench.

She thought she realized now what the stink was.

Wanted, desperately, to be wrong.

Tried, and failed, to block it up at the back of her mind.

Pike.

'My heart!' Patty Jackson cried out suddenly. 'I think I'm having a heart attack!'

Her stricken voice cut through the semi-dozing mood in the nave, made people all over sit up, alarmed.

'Mom?' She turned to Ann Jackson, both hands clenched in the center of her chest. 'Pain. *Real* bad.'

Across the aisle, one row along, Stephen Plain stood, looked around, found Michael Rider. 'May I?'

'Please,' Michael said. 'Go.'

'*Oh*,' Patty Jackson said, and collapsed against her mother.

'Patty!' Mark Jackson jumped up. 'Oh, my God!'

'All right,' Stephen said. 'Let's get her lying down in the aisle.'

Jackson carried his daughter from the pew and laid her down.

Stephen knelt, put his cheek to the middle-aged woman's mouth. 'She's breathing.' He put two fingers to her neck, checked his wristwatch and concentrated.

'Is she OK, Doc?' Jackson asked.

'Quiet please, I'm taking her pulse.' Stephen paused. 'OK, she's back.'

Patty was white-faced, staring up at them. 'What happened?'

'You're OK.' Ann Jackson was kneeling too, stroked her hair. 'The doctor's going to take care of you.'

'Patty, can you describe the pain?' Stephen asked her gently.

'I don't know,' she said, still scared. 'Bad.'

'Is it just in your chest or anywhere else?'

'Not in my arm,' she told him. 'In my back, though.'

'Panic attack?' Rosie Keenan had come from the front and asked the question softly.

'Possibly not.' Stephen twisted around to face Michael, behind them in the aisle. 'She needs to get out of here.'

'Not possible,' Michael said. 'I'm sorry.'

'Of course you are.' Stephen turned back to the patient. 'I'm just going to listen to your heart, Patty, OK?' He bent low, rested his right ear against her chest. 'I know this seems a little strange, but with no stethoscope . . .'

'It's OK,' she whispered.

'Just be still and quiet for a few moments.'

He listened for a while, then straightened up. 'I think you're going to be fine.' He turned back to Michael. 'But we really do need to get her out.'

'You people wired those doors, you son of a bitch.' Mark Jackson's face was scarlet. 'You must know how to defuse them.'

'Just one door,' his wife said. 'Please.'

'I don't know any more about those wires than you do,' Michael said.

'Doc,' Joel said, feet away. 'Can I help at all?'

'Don't you even *think* about touching my daughter,' Jackson snarled.

'I'd like to give Patty an aspirin,' Stephen said.

'Does anyone have any aspirin?' Michael's voice was loud and clear.

'I do.' Rosie ran back to where she'd left her purse.

'Is the pain any easier, Patty?' Stephen asked.

'A little.'

'Here.' Rosie came running back.

'Good.' Stephen took the tablet, then gave it to Patty. 'I want you to chew this. It's bitter, but don't swallow it, just chew.' He smiled at her. 'I think this might just be some kind of reaction to all this upset, Patty, but it might possibly be angina.'

'Not a heart attack?' Ann Jackson asked.

'I don't think so.' Stephen kept his voice low. 'Hard to be sure. We need an ECG and other tests. But for now, Patty needs to be kept calm and quiet.'

'Hear that?' Mark Jackson marched up to Joel. '*Hear* that, you scum?'

'I'm not the one yelling,' Joel said, and walked away.

'Don't you turn your back on me!'

'Mark, stop it,' his wife pleaded. 'You're just making things worse.'

Michael and Joel crossed in the aisle, eyes searching around, both edgy and vigilant, shotguns gripped, and Joel stopped. 'I'm not going to have another death on my conscience, Isaiah.' His voice was low but desperate. 'We need to get Reaper up here, get him to open a door so we can at least get her out.'

'I'm not sure he'll do that,' Michael said.

'We have to try. You have to talk to him.'

Michael knew that Joel was right, and he'd been burning to get down below, to find out what the *hell* was taking so long, to make sure, more than anything, that Liza was safe. Now he glanced around. 'You'll be on your own.'

'I don't care. Just tell Reaper I won't let another innocent person die, *tell* him.'

'What's happening?' Keenan had come up behind Michael.

'Joel wants me to persuade Reaper to let the sick woman out.'

'What if he won't agree?' the vicar asked.

'Then I'll get a door open myself,' Joel said.

'You know how to do that?' Keenan asked.

'He does not,' Michael said. 'Don't do anything nuts, Joel.'

'He won't,' Keenan said. 'I won't let him. You go, Michael.'

It felt crazily good to hear the vicar use his real name.

'Just *go*,' Joel echoed.

Michael turned, headed for the undercroft door.

His mind flying now, his thoughts more mixed up, more *screwed* up, than ever.

Only two things he was sure of.

He had to find a way to end this madness.

And find Liza.

Seventy-One

'Turn around, Ms Plain,' Reaper told Liza.

'What for?' A quiver of dread shook her voice.

'Just do it.'

She turned.

'I've decided I want you to hear my confession.'

'Me?' she said, shaken. 'I'm not a priest.'

'I wouldn't confess to a priest,' he said. 'In fact, I never imagined I'd have any interest in confessing to anyone, but as tonight has moved along, I find that I do want to. And here you are.'

'At gunpoint,' she said.

'True. But will you hear it?'

'Not if I have a choice.'

'You're a journalist. You must want to hear it.'

'I'm a human being. I'm your prisoner.'

'Nevertheless, you are here, and what I'm going to tell you and *show* you is most definitely news-worthy.' Reaper paused. 'And clearly you are still a journalist, because otherwise you wouldn't have accepted this assignment.'

'I accepted it so that I could tell the outside world what was happening,' Liza said. 'I didn't bargain on this.'

'You don't know what *this* is yet.'

Fatigue hit her again, like a truck, took any vestige of courage with it.

'That's how I'd rather keep it,' she said.

'I'm sorry,' he said. 'But you don't get to choose now.'

She stared at him, fought to gather back a little strength.

'What is that terrible smell?' she asked.

Though she knew.

'I don't smell it anymore,' Reaper said. 'They say you can grow accustomed to almost anything. It does seem to be true.'

Ask it.

'Is it Pike?' she asked.

'Will you hear my confession, Liza Plain?'

'You can tell me whatever you want,' she said, 'but it won't give you absolution.'

'I gave up hoping for absolution a very long time ago,' Reaper said.

And smiled.

* * *

310

They were not in the office, or anywhere in the undercroft.

Neither Liza nor Reaper.

'Christ,' Michael muttered, and went on looking around.

The fire exit at the end of the narrow corridor was still wired, the door leading to the parish hall still locked – was usually kept locked, Michael remembered reading in the notes on the scale drawings, unless some church event was going on.

Which meant they had to have gone down. Reaper had *taken* Liza down there into the tunnel system through which Michael knew that the others had fled – and was it possible, it struck him now, that their leader had taken her as insurance for his own escape, a hostage in case the FBI knew about the tunnels?

No easy way of finding out exactly where they were. No cell phones, no radios, no means of contact; simplicity keeping the mission safer, Reaper had insisted. Nothing that might draw attention before 'Revelation', nothing to aid law enforcement after.

Evidence of the robbery lay on the desk in the vicar's office. Three large, buff-colored, cash-stuffed envelopes: one marked with a bold 'J', one 'L' (the dead man's cut), one 'M'.

Reaper had described the theft to Michael as a redistribution of ill-gotten gains, and Michael had said he wanted no part of it, but Reaper had clearly left a cut for him anyway.

Michael looked at the fat envelope now, recognized that it had to be a life-changing sum of money, remembered the dead child upstairs and knew, with a small sense of relief, that he had not changed his mind.

The phone on Keenan's desk was off the hook, as he'd guessed.

Lives on the line here. Depending on what he did next.

He made up his mind. Put the receiver back.

The phone rang and he picked up, spoke rapidly, gave the man on the line no chance to speak, identified himself, described Patty Jackson's possible heart attack and the need to get her out as soon as possible. Said that the longer this rolled on, the greater the likelihood that someone might do something crazy, that they needed to find a way of ending this without more bloodshed. Said that at this moment, there was only one armed man in the nave, a man he was almost certain would willingly lay down his weapon in the name of commonsense. Said that all the exits were still wired.

'But there are no wires on or around the stained-glass windows,' Michael told the man. 'And the windows center of the north and south walls are some distance from the wired doors, but I have no idea what the explosives are, or how sensitive they might be.'

He took a breath and the negotiator dove in.

'Mr Rider—'

'Patty Jackson needs to get out soon,' Michael said, and put down the phone.

Considered the fact that he had just betrayed Reaper, a sick old man who had probably descended to this madness because of his own father's betrayal.

But Reaper appeared to have gone, maybe for good, and Liza had to be with him.

Something terribly wrong about that.

The phone started ringing again but Michael ignored it, picked up the vicar's chair, carried it to the door at the bottom of the steps up to the nave and jammed it beneath the handle. Not much of a barricade, but something to slow the cops down at least briefly if they came this way.

Not ready to face the law yet, perhaps not ever.

He wavered. If he took the time to go up now, to bring Joel and Keenan up to speed, maybe give Joel a last chance to come down and escape through the tunnels, all hell would very likely break loose, with possibly catastrophic consequences.

And Liza was missing.

Right or wrong, that suddenly seemed to transcend all other considerations.

Decision made.

He unzipped one of his jacket pockets, and took out his flashlight.

Went looking for the trapdoor.

Seventy-Two

'So,' Liza said, 'this confession. Will you let me record it? I don't know if it will transmit or not from here.'

'You can record,' Reaper said. 'Though I'd ask you not to be specific as to our whereabouts.'

313

'Is that "ask" as in you'll shoot me if I do tell them?'

'Perhaps,' Reaper said. 'Though I'd probably be gone before they reached us.'

'The way Nemesis went?' Liza asked. 'And I'm presuming the others.'

'Perhaps,' Reaper said again.

He leaned his right shoulder against the rough tunnel wall, the backpack in the way.

'Maybe you'd be more comfortable taking that off for a while?' she said.

'It's fine,' he said shortly. 'May I begin?'

She blew on her fingers, trying to warm them, checked the microphone, then raised the camera.

'Go ahead.'

'The first thing you need to understand, Ms Plain,' Reaper said, 'is that I have, for the most part, been in control of the wicked things I've done. I have become, over time, devoid of conscience. I don't know if I'm a sociopath, but I am a psychopath, though I don't believe that was always the case.'

'You mean when you were still "the boy",' she said, her heart beating faster.

'Do you plan to interrupt often?' Reaper enquired.

'As little as possible. Just when I need something clarified. For the record.'

'Yes,' he said. 'When I was still young Joshua, I was a true innocent. Since those days, however, I have been subjected to imprisonment, electro-convulsive therapy, force-feeding, anti-psychotic drugs of all kinds, beatings and rape. All of which I survived physically, but I suppose it would be fair to say that my psyche, such as it was, was shot.'

314

No actual confession yet, more self-justification, Liza thought, with a sense of being on a precipice, horrors yet to come.

'After that, whenever I saw a church, I felt cold dread, and when I saw any kind of minister, I saw evil and ugliness.' He paused. 'Bear in mind, Ms Plain, that such experiences were very rare because I was locked away most of the time.' He coughed, shifted his position, kept his grip on the shotgun, his gaze on Liza, and went on coughing.

'Can I do anything?' she asked, wishing again that he would collapse.

He shook his head, and in another moment, the fit reduced in intensity, then stopped.

'There's some blood,' Liza said.

He didn't flinch, just raised his right arm, his shotgun arm, wiped his sleeve across his mouth, nodded, then gave a slight smile.

'Where was I?'

'You said you were locked away,' she said.

He nodded again. 'In the Garthville library, I read about little Alice Millicent and felt surprised that Cromwell had been charged. Because even though I knew he'd helped put me away, and I hadn't ever really known him, I couldn't picture him as a child killer.'

Another cough erupted, but he controlled it, sped up.

'When I was first on the run, a young man, I came here and was staggered by the safety and empowerment these tunnels gave me. I could be invisible, move around beneath the village. I found it easy to get my bearings, to map mentally, find my way up to John Tilden's restaurant . . .'

The words tailed off, and then, suddenly, he asked: 'Would you like to see my place now?'

Her heart seemed to fly up into her throat.

'I'd rather you went on with your story,' she said.

'But I haven't actually confessed to anything yet, and when I do we will need to be *there*, because, as I think I've told you, it was always very special, even to the boy.'

'One more question first,' Liza said, desperate for delay. 'Why have you wanted all of this recorded?'

'For justice, as I've said.'

'For Donald Cromwell.'

'I never lost sleep over Cromwell, though I have enjoyed the notion of getting posthumous justice for Isaiah's sake.' Reaper paused. 'The real justice I've sought is for the boy who spoke to angels.'

'What about Cromwell's wife and daughter?'

'Stop time-wasting, Ms Plain,' he said. 'My place beckons.'

The stench seemed to wrap itself around Liza's head, choking her.

'I can't breathe this air,' she said, faintly.

'You'd be amazed,' Reaper said, 'what you can do.'

Michael had fallen down.

Less than twenty yards, give or take, from the foot of the ladder, his hunt for Liza barely begun, he'd tripped over an old broken brick, lost his footing and gone down hard.

He'd cursed and tried to get up, but he'd injured his right knee, and it seemed at first that it wouldn't hold him, but he doubted that it was fractured, and anyway, this was a case of mind over matter, because he had no choice.

So he'd gotten himself up and limped on. The pain was nothing, *nothing* compared with what he'd done to those people up in that church, nothing compared to the death of a *child*. Nothing compared with what he'd done to Liza, and yes, it was Reaper who'd brought her down here, but if anything bad, anything *worse*, happened to her, it was on Michael Rider's head, and no one else's.

But the fall had slowed him right down, and every time he tried speeding up, the knee gave way again, so he was having to maintain a slower pace, was using the shotgun now as a makeshift cane, keeping his fingers well clear of the trigger.

'I'm coming,' he told Liza under his breath.

And limped on in the dark.

Things going real slowly up in the nave of St Matthew's, too.

More waiting for everyone, but especially for Keenan and Joel, because Rider hadn't come back yet, and they didn't know what was happening down below, but Joel knew about the tunnels, and loyalty to Reaper was starting to stretch a little thin, because that woman might be very sick, and there were limits . . .

He didn't see them coming.

They came fast and hard. Leary, Roper and Nowak, adrenalin in motion, all iron fists and kicking boots; and Joel was on the ground in an instant, no fight in him, his arms instinctively shielding his head, and Nowak snatched his shotgun, brandished it in the air, and women nearby were screaming hysterically.

'Please!' Keenan was running toward them.

'Stop it!' Rosie pleaded, horrified.

'Mind he doesn't bleed on you,' Mark Jackson shouted.

'For the love of God, be quiet, you *ignorant* man,' Gwen Turner told him.

'You're lucky we don't kill you,' Eddie Leary told the man on the ground.

'We need to tie him up,' Roper said.

'No one is tying anyone up,' Keenan said. 'That man wants to end this as much as we do. He wants to help your daughter, Mr Jackson.'

'Sorry, Rev, we're not letting him go,' Eddie Leary told him, gasping, as Adam Glover, joining the fray, took off his belt and gave it to Roper to bind Joel's wrists. 'Give me yours, for his ankles,' he told Nowak.

'Not his ankles,' Keenan protested. 'I told you, he wants to *help*, and he has to be able to walk if anything happens.'

'The vicar's right,' Nowak said, and held out the shotgun to Keenan. 'You'd better take this.'

'I'm a vicar, not a sheriff,' Keenan said angrily.

Three pews nearer the front, beside his folded wheelchair, the former sheriff shook his head and closed his eyes.

'Fuck's sake, take the goddamn gun, Vicar,' someone said.

'Is the safety on?' Keenan asked.

'I'm not sure,' Joel said from the floor.

Keenan took it, warily.

Someone whooped triumphantly.

318

'Better you hold on to it, Reverend, than anyone else,' Joel said.

'You shut the fuck up,' Leary told him.

'In case anyone's forgotten,' Adam Glover said, 'my daughter's lying dead and alone in the vicar's parlor.'

'And my husband's been missing for hours,' Freya Osborn added.

'My granddaughter, too,' Stephen said.

'Your granddaughter was having a ball,' Eddie Leary said.

'Don't be ridiculous,' Gwen Turner said. 'I'll bet our house she's the reason the FBI are out there.'

'Much good that's done us,' Jackson said.

'Patience,' Keenan said, and stepped forward to help Joel off the floor.

'Hey,' Roper said. 'Leave him where he is.'

Keenan ignored him, got the fallen man to his feet, looked at the young men and the organist, and held the shotgun high, barrel upward.

'I'm the man with the gun now,' he said. 'So please, all of you, sit down.'

He waited, marveled at their obedience, put his left arm around Joel and walked with him to the front.

'Mr Tilden,' he said to the killer in the front pew. 'Move up, please.'

'I don't want him next to me,' John Tilden said.

'Move *up*, you bastard,' his wife told him.

For one second, he stared at her, then he shifted across, and Joel sat down between him and Eleanor Tilden.

'Thank you,' Joel said to her.

'You're welcome,' she said.

'Now I, for one,' Keenan said, 'am going to pray.'

Seventy-Three

Reaper had lit candles in his *place* – seven white pillar candles that had been ready and waiting.

'Welcome,' he said.

And Liza knew for sure.

Not a fractured sewage pipe, that last vain hope quashed as she saw him.

She clamped her left hand over her nose and mouth, let out a great moan and felt her heart beating out of her chest.

Stared at the old man, tethered to a large wooden cross.

Naked, but for his stained gray shorts. His fragile arms tied to the crossbeam with thin rope, his withered legs fastened to the upright, and his head, too.

Not yet dead, Liza realized, an irregular fluttering visible in his bony chest.

'Not quite a conventional crucifixion,' Reaper said.

His voice came to Liza like eddies through thick, nauseating liquid.

'If his arms were his sole support, his head would have cut off breath, and he'd have asphyxiated long ago, and I didn't want that. He's had bread and a little water now and then.'

The remnants of a groan came from the man.

'Untie him.' Liza's voice was harsh.

'Not yet,' Reaper said. 'Soon.'

320

Liza tore her eyes from the man, and stared at his captor, his tormentor.

'You wanted to know,' Reaper said. 'You kept asking, over and over.'

'Give him water,' she said. 'Please.'

'No,' Reaper said. 'No more water.'

Rage engulfed Liza, impelled her forward, the camera dropping from her hands, dangling from its shoulder strap and the cable that still attached it to the device in her backpack.

'No.' Reaper stepped forward, stuck the snout of the shotgun between her and the gibbet. 'You're not here to save him, Ms Plain.'

Thomas Pike moaned.

Liza caught the stink that came from him, retched and took a step back, away from the man who had once been the vicar of St Matthew's. Anyone who could do this to another person would shoot her without hesitation, and she wanted to survive this, wanted to report this, needed people to *know*.

And then she saw Pike's chest more closely.

And his shoulders.

Looked up and saw his forehead.

She tried to speak, but had no words, and no courage left to say them anyway.

The old man had been branded, the wounds raw and seeping blood, pus and dirt, but no doubt as to their shape. Crosses burned into him.

'I've already told you what I am, Ms Plain,' Reaper said. 'A psychopath.'

'You're a monster,' Liza said, her voice returning.

'Man-made. At least partially.'

Liza forced her mind to begin working again.

'You said you wanted to make a confession. You can't confess your sins and keep him tied to *that*.'

'I shan't keep him there much longer,' Reaper said. 'Once he's finished, he'll be buried with the others.'

Others.

Liza shut her eyes, slammed a hand back over her mouth.

She had realized the instant she came close to Pike that the particular stench she'd smelled earlier, far stronger here, was not emanating from him. She was as sure as she could be what it was, though she had never previously experienced the stink of decomposed flesh.

No doubt about it now.

She turned, stumbled against the wall and threw up.

In the bar at the Shiloh Inn, one of the guests, a middle-aged part-time piano tuner whose work required, among other things, manual dexterity, had finally, after hours of struggling, managed to untie his own hands and remove his gag, had swiftly attended to his wife, and after her the duty manager; and pretty smartly after that, considering all they'd endured till then, all thirteen prisoners in the room had been freed.

That freedom still in question.

No one entirely sure when they'd last seen the two Halloween-masked gunmen who'd stayed to guard them after their colleagues had departed and the exits had been locked, bolted and rendered lethal to open – or so they had been told.

No one daring to venture out of the bar.

'If we stay in here,' the manager said, 'at least we're safe till help comes.'

'Unless they come back,' his wife said, and burst into tears.

'I think they've gone,' the manager said, and put his arms around her.

'But how could they have,' one of the guests, white-faced and trembling, asked, 'with the doors wired?'

'Maybe they're not wired,' the duty manager said.

'But maybe they *are*,' his wife said.

No one had heard so much as a floorboard creak for hours, they all agreed, but still, no one felt willing to take a chance, either of meeting the gunmen or getting blown up.

Meantime, the phone in the bar didn't work, and no one had a cell phone or tablet, and what they all cared about most was getting to a bathroom, but that meant venturing out of this *safe* room.

'I'm going to open the shutters,' the manager said. 'Take a look.'

'What if they see you?' his wife said.

'Everyone move to the far end,' her husband directed.

'For God's sake,' his wife said, 'be careful.'

He drew back the drapes a little way, took a breath, opened one of the shutters a crack, peered out and saw that the sun was rising.

'Holy guacamole,' he said. 'You never saw so much snow.'

'What else?' the piano tuner asked.

He went on peering.

'Something's going on,' he said, 'up at the church.'

Seventy-Four

'Pike was the last,' Reaper said. 'As seemed fitting. The final act of vengeance, if you like.'

Liza felt beyond speech again, knowing now that she was in the presence of an unfathomable insanity.

Her eyes having grown accustomed to the dim, flickering light, she had begun to search around for something, *anything* that might help her, knowing even as she hunted that there was no real possibility of escape. And though she had found nothing to help her, she had seen what lay beyond poor Pike on his gibbet.

Mounds of dirt, the size and shape of graves, roughly dug and filled.

Four that she could see, though there might be more.

'Seven altogether, Ms Plain,' Reaper said. 'A lamb in one, a man from Chopmist in another. But the one I regard as the true *first* lies in the third grave. A nun.'

The unsolved church-linked disappearances.

'I didn't find her in a church or even a convent. She was walking all alone along a quiet road while I was out one early evening in the gardener's truck. She seemed to have been placed there for me, and the Messenger took care of the rest.' He paused. 'The camera, Ms Plain, please. To record my confession.'

324

She fumbled for it, going through the motions mechanically, unsure if the settings would cope with the candlelight, or if the equipment was even working at all, and she remembered now that Nemesis had hot-swapped batteries a couple of times in the camera and gizmo, but even if it had ceased working, it seemed to comfort her just a little to have the camera back in her hands.

Who was the *messenger*? she wondered, but stayed silent.

'I brought her here, ended her life, buried her. It was swift for her, but for me, it was overwhelming. The boy had been long gone, but at those times I sometimes think the man was absent too, sucked into a vacuum while a stranger inhabited my skull—' He coughed once, then went on. 'I'm not claiming that it lived there independent of me – that would be nonsensical and dishonest. I've fed it over time, encouraged it, if you will.'

'If we untie Pike,' Liza said, her voice hoarse, 'it might help you.'

'The next was a woman from Foster,' Reaper went on. 'The Messenger and I were more organized that time. She'd been preparing the high altar in her church for Thanksgiving Eve. I've already told you how I planned my missions, made sure I'd have enough time to get back to Garthville. And the more lucrative I made things for my helper, the more he ensured my safe return to bed.'

'Was he the messenger?' Liza dared to ask. 'This gardener?'

Reaper's brittle laugh triggered another bout of coughing. 'No, as I told you, he was just a man who liked what I brought him. Not always from churches. Have I mentioned that I stole from the Shiloh Inn?'

'Your father's place.'

'John Tilden's place.' His voice had grown sandpaper rough. 'It amused me to be able to do that. I came a few times while he and wife number three were sleeping. They slept very soundly. Hard work, wine and whiskey. I stole cash, which the gardener appreciated most.'

'Was that when you found Alice Millicent's ribbon?' Liza said.

Reaper nodded absently. 'It was a young man next, an organist at a church in Nooseneck. His death was slower.' He shifted, tiring, leant on his cane, then pushed on. 'Then another woman from Primrose. I think she was a rector. She really wanted to die at the end.'

Liza looked past him again at the mounds, a little more strength returning to her, because the one worthwhile thing she could do for all those victims was to make sure they were found and their murderer identified. Which meant that, with no way of knowing if she'd been transmitting, she had to get *out*.

'Then the gardener got sick and I was stuck for a long time until he came back, and I got out again and found a man working in a church near Harmony. And then my good friend, the gardener, died.' Reaper smiled. 'Our partnership had lasted longer than many marriages.' He shrugged. 'And finally, as you can see for yourself, we have the once-Reverend Thomas Pike.'

Liza didn't allow herself to look back at the man on the cross.

'You said they let you out after they knew you were dying,' she said. 'Why not before? You were sharp enough to buy the gardener, do all that research. Couldn't you have persuaded them that you were sane, safe to release after so many years?'

'Maybe I didn't want to,' Reaper said. 'Until I was ready.'

'For this?' Liza said.

Reaper took a moment. 'Pike was more afraid than any of them had been. Especially after he realized who I was. I've kept him alive, which is very cruel, of course, but I wanted him to suffer, to understand what he'd done to the boy and, if you follow that line of thought, to these others too.' He paused. 'I'd considered bringing Reverend Keenan down here for my confession, but I knew he'd have tried to absolve me and I have no interest in that. You kept on asking about Pike, Ms Plain. I felt it only right to show you.'

A ghastly sound, part gurgle, part whimper, emanated from the dying man.

'Maybe, if you show compassion now' – she wanted to weep or maybe scream – 'after all the terrible things that were done to you—'

'No more,' Reaper cut her off, his voice echoing.

Liza changed tack swiftly. 'So who is the messenger?'

'Just a fiction of mine,' he answered flatly. 'Biblical angels were messengers. He seemed real to me for a long time, but later, I knew that I'd conjured him up.' He smiled again. 'Protecting myself, perhaps, from the full comprehension of my own depravity.'

He stopped talking, and Liza's heart began to pound again.

'So that's about it,' he said. 'My confession. All wrapped up.'

They both heard the sound.

Of someone coming.

Reaper raised his shotgun.

Seventy-Five

'Hey,' Michael called. 'It's Isaiah. I'm alone, Reaper.'

'Look to your right,' Reaper called. 'Narrow tunnel – you'll see candles.'

'Be right there,' Michael called back.

No more using his shotgun as a cane, aware that he might need it now, and that was slowing him down even more because his knee was painful as hell, not that it mattered.

Only one thing mattered now.

Getting Liza safely out.

He'd heard the last part of what Reaper had just called his 'confession'. Enough to have raised the hairs on the back of his neck and to finally give him a true idea of what he was really dealing with.

Nothing he could have dreamed of. Definitely nothing he was equipped for.

'Is Liza with you?' he called now, fully aware that she was.

The pale, flickering glow was just ahead on his right.

'I'm here,' she called back. 'I'm OK, but—'

She stopped too abruptly.

Reaper had stopped her.

Michael began edging closer. 'Liza?' he called.

'Come and join us, Isaiah,' Reaper's voice answered.

Michael turned the corner, walked a little way through the tunnel toward the dim light, and saw the man on the cross.

'Oh, good God.' Blood draining from his face, he stared around wildly for Liza, found her to his right, eyes huge and terrified, Reaper's gloved hand covering her mouth, his shotgun aimed at the side of her head, his cane on the ground, Liza's camera dangling from its cable. 'What the hell, Reaper?' His voice was almost even. 'Let her go.'

'Of course.' Reaper took his hand away. 'I didn't want her warning you off.'

'What about the gun?'

Reaper moved the shotgun's muzzle away from Liza's head but kept the weapon firmly gripped, its stock in his right armpit, finger on the trigger.

'I'm sorry, Ms Plain,' Reaper said, 'if that scared you.'

Liza took a shaky step away from him, watched him pick up his cane. 'That's Thomas Pike,' she told Michael quickly. 'Reaper's been killing people for years. There are graves down here. He's been *confessing* to me.'

Michael cast another look at the poor man on the cross, at the obscenity of it, recognized the stink all around them, had smelled it once in prison, knew it was death.

329

Then he looked back at Liza and shut down his own panic.

'I came to tell you what's happening in Saint Matthew's,' he said, easily, as if the evidence feet away was just a piece of fiction on a movie screen. 'One of the women got sick – possible heart attack. Dr Plain says she needs to go to a hospital. Joel says that's right, thinks we should open a door to let her out.' Another pause. 'I agree.'

'So Joel's given up?' Reaper asked. 'I thought he might.'

'Only so they can get that woman to safety.'

'Who is she?' Liza asked. 'The sick woman?'

'Patty Jackson.' Michael watched her face. 'You know her?'

'Not well,' Liza said. 'I'm glad they're going to try to get her out.'

'If they don't blow themselves to hell first,' Reaper said.

'I told them to wait till you were back.' Michael took a breath. 'And I answered the phone before I came down here.'

'I took the phone off the hook,' Reaper said.

'I put it back. I told the FBI about the sick woman.'

'And what did the FBI say?' Reaper asked ironically.

'I didn't wait around to listen.'

Michael felt Liza's eyes on him, looked back at her, knew she could not possibly be certain of him.

'All right.' Reaper nodded. 'We're almost done here. Just one more thing to tell you, Ms Plain, you and your public, so your camera, please.'

Michael saw the dread in her, felt the sheerest admiration as she took hold of the camera and began recording, her hands shaking.

'They already know where to find the ribbon,' Reaper said. 'But John Tilden wrote notes about what he'd done in a small black leather-bound book. Including his curious need to keep the ribbon. Another kind of confession, written long ago by a guilty man perhaps trying to find a way to live with what he'd done.' He paused. 'Which he managed very well, it seems.'

Michael was listening now with a terrible curiosity.

'There's a barn,' Reaper said, very clearly. 'An old apple barn one mile west of Shiloh Village, near the end of Lark Road, at the tip of a track that used to lead to a farm. They'll find a trapdoor to a tunnel, but the notebook isn't down there. It's up on one of the storage shelves, wedged tight in a corner. Just in case Tilden's lawyer claims he was coerced by us.'

'You've thought of everything,' Michael said, and he'd known about the barn and the covered SUV, left there, Reaper had said, for the last one out.

'I told you Whirlwind wouldn't let you down, Isaiah,' Reaper said.

'Why Isaiah?' Liza asked.

'According to Reaper,' Michael answered, 'he was a prophet who brought messages of vengeance.'

'Another messenger,' she said, quietly.

'Don't confuse Isaiah, Ms Plain,' Reaper said.

The pain in Michael's knee suddenly jabbed at him and he winced, shifted his weight.

331

'You're hurt,' Liza said.

'It's nothing.' He looked at Pike. 'I want to cut him down.'

'There'd be no point,' Reaper said. 'He died just before you arrived.'

Michael looked away from the crucified man and back at Liza, saw she was close to tears, wished he could hold her, wanted to kill Reaper – but old and dying as that man *claimed* to be, his fingers were still locked on the trigger of his shotgun, and Liza was too close . . .

'You surely don't imagine he could have recovered, Ms Plain?' Reaper said.

'And do you imagine that he deserved *that*?' Her anger surged again. 'To be terrorized, tortured, subjected to this *sacrilege*. A priest, not even allowed last rites, you *bastard*.'

'A little respect, please,' Reaper said, coldly. 'We're almost done here, and then you can go, take your story, your *scoop*.'

'You're letting her go,' Michael said. 'That's good.'

Reaper raised the shotgun. 'Let's not get ahead of ourselves. I said *almost* done. I'm not quite finished with Ms Plain yet.'

'What more do you *want* from her?' Michael said.

Seventy-Six

He wanted her, he said, to complete her assignment, to take a good look around his *place*, record all she could and report what she was seeing.

332

'Mind you watch your step around those graves,' he said.

Liza stared at him, nodded. 'All right.'

'You'll need my flashlight,' Reaper said.

She put out her hand, saw it was shaking again.

'Take mine,' Michael said.

Reaper turned the shotgun on him. 'I want you to keep yours, Isaiah. Ms Plain, you'll have to take mine from me, since my hands are full.'

Liza stepped close enough to tug the flashlight from his belt, then backed off, turned and made her way unsteadily to the area beyond the candles where she'd seen the mounds. There were two more graves farther back – five altogether, as he'd said – the dirt piled around them more untidily than the others; rats sniffing around, though she was past worrying about them now, because they were simply existing, doing what was needed for survival.

'Two in that last one,' Reaper called to her. 'I had no strength to dig a new grave after the organist, so the rector from Primrose is lying with him. She made no objection.'

Liza used the camera, said nothing, filmed what she could, then turned back.

'There's no grave for Reverend Pike,' she said.

'He won't need one,' Reaper said.

Liza stepped carefully past Michael, to the gibbet, looked through the viewfinder up at the dead man.

Remembered his last sounds and let her tears come, felt them heat her cheeks.

'I'm sorry,' she whispered, and created a visual record of what had been done to him, forcing herself to absorb every detail, because if the equipment failed or the light was too poor she would need later to describe the enormity of the horror, of this human being's degradation and suffering.

Those words not nearly enough.

Hate rose in her again.

'When you've finished,' Reaper said, 'I want you both to go. I want to be left alone. Though I hope you'll remember, Ms Plain, my request regarding the cash.'

'I gave you my answer.' Liza felt Michael's eyes on her. 'Joel wanted his share to go to certain charities, and Luke wanted—'

'Clearly I can't force you now to do the right thing, just assure you again that it was tainted money before it came our way.'

'It didn't *come* your way,' Liza said. 'You stole it from an old man, who's probably died by now because neither you nor Amos would lift a finger to help him.'

'If Osborn's dead, he won't miss the cash,' Reaper said. 'And dead or alive, neither he nor his wife will be admitting to its existence, so if you leave it behind, it will be a considerable waste.'

'What's in your backpack?' Michael asked suddenly.

'All I need to ensure that I won't be taken.'

Michael blinked, then understood. 'Explosives?'

'God.' Liza felt raw fear fly through her again, remembered how carefully he'd leaned against a wall earlier, and suicide had not occurred to her, or maybe she'd blocked out the thought as she'd fended off so many other terrors.

'So, Ms Plain, since your job here is now done,

I'd say that you should get out while you still can.' Reaper shrugged. 'You have that choice. Leave now or stay, if you prefer.'

'She'll leave,' Michael said.

'With you,' Liza said.

'What for?' he said.

'To stay alive.' She stared at him, saw absolute desolation in his eyes, was terrified by it, tried to fight it. 'For my sake, if not for your own.'

'To rot in jail? In maximum security, probably, like my grandfather – except that I deserve it.' He shook his head. 'I wouldn't survive, Liza – I wouldn't *want* to. And you need to forget about me. You have a future. I don't.'

'You can't tell me what to forget.' Her eyes were stinging. 'Please, Michael.'

'You have options too, Isaiah,' Reaper said. 'You can probably still make it out, same way as the others.'

'Get out now, Liza.' Michael ignored Reaper. 'Tell your story – and think about getting the cash to those charities. Do whatever you feel is right, but you need to *go*.'

'And if I don't?' She looked at Reaper.

He twitched the shotgun toward his backpack. 'One shell into that, and we'll all be gone.'

'For God's sake, Liza.' Michael's eyes were fierce now. 'Get *out* of here.'

She stared at him again and knew she had no real choice.

'Tell them all I'm sorry,' Michael said quickly. 'Except John Tilden.'

She bit back her tears. 'I will.'

'Now just *go*,' he said.

She took one more look and then she turned away, from the man she thought she would have loved, if life had turned out differently, and away from the monster and his suicide backpack and his macabre *place*.

And then she started running.

Reaper's flashlight made it possible, the mad, terrifying sprint back through darkness, the intersecting coal-black tunnels passing in a flash now, Nemesis's gizmo with all its evidence – stored, she prayed – banging painfully against her back, her left hand clenched around the camera, the flashlight in her right hand, its white beam swinging crazily as she ran, tripped, slipped and ran again, each breath painful. And all the while, her mind was filled with the graves and what might lie beneath the dirt, with Pike on the gibbet, the oozing branded crosses on his forehead and torso; her nose and throat still filled with the stench that she felt she would never be rid of; with Reaper and his sickness and his physical *ordinariness* . . .

With Michael, fierce-eyed, pushing her out, giving up.

No future for him if he'd come with her, he was right about that, but *maybe* he was doing what Reaper had suggested, maybe even now he was limping through that escape tunnel, maybe he would escape and live . . .

Though she doubted that.

Turned her mind from it and the rest, unable to process any more.

Insane. All of it.

And suddenly there was the *ladder*, and she

stuck the flashlight in her waistband, started to climb, fell back, all power suddenly drained from her limbs, and she had to rest, but there was no *time* for that, because any minute now the madman might detonate his explosives – unless he'd changed his mind and was getting out with Michael, his 'Isaiah' . . .

Enough.

Liza cut off her ragged, gasping thoughts.

She had to make her legs work, had to get *up* there.

Now.

Seventy-Seven

'Decision time for you now, Isaiah,' Reaper said. 'Are you leaving or staying?'

'It doesn't have to be this way,' Michael said.

Coming to the end, finally. As he'd known it would.

'It does,' Reaper said. 'For me, it does.'

'You could still go back, let them all go, face what you've done. You could die peacefully.' And Michael wasn't sure why he gave a damn about how this murdering sadist died, or maybe this just seemed too easy a way out for Reaper, or maybe it was himself he was thinking about.

'In the prison hospital, you mean, shackled to a bed, some *priest* lurking, waiting to absolve me?' Reaper smiled. 'Why does it matter to you how I go, Isaiah?'

'My name is Michael Rider, for Christ's sake.' His voice rose with angry frustration. 'I'm no prophet, and I'm not interested in vengeance.'

'You must be, deep inside.'

'No,' Michael said. 'I'm not you. And it's good that you cleared my grandfather's name, and that your father's going to get what's coming to him, but the only person I can blame for the ruination of my life is *me*, and if I die now, I won't be kidding myself I'm going in any blaze of glory or retribution.'

'That's fine,' Reaper said. 'I'm glad for you. And it's why you should get out through that tunnel while you can, but it's your last chance.' He held up the shotgun. 'I'm waiting just long enough for Ms Plain to make it back up to church. And if you choose to go, I'll wait a little longer.'

'I have one request,' Michael said.

The other man sighed. 'I'm very tired. I've been waiting for this moment for longer than you've been alive.'

'Let me cut Pike down.' Michael looked at the dead man. 'Surely he suffered enough? Can't you accept that he probably didn't know what else to do back then?'

'I was ten years old, and he helped finish me,' Reaper said. 'He was the start of it, the worm in the apple, and everything wicked that I've done started with him.'

'And John Tilden,' Michael said.

'And ideally, he'd be down here too, only he wouldn't be dead like Pike. I'd be making him wait till the bitter end.'

Michael saw something change in the other man's face, in his eyes.

Saw his right hand begin to tremble.

'I have a request too,' Reaper said. 'My last to you, Isaiah, or Michael, if you prefer. That you do get out, find some way to live your life, let Liza Plain wait for you if she will.'

Michael let his mind go to her, to the blue, honest eyes beseeching him to live.

He wondered if perhaps he could, for her.

'You'll go,' Reaper said.

Michael looked at him, saw wreckage in his face, in his eyes.

'I wish—'

He stopped, saw the killer lift his hand, saw the tremor seeming to accelerate.

Knew, suddenly, that he was all out of time.

'Now,' Reaper told him. 'Please. Go *now*.'

Seventy-Eight

The darkness he had always craved came to him at last.

First, there was exquisite pain and the world's-end of reverberation and brilliant, dazzling fire.

Then silence.

And then the dark. Total, black as coal, wrapping around him as tight as a swaddling cloth. And he dreamed that his mother was with him, and that somewhere, not far away, a boy was singing.

And then the sweetness was gone.

Along with pain and breath.

And his mother left him again.

Obliterated forever.

Together with the man who had once been the boy who spoke to angels.

And the monster he had become.

The boom of the blast might almost have been taken for thunder if it hadn't thrown Liza right off her feet, and if she hadn't known exactly *what* it was. And there were other sounds within the boom and surrounding it too, seconds of indescribable noise, remote, yet *inside* her head and body, followed by a howl of wind blowing down the tunnel toward her.

Then silence.

Waves of it, except for a clanging in her head and a swirling in her brain, before everything came crashing down onto her, and all she knew for sure was that she had waited too long.

There was no pain. Just a great weight and darkness and *fear*.

Of being trapped.

Of suffocating.

Of dying alone.

Seventy-Nine

Above, there was chaos. The old church shaken to its foundations by something no one could comprehend, the walls and vaulted ceiling standing solid, a tribute to their architecture and construction, the altar unmoved, though everything neither cemented nor nailed down had gone tumbling, a pair of candlesticks and the chalice from which Reaper had drunk still rolling on the floor below the chancel.

The hostages, already drained almost beyond endurance, were clutching each other again, utterly bewildered as to what had happened, because there had been an explosion, but the wired front and side doors were still intact, and they were still not free.

'Back entrance?' Rosie Keenan said, clinging to her husband.

The vicar shook his head. 'I'd say it came from below.'

'Think we're safe up here?'

'Seem to be,' Keenan said.

He crossed himself.

And spotted Joel.

Up on his feet, wrists still bound with Adam Glover's belt, walking quickly and with determination toward the north-east door.

'*Stop* him!' Keenan yelled.

People turned and stared at him, their reactions sluggish.

Only Freya Osborn appearing to notice the man and realize the danger, and she didn't budge, merely watched, her face implacable.

As the man called Joel thrust out his hands and ran at the door.

It went up with a deafening roar, engulfing door and man in a wall of flame and smoke, and the force of the explosion knocked Osborn's wife and Grace Glover's mother and grandfather out of the front pews, onto the wooden floor.

'Holy shit,' said Eddie Leary, back in the eighth row.

'Fuck,' said Mitchell Roper, awed.

The smoke spread, layered like fog.

'Jill!' Gwen Turner screamed.

'I'm OK!' Jill yelled back. 'Stay down.'

'Betty!' Annie Stanley called. 'Are you hurt?'

'They'll have to do better than that to get rid of me,' Betty Hackett said shakily.

'Thank God.' Keenan held Rosie at arm's length, still checking her over. 'Thank God you're all right.'

'Is it over?' she asked him.

'I don't know.' Keenan got up. 'I need to go to Joel.'

The dead man, blown like a puppet halfway across the nave, lay flat on his back below the chancel, his face and hair blackened.

The vicar fell to his knees beside him.

'You can't help him now, Simon.' Rosie was behind him.

'He wanted to get Patty out.' Keenan was distraught. 'He did this to end it. The least I can do is pray for him.'

'Pray for him later,' Rosie said. 'A lot of people need our help first.'

Keenan looked around, taking in the scene, shook his head, made the sign of the cross on the dead man's forehead, then stood up.

And saw that the undercroft door was open.

Someone just disappearing through it.

Stephen Plain.

'Oh, dear Christ,' Keenan said.

342

Eighty

Liza came to with a great start of terror.

Dirt in her mouth.

She coughed, spat, expelled some of it, opened her eyes, saw only blackness and panicked.

Buried, entombed, helpless, finished.

So *stupid*.

She should have gotten upside quicker.

Should never have come down in the first place, should never have accepted that wicked man's *assignment*. She should have stayed put with her grandfather and the rest of the village, stayed loyal to them rather than grasping at damned journalism, which she'd never even been any good at.

Though maybe it hadn't been the story that had drawn her into this so much as Michael Rider, codename Isaiah, a man with a lousy past and no future.

And dark, sad, gentle eyes.

Not now, she told herself.

The silence was strangely heavy, like quilting shoved into her ear canals, inside her head.

Yet her mind was working.

Whatever had fallen on her, she was still *breathing*, so maybe . . .

She dared to see if she could move. Feet first, too afraid to try her arms or even her hands, in case . . . She shuddered, moved her right foot, met

343

resistance, but she could *move* it, so she tried with her left – that one a little easier, space around it.

Liza took a shallow breath, afraid of choking on the dirt, and kicked with that foot, and a spray of dirt spattered back into her face, into her nostrils, and she blew out, cleared them, and small triumph washed through her because she could move her legs and, though she was becoming conscious of discomfort in her back, it didn't feel worse than what one might expect after being knocked off one's feet and half buried – and clearly it was infinitely better to be feeling some pain than not to be feeling anything.

'I'm OK,' she said, not hearing the words but feeling their vibration.

Gritting her teeth, she started over, found that both hands were working, and gave thanks. No injuries to either arm, so far as she could tell, and she freed her right hand, moved it up to her face, brushed filth off her lips, nose, *eyes* – but the darkness did not relent, and tears surfaced in a sob, and she let them come for a moment – then stopped because her left hand had made contact with something hard.

Reaper's flashlight.

Not *working*, and despair overwhelmed her until she realized that even if its real purpose was screwed, she could still use it as a tool, dig with it if she had to.

She rested for a few seconds, trying to orient herself. Just before the blast, she'd reached the foot of the ladder, and she might have been blown some way from it, but since the tunnel itself didn't seem to have totally collapsed, she rationalized that she could be no more than feet away from the exit.

New fear struck home.

What if this space was just an air pocket? One heard about people buried after earthquakes or avalanches who survived that way but had to wait hours or days to be found. And one read about bodies dug out, victims who'd clearly lived on for a while before succumbing to the inevitable.

Shut *up*, she told herself.

Find the ladder.

She shifted carefully, sat up, her heart pounding violently, afraid of colliding with an invisible pile of debris or wrecked wall.

Nothing there. Just space. Air.

'Thank you,' she whispered.

Thought she heard herself this time, and said it again, more loudly.

'Thank you.' Distant, muffled, but *there*, her hearing returning, and she considered yelling for help, but decided that would take too much strength – that in any case, logically, no one would hear her, not for a while anyway.

Find the ladder.

She tried the flashlight again, smacked it smartly. No light.

So be it.

She stretched out both arms, feeling around as a blind person might in unknown territory. Panic surged again and she pushed it away with a low growl of anger, reminded herself that given the circumstances she was in good shape and in a good position; farther back in the tunnel, she'd have stood much less of a chance.

She started to get up, struck something hard with her left shoulder, yelped, heard and felt more dirt descend in a shower, cried out in fright.

It stopped.

Thoughts of Michael slid into her mind, but she pushed them away.

Not now. Later.

Staying in a crouch, not daring to straighten up again, she felt around, hardly moving her feet, aiming to stay rooted where she'd fallen, still believing she had to be at least in the proximity of the ladder and the exit.

She felt something hard and cold to her left, and it wasn't rubble, it was a real, solid *wall*, still standing, and with a rush of hope, she extended her arms straight ahead.

Nothing there.

Concentrate.

She needed to remember if there had been wall to her right when they'd come down the ladder and turned left, but she couldn't because both times her descent had been at gunpoint, and she hadn't looked to the right, because it had all just been *dark*, and all that had mattered then had been staying with the Whirlwind flashlights.

'Come on,' she told herself, extended her arms again and circled around to her right.

Nothing.

She took a step forward, did the same exercise again.

The flashlight in her right hand struck something solid.

Optimism surged and she took another step forward, but her right knee collided with the hard object and she stumbled, tried to catch herself, but fell, dropping the flashlight.

She swore, tried to find it, failed, then wondered suddenly if the camera had a flash.

And realized for the first time that it was gone – the camera had *gone*, had probably fallen with her at the time of the explosion, so no hope of finding it now.

The gizmo was still on her back, though, so, if Nemesis had been truthful, the recordings were probably secure.

Tears welled again, but she wiped her eyes roughly with her parka's sleeve, stayed where she'd landed, on her backside, and told herself to find out what she'd just walked into.

A mound of debris, it seemed, as she located it and poked at it with both hands; no more than two feet high, therefore easy enough to climb over.

She leaned forward, reached past it and touched something with her middle finger.

Hard. Different.

Metal maybe.

She touched it again.

Metal, for sure.

She tried to stay calm, but her breathing was quickening, and she groped at the metal thing and knew it was what she'd hoped for.

A *rung*.

'Thank you,' she said again, leaned farther in, felt around six inches or so higher, found the next rung, grasped it, felt the weakness of sheer relief, but did not let go.

Last time she'd surrendered to exhaustion, the world had blown up.

347

Reaper igniting his backpack, taking himself and Michael—

Shut *up*, she told herself again.

Keeping firm hold of the second rung, she stood up and clambered slowly and carefully over the rubble, caught her left shin on something sharp enough to rip her leggings, barely noticed and definitely didn't care.

Two hands on the ladder now.

She looked up, saw nothing, felt dizzy.

Waited a moment, took a breath.

'Here goes nothing,' she said softly.

And climbed.

Eighty-One

'Dr Plain, what are you *doing*?'

Keenan had caught up with Liza's grandfather at the foot of the undercroft steps.

'Simon, please be careful,' Rosie called from above.

'I can't get this damned door open,' Stephen said.

'Let me try,' Keenan said.

'I'm doing it.' Stephen wrenched at the handle. 'I can *do* it.'

'Mind you don't break it off, Dr Plain,' Keenan said.

'Maybe they've locked it,' Rosie called.

'There's no key,' the vicar called back up.

'We need to break it down.' Stephen was breathless.

'Dr Plain, you won't help anyone if you give yourself a coronary.'

'I'm as strong as an ox,' the old man said. 'We need to find Liza.'

'We will,' Keenan said. 'If you'd please let me by.'

'It's giving slightly,' Stephen said, panting, 'but something's blocking it.'

'It opens inward,' Keenan said.

'Can you try to kick it open?' Rosie called.

'I can try,' Keenan said. 'Please, Doctor, just let me get past.'

'I'm not completely useless,' Stephen said.

And kicked it.

Three failed attempts at getting the trapdoor open.

Perspiring, heart slamming in her chest, tears of frustration.

'*Fuck* you,' Liza said the final time.

It flew up, light dazzled her and she scrambled up and out onto the floor.

Blinking, trying to get her breath.

She was *out*.

Able to see again, she looked at the archive room.

Everything looked as it had.

She got to her feet and made her way slowly and weakly to the narrow corridor.

And heard them.

On the other side of the door.

'Jesus, Mary and Joseph!' a man said, exasperated.

Her grandfather's voice.

* * *

349

At pivotal moments in life, it's often impossible to say exactly what drives a person to normally unimaginable acts.

The Liza Plain of yesterday – even hours ago – would have gone to the door that she could now see had been barricaded by someone – the last person down here, *Michael,* with a chair.

That Liza would have removed it, and let her grandfather through.

Let him know she was *alive.*

Instead, she ran to Keenan's office.

Saw the envelopes still on his desk. Three of them: one for Luke, one for Joel's charities – the paper with the list on the desk too; and the third, marked 'M'.

More noises came from beyond the door, voices raised.

She ignored them, heaved the gizmo backpack off her shoulders, yelping with pain, disregarding that too, because it was *nothing*, as were the sounds, and she could hear that Stephen sounded angry, and nothing new there.

Not much time.

She unzipped her parka and yanked up her sweater, every movement hurting, sweat dripping off her forehead, running between her breasts, and quickly she wiped herself with the sweater, needing her skin to be dry, then, fingers trembling, pulled out the waistband of her leggings, felt for the elastic of her panties, pressed Luke's envelope as flatly as possible against herself, folding it around her curves, pulled up the panties, did the same at the back with Joel's, adding the piece of paper, then drew up the leggings over them.

The bang made her jump, start to shake again, but it was only the door, someone trying to break through.

She stared at Michael's envelope, then laid that vertically beneath her thermal vest, the top of the envelope just below her breasts, the base under her waistband.

Pulled down her long sweater, dragged on her parka, zipped it up.

Heaved the backpack on again.

Took a breath.

Yelled: 'Granddad?'

Went to the door.

'Liza?'

'There's a chair – wait a moment!'

She made a noise about removing the chair and knocked it over.

The door opened, and there they were, Stephen and Keenan and his wife behind them.

'Thank God,' the vicar said.

'Are you all right?' Rosie asked.

'Don't ask the poor girl stupid questions,' Stephen said. 'Look at her. Of course she isn't all right.'

He put out his arms to her, but Liza stepped back.

'I'm sorry,' she said. 'I just want to get upstairs.' She realized then that they had what looked like soot on them. 'What's happened?'

'One of the fire doors blew,' the vicar said. 'Didn't you hear it?'

'No,' she said, which was true, and she wondered if it had happened at the same time as the blast below, or while she'd been knocked senseless for however long that had been – or maybe it had been the *door* exploding that had knocked her out, and maybe not Reaper's backpack at all?

But then she remembered the wind howling through the tunnel, and knew exactly what and who had caused it.

'Is it very bad?' She forced herself to ask the right question.

'Not as bad as it might have been,' Rosie said.

'Bad enough,' Keenan said.

'Main thing is we're all getting out,' Stephen told her. 'And you're with us.'

'But what happened to you?' Rosie was staring at her. 'Are you hurt?'

'I'm OK,' Liza said. 'Right now I just want to get out.'

'Of course,' Keenan said. 'But where's Reaper?'

'Gone,' Liza said.

'And the other one?' Rosie said. 'The one called Isaiah.'

'Gone, too,' Liza said tightly.

They began making their way up the narrow steps, Stephen first, Rosie trying to help her and Keenan attempting to relieve her of the backpack, but Liza shook them both off and, at the top of the steps, pushed ahead of them all.

'I'm sorry,' she called back, 'but I need some air.'

'We'll help you,' Rosie told her. 'Wait for us.'

'I can't,' she said, and accelerated.

Jelly legs gone now, functioning on pure adrenalin again, no time to ask herself what she was doing.

Not now.

Later.

Eighty-Two

'My God.' Liza ground to a halt in the jam of people gathered near the ragged, blackened, still-smoking hole in the north-east wall of the church.

Daylight beyond it. Christmas Day.

'I thought it would be bigger.' The young man with the black hair and ear stud was beside her. 'Didn't you think it would be—?' He stopped, staring at her. 'What the fuck happened to you?'

Liza said nothing, edged away, wanting to lose him, to lose herself in this crush of hostages with everyone wanting *out*, saw how hard it would be to get through at all, let alone do what she'd already planned out in her head.

Temporary insanity.

It was chaotic, the clamor hurting her ears, her head. Uniforms present, Fire Rescue, cops, FBI, visible in their parkas, paramedics. Men and women talking into radios, breath steaming. The narthex, main and south-east doors, and nine out of the ten rows of pews all sealed off with crime-scene tape – a risk, still, Liza realized, of the other doors blowing – and creating the jam in this area. She saw Steve Julliard being wheeled out, and someone else on a gurney, Patty Jackson, her parents either side; looked at the dazed people apparently waiting in the front row, Betty Hackett and Freya Osborn among them, both being tended to by paramedics and the pharmacist, Norman

353

Clay. Freya, with a cut on her forehead, was being comforted by the female deacon Liza remembered from hours ago, a calm person as she recalled, Freya talking agitatedly to her now. And however much Liza longed to escape, she knew she had to pass on what she knew. Though not first-hand, not yet, and, turning quickly before Freya saw her, Liza spotted Gwen Turner, felt she could entrust this to her, and made her way across, grabbed her arm, saw relief in Gwen's eyes at seeing her safe, gave her no chance to speak, just said: 'Gwen, I need your help.'

'Anything. Are you OK?'

'I'm fine.' Liza leaned close and spoke against her ear. 'I need you to tell Freya Osborn and the police that Bill was badly hurt hours ago by the one called Amos, and they just *left* him in the library in Shiloh Oaks, so he needs urgent help' – she had to take a breath – 'but they *can't* just go steaming in, because they've booby-trapped the doors there too.' She pulled away. 'Have you got that?'

'Yes, but you should tell them yourself.'

'I can't,' Liza said. 'I *can't*, OK?'

'Sure. I'll deal with it right away – but you need to get checked out.'

'She will be.' Keenan came up behind them, and turned to his wife. 'Rosie, can you make sure Liza gets to a paramedic?'

Liza watched as Gwen reached Freya Osborn, then quickly turned again, back into the throng, but Rosie stuck with her, told her about Joel apparently setting off the explosives deliberately, said that Simon felt certain he'd given his life to free them.

'Liza, I'm sure you should be sitting down.'

'I don't need to.' Liza wanted to be rid of her, of *everyone*, but Rosie wasn't going anywhere, was asking her questions about what had happened down in the undercroft.

'We weren't in the undercroft,' Liza told her quickly, quietly. 'Reaper had a backpack of explosives. There are tunnels below the church, below most of the village.'

'And that's where you've been, with *him*?' Rosie looked horrified. 'Oh, my God, you could have been killed.'

'But I wasn't,' Liza said.

'And right now' – Stephen Plain materialized beside her and took her arm – 'you just want to get out of this place, right, Liza?'

She looked at him, startled, and then, instantly, driven by some curious instinct, decided to trust him, kept her voice low.

'I have to get to our house, Granddad.'

'I see.' Her grandfather was calm. 'Leave it to me.'

'I just heard they're going to evacuate the whole village,' Rosie Keenan said.

'In those conditions?' Stephen nodded toward the cavity through which people were being slowly moved, his height giving him a vantage point. 'Have you seen it out there? It's like the North Pole, and I heard a paramedic say they can't risk bringing vehicles in.'

'The police are going to want to talk to Liza,' the vicar's wife said.

'Not yet,' Liza said sharply. 'I can't.'

She had to get *out*, had to find a way, wished she'd never *seen* those envelopes.

'Reaper's gone – you can tell them that, Rosie, if they ask. I think he blew himself up, but I wasn't there. He told me to get out, and then . . .' She stopped, starting to tremble.

'Easy.' Her grandfather gripped her arm more tightly.

Liza became aware that people all around were staring at her.

'I need to get out *now*, Granddad,' she said.

'No problem.' His voice was even lower. 'Just leave it to me, Liza. Better not say much from now on – you're suffering from shock, so stop talking and take my lead.' He turned to Rosie Keenan. 'I'm going to get her to the house.'

'But people are saying it's dangerous.'

'Poppycock,' Stephen said. 'We'll go ahead. See you soon.'

The retired doctor used a blend of authority and a charm that Liza had never witnessed before, though when necessary he turned curmudgeonly and people stepped aside, let him through, assuming perhaps that he had special dispensation. And a few times, hearing her name spoken, Liza was aware of people staring, saw Jill Barrow waving, glad too that she was safe, and wanted to acknowledge her.

'Not now,' Stephen told her. 'Ignore them all.'

Outside – really *outside*, at long last – the sky blue with just a few fluffy clouds, *walls* of snow everywhere, great drifts piled up, the icy, crystalline air acted on Liza like some high-octane energy drink. Listening to agitated conversations here and there, they learned that the freed hostages were being divided into those needing assistance and those able to walk to buses waiting on Shiloh Road beyond Elm Street, ready to take them to Shiloh Town Hall. And in less abnormal conditions, there would, she guessed, have been buses and ambulances lining up on Main Street to get them out fast, but the Blizzard-to-End-All-Blizzards and still-present danger had rendered the village a no-go area.

'Home, right?' Stephen asked.

And here was yet another of these surreal experiences: having her grandfather on her side and asking no questions, just seeming to know that she needed his help, which seemed quite a Christmas gift – along with freedom and *life* – so she wasn't going to let herself think about anything else, was just going to stick her freezing hands in her pockets and move forward, cut off all the mess and pain crowding her mind.

'OK, here we go then,' Stephen said, and began to guide her through the deep snow, heading for home.

'Ms Plain?' a voice said.

They turned and saw a pleasant-faced, ruddy-cheeked middle-aged man in a parka and woolen hat, holding out an FBI badge.

'Special Agent Clem Carson,' he said. 'Are you Liza Plain?'

'She is.' Stephen tightened his grip on Liza's arm. 'I'm Dr Stephen Plain, and this is my granddaughter. Right this minute, I need to get her back to my surgery, which is just up there.' He pointed vaguely.

'There's a chance it might be unsafe, sir,' Carson

said. 'That's why we're moving everyone out as quickly as we can.'

'Quite a proposition,' Stephen said, affably. 'So you people must have your hands full, which is why I'm going to take care of my granddaughter, who has been through more than enough.'

'Granddad,' Liza said, 'I think I should give Agent Carson what the FBI are going to want most.'

'And I think the FBI can wait a half-hour.' Stephen glared at her.

'My backpack,' she said. 'If you could just help me off with it, sir?' She gave him a weak smile. 'It's the equipment the gang gave me so I could transmit. It's evidence, obviously.'

'It most certainly is, ma'am,' Clem Carson told her. 'You did a great job.'

'You do realize she had no choice,' Stephen said. 'They all had shotguns. I take it that's understood.'

'I'm sure it is.' Carson helped to ease the backpack from Liza's shoulders, saw her wince, heard her groan of pain. 'I'm betting you're glad to be rid of that, ma'am.'

'You have no idea,' Liza said. 'I lost the camera underground but I'll be able to tell you where to find it, if you'll just give me some time to rest.'

'Best place for now would be my car, ma'am.' Carson hoisted the backpack onto his right shoulder.

'Best place for now is our house.' Stephen put his arm around her.

'*Hey!*' a male voice yelled, and they all turned toward a commotion starting up, because some people had just emerged from two narrow town houses on Main Street, and other doors were opening.

358

'Oh, dear Lord,' Clem Carson said. 'They need to be staying inside until they're called.'

'Best go help your colleagues then,' Stephen told him. 'We'll wait for you.'

'I'd rather see you both to safety first, sir.'

Someone started calling on a loudhailer, and Liza put her hands up over her ears.

'Just go deal with that, for pity's sake,' Stephen said.

Carson looked at them both. 'You'd better join the line, get yourselves to the town hall. We'll come find you there.'

'We'll look forward to it,' Stephen said.

'Please take good care of the backpack,' Liza said urgently, wondering suddenly if she'd done the right thing handing it over to a stranger with a badge. 'It's evidence of a lot more than you think.' She took a shaky breath. 'At least six murders, for one thing.'

Clem Carson stared at her.

'Now *go*,' Stephen barked at him.

Carson turned and ran.

'My God, Granddad,' Liza said. 'That was amazing.'

'Time for compliments later. Let's get you home.'

They turned, made it to the corner of South Maple and waited to be stopped, but no one bothered them.

'What happened to John Tilden?' Liza asked as they trudged past buried cars. 'I didn't see him.'

'Arrested,' Stephen said, panting. 'I saw them take him out just ahead of us.'

'Poor Eleanor.'

'Strong woman, Ellie Willard.'

359

'Willard,' Liza repeated, never having heard Eleanor's birth name before.

'I've always liked strong women.' He paused for breath, the going very heavy. 'Seems to me now that I have a remarkably strong granddaughter.'

Liza flushed, then hesitated. 'I need to ask you something, Granddad.'

'Fire away.'

'Were you involved as a doctor in having Joshua Tilden put away back then?'

'I was not.' Stephen stopped walking and looked her in the eye. 'No one called me. If Cromwell did help John Tilden, which is likely, he presumably used his own man.' He started moving again. 'Though a cover-up would have been costly, and Tilden wouldn't have had the means in those days, and I doubt that Cromwell would have used his own money.'

'Whose then?' Liza asked.

'Only one man in Shiloh people turned to when they needed money fast.'

'Osborn.' Liza remembered Amos's loathing of the old newspaper man, thought about the cash, grew hotter, sped up.

'I always told you no good would come from raking up the past,' Stephen said.

'At least people know the truth now,' she said.

'At what cost? A child's life? All those people terrorized.' And then, seeing her face, he added: 'I always felt bad about the letter, but I couldn't do anything about it, and there's an end to it.'

Liza looked up at him and managed to smile. 'I hope the house is safe. I'd hate to get you blown up after all this.'

'Those thugs were bent on keeping people locked in,' Stephen said grimly. 'There was no one left in our house for them to worry about.'

Liza looked back over her shoulder. No one was following.

'We can stop again if you need to rest, Granddad.'

'Not me,' he said. 'I never felt better.'

At the foot of the driveway, they halted, both panting, Liza feeling weak again, afraid of collapsing before they reached the house. And her grandfather had to be aware of that, had surely to be near the end of his tether too, yet he wasn't fussing, was simply *helping*, the last person in the world she'd have expected that from.

'I see no bombs from here,' Stephen said, humorously. 'Shall we approach?'

'Definitely,' Liza said.

They clambered over and through the mounds of snow heaped on the driveway and in drifts against the wall of the house and front door, and cleared away as much as they needed to.

She stopped again, abruptly, breathless. 'I don't have my keys – I don't even remember when I last saw my bag.'

'Not a problem,' Stephen said.

He fished in his coat pocket and found his set.

'Better stand back when I open up, just in case,' he said. 'I'm old, after all.'

Liza laughed, staggered that she could do that after what she'd seen down below, in Reaper's 'place', quickly set it all aside again, a portion of horror to be dealt with later. And then she looked anxiously back over her shoulder.

'It's all right,' Stephen said. 'Come along.'

Inside, all was as it had been, except for the snow spilling into the hallway with them.

'Would you mind,' Liza asked, 'if I go upstairs for just a little while?'

'Alone, do I take it?'

'Please,' she said. 'I'm sorry, Granddad.'

'No need.' He smiled down at her. 'Tragedy aside, it's been the least agonizingly dull Christmas I can remember for decades.'

Liza reached up and kissed his icy cheek. 'Thank you. More than I can say.'

'You just go ahead,' he said. 'I'll be in the living room, having a bit of a sit down.'

'Are you really OK?' she asked, remembering his own ordeal.

'In one piece, and plenty to think about,' he said. 'Very glad to be home.'

'I won't be too long,' Liza said at the foot of the stairs. 'If anyone comes—'

'I'll tell them you're unwell, taking a little time out,' Stephen said. 'Now go on.'

She went.

Eighty-Three

If they caught her, she thought, walking shakily upstairs, if they found out what she was doing, she guessed that her grandfather would probably try to defend her, would say she wasn't in her

362

right mind because of what she'd been through, and maybe that was true.

Except it was not exactly true.

She might not be in her right mind, might never be again, but she did know exactly what she was doing.

Aiding and abetting criminals. Not because Reaper had asked her to do it, but because Michael had.

Hurry.

She reached the second floor, went into the bathroom, locked the door behind her, unzipped her parka and tore it off, pulled out the envelopes – more money than she'd ever had in her hands, that was for damned sure – and dropped them on the floor on top of the parka.

She opened the mirrored cabinet, found the metal nail file that she'd seen when she'd looked for soap before her bath on Christmas Eve – and even while she'd been hiding the cash inside her clothes, she'd remembered that file, had known what she would do with it.

'Calculating,' the prosecution would say.

She turned and looked at the side panel of the old-fashioned tub.

It was as she'd remembered.

She turned on the faucets in the hand-basin to disguise any sounds.

Got down on her knees.

Unscrewed the panel and withdrew it quietly, carefully.

Space enough in the cavity. She slipped in the envelopes and Joel's list, then replaced the panel and screws, stood up, legs trembling, wiped the end of the nail file and returned it to the cabinet.

Voices below, all male.

Slow footsteps coming upstairs.

She kept the water running in the basin, began coughing.

Tucked her vest into the top of her leggings, pulled down her sweater.

Went on coughing.

Thought of Reaper.

And of Michael.

Stared at herself for the first time, saw her blackened face and hair, let the tears in her eyes roll down her cheeks, thought about washing her face, then realized that the dirt was an important backup to her story.

A bottle of Listerine stood on the shelf.

Good idea, if she wanted them to think she'd been throwing up.

As good a reason as any to want privacy.

After all she'd been through.

'Liza, are you all right?' her grandfather called through the door.

She pulled on her parka. 'I'm OK, Granddad.'

She let the water run for another moment or two.

Saw the bottle of air freshener on the shelf and used that too.

Thinking like a criminal.

'Only there are two FBI agents downstairs,' Stephen said.

'I'll be down in a moment.'

'All right,' her grandfather said. 'Take your time. I'll offer them tea.'

She heard him going back downstairs.

Her accomplice, she thought, and shook her head.

The two agents, drinking tea that one of them had insisted on making, were both polite to her. Carson hatless now, his hair white and very short, the gentler of the pair; the other man, named Walker, younger, dark-haired, keen-eyed. Both *appearing* to accept the story of her desperate need, unwell and beyond exhausted, to get back to familiar territory, Stephen firmly backing her up and no one arguing with him.

'So are we safe to stay here now?' Liza asked.

'Word is you're far enough from Main Street,' Carson said.

'Has everyone down there been evacuated now?' Stephen asked.

'Apart from the people in the inn,' Carson said.

'Are they all right?' Liza felt a rush of empathy.

'We believe so,' Walker said.

'What about Bill Osborn at Shiloh Oaks?'

'No word yet on Mr Osborn,' Carson said.

'Having come back here against advice,' Agent Walker said, 'orders are that you stay inside until further notice.'

'House arrest now,' Stephen said dryly. 'What if I'm needed?'

'Plenty of doctors on the scene,' Walker said. 'I believe you're retired, sir.'

'From what I've heard, they couldn't have coped without Dr Plain,' Carson said. 'Though you both do need to get yourselves checked out – you especially, Ms Plain.'

'There's no need, I'm OK,' she said. 'Just a few bruises.'

'Sleep needed,' Stephen said. 'And *food*,' he added.

'Plenty in the fridge,' Liza said. 'All the stuff I brought from Glover's.'

'Excellent,' he said.

'If you're up to it, Ms Plain,' Walker said, 'we do need to speak to you.'

'Of course.' Liza stared at Carson. 'Where's the backpack?'

'Safe,' Carson assured her. 'Don't worry.'

'If the equipment worked, it's crucial evidence,' Liza said. 'Nemesis set it all up.'

'That's one of the gang,' Stephen added grimly. 'Female.'

'She got out first,' Liza said. 'Through a tunnel.'

She paused, remembered that she hadn't had the equipment with her during the robbery, and, oh, dear God, she'd have to tell them about that, and then they'd be looking for the money . . .

'You do know about the tunnels?' she asked.

'We do,' Walker said.

'I need to tell you what happened down there.'

'Take your time,' Carson said. 'The vicar's wife told us you said that Joshua Tilden had probably blown himself up.'

'He told us he had explosives in his backpack,' Liza said.

'Us?' Walker queried.

And there it was, the proverbial elephant in the room. Her relationship – brief, but more than intense – with Michael.

Her angst about the money faded, his face taking its place.

366

'Michael Rider,' she clarified. 'Reaper took me down into the tunnels, and Michael came after us. If he hadn't . . .' She closed her eyes.

'Drink your tea, Liza,' Stephen said. 'Questions later.'

'I would just like some water, if that's OK,' she said.

'Sure it is,' Carson said, and went to fetch it.

'We're going to need to take some photos, Ms Plain,' Agent Walker said.

'Of what?' she asked.

'Of you,' he said. 'You're evidence too.'

Liza put a hand up to her face, saw it come away smeared with filth and began to cry. 'I'm sorry, I'm making everything dirty.'

'Good Lord,' Stephen said. 'Who cares about that?'

Carson came back with the water, and Stephen took the glass from him, held it out to Liza and she took it, but then her hands began shaking, and he took hold of it again.

'Let me help,' he said.

He knelt stiffly beside her armchair and tilted the glass against her lips, and Liza did not resist, managed a little.

'I think it's abundantly clear, gentlemen,' Stephen said, 'that my granddaughter needs a good long rest before she talks to you.'

'No.' Liza pushed away the glass. 'It can't all wait, Granddad.'

'You mentioned murders earlier,' Clem Carson said.

Pike on the gibbet came into her mind, made her shudder.

'There are *bodies* down there.' The shaking grew worse, and suddenly it was hard to speak, but she had to get it out, they had to *know*. 'Thomas Pike and six – or maybe seven, I can't seem to think straight, I'm sorry – but there are *graves*.' She was having trouble breathing. 'Reaper killed them all. He told me, and I recorded it.'

Dizziness hit her hard.

And the world turned black again.

Eighty-Four

In the days that followed, people were very kind. Word got out about some of what had happened down there below their village, and most people who had questioned Liza's role in the siege no longer felt that way.

William Osborn had not survived.

The man called Amos now wanted for his murder.

The whole gang wanted for a host of crimes.

Once she had begun to recover, Liza began the lengthy process of debriefing, giving endless statements and answering repetitive questions by the FBI and State Police, holding back as little as possible. She explained her brief history with Michael, including the hours they'd spent together on the night of December 23, and told them about his strange attempts to persuade her to leave Shiloh. About her profound shock at seeing him in St Matthew's as part of the gang.

She told them about the robbery, about the safe

368

and the jewelry given by Amos to Nemesis. About the money beneath the floor. 'I don't know how much there was,' she said. 'I've never seen so much cash.'

'What happened to it?' one of the Providence investigators asked.

'Nemesis stuffed as much as she could carry under her clothes before she left through what I assumed was an escape tunnel, and Amos brought the rest back to Reaper, who was waiting in the undercroft at Saint Matthew's.' Liza paused, her heart hammering. 'And after that, from what I could tell, Reaper divided what was left between Amos and Jeremiah.'

'All of it? Including the dead men's cuts?'

'So far as I know. Joel was still alive then, but he told Reaper he didn't want his cut.'

'And Rider? Didn't he take a cut?'

'If he did, I didn't see it. I don't remember him carrying anything except a shotgun and a flashlight when he came down into the tunnel to find me.'

'Are you sure that's why he came down there?'

'Not entirely,' Liza said. 'But he wanted me to escape, I know that.'

'You said that Reaper told you to get out too.'

They referred to him mostly as Reaper, avoiding any confusion between the two Tildens.

'Yes,' she said.

'Why do you think that was, Ms Plain?'

Liza shut her eyes. 'That's what he called me all through the whole thing. "Ms Plain". As if being courteous made it better.'

'A courteous psychopath,' someone said.

'He called himself a psychopath,' Liza said.

'So why do you think Reaper told you to get out?' The investigator returned to the unanswered question.

'I don't know.' She paused. 'Anyway, he didn't wait for me to get out, did he? I was still in the tunnel when he detonated his backpack.'

'Did he offer you a cut, Ms Plain?'

'No!' Outrage made her shake again, and for the first time she wondered if she might need a lawyer. 'Of course he didn't. I was a hostage, same as all the others.'

'Not quite the same,' the investigator said.

She was believed, so far as she could tell.

Law enforcement agencies were not the only ones wanting to talk to her.

Segments of her reporting of the 'Christmas Eve Siege of Shiloh' – as it was largely being called, though there were some references to the 'Midnight Mass Siege' – had been heard and seen by vast numbers of people after snippets had escaped onto YouTube, trending for a while on Twitter and other social networks.

Newspapers and media all knocking on the door.

Not a good feeling.

'So,' Stephen said before her return to Boston, 'you finally got what you wanted.'

'You can't think I *wanted* any of that to happen, Granddad,' she said.

'Nevertheless, you got your big story,' he said. 'No shame in that.'

'I'm not ashamed,' she said. 'Though in some ways, I did feel dirty for doing what Reaper wanted.'

She paused. 'I still do, because it's the horrors that are getting the most attention.'

'Isn't that the nature of your kind of journalism?' he said.

She wanted to argue with him, wanted to tell him that good journalism was about truth, that she didn't know yet what *kind* of journalist she was – if, in fact, she was any kind at all.

Before this, she had at least believed herself to be honest.

She wasn't sure of that anymore.

Not really sure of anything.

Eighty-Five

It took time for the tunnels to be made safe enough for the investigative and forensic teams to make their way to Reaper's torture and burial chamber, the processes slow and painstaking, especially since the explosion that had trapped Liza had all but demolished the major crime scene down there.

First indications – minimal information only being passed to her as a courtesy – were that at least the sound recordings of Joshua Tilden's confession were clear enough to be helpful for legal purposes.

Not that the killer would ever face trial, his remains having been conclusively identified. Along with those of Thomas Pike. DNA and dental matching of the other victims was to be a lengthier process.

Michael Rider's body had not yet been found.

Placing him, along with Amos, Jeremiah and Nemesis on the FBI's Ten Most Wanted list.

That alone enough to make Liza want to weep.

Better dead, she thought now, hard as that was for her to contemplate. Trying not to wait for news of him, yet still doing that every day.

She knew, with absolute conviction, that even if he had made it out, Michael would never contact her again, would keep himself far from her, for her sake. She asked herself harshly how she could be sure of that when she'd hardly known him, when he had, after all, become one of Reaper's gang, had allowed himself to be used that way.

Each time, the answer came in the form of two memories. The first, of the young, gentle, bright-eyed teacher at Walden Pond School. The second, of their kiss.

Meantime, Michael's share of the proceeds of the robbery were still secure.

She had waited until the day of her return to Boston to remove the envelopes from the side of the bathtub. Had run herself a long, foamy tubful as cover, had locked the door, taken the cash and Joel's list of charities and wrapped them up in a large towel before taking them to her bedroom and packing them in her travel bag.

No word to Ben about it when she got back to Snow Hill Street.

Beyond unfair to turn him into an accomplice.

Her biggest quandary was what to do with the money.

She considered taking a safe deposit box, but feared that she might be under scrutiny, realized that donating large sums to Joel's or Luke's charities would be idiotic, and that likewise, trying to get Luke's money to his parents, now that he had been identified, would be dangerous for her and for them.

She had shredded Joel's list one weekend while Ben was away with Gina, had disabled the smoke detector in the kitchen and burned the shredded pieces in the sink, watching the ashes disappear.

Not so easy to get rid of hundreds of thousands of dollars.

Not that she'd actually counted, because she had no wish to know, because all that taking it had brought her was ongoing guilt and fear. Because investigators had already visited her twice in Boston, asking questions about anything that Michael might have told her, anything that might have 'slipped her mind'.

'Nothing,' she'd said, terrified both times that they might search her room.

Knowing that they might return again, perhaps with a search warrant.

She wavered about her final plan for a while, realizing the risks, knowing too that the only alternatives – keeping the money or calling the FBI – were untenable. The decision made, she burned the original envelopes and, wearing gloves, divided the cash into six parts, placing the wads of notes into new envelopes, hiding one away before setting off on two separate excursions to drop the other five at soup kitchens and homeless shelters around Manhattan, Queens, the Bronx and Brooklyn. Afraid to donate closer to home or anyplace that might link to Michael, always disguising herself in a gray hooded jacket and large sunglasses, in case of surveillance cameras.

Some good done with it, at least.

On the upside, she had received a number of offers since the holidays: from magazines, publishers and even one from a TV movie production company.

Had not decided which, if any, to accept.

'You have to write this,' Ben encouraged her. 'You'd be certifiable not to.'

'I need more time,' she told him.

'Don't wait too long,' he said. 'People have short memories.'

'Not always,' Liza said, thinking of Reaper.

Still, she knew that Ben was right. Knew too that it might actually be healthy for her to write it all down, though catharsis did not necessarily mean that she would achieve a worthwhile finished product.

And she did need time.

To sift through the emotional wreckage, to consider all the human stories that had been thrown at them in church that long night. To think about John Tilden, a monster in his own right, his trial still to come if and when the Rhode Island Attorney General's office was ready. Whole gobbets of her story, therefore, sub judice for the foreseeable future.

The list of victims horrifically long, starting with Naomi Tilden, Alice Millicent and Donald Cromwell, continuing with Reaper's victims, ending with poor Thomas Pike and, finally, with the suicide of the serial killer himself.

And then there was Michael.

Dead or alive, folly or not, she knew she would keep his money for him.

Suspected that her own crime made her feel closer to him.

Chose not to analyze that any more deeply.

For now, her plans were loose, few things certain. She would steel herself to return to Shiloh for a special service following the completion of St Matthew's restoration works, and she would force herself to go home more often, try to become the granddaughter that Stephen deserved.

As to Shiloh itself, she would never be able to forget what lay beneath, what her dreams reminded her of most nights. Of endless black tunnels and the stench of Reaper's 'place', ingrained in her memory along with the sight of Pike's branded flesh and agonized, dying eyes.

And the terror of being trapped after the explosion.

She had decided that she would write her story, find out in the process what talent she really possessed, feared learning that she might, after all, be mediocre. Long-ago daydreams of a career in broadcast news laid irrevocably to rest after the siege.

Not yet ready to commence writing, she had begun piecing together Michael's life and the family history that had dragged him toward what seemed an almost predestined direction; learned that Thad Rider, the father he'd never known, had died five years ago, and wondered how differently things might have unfolded if the rock singer had stayed; found, as she followed Michael's journey, that its kindlier uphill paths and dark downward dives brought to mind a graphic visualization.

Calm, steady climbs. Then mostly downhill all the way.

Michael's private past not for publication, that much non-negotiable.

The notion of getting her own professional break through the ordeal repugnant but perhaps inevitable.

It was *after* that would count, what she'd learned from it all.

What she did with it.

She found it hard to concentrate for long.

Michael in her thoughts too often.

She thought she saw him now and then, a flash of a thin, dark-haired, sharp-featured man, hurrying through the crowds at rush-hour or strolling through the Public Garden or spied from a window seat on a bus.

It was never Michael.

Even if he had survived, he would never come to Boston.

And even if, someday, it *was* him, they had no future together.

Just another fantasy to learn to live without.

Michael Rider would never be truly *with* her, never keep her warm at night.

The only tangible remnants of him a framed photograph of a charcoal drawing on her wall and an envelope full of stolen hundred-dollar bills.

Maybe, one day, the cops would arrive with a search warrant.

Or maybe, one day, she would finally take it out from its hiding place, give it away or burn it, or even spend it. Rid herself of that guilt, cease searching for a ghost.

Maybe, in time, the Reaper nightmares would die away.

Not likely to happen any time soon, she thought.